THE HEADMISTRESS

Angela Thirkell

virago

VIRAGO

This edition published in Great Britain in 2016 by Virago Press
First published in Great Britain in 1944 by Hamish Hamilton Ltd

1 3 5 7 9 10 8 6 4 2

A CIP catalogue record for this book
is available from the British Library.

ISBN 978-0-349-00747-2

Typeset in Goudy by M Rules
Printed and bound in Great Britain by
Clays Ltd, St Ives plc

Papers used by Virago are from well-managed forests
and other responsible sources.

MIX
Paper from
responsible sources
FSC® C104740

Virago Press
An imprint of
Little, Brown Book Group
Carmelite House
50 Victoria Embankment
London EC4Y 0DZ

An Hachette UK Company
www.hachette.co.uk

www.virago.co.uk

VIRAGO
MODERN CLASSICS
667

Angela Thirkell (1890–1961) was the eldest daughter of John William Mackail, a Scottish classical scholar and civil servant, and Margaret Burne-Jones. Her relatives included the pre-Raphaelite artist Edward Burne-Jones, Rudyard Kipling and Stanley Baldwin, and her godfather was J. M. Barrie. She was educated in London and Paris, and began publishing articles and stories in the 1920s. In 1931 she brought out her first book, a memoir entitled *Three Houses*, and in 1933 her comic novel *High Rising* – set in the fictional county of Barsetshire, borrowed from Trollope – met with great success. She went on to write nearly thirty Barsetshire novels, as well as several further works of fiction and non-fiction. She was twice married, and had four children.

By Angela Thirkell

Barsetshire novels

High Rising
Wild Strawberries
The Demon in the House
August Folly
Summer Half
Pomfret Towers
The Brandons
Before Lunch
Cheerfulness Breaks In
Northbridge Rectory
Marling Hall
Growing Up
The Headmistress
Miss Bunting
Peace Breaks Out

Private Enterprise
Love Among the Ruins
The Old Bank House
County Chronicle
The Duke's Daughter
Happy Returns
Jutland Cottage
What Did it Mean?
Enter Sir Robert
Never Too Late
A Double Affair
Close Quarters
Love at All Ages
Three Score and Ten

Non-fiction

Three Houses

Collected Stories

Christmas at High Rising

I

The pretty and formerly peaceful village of Harefield lies in a valley watered by the upper reaches of the River Rising, under the downs. The Rising, here no more than a stream, flows in many silvery channels through the rushy meadows to the north of the village. The wide High Street is on a slant. The houses on the north or lower side have gardens that run down towards the water meadows. The south side, where the houses are larger and look away over the north side to the hills beyond, has gardens running gently uphill and bounded at their further end by the grounds of Harefield Park, a plain-faced Palladian house which stands connected by a covered arcade with a pavilion on each side, commanding but a little gaunt, half a mile or so away from the village. Here have lived for a hundred and fifty years or so the Belton family, pleasant undistinguished people who burst into comparative affluence with a nabob under the Honourable East India Company and have been gently declining ever since. This decline was attributed by Mr Carton, a middle-aged Oxford don of a genealogical turn of mind who lived at Harefield out of term and liked 'going into families' as he called it, to their having married more for love than for money or lands. The result had been a very happy home life, the right number of sons for

Army, Navy, colonial service, law and other useful public work, and nice daughters who had usually married younger sons or clergymen, so that the Beltons were as much interrelated with the county as any other family in Barsetshire. They also owned some of the fine red-brick houses in the town and had always farmed their own land.

But gentleman-farming is no inheritance and by the time the war settled down upon the world the Beltons were living on overdrafts to an extent that even they found alarming, and two years later were unhappily making up their minds to sell a house and estate for which there would probably be no demand, when Providence kindly intervened, in the shape of the Hosiers' Girls' Foundation School. This old and very wealthy city company supported two excellent schools. The boys' school had been evacuated at the beginning of the war to Southbridge, but was now back in London. The girls' school had gone to Barchester and had a working arrangement with the Barchester High School. Their school buildings in London had been almost completely demolished in 1940, so they remained in Barchester. Their parents, who were mostly doing pretty well, were so glad to find their daughters healthy and happy that when they had also realized the great joy of only seeing them in the holidays, instead of five days in the week from half-past four in the afternoon to nine o'clock in the morning, not to speak of all Saturday and Sunday, most of them gladly agreed to their remaining as boarders.

If this decision had been made earlier in the war it would have been easier to find a house, but now, what with Government offices, insurance companies (which had an insatiable appetite for country mansions), banks, hospitals and the Forces, there was not a good house available in the district. Miss Sparling the headmistress spent all her weekends looking at impossible places and grew more and more anxious. Not only did she wish to please her employers, with whom she was on excellent terms, but her heart sank at the thought of another year, nay even another term, in Barchester. Not that she was unpopular. The Close had taken her to its bosom and the professional families much enjoyed her company, but she was not happy. Soon after the Hosiers' Girls came to Barchester Miss Pettinger, the headmistress of the Barchester High School, had very graciously pressed Miss Sparling to stay with her. Miss Sparling, worn out by a succession of rooms and landladies each more repellent than the last, had gratefully accepted this invitation and eternally regretted that she had done so. It was not that she was starved, or beaten, or given an iron bedstead with a thin mattress, or made to sit below the salt, but there was something about Miss Pettinger that made her whole life acutely uncomfortable. What it had meant to be at close quarters with Miss Pettinger for two years, only Miss Sparling knew, though many of Miss Pettinger's ex-pupils could have voiced her feelings; notably Mrs Noel Merton, now living at her old home near Northbridge, who went so far as to remark to Miss Lavinia Merton, aged six months, that if she didn't hush her, hush her and not fret her, that old beast Pettinger would in all probability get her.

Then, one Sunday afternoon at the Deanery, the Archdeacon's wife from Plumstead happened to mention that Lady Pomfret had told her that she heard the Beltons were going to try to let the Park. Miss Sparling, always with the welfare of her school at heart and spurred by the ever-springing hope of getting away from Miss Pettinger's society, rang up her employers that night. Within forty-eight hours the Hosiers' solicitor had telephoned to Mr Belton, come down to Barchester with a surveyor in his train, extracted a car and petrol from the Old Cathedral Garage, seen Mr Belton's lawyer, been all over the house with Miss Sparling and the surveyor, and gone back to London. Within a fortnight the Beltons had moved into the village, workmen had been produced, the necessary alterations made, and by the beginning of the autumn term Miss Sparling was installed at Harefield Park with her staff, her girls, and a delightful little suite of her own in the West Pavilion. No longer would she have to listen to Miss Pettinger's views on politics or her account of her motor trip in Dalmatia; no longer would she be cross-examined as to the probable results of her girls in the School Certificate examination; no longer would she have to hear herself introduced with a bright laugh as 'my evacuee, but *so* different, quite an old *friend* now'; no longer – but when she came to think about it, she could not honestly say that Miss Pettinger had ever been spiteful, ungenerous or unkind in word or deed. It was only that she simply could not abide that lady; and here again Mrs Noel Merton would have entirely agreed with her.

Most luckily Arcot House, a small but handsome house in the village belonging to Mr Belton, fell vacant about this time, owing to the death of old Mrs Admiral Ellangowan-Hornby. That lady, the daughter of a Scotch peer, had a taste for white walls, good furniture and ferocious cleanliness, so when her heir, a nephew who did not in the least wish to live there, suggested that the owners might like to take it furnished, very little was needed in the way of preparation, and a few days before school reassembled Mr and Mrs Belton, who had been living at the Nabob's Head at the upper end of the village, walked quietly down the High Street and entered Arcot House. In the drawing-room, which commanded the village street in front and the garden with a distant view of Harefield Park at the back, a bright fire was burning, the furniture caught the gleam of the flames, Mrs Admiral Ellangowan-Hornby's Scotch ancestors and ancestresses looked down with immense character from the walls, and tea was laid. A tall, plain, middle-aged woman who looked like a cross between a nurse and a housekeeper, as indeed she was, came in with a kettle and set it down by the fire.

'That's in case you wanted any more hot water, madam,' she said. 'And Mr Freddy telephoned to say he'd be here any time, and Miss Elsa telephoned to say she might turn up tonight or tomorrow morning, and Mr Charles did ring up but I couldn't hear what he said, but Gertie Pilson at the exchange says if he rings up again she'll take the message herself. I've got all the beds ready and Hurdles says he'll see there's a nice bit of meat if it's for the Commander and I was to tell you he'll get you something nice off the ration if Miss Elsa comes and Pratt's got some lovely kippers Mr Charles can have for his breakfast. I lighted the fire and there's enough coal in the old lady's cellars to last six months and plenty of wood in the park so don't you worry.'

Having issued these orders of the day, the woman turned on her heel and left the room, not exactly slamming the door, but shutting it with a degree of firmness which anyone unaccustomed to her ways might have taken as a sign of ill-temper. Her master and mistress (by courtesy), who were used to her ways, remained unmoved. When Mrs Belton was engaging a nurse before the birth of her first child, a young woman had applied for the post who was so obviously the right person to rule a nursery that young Mrs Belton had engaged her almost without inquiry. Her family was well known and respected in Harefield, her uncle Sid Wheeler being landlord of the Nabob, her cousin Bill Wheeler a first-class chimney sweep and the only person who really understood the chimneys at Pomfret Towers, and her mother an excellent laundress. Her father chiefly lived on his wife, supplemented with odd jobs, but as Harefield, like many villages, was at bottom matriarchal, no one thought much the worse of him. When asked her name the young woman had said Wheeler; and on being pressed had grudgingly admitted to S. Wheeler, adding that she was properly christened and didn't wish to say no more, and such was her strength of character that no one had ever dared to call her by anything but her surname.

Mr Carton, whose interest in genealogies and families boiled over in every possible direction, had given it as his opinion after spending several evenings at the Old Begum, an alehouse patronized by Mr Wheeler père, that her dislike of her name being known, while largely based on a fine primitive feeling that by letting your name be known you gave unknown powers a handle over you, was also due to a class feeling that upper servants, such as butlers and head parlourmaids, were always called by their surname and one was not going to demean oneself before such. Therefore into the nursery she had come as Wheeler, and Wheeler she had remained. By such interfering and inquisitorial visitations as censuses and later identity cards and ration books, not to speak of her mother when she brought the personal wash up to the Park, or general conversation in the village, it had long been known that her name was Sarah, but no one had ever dared to use it. Even Charles Belton, her latest and best-loved nursling, had only once, flown with a century made for Harefield v. Pomfret Madrigal on the home ground, attempted to call her Sarah and had been so awfully set down in the tea marquee, in front of both teams, that he had never tried again.

'Why so many cups and saucers, do you suppose, Lucy?' said Mr Belton, who had been studying the tea equipage in silence.

His wife looked at the table, where six or seven cups, saucers and plates of delicate china were set out.

'I can't think,' she said. 'But I'm very glad Wheeler is going to be our houseparlourmaid. Anyone else would break that china at once, and Mrs Ellangowan-Hornby's nephew might go to law about it, for we could never replace it and it's probably worth a million pounds. Come and have your tea, Fred, and use one of them. How funny it is to be living in someone else's house.'

'Only leasehold. My house if you come to think of it,' said Mr Belton, who held strong views about property, though a very long-suffering landlord with his small tenants. 'My house twice over if it comes to that. Property belongs to me and I'm tenant of the old lady's nephew as well.'

'I wonder what Captain Hornby is like,' said Mrs Belton, sitting down at Captain Hornby's table, in his chair, and beginning to pour out tea from his teapot.

'Like?' said her husband. 'Like anyone else I suppose. Where's my saccharine? Where *is* my saccharine? Damn the filthy stuff. Can't think why old What's-his-name in Harley Street told me to take it. Partner in a saccharine factory probably. That's the way all these doctors live.'

Mrs Belton gently pushed towards her husband the little silver box in which his saccharine was kept. She did not answer, because she knew his gruffness was merely a screen for a wounded pride. He had been as good as gold about leaving his family home, for he had the courage to face disagreeable facts, but his wife knew how deeply he felt it that the inevitable blow had fallen in his lifetime and how, in spite of valiant efforts, he could not help feeling that he had come down in the world. For five generations the Beltons had sat in their Palladian mansion looking over their own parkland. Now the sixth Belton since the nabob was sitting in a drawing-room, a parlour, in a house in the village street, a house which, except for the lucky fact of its being up four steps from the pavement with rather terrifying barred basement windows looking on to tiny areas with a grating over them, would have had to have blinds in the front rooms to prevent passers-by looking in. Mrs Belton was a humble creature in some ways but her pride too was wounded, for she knew she had brought her husband little dowry. A Thorne, one of the many cousins of the very old Barsetshire family at Ullathorne, she was of good blood, but no amount of blood could keep Harefield Park from turning into a girls' school. In happier days she had hoped that in her children the family might at last come into its proper place again. Freddy was to marry a very rich delightful heiress and put proper bathrooms all over the house when his father died and he left the Navy and came into the place, Charles was to make an immense fortune in business, be a kind wealthy bachelor uncle and leave all his money to Freddy's children, and Elsa was to marry very well, preferably the heir to a dukedom or at least a marquisate, and present Freddy's girls at court. These things would surely come to pass with children as good-looking, gifted and charming as her own; and if Freddy and his wife wanted to live at Harefield Park, why his parents could well retire to one of their houses in the village and let the young people have their fling. But to retire in favour of a girls' school, to confess oneself beaten by one's own estate, to take away from one's children the home of their childhood, the nursery where they had quarrelled, the kitchen where they had teased the cook, the disused hay lofts in the stables where they had played, the lake where they had muddily bathed in summer and dangerously (for there was a very cold spring in the middle of it) skated in winter, these were very bitter thoughts, and Mrs Belton's pretty, anxious face was contorted by the unbecoming grimaces one makes to show that one has no intention of crying; no, not the least idea in the world.

'What *is* the matter, Lucy?' said Mr Belton, almost glad to turn upon his wife as a relief from the very similar feelings that were tearing him. 'I mean, my dear, is anything *really* the matter?' he added in a more gentle voice.

His wife would have found it almost easier to deal with his more truculent mood, but so touched was she by his effort to be sympathetic that she gulped down all her unhappiness and said,

'I was only wondering if the children would be allowed to skate this winter if they get leave.'

'Allowed? What the devil do you mean *allowed*?' said Mr Belton. 'We haven't sold the whole place, my dear, only let the house and garden. That Miss Sterling—'

'Sparling,' said his wife.

'Sparling then,' said Mr Belton, 'though it's a name I don't know, queer sort of name, seems a nice sort of woman. It was her idea that we should keep the East Pavilion. And to tell the truth, if I'd had to move the estate office it would have been very inconvenient. I couldn't very well see the tenants here. And this is a good house, Lucy. Old Dr Perry, not this man, his father, always said it was the best house in the High Street. I'm sorry, Lucy, I'm sorry.'

So noble did Mrs Belton think her husband for confessing, or at any rate recognizing, his fit of temper that she felt more like crying than ever, when a loud peal distracted her.

'Damn that bell,' exclaimed Mr Belton, glad of a legitimate excuse for working off his feelings. 'It's been like that for twenty years. One touch and it rings like a fire engine. The old lady complained more than once and Icken has been down to see it again and again. He's the best estate carpenter in the county, but he couldn't get the damned thing right. What is it, Wheeler?'

'It's the Vicar, sir,' said Wheeler. 'He says to say if you are tired he won't come in. And Lady Graham has sent two rabbits and a basket of mushrooms by the coal man, madam, with her love and you must let her know if there's anything she can do.'

'How kind of dear Agnes,' said Mrs Belton. 'Yes, of course we want to see Mr Oriel, Wheeler.'

Wheeler retired and came back with the Vicar whom, quite apart from his collar and black vest, anyone would have known for a clergyman at once on account of his large and flexible Adam's apple, which fascinated the rash beholder's eye and had once caused Charles Belton, aged four, to ask him why he couldn't swallow it.

'How *very* nice of you to come, Mr Oriel,' said Mrs Belton getting up. 'Have you had tea?'

'But you are expecting a party,' said Mr Oriel, looking nervously at the array of china.

'That was our faithful Wheeler,' said Mrs Belton, 'and why all that crockery I can't think. But we aren't expecting anyone and are so delighted to have you as our first guest.'

'I confess I am relieved,' said Mr Oriel, shaking hands with Mr Belton. 'I saw Lady Pomfret's lorry outside the Town Hall and made sure she would be here. Milk if you can spare it; no, no sugar thanks. I have a small bottle of saccharine tablets which I carry about in my pocket,' said the Vicar, feeling with every hand in every pocket.

'Have some of mine,' said Mr Belton, opening the little silver box, 'filthy stuff.'

'It seems ungrateful to say so, but it *is*,' said the Vicar, obviously relieved, 'and why we take it I cannot think.'

'Instead of sugar. And a damn silly thing to do,' said Mr Belton. 'Stuff isn't sweet, it's bitter. And the more you put in the nastier it is.'

'I never did take sugar in my tea, or in coffee,' said the Vicar. 'I have always disliked it. But I understood that by taking saccharine, we were somehow assisting the war effort. There are so many ways of helping the war and one sometimes finds them a little bewildering. Now, we were told that His Majesty has only five inches of water in his bath, so of course I marked a five-inch line on the Vicarage bath – and I cannot tell you how difficult it was, for as you know there is no corner in a bath, no square corner if I make myself clear, by which you can really judge. If you put a ruler against the side of the bath it is all so round and slanting, the bath I mean,, that you cannot tell exactly where the mark should come. But I had an inspiration. I filled the bath rather full and stood a ruler upright with its low end, I mean the one where it says one inch, resting on the middle of the bottom. I then pulled out the plug, and when the water had dropped to the figure five, I put it in again. While I was putting it in a little more water ran away, but this made it about fair, for as you know there is on many rulers, and on the particular ruler in question, a little bit at the beginning, or rather at each end, which is not included in the inches, which would have given me an unfair advantage.'

'Some cake,' said Mrs Belton sympathetically.

'But now – oh, thank you,' said the Vicar, helping himself to a slice, 'I am again in a quandary.'

'I don't see why,' said Mrs Belton. 'You've got your five inches.'

'Yes; but here is the rub,' said the Vicar. 'If, in error, I fill the bath up to the five-inch mark with boiling water, for my housekeeper keeps the water delightfully hot, is it fair to add sufficient cold water to make it bearable?'

'You'd be boiled like a lobster if you didn't, Oriel,' said Mr Belton. 'I can't think why we never had cake like this at home, Lucy. Reminds me of my tuck-box at my first school.'

'That is exactly what I meant,' said the Vicar, gratified that he had made himself so clear. 'So, even at the risk of disloyalty, I have to add cold water, which does not of course increase my own fuel consumption, but does, so I am told, increase the fuel consumption wherever it is that the cold water has to be pumped from. And then again if I put my cold water in first—'

'Which you always ought to,' said Mrs Belton earnestly. 'That is the first thing any good nannie has to learn, or she may scald the baby when she puts it in.'

'—I may put in too much and so be obliged to fill up with so much boiling water that it comes well above the five-inch mark. How very good this cake is.'

'Well, Oriel, I wouldn't worry too much if I were you,' said Mr Belton. 'There's that bell again.'

Another violent peal resounded from basement to attic. Wheeler appeared.

'It's Lady Pomfret, madam,' she said. 'She says to say if you're too busy. And I forgot to tell you, Mrs Brandon brought the cake when she came over to see about the Land Girls. She says it is real flour she had hoarded, not this nasty healthy stuff, and if she can do anything please let her know and Mrs Hilary's new baby is a dear little girl.'

'But of course ask Lady Pomfret to come in,' said Mrs Belton, for she was very fond of the young countess whose mother-in-law had been a distant Thorne cousin. So in came Lady Pomfret with Lord Mellings aged four and a half and Lady Emily Foster aged three.

'Dear Lucy, how very delightful to find you,' said Lady

Pomfret. 'The home farm lorry was going to Northbridge, so the children and I came in it and it is going to pick us up in half an hour. What a beautiful room, Mr Belton. I have never been in this house before.'

'Do you know our Vicar, Mr Oriel?' said Mrs Belton.

'I have not had the pleasure of meeting you before, Lady Pomfret,' said Mr Oriel, 'but I knew your dear mother-in-law well. In fact we were some kind of connection, but it always puzzles me.'

'Let's see, Lady Pomfret was a – bless my soul, *what* was she?' said Mr Belton. 'I know as well as I know my own name, but it is just where I can't get at it.'

'She was Edith Thorne, Fred,' said his wife. 'I didn't know you had Thorne relations, Mr Oriel. We must have been cousins all these years without knowing it.'

'It is hardly so near as that, I am afraid,' said Mr Oriel smiling. 'The connection is through the Greshams.'

'Wait a bit now,' said Mr Belton, as if Mr Oriel were trying to take an unfair advantage. 'There was a bit of a scandal, wasn't there? Something about a queer – if that bell rings again, Lucy, I'll have Icken down tomorrow to dismantle the whole thing and have an electric one. What is it, Wheeler?'

'Mr Carton's called and he says if you are busy he won't come in,' said Wheeler. 'And Miss Marling brought some grapes and a brace of partridges, madam, with Mr Marling's love. Miss Marling was in the pony-cart and said she couldn't stop, but if you wanted a small load of manure she could tell you where to get some. Excuse me, my lady, but would his lordship and Lady Emily like to have tea with me in the pantry? We have plenty of milk.'

'I am sure they would love to,' said Lady Pomfret. 'Now

Ludovic, take Emily's hand and go with Wheeler. Old Lady Lufton would insist on being a godmother,' she said apologetically as her children went away with Wheeler, 'but I suppose we shall get used to it.'

Then Mr Carton came in. And if any reader wishes to know what he was like, he was exactly like what an Oxford don nearer sixty than fifty ought to be; tall and rather untidy, with receding hair, and spectacles which he was always putting on and taking off; of precise speech, capable of vitriolic rancour in the field of scholarship, secretly very kind to his pupils, with no known ties except a mother of eighty who lived at Bognor and did a surprising amount of gardening. With Mr Oriel he had a perpetual friendly difference of opinion about the singing in church, Mr Carton upholding *Hymns Ancient and Modern* with violence, while Mr Oriel who had High Anglican leanings rather affected a little book called *Songs of Praise*.

'You do know Mr Carton, I think, Sally,' said Mrs Belton to Lady Pomfret. 'Will you have tea, Mr Carton? You have come just at the right moment, because we can't quite make out how Mr Oriel and old Lady Pomfret were connected and you are so good at families.'

'My great-uncle at Greshamsbury—'

'Edith Pomfret's mother's cousin—'

'That girl there was a queer story about that brought all the money into the Gresham family—'

'I often heard Lady Pomfret speak of an old Dr Thorne who married an heiress—'

Said Mr Oriel, Mrs Belton, Mr Belton and young Lady Pomfret all at once.

'Stop,' said Mr Carton. 'Wait. I'll tell you exactly how it is.'

He put his spectacles on, looked piercingly at the party over the top of them as if they were undergraduates, and putting his finger tips together, pronounced judgment.

'Your great-uncle the bishop, Oriel, married some time in the 'sixties one of Squire Gresham's daughters whose name for the moment escapes me. His wife's brother, Frank Gresham, the present man's great-grandfather, married Mary Thorne who was the illegitimate niece of the Dr Thorne who married Miss Dunstable whose money came from a patent Ointment of Lebanon. Dr Thorne was only a distant cousin of the Ullathorne Thornes, to whom old Lady Pomfret belonged, but the connection is there all right, though I couldn't give the precise degree.'

He then took off his spectacles, put them into their case, snapped the case shut and put it in his pocket. There was a short silence while his audience digested these facts.

'My great-uncle had fifteen children,' said Mr Oriel thoughtfully. 'His fifteen little Christians he used to call them. Dear, dear.'

There seemed to be no adequate comment on this picture of scenes from clerical life, so it was almost a relief when the bell suddenly rang again and Wheeler came in.

'It's Dr Perry, madam,' she announced, 'and he said not to disturb you if you were engaged. And did you wish Lady Emily to have a piece of cheese with her tea, my lady? His lordship said she always did at the Towers.'

Lady Pomfret said certainly not and Ludovic was being most untruthful and would Wheeler let her know as soon as the home farm lorry came, because it was high time she took the children home, and then Dr Perry came in, a stout jovial little man who had been the Beltons' family physician, just as his father before him had been family doctor to the previous generation of Beltons.

'I was telling my wife, Perry, that your father always said this was the best house in the High Street,' said Mr Belton. 'You know everyone, I think.'

Mrs Belton said she would have fresh tea in a minute but Dr Perry refused, saying he was on his way home and had only looked in to give them his wife's love and bring two pots of her peach jam.

'I've just been up at the Park,' he added. 'One of the girls had a nasty boil and I had to lance it. Lots of boils going about now. We're going to have a nasty winter among the civilian population, Mrs Belton, mark my words. How are your young people?'

Mrs Belton said they had all been ringing up and she hoped to see them, but one never knew till they arrived without any rations late on Saturday.

'I like the headmistress,' said Dr Perry. 'Good-looking in her own style and a lot of character I should say. A nice lot of girls too. They were arriving when I was there and they begin lessons tomorrow. I hope they won't get measles. There's any amount about, chicken-pox too. We only want a typhus epidemic. You know Dr Buck has been called up, so I'm single-handed except for Dr Morgan and I can't abide the woman. She does well enough for half-baked highbrows, but she will talk about psychology to the cottagers and they don't like it. Quite enough trouble with their children and their rheumatics without all this talk. And if they want a spot of libido they'll have it all right with all these soldiers and girls about. No need to tell them about that.'

Mr Oriel said it was most distressing and he for one was ready to marry young couples at any moment, if only for the sake of the unborn child.

'We all know that, Oriel,' said Dr Perry, who was fond of his pastor though with no very high opinion of his worldly wisdom.

'But it's not the unmarrieds; they usually get married all right. It's the married women with their husbands away. Mrs Humble down near the Three Tuns has just had her second, a fine baby too. I'd like to see Morgan talk psychology to her!'

Upon which Dr Perry laughed rather boisterously, and though all his hearers liked him and knew how good and patient he was on his professional side, it was a distinct relief when Wheeler came in to say the lorry from the Towers was there and Cook was just washing Lady Emily's hands and face.

'And I hope, my lady, that the Honourable Giles is keeping well,' said Wheeler to Lady Pomfret.

'Splendid, thank you, Wheeler,' said Lady Pomfret. 'He cut a tooth yesterday on his sixth birthday; I mean his six months old birthday. Good-bye, Lucy. Let me know if Freddy or Charles want any shooting. Poor Jenks says it isn't like being a head keeper with no gentlemen out with their guns. His boy in the army who was in hospital is quite fit again and engaged to a nice girl in the Land Army. Come along, children.'

When the ripples of farewell had subsided, Dr Perry said he must be going.

'Go and see that schoolmistress, Mrs Belton,' he said. 'You'll like her and I think she will be lonely. She's a cut above the other mistresses. You'd like her, Oriel. A good churchwoman and all that sort of thing. You'll have to confirm her girls – no, it's the Bishop that does that of course, though I'd as soon be confirmed by one of the Borgias myself. You'll have to tell them what it's all about anyway. You'd like her too, Carton. Talk about Cicero and all that sort of thing. She's one of that classical lot. Tell your young people to let me know when they want to go to Barchester, Mrs Belton. I'm often at the General Hospital and I can always give them a lift. And I'd like to say,' said Dr Perry, suddenly showing signs of embarrassment, a state most uncommon with him, 'that the whole village will miss you at the Park, but it will do us all a lot of good to have you down here, among us. Jove, I've kept my surgery waiting twenty minutes.'

Upon this he shook hands with his host and hostess, and bolted out of the house with a red face.

'A very good man,' said Mr Oriel slowly, 'though he pretends he isn't. But I wish this new headmistress wasn't a good churchwoman. No, I don't mean that, but good churchwomen are so apt to want to tell one things and I'd rather not. I suppose this is cowardly though. Are you coming my way, Carton?'

'"One of that classical lot"!' Mr Carton exploded with withering scorn. 'Educated women are no treat to me. Cicero indeed! She probably says Kikero. Thank God the creatures that come to Oxford now are all doing economics; they and their subject are just about fit for each other. Pah!'

Everyone secretly admired a man who could say Pah, one of those locutions more often written than spoken.

'Well, good-bye,' said Mr Oriel, looking very hard at the highlight on the nose of Raeburn's portrait of a former Lord Ellangowan. 'You know, Perry is a very sensible man. If I'd tried all day I couldn't have put it better. About the Park I mean. As a matter of fact,' said Mr Oriel, shifting his gaze to the raven locks of the lovely Lady Ellangowan who was carried off in a decline at twenty-five, 'we all feel that the Park is Here. Arcot House will be the Park as far as the village is concerned. God bless you both.'

He then felt he had gone too far, looked wildly at the knob on the teapot, shook hands violently with the Beltons and said, 'Coming, Carton?'

Mr Carton, who had fallen into a kind of trance or dwam

during Mr Oriel's last heartfelt words, suddenly came to and uttered violently the word, 'Patience.'

'We do,' said Mrs Belton earnestly.

'Tut-tut, I don't mean that,' said Mr Carton, whose hearers were again filled with admiration of his vocabulary. 'And when I say Patience I am wrong. I mean Beatrice. Beatrice Gresham was the girl Oriel's great-uncle married. I knew it would come to me. Good-bye. I cannot tell you how much I look forward to seeing more of you both, if I may. In fact I have, selfishly, only one regret at your having left the Park – the library.'

'It's locked and I've got the key,' said Mr Belton. 'I've got a duplicate. You can have it. No one else wants to go in. I don't believe any of the children can read at all.'

Mr Carton expressed his thanks, would have liked to say God bless you, but as Mr Oriel had said it already; he felt it would be poaching on his clerical preserves. So he went off, carrying Mr Oriel with him.

Wheeler then came to take away the tea things.

'I knew you would be having callers,' she said, looking with gratification on the dirty cups. 'If anyone else comes I'll send them away. You need a lay down, madam, and if you want your bath the water's nice and hot any time. Cook says it's a lovely little boiler and now she can do it herself the water will be properly hot, not like that boiler up at the Park eating the coal all the time and old Humble too lazy to stoke it up properly at night. Oh, and there's a big tin of biscuits come from Lady Norton, madam. One of the soldiers that's billeted at Norton Park brought it over on his motor bike and she says if you want any more to let her know.'

When Wheeler had gone Mr and Mrs Belton sat quietly by the fire. Mrs Belton was very tired and blamed herself for the feeling. A woman in her middle fifties, she said angrily to herself, had no business to be tired. At that age one ought to be full of horrible energy, dashing about in old but well-cut tweeds organizing everything, a jolly elder sister to one's children, or at least a very competent grandmother romping with the grandchildren while their parents were on war work or abroad. At any rate there weren't any grandchildren, so that was that. All three children ought to have married years ago, but they never seemed to want to. Nor did they want a jolly elder sister. All they wanted was a purveyor of beds, fires, food, such drink as there was, cigarettes; someone who could take all telephone messages accurately, never ask where they were going or had been, tireless, self-effacing. All of which she had tried to be and she knew that her husband had too, but at the end of each leave, whether it was Freddy from his ship, Elsa from her hush-hush job, or Charles from the army, she felt she had not given satisfaction. As for her tweeds, they were certainly old; but not particularly well cut, for the children's allowances and the expenses of the house and estate did not leave much margin for a good tailor now, and her Mr Levine in Bruton Street, who cut coats like an angel and skirts like a genius, had gone up in four years from twelve guineas to thirty. What she would really like, she thought, would be to throw every single thing in her wardrobe out of the window and have everything new and to stop feeling tired and looking her age and go somewhere warm, if there was any warm place left in this horrible world now, and exercise *allure*, and be admired. All this made her laugh at herself, and her husband looked up, pleased to see that Lucy was happy, for much as he hated leaving his home he had dreaded the change even more for his wife.

'Dr Perry was quite right,' said Mrs Belton, stroking her

husband's tweed sleeve. 'It is the nicest house in Harefield, and it is lovely to think we shan't be cold this winter.'

Mr Belton said nothing, but his heart gave a leap of thankfulness that Lucy was settling down so quickly. And everyone had been so kind. People sending presents of food – even old Lady Norton who had frightened him ever since he could remember her. The nice things Oriel and Carton had said, and Perry; and that nice little Sally Pomfret, who didn't have too easy a time herself with her great barrack of Pomfret Towers and every committee in the county and three small children.

'I'm glad you're pleased, my dear,' he said. 'A little peace and quiet will do you good. And when you have got things straight, perhaps you'll do something about that Miss Starling.'

'Sparling, darling. Of course I will,' said his wife. 'Perhaps Mr Oriel might marry her. Anyway I'll go and call on her. Or ought I to write and ask if I may? A headmistress seems rather glorious. Oh, what a lovely little room this is and so extraordinarily peaceful.'

Little perhaps it was after the great rooms at Harefield Park with their finely decorated ceilings and furlongs of carpet and curtains, but large in its proportions and Mrs Admiral Ellangowan-Hornby's taste, breathing an ordered peace which was infinitely soothing to the shipwrecked voyagers in their temporary harbour.

This pleasant warm content was suddenly broken by a shattering noise outside the house and a violent ringing of the telephone from across the hall. Wheeler could be heard answering the telephone; the shattering noise continued, diversified by voices trying to outshout it, and after a moment the front door bell pealed through the house, followed at a very short interval by another peal equally violent. They now heard Wheeler hurrying to the front door and the well-known voice of their younger son Charles.

His parents, though they would have died rather than admit it to any outsider, to each other, or even to their secret selves, experienced a peculiar sinking of the heart, or rather of the spirits at this sound. Not but that either of them would cheerfully have gone to the scaffold for Charles, or given him the best bed, all the butter ration and the most comfortable chair; but they knew from fatal experience that whatever they did would be just wrong. They also each knew, though they had never come within miles of discussing the subject, that Charles really had much the same feelings himself; that he always came home full of the best intentions, prepared to walk round the place with his father, or accompany his mother to tea at the Perrys', or even to discuss his own future; that even as he entered the house all those sincere feelings were overlaid by a nervousness and irritation which caused him to be on the whole selfish, graceless, cross if questioned about himself and resentful if he wasn't. And it was much the same with Freddy and Elsa, though Freddy at twenty-nine was approximating to something human in his parents' house. Mrs Belton often wondered if all the other parents felt the same. It was not apparent that they did. Hermione Rivers for instance, Lord Pomfret's cousin who wrote all those successful novels, was always boasting about her boy Julian and his painting; Mrs Tebben at Worsted was more than boring about the devotion of her Richard; that dreadful Mrs Grant who was some connection of Mrs Brandon's used to speak far too frequently of her son Hilary's complete oneness with his *madre amata*. Mrs Belton had sometimes wished she could have sons like that. But yet some inner freemasonry of mothers told her that much of this was wilful self-delusion, façade, whatever one liked to call it, even perhaps a gallant making the best of things.

She had seen Mrs Rivers, usually so arrogant and overbearing, go white and silent under one of Julian's rebuffs; she had seen Mrs Tebben turn her face away for a moment at some careless or exasperated stab from Richard. Mrs Grant, it is true, had never been seen to blench, but then Hilary, at any rate till his mother was finally stranded in Calabria and he married his cousin Delia Brandon, had been rather milk-and-water. And Freddy, Elsa and Charles, thank goodness, were not milk-and-water at all. And then, with a mental shrug of her shoulders, she realized that in thanking goodness for her children being not milk-and-water she was only being exactly like all the other mothers. There seemed to be no way out.

An echo of all these thoughts may have run through Mrs Belton's mind while the echoes of the front door bell died away. Then the pressing present moment returned in full force as several loud bumps as of heavy parcels being thrown onto the floor sounded from the hall and Charles appeared, wearing a gigantic and dirty raincoat with a storm collar over his uniform and a very tight pale green beret.

'Twenty-four hours,' said Charles, 'but a man had a motor-bike so it'll be thirty-six. We did about seventy most of the way.'

Then catching sight of himself in a pillared and gilded mirror over the fireplace he strode up to it, settled the beret more tightly on his head and admired it.

'How do you like it?' said Charles carelessly.

Now if Mr Belton had been a real parent, he would have said, 'Take that thing off at once, my boy, and kiss your mother, and don't let me see you wearing a hat or whatever you call it in the house again.' And if Mrs Belton had been a truthful mother she would have said, 'What a hideous colour, darling, and your face looks just like a pudding boiled in a cloth under it.'

But neither courage nor truth was uppermost in Mr and Mrs Belton at the moment. Mr Belton said, 'Queer colour, isn't it,' in what he hoped was a man-of-the-world voice, while Mrs Belton said, 'It's very nice, darling, but you look even nicer with your peaked cap.' They then realized at once that they had probably blighted the whole of Charles's leave, if not for him, at least entirely for themselves and wished they were dead. But they were also very glad to see that Charles looked even broader, redder in the face and generally healthier, if possible, than on his previous leave.

'Do you want tea, darling?' said his mother. 'Wheeler will get it in a minute.'

'No, thanks. I'll be going round to the Nabob presently,' said Charles. 'Copper and I had one coming down the street and we told them we'd look in again. So this is where we are to live, is it?'

Mr Belton rashly asked who Copper was. In normal times Charles would have got up and walked out of the room on less provocation than this, but so tolerant had army life made him that he merely answered, 'A man. The one with the bike. It's not his name really,' after which his father knew better than to ask what his name really was.

'I'll tell you a funny thing – where do the cigarettes live, Father? Oh, never mind, I've got one here. I quite forgot,' he continued, extracting a battered cigarette from the bottom of a pocket, together with some cotton waste which he threw at the fender, just missing it, 'that it was the last day in the old home and all that and I told Copper to take me to the Park. I got the shock of my life when I walked into the hall and found a lot of girls. My word, what a set! Talk of legs!'

'Pretty, eh?' said his father, trying to affect a roguishness quite out of keeping with his nature.

24

'Hideous,' said Charles briefly. 'There may have been a nice pair hidden away somewhere, but most of them looked like our A.T.S. corporal, beef to the instep. And all wearing gym tunics. And then a kind of mistress came out and said did I want anything. So I said no, and it was all a mistake and my father and mother used to live there, and my name was Belton, and I suppose she thought I was dippy; she said she was sorry. So I yelled to Copper and luckily he hadn't been able to start up the bike, so he brought me down here. I say, Mother, where do I live?'

Rightly interpreting her younger son's question as a desire to know where his bedroom was, she said on the second floor, just at the top of the stairs.

'There is a basin with hot and cold,' she said, hoping to placate him, 'and a bathroom next door. Elsa's room opens into it too.'

'Good. I'll lock her door on the bathroom side,' said Charles. 'Where's the telephone?'

As he spoke the telephone bell sounded.

'I'll find it,' said Charles. 'I'm expecting someone to ring me up,' and shedding his beret and gloves he strode out of the room leaving the door open. His parents put up a very good show of neither seeing the mess nor feeling the draught, knowing well that any attempt to tidy the room would be taken as criticism and fuss, and resented accordingly. So they sat saying nothing, acutely conscious of the shattering noise which still burst out at intervals.

'It's Elsa,' said Charles, reappearing. 'She got a lift as far as Southbridge and can't get on. Copper hasn't got his bike started yet so I'll tell him to go and fetch her.'

Before his parents could answer he had gone into the hall, flung open the front door and was shouting to the invisible Copper in a voice that dominated all other noise. The engine

25

gave a last desperate death-rattle and the shattering noise went away towards Southbridge.

'I like this house,' said Charles, letting himself fall into a large chair. 'I've wanted a fixed basin in my room all my life, and a bathroom next door. I wish old Mrs E.-H. had left it to me instead of her nephew. Why haven't I a rich aunt with fixed basins? I saw the nephew in church once – one of those black-shaving rather sad-looking naval fellows. Funny how a naval uniform shows up dirt. They need much more brushing than khaki.'

'Navy blue is the very worst colour for showing dust and fluff,' said his mother, grasping at a subject on which she could speak with authority. 'When I had a maid, years ago, she used to sponge and press my blue tailor-mades every time I had worn them.'

'Well, I wish you had one now,' said Charles kindly. 'I'd get her to press my trousers. But I dare say Wheeler will. Now, I think green is a jolly good colour.'

Having brought the conversation to this point he paused. His parents felt there was a clue which they ought to take up, but couldn't quite guess what it was. His mother, looking once more at the horrid heap of clothes which she had not the courage to tell him to remove, began to talk at random, as her nervousness with her beloved child so often made her do, and said, for the second time that afternoon, that his beret was very nice colour. Instead of being offended he assumed a gratified expression, much to her relief.

'It's all right,' he said carelessly. 'Striking.'

Mr Belton said he must have seen some like it somewhere but couldn't exactly say where.

'You couldn't have,' said Charles. 'They're only just out, Triple-A.'

'What is Triple-A?' said his mother, guided for once by maternal instinct to what proved to be the right remark.

'Well,' said Charles, leaning forward with his elbows on his knees thus causing both his parents to feel how very handsome his face was with the firelight on it, 'all this is very secret, but everyone knows it, so I might as well tell you.'

His parents made noises expressive of readiness to die under torture before betraying a word.

'You know Tanks,' said Charles.

His mother said 'Yes,' a little too eagerly and his father said 'Carry on,' which was quite the wrong thing to say. But, being anxious for an audience, Charles magnanimously forgave him and continued.

'And you know anti-tanks. And of course we've got something that goes one better now; anti-anti-tanks they're called. So some genius has brought out something very hush-hush that knocks out the anti-anti stuff; and that's what I'm on now. That's why it's called Triple-A.'

His father nodded wisely. Charles decided to overlook this and pursued his theme.

'We are the only ones that wear the light green beret. It's a marvellous show. I can't tell you about it of course, but it's going to be an absolute knock-out. Three of our fellows got themselves killed on manoeuvres, which just shows.'

'Oh, Charles!' said his mother.

'Silly chumps stuck their heads out against orders,' said Charles.

'But supposing it had been *you*,' said Mrs Belton.

'My dear good mother,' said her son with slight impatience, '*I'm* not a silly chump. At least not when it comes to looking after myself. But I can tell you one thing that isn't generally known.'

He then, to his parents' intense pride and interest, talked for ten minutes or so about his work, moving them deeply by his young seriousness and absorption in his deadly games and his entire unselfconsciousness. The September daylight was fading, the fire flickered on a young face full of life and vigour though more finely drawn than it used to be, and his parents wished that time would stand still. Then Wheeler came in to do the blackout, the telephone bell shrilled again, and the spell was broken.

'It's old Freddy,' said Charles, who had rushed out to answer the telephone. 'He's got the weekend off from the Admiralty and he's stuck at Nutfield station. He'd forgotten the bus was taken off. I told him to wait and I'll get Copper to go over and fetch him as soon as he has brought Elsa. What time is it? Seven. He can easily get Freddy here by half-past and then we'll all go to the Nabob.'

'Dinner's at half-past, Mr Charles,' said Wheeler.

'Not tonight,' said Charles. 'Give Cook my love and say just to stop cooking for half an hour. Here's Copper.'

The noise again drew up at the door. Charles went out to speak to it, there was confusion in the hall, the noise went shatteringly away again and a good-looking girl, with her father's expression, came in and kissed her parents.

'Back in the mud hovel,' she said, and sat herself on a hassock near the fire. 'Never mind, the fisherman and the fisherman's wife look very nice. And how lovely to be home, even if it isn't home. It's a heavenly house, Father.'

'I hope you will like it even more when you have seen it,' said Mr Belton, very glad that his daughter approved. 'Your mother and I had to decide everything so quickly we couldn't let you all know in time to come and inspect it.'

'Oh, I've seen it all right,' said Elsa. 'That's why I asked you if I could have that bedroom in front with the view north.'

'When was that, darling?' said her mother. 'I didn't know you had been here before. I somehow never got to know old Mrs Ellangowan-Hornby.'

'It wasn't her,' said Elsa inelegantly, 'it was Christopher. You know, the old lady's nephew, the one the house belongs to now. He took me all over it.'

'You never told me,' said her mother. It was said merely as a statement, not as a reproach, and her daughter took it as such, quite in good part.

'It was when she had a stroke, Mother, two years ago, and Christopher was on leave because he was at sea then and he came down to see her and I'd met him somewhere in town, so he said would I like to see the house. I simply adored it and I specially liked that bedroom in front with the bathroom next door.'

'Charles is at the back, so you'll share the bathroom,' said Mrs Belton.

'Then I'll take the key out of my door or he's sure to lock it,' said Elsa. 'I'd better do it now. Oh bother, I expect he's gone up to take it himself.'

With a scurry she jumped to her feet and fled upstairs. From the second-floor landing sounds of friendly argument conducted with stampings and shriekings drifted down. The telephone rang again several times with friendly greetings from various county neighbours and offers of home produce ranging from a young cockerel to fatten for Christmas to the offer of a mount for any young Belton who was on leave during the cubbing season. By the time all these calls had been answered Mrs Belton was feeling that a bath before dinner was the most important thing in the world, and if dinner was to be at eight, as she supposed it now would be, she had time to go and have one. But even as she set her foot on the lowest step of the perfect staircase the shattering noise came tearing down the street and rose to a hideous climax at her front door. The door bell rang through the house, Elsa and Charles rushed downstairs like thunder, Wheeler came through the hall and opened the front door and disclosed Commander Frederick Belton, R.N., on the doorstep.

'Hullo, Freddy,' screamed his brother and sister in chorus. 'Come on, we're all going to the Nabob.'

Commander Belton, ignoring their outcries, forced his way like a strong swimmer into the hall, hugged his mother, shook hands with his father and saluted Wheeler.

'Now I'll attend to you two,' he said to his brother and sister. 'What time is dinner, Mother? Eight? Very well. One quick one at the Nabob and back you both come.'

'Charles dear, what about your friend on the motor-bicycle?' said Mrs Belton whose first instinct was to hospitality. 'Won't you bring him back to dinner?'

'Who? Oh, Copper,' said Charles. 'If he stops the engine he'll never get her going again. He's all right, Mother. Come and talk to him.'

He propelled his mother out of the door, down the front steps on to the pavement. The man on the motor-bicycle pushed back his crash helmet, revealing a pale, long-nosed face and ginger hair.

'How kind of you to go to the station for my son, and to fetch my daughter, Mr Copper,' said Mrs Belton. 'Can't you stop and have some dinner? It's rather a scratch meal as we've only just moved in, but we would be delighted.'

Even as she spoke she became aware that the obliging Copper would not be in the least a suitable dinner guest. He grinned sheepishly, showing rather unpleasant broken teeth, and went bright red, mumbling that the officer would know.

'It's all right, Copper,' said Charles. 'It's only my mother. I told you Copper wasn't his real name,' he added, addressing his mother. 'His name is Bobby, so he's called Copper. He's one of the ground staff at the aerodrome near us and he's got leave and a motor-bike and petrol, which is more than we ever get, and he's going home to Rickmansworth tonight, but he doesn't want to get there till his mother-in-law has gone to bed. That's right, isn't it, Copper?'

The amiable Copper grinned again.

'Well, come on and we'll see what the Nabob can do,' said Charles. 'Rev her up, Copper.'

The ginger-haired bicyclist shoved his helmet onto his forehead again, saluted and roared away up the street, followed by Elsa and Charles. Commander Belton lingered for a moment on the doorstep.

'Go and have your bath, Mother,' he said. 'I'll bring the liberty men aboard at ten minutes to eight, so don't worry. I think I like our new home very much. I've always wanted to go over Arcot House since I was a little boy and Mrs Ellangowan-Hornby gave me some preserved ginger because I got her cat down out of a tree. Hornby's a good fellow too. We must have him down here.'

He went up the street with long strides and Mr and Mrs Belton went back into the house. Wheeler shut the door, collected Charles's things from the drawing-room and took them upstairs. Then she turned on Mrs Belton's bath.

'Oh, Wheeler,' said her mistress's voice from her bedroom, 'do you know if Mr Charles has got the key of Miss Elsa's door into the bathroom? They were arguing about it and I really don't want a bear-fight over my head.'

'I've got the keys of both the doors, madam,' said Wheeler, 'and that's where they'll stay. They're just the same as they was in the nursery, always up to some mischief. There's a bolt inside Miss Elsa's door and that's quite enough. Now you have your bath, madam, and I'll get those bedrooms a bit tidy before dinner. And one of Lord Pomfret's men came over, madam, on one of the farm horses and he brought a bottle of whisky with his lordship's compliments and he wished it was a dozen of champagne.'

Mrs Belton, getting with a sigh of relief into a steaming bath, felt that though she had a thousand things to be thankful for, life at this particular moment was just a little too much for her.

2

By a miracle, not unassisted by the unobtrusive efforts of
Commander Belton, the whole family were down to breakfast
on Sunday morning quite soon after nine. Mrs Belton knew
better than to ask if anyone was coming to church, but to her
surprised pleasure Charles offered to accompany her. Freddy
and Elsa proposed to do some work in the garden, which had
been gently running to seed during Mrs Admiral Ellangowan-
Hornby's illness, and plant out a lot of winter greens that the
old gardener from the Park had brought down.

To Mrs Belton's feeling of pleasure that one child at least
would accompany her, there succeeded as the morning wore on
the familiar feeling that he would never be ready in time. So at
half-past ten she went up to see how he was getting on. Rather
as she expected his whole bedroom was strewn with equipment,
and as she had feared the bathroom was also one litter of boots,
belts, brass polish, shoe polish and dirty rags. Her youngest son
in shirt sleeves, smoking a pipe, his hair tousled and on end,
was sitting on the side of his bed cleaning his leggings on the
counterpane.

'We will have to be starting for church quite soon, Charles,'
she said anxiously.

'What do you think of these buttons, Mother?' said Charles, taking no notice at all of her question. 'I can't get my batman to do them like that, the lazy brute.'

'They are splendid!' said his mother with forced heartiness. 'You will be ready by a quarter to, darling, won't you. And would you like my nail scissors? Your nails really won't *quite* do for church.'

'No thanks,' said Charles, breathing on a button and rubbing it to a yet more glistening polish. 'Anyway I don't need scissors. A matchstick will do.'

'Well, I must get ready,' said his mother. 'If you aren't down by a quarter to I'll walk on slowly.'

She looked imploringly at her youngest son. He did not say the words, 'Oh, don't fuss,' but they were so clearly implied by the earnestness with which he applied himself to another button that his mother gave it up and went away. At a quarter to eleven she was ready in the drawing-room, at twelve minutes to eleven she was standing in the hall looking up the stairs, not quite daring to call her son. At ten minutes to eleven she very slowly left the house and very slowly walked towards the church, whither her husband had preceded her, as he liked to make sure that the markers were in the right place for him when he mounted the eagle to read the lessons. In the little avenue of pollarded limes that led to the church she met several friends and acquaintances and lingered to speak with them, casting an occasional look over her shoulder; but no khaki-clad figure was in sight. So she went in and took her usual place in the Harefield Park pew and knelt in meditation which was less directed to heavenly things than to trying to choke down her disappointment that Charles had not come. True he had offered to come and usually kept his word sooner or later; but it was so much more often later, as she knew by long experience, that she resigned herself and looked round the church.

The usual village people were in their places; mostly elderly men and women now, and a sprinkling of young mothers rather anxious over their children's behaviour. The pews in the north aisle were filled with what were obviously the Hosiers' girls, quite a pleasant, uninteresting, fresh-faced lot in the school uniform of grey flannel skirts and a rather shapeless purple flannel blazer with the Hosiers' badge (an unknown object supposed to represent a hand loom and the motto *Fide et Industria* which, as Miss Sparling had remarked in moments of exasperation with her Governors, had nothing to do with the case), later in the year to be covered by the school overcoat of grey cloth with a purple collar so that no one could wear it without shame in the holidays. A pudding-bowl grey felt hat with a purple ribbon completed the outfit, but as the manufacturers' stocks were now practically exhausted, an Act of Grace had been passed permitting girls to wear their own clothes provided they were suitable: a concession of which the dressier girls were going to take every advantage.

There were one or two elderly or obviously slightly deformed mistresses in charge, but no one whom Mrs Belton could place as a headmistress. The choir, now reduced to three boys, the tailor's daughter who was exempt because of her eyes, and the grocer's one assistant who was over fifty, took its place; the organ made a kind of noise; Mr Oriel hurried out of the vestry, and at the same moment Mrs Belton felt rather than saw (for the Park pew was in the front) the heads of the whole congregation turned towards the door. The mass movement compelled her also to turn and she saw her youngest son pausing just inside the church, every button winking in the sun which slanted down from the

35

clerestory windows, his green beret at what she privately thought an extremely vulgar angle. Apparently unconscious of the effect he had made, he removed his beret, came with reverent haste up the aisle, walked with solicitous deference over his father's legs, sat down between his parents, and placing the beret tenderly on the seat, knelt, absorbed in prayer.

Mrs Belton went through the service in a kind of waking swoon, gradually recovering consciousness as she perceived that her son was not showing off and had even gone so far as to clean his nails: sketchily it was true, but the readiness was all. And by the time Mr Oriel began his sermon and everyone settled down to try to think of something to think about, she was so bursting with pride over Charles's good looks and martial bearing, that if Mr Oriel had read aloud a Declaration of Indulgences she would have been none the wiser.

The service concluded, and two shillings supplied by Mr Belton for Charles to put in the plate, or rather the embroidered Liberty-green lozenge-shaped bag supported on a kind of small ecclesiastical turned broom handle, the congregation moved shufflingly out into the lime avenue. The Hosiers' girls emerged in a neat crocodile with the mistresses walking beside it and among them a woman who must have been concealed from Mrs Belton by a pillar, so obviously was she the headmistress.

On an impulse Mrs Belton went up to her and asked if she were Miss Sparling. The crocodile wavered and stood still, its eyes mostly fixed on Lieutenant Charles Belton's green beret and on the wearer below it.

'Yes, I am,' said the apparent headmistress in a very pleasant voice and with a questioning smile.

'I am so sorry, but I'm Mrs Belton,' said the former mistress of Harefield Park. 'I do hope the engine for the electric light is working all right, because it mostly doesn't. Fred!' she called to her husband, 'This is my husband – Miss Sparling. And this is my second boy, Charles!'

Charles, who was gently scowling (though it suited him very well) at his mother's slow progress, came forward and saluted.

'Oh, it was you that came in yesterday,' said Miss Sparling. 'I wish you could have stopped to tea. My girls were quite excited.'

Charles, who had not been unaware of the havoc his béret was making, looked sheepish. Miss Sparling, who obviously looked upon him as a mere child (much to his annoyance), then turned to his mother, and speaking as an equal, though with a pretty air of deference to fallen Royalty, said so far the engine had behaved beautifully and she was sure the girls would be very happy in a real home, and would do their very best to treat it kindly. Mrs Belton then asked if she might come and call. Miss Sparling said she would be delighted, and if Mrs Belton would not think it too abrupt, would she come to tea that afternoon, as the first Sunday in the term was always a good day for visitors.

'If Mr Belton would come too, it would be a great pleasure,' said Miss Sparling. 'And do bring—' Charles thought she was going to say 'your little boy,' but she finished the sentence – 'your son with you.'

Mrs Belton said they would love to come and if her elder son and her daughter had not made other plans for their short leave, might she bring them too. The crocodile re-formed. A large girl, who had been looking at the talkers, dropped her prayer book and picked it up again and the school went away.

Mr Oriel then approached.

'Oh, Mr Oriel,' said Mrs Belton, 'I wish you had been here. I was talking to Miss Sparling and she seems very nice. We are all

37

going up to tea with her this afternoon. You might have come too.'

'I have already been invited,' said Mr Oriel nervously. 'Miss Sparling was at the eight o'clock service with a few of the elder girls. They came on bicycles and we had a few words afterwards while some of them were pumping up their tyres. I feel I may have prejudged her unfairly. Perry has such a way of jumping to conclusions and he gave me a totally erroneous idea of her.'

'Then we'll all meet later,' said Mr Belton, who was tired of all this gossiping. 'Come along, Lucy, we'll be late for lunch.'

At the lunch table Mrs Belton conveyed Miss Sparling's tea invitation to the rest of the family.

'I do want to go and yet I don't,' she said. 'I think Miss Sparling is nice and I'd like to show we feel friendly to her, but I am feeling rather a coward about the Park. I might suddenly forget I don't live there and try to go up to my own bedroom and find it full of giggling girls.'

'Poor Mother,' said Elsa kindly but bracingly. 'I expect a mistress is in my room, with a nightgown case embroidered with lilies of the valley and a hairbrush with the bristles worn down.'

'There's only one person I'd hate to think of in my room,' said Charles, 'that's the beef to the instep girl. Did you see her after church, Mother?'

Mrs Belton said which was it.

'Oh well, if you didn't *see* her,' said Charles with slight scorn. 'The one that dropped her prayer book. I suppose she thought I was going to pick it up.'

'Rather a large girl?' said his mother.

Charles merely said she had said it. The sort that would play back at hockey, and give you an almighty swipe across the shins and could he have a lot more of that apple pudding.

As Mrs Belton looked at his plate and indeed the plates of all her children, she felt extremely glad that they still had some of the fruit and vegetables from the Park to depend on and the milk and cream of their own cows. For the Hosiers' girls were registered with the Pomfret Towers Dairy Ltd., and the Beltons' cows remained their property, which was just as well, for William Humble, the old cowman, would sooner have thrown all the milk into the lake than let anyone but the family have it, or lost the illegal profits he made by selling to some of his friends.

'Well, Lucy, what do you think of that Miss Sterling?' said Mr Belton. 'Quite a pleasant woman, I thought, and not bad-looking. It might be much worse.'

Elsa said she had seen enough of headmistresses when she was a boarder at the Barchester High School, and if it had been Miss Pettinger at the Park she would have refused to visit her. Anyway, she said, this one seemed to be a lady and the Pettinger wasn't.

A shocked exclamation from her mother led to a most interesting discussion as to what a lady really was; or what really was a lady. In this debate Mr and Mrs Belton did not take much part, for Miss Sparling was in a sense their guest and it seemed to them the height of ill-breeding to discuss the question of her being a lady at all.

'I suppose to a duke, or even a marquis, we all seem pretty common,' said Elsa. 'But if one of us married a duke I suppose we'd manage all right. As a matter of fact it must be much nicer not to be a lady now, because then one would have a lot more friends. Being a kind of lady makes one a bit particular even if one tries not to be. Some of the girls at my job are real ladies. I mean, like me if I am a lady, but the rest aren't. I mean they are awfully clever and good-looking and say the right things, but somehow they aren't just right. And all their people seem quite rich, but I don't think they'd fit in at Harefield. I suppose I'm a perfectly beastly snob, but I can't help it.'

Mrs Belton thought of her own youth, so sheltered, among girls of her own sort who might look funny now with their heavy knobs or puffs of hair, their long skirts, their unadorned lips and finger-nails, their mothers' eye always more or less over them, but were all what she roughly called one's own sort. And then she thought of her Elsa, brought up in what had almost amounted of late to genteel poverty, and now absorbed in whatever her secret work was, among a lot of young women who must undeniably have brains or they wouldn't be there, but many of whom her daughter, in normal times, would never have come across. All this mixing might be a good thing, but she felt too old for it and frankly hated it.

'It's a queer mixed lot everywhere now,' said Mr Belton. 'There are men on the Bench that don't know a gamekeeper from a poacher and think kindness pays with young hooligans that steal and destroy other people's property. There's a man sitting with me now that employs two thousand men at Hogglestock and heaven knows how many more over the other side of Barchester, and dresses like something on the stage. He may be all right, I don't say he isn't, but he throws his weight about and gets petrol when nobody else does, and frankly the less of him I see the better pleased I am.'

'Bad luck, Father,' said Commander Belton sympathetically. 'Of course we do get a few queer fish at the Admiralty, but taking it by and large the Navy isn't too bad. When you're all doing things together everything shakes down; and when we're at sea we don't worry much about whom we'll meet on land.'

'As a matter of fact,' said Charles, who had obviously been

wrestling with an unformulated thought for some time, 'if you get awfully mucky and sweaty with a lot of fellows over your tanks, you find they're all right. At least our lot are.'

Having brought this thought to birth he scraped the rest of the apple pudding on to his plate and covered it with the rest of the cream.

'If only life were one long crisis, everyone would be perfect,' said Mrs Belton.

'But luckily it isn't,' said her husband. 'Don't talk nonsense, my dear.'

'Well, I do hope my son-in-law and daughters-in-law will be our sort,' said Mrs Belton wistfully. 'Of course I'd love anyone any of you married, but it would be much more fun if it was someone like ourselves.'

'In books girls marry their bosses,' said Elsa, 'but all mine have hundreds of wives and children. I'm concentrating on a career. If you get engaged the man only goes and gets killed or taken prisoner, and by the time the war's over there won't be a spare man left. So I'm going to be the perfect woman secretary and marry a Cabinet Minister as his second wife and be photographed looking quite hideous.'

'There won't be a single gentleman in the Cabinet in five years,' said Mr Belton gloomily.

'I suppose I'll get killed,' said Charles, who was making havoc among Lady Norton's biscuits, 'so I needn't worry. But I do wish there were some nice girls here for my leave. Even what you call nice, Mother, would do.'

'Perhaps we'll find some at Miss Sparling's school,' said Commander Belton. 'If I can find an heiress, Father, I'll marry her however common and pay off the mortgage and rebuild the almshouses and restore the family fortunes.'

His father was about to protest violently that the place wasn't mortgaged and the almshouses were in perfectly good condition, but suddenly realizing that it was a joke he said Freddy had better marry that stout girl that was Charles's friend, and the conversation moved to other topics.

A pleasing feature of the houses on the south side of the High Street was that the long gardens each communicated directly with the park by a door in the end wall. The keys remained the property of the reigning Belton and were not lightly bestowed. The Perrys at Plassey House had one, so had Mr Updike the solicitor at Clive's Corner, Mrs Hoare the widow of the former Pomfret estate agent at Dowlah Cottage, and a few other well-deserving tenants. Arcot House possessed one till Mrs Ellangowan-Hornby had her stroke. A month or so after this the old lady had sent for Mr Belton and summoning all her will-power, which was considerable, had forced her swollen tongue to utter and her almost helpless hand to write a few words stating that the key had been returned to her landlord. Having so delivered herself, in the presence of both her nurses (the interview having been expressly arranged at an hour when the day nurse went off duty and the night nurse came on), she made a few inarticulate sounds interpreted by the night nurse as 'so that the nurses shan't use it,' and relapsed into her usual immobile state, only showing by a fitful twinkling of her eyes her extreme pleasure at having got the better of her attendants.

So instead of going out of the front door, up the street, past the church and the Nabob's Head, in at the lodge gates and up the mile of winding drive, the Belton family walked through their garden, went through the door at the end, and emerged upon a rough lane by which wood and coals were apt to deliver themselves. They then climbed a stile almost opposite their garden door and took a footpath which ran slanting across the park to the house. This path was at once the treasure and the plague of its possessor. It was a very old right of way which had been used by the villagers for hundreds of years to get to Little Misfit, skirting the Park grounds as they went, and passing directly under the windows of the West Pavilion. Under the orders of the War Agricultural Executive Committee Mr Belton had put that part of his land under the plough. But sooner than interfere with the people's rights, he had the roller taken over the course of the path every year and took each summer a sad pleasure in seeing his neighbours walking on their ancestral way between the ripening corn. No one was grateful and the faithful tenantry were more than apt to walk two and even three or four abreast, thus contributing their mite to the war effort by treading down the corn. But no one was more annoyed than the secretary of the local branch of the Hikers' Rights Preservation Society. This gentleman, who was a small chemist and a keen opposer of what he called feudal arrogance, spent most of his time walking over the field paths of the district (a job which owing to the excellent and complex network of rights of way took him roughly eleven months of every year), hoping to find evidence of arrogance in blocked, overgrown or ploughed-up paths. But much to his fury the landlords, large and small, appeared to be as interested in the paths as he was, and Roddy Wicklow, the Pomfret estate agent, back on leave with a wound in his leg, meeting him one day near Six Covers Corner, had taken a malicious pleasure in forcing the champion of the people's rights to walk through three-quarters of a mile of a small sunk lane deeply embedded in thorn trees and brambles with a stream running down the middle of it, which lane had fallen into disuse simply because the public, and hikers in particular, were too lazy to use it, preferring to tread down Lord Pomfret's corn on one side, or frighten his gravid Alderney cows on the other. Each successive autumn since Mr Belton ploughed the park had this elderly Gracchus watched the ploughing with an auspicious (as hoping to get Mr Belton into trouble by its means) and a drooping (as one mourning the final extinction of Magna Carta) eye. And each successive autumn had he experienced the mortification of seeing the path neatly rolled out and Mr Belton taking a ceremonial walk across it, which did not prevent his doing a good deal of boasting at the H.R.P.S. yearly meeting.

At this moment of the year the stubble lay pale and mangy, not yet touched by the plough. The clumps of beeches, where a branch here and there was just beginning to flame into pale gold, looked strangely isolated to Mr and Mrs Belton, who still always thought of them as standing on a grassy slope, with sheep wandering among them.

'There were still some deer here when my father was a boy,' said Mr Belton as they breasted the gentle slope.

His three children looked at one another. As far as they could remember their father had made this remark when crossing the park ever since they could walk with him. At ordinary times it would produce an irritation which caused them to make hideous faces at each other, or even mutter under their breath, but today, what with the good lunch, the excitement of the new home and the feeling of how rum it was to be visiting their own house as guests, they only smiled in a tolerant way, Commander Belton going so far as to reply, 'Nice little things. Very pretty they must have looked.'

As they approached the West Pavilion there was a short discussion as to whether they were expected to go up to the front door, or slink in at the side, ended by the appearance of Miss Sparling at her private entrance.

'Please come in,' she called to the visitors. 'I thought we would have tea here first and look at the school afterwards. I can't tell you,' she added to Mrs Belton as she took them into the pavilion, 'how heavenly it is to have a kind of home of one's own again. I have managed to get my books and some of my furniture down and no one's allowed to come here unless I ask them. The Governors very kindly got me an extension telephone put in.'

So speaking she took them into what had been one of the bachelors' bedrooms, shut up of late years as there was no one whose business it was to keep it clean. There were books all along one side, uninteresting but quite presentable chairs and tables, and on the walls what Mrs Belton recognized as the very large excellent photographs of Greek and Roman remains taken by Mr Belton's grandfather, a keen amateur of the wet plate, when abroad on his honeymoon, long ago banished to the billiard room.

'I hope you don't mind,' said Miss Sparling, following Mrs Belton's glance. 'I like them so much, and it seemed a pity for no one to look at them.'

'Quite right,' said Mr Belton. 'Not a bit the sort of thing for the billiard room. Enough to put you off your stroke. Aren't you using the billiard room then?'

'I'm afraid we can't this term, because of the heating,' said Miss Sparling. 'But in the spring I shall let some of the elder girls play.'

'Good God!' said Mr Belton, and checked himself. What he was going to say was, 'They'll cut the cloth,' but a sudden recollection that the Hosiers' Company, and thus Miss Sparling as their representative, were for the present the legal owners of his

45

billiard table and paying the insurance on it, besides his gentle-manly wish not to embarrass a lady, made him leave it unsaid.

His son Charles, less inhibited, said, 'Oh Lord! I mean is it all right? I mean a cue's an awkward thing if you aren't used to it. I remember cutting the cloth at Pomfret Towers when I was a kid and getting told off like anything.'

Miss Sparling smiled at Charles in a way that made him slightly uneasy and said to Mrs Belton, 'Please sit down and we'll have tea at once.' She then rang the bell and continued, 'I hope you won't feel nervous about the table, Mr Belton. As a matter of fact a good many of our girls play at home. And Miss Holly, my secretary, whom I would like to introduce you to later, is a very good amateur.'

At this moment the door opened and tea was brought in by a stout girl of about fifteen whom Mrs Belton at once rec-ognized as Ellen Humble, granddaughter of her cowman. On seeing Mrs Belton Ellen nearly dropped the tray, but was saved by Commander Belton who helped her to steady it and place it on the table. Mrs Belton asked after her mother, but Ellen, overcome by the attentions of a real naval officer, was reduced to idiocy and bundled herself out of the room.

'A very good girl,' said Miss Sparling, taking no notice of her handmaid's behaviour. 'My Governors didn't like the idea of my sleeping alone out here, so Ellen is sleeping in the little room at the back, in case burglars come.'

'But would she be much use?' said Elsa.

'Not a bit,' said Miss Sparling calmly. 'But after she has gone to sleep at nine o'clock nothing wakes her. As she couldn't do anything to a burglar except stare or giggle, it makes me feel much more peaceful.'

Mr Belton looked at Miss Sparling with a mixture of pity

and admiration, which made no apparent impression on that lady at all. Seen at close quarters and in her own surroundings, Miss Sparling was far from unattractive; a tall, well-built woman, about forty-five at a guess, with a not unbecoming majesty of figure, dark wavy hair cut rather short and lying close to her head, large brown eyes, good teeth, neat feet and well-shaped, competent hands. Her voice as we already know was pleasant, and though her face had in repose a rather commanding expression, her smile softened it very becomingly.

'I am expecting Mr Oriel,' she said. 'He has probably gone to the front door, and I left word that he was to be brought here.'

'Miss Sparling,' said Charles, with the desperation of one who has been waiting to ask an indiscreet question for some time and can contain himself no longer, 'when you said your girls played billiards at home, I thought the Hosiers' Girls' School was a kind of secondary school. I don't mean rudely, but I saw some of the Hosiers' boys when they were at Southbridge School and they weren't quite what you would call a public school, I mean they did awfully well in exams, but they weren't – oh, well, you know what I mean, only it's so awfully difficult to say what one means, only they didn't seem as if they'd have billiard tables at home if it isn't rude to say so.'

By this time Charles's family would have been quite glad if he had been back in his billet at Shrimpington-on-Sea, and indeed Charles himself, hearing his own voice faltering in an embarrassed vacuum, wouldn't have been sorry if he could have been miraculously transported elsewhere. But Miss Sparling appeared to take his tactless questions quite as a matter of course, and was about to answer him when the extension telephone rang to say that Mr Oriel had been rescued from the front door and was even now on his way to the pavilion under the guard of Miss

Holly. There was a slight rearranging of chairs to make room for the newcomers and then Miss Holly, a short stout woman with small black eyes and a very businesslike air, came in with the Vicar. Miss Sparling greeted her guest kindly, introduced Miss Holly to the Beltons and told Ellen Humble to bring some more hot water.

Conversation was made easy by Miss Sparling and Mrs Belton, both accomplished hostesses, and Mr Oriel who could always be relied upon. Elsa discovered that Miss Holly had two friends in the hush-hush business and had very sound views about Miss Pettinger, Mr Belton talked to his eldest son about the estate, and Charles made a very hearty tea in spite of his tactless remarks a few moments earlier.

'I was thinking,' said Mr Oriel, whose hospitality was as unbounded as his housekeeper's cooking was good, even in the fifth year of a totalitarian war, 'of a little dinner party to honour my new parishioner. I hardly like to ask a lady to come out at night, but the blackout is still well after seven o'clock, we would dine at half-past, and I will get the Nabob's Head to send its little car for you and take you back. They will always do this for me if it is a short distance and due notice is given. Would you feel equal to it, Miss Sparling? And if so, will you name a day convenient to you perhaps next week, before the blackout gets any earlier. Not Sunday, for it would mean a cold supper, I fear, rather late; and not Friday because it is the Confirmation Class.'

Miss Sparling thanked him and said perhaps a Wednesday then, which was quite a good evening for her.

'Wednesday, how stupid of me, is the British Legion smoking concert,' said Mr Oriel, 'and though they would feel honoured if I brought you, it begins at seven o'clock and usually goes on till about half-past nine with the interval for refreshments.'

Miss Sparling said Thursday would make a pleasant break in the week.

'Thursday then,' said Mr Oriel, much gratified. 'Oh dear, my housekeeper goes out on Thursday, and though she is very kind about changing her day to suit me, she has done it twice running, once because I had a cold and once because she had, so I feel a certain diffidence about asking her again.'

Miss Sparling said Monday, if not too short notice, would be a very pleasant way of beginning the week.

'Excellent, excellent,' said Mr Oriel. 'I hope, Mrs Belton, that you and your husband will come. I shall ask the Perrys, and that will make us six.'

Mrs Belton, who always tried to accept evening invitations in the village as it was the only way of getting her husband to see people at leisure, said they would be delighted.

'Good, good,' said Mr Oriel, pulling out a notebook. 'I shall make a note of it. That is next Monday evening then. There is something down here, but I must have written it without my glasses on, for it is quite illegible. Siskin? No, it can't be that. Bisley? I often say to myself,' said Mr Oriel, looking up from his engagement book, 'that I must learn to do things slowly and in order. I have some new glasses and I cannot get used to them, so I don't put them on; and I am brought to confusion. Oh!' he continued with a change of tone, 'I have got it. Bishop. Of course he would choose that date; just like him,' said Mr Oriel, who in common with practically all the clergy of Barchester, except old Canon Robarts who had been gently mad for years, entertained most unchristian feelings towards his overlord. 'He has summoned me to the Palace,' he continued with what he felt to be an accent of biting sarcasm on the *summoned*, 'at six o'clock and that means I can't possibly get a bus back till the

7.25. There is much to be said for the constitution of the Church of Scotland. I doubt whether even a Moderator would exercise such petty tyranny as his present lordship. But I forget myself. If the Bishop is a friend of yours, Miss Sparling, I must apologize most sincerely.'

'Please do not,' said Miss Sparling. 'The Bishop and his wife are great friends of Miss Pettinger with whom I have been living. Miss Pettinger did once take me to a meeting at the Palace where I sat in a corner and didn't know anyone, but that is the beginning and end of my association with them.' This was said in a pleasant level voice, without any tinge of acrimony, but it was common knowledge, though not through any indiscretion of Miss Sparling's, that her bread had been bitter and Miss Pettinger's stairs very hard to her, and her hearers expressed their sympathy in a kind of hum or murmur as of a Puritan congregation applauding an inspired corporal's words of edification.

Mr Oriel almost said Hurrah! but checking himself, and deciding with the incredible swiftness of unworded thought that neither Alleluia nor Kyrie Eleison though exactly expressing his feelings would be entirely in place, he put his notebook back in whichever pocket a clergyman keeps his notebook in.

'Then I fear that leaves us only Tuesday,' said Mr Oriel penitently. 'That is if you would not mind my being a little late as I have to take a funeral for a dear old friend at Nutfield that afternoon and stay to tea with the family and there is only one bus back which is usually behind time.'

Miss Sparling said that would be delightful.

'You can't, Mr Oriel, if it's the bus I didn't come in,' said Elsa, 'because it's off. I got a lift on a motor-bike with a friend of Charles's, but he's gone to Rickmansworth.'

This depressing news threw everyone into a fever of trying

to arrange Mr Oriel's Tuesday afternoon for him, but short of cutting the funeral altogether, there was nothing for it but that he should go by train from Nutfield to Barchester and come out by the 7.25 bus. Silence fell.

'I say, Mr Oriel,' said Charles, 'when you said it was a dear old friend you were doing the funeral for, was it the one who's dead or the parson?'

Mr Oriel looked puzzled. Mr Belton said What was that Charles was saying.

'Don't be an idiot, Charles,' said Elsa. 'He means are you taking a friend's funeral or a funeral for a friend, Mr Oriel.'

'I suppose one would call it my friend's funeral,' said Mr Oriel doubtfully. 'It is the Vicar of Nutfield.'

'But he's not dead,' said Mr Belton. 'At least he rang me up this afternoon. Must be some mistake.'

'Of course he isn't dead,' said Mr Oriel, with what in so mild a man was almost indignation. 'How can he be dead if I am taking Horton's funeral for him – the Bartons' old butler, you know. He is going away for a few days' much-needed change. Miss Sparling, this is most distressing, but I fear we shall have to put the party off till the following week.'

'You haven't tried Saturday,' said Miss Holly.

'Miss Holly always sets us right,' said Miss Sparling, making Mrs Belton think of Miss Trotwood and Mr Dick. 'Saturday then, Mr Oriel, if it suits you.'

There was no impediment to Saturday, so the engagement was made, and the Perrys were to be bespoken. Miss Sparling then suggested that they might care to see her little apartment before going over to the school. Mr Oriel, from a kind of delicacy, declined the first treat and remained in the sitting-room, talking with Miss Holly and Commander Belton. But the rest of the Belton family saw her neat bedroom, and the little room where Ellen Humble slept, both comfortable, both curiously lacking in personality.

'How do you manage about your bath water?' asked Mr Belton, intent on practical things. 'My father put a bath in when we used this as the bachelors' wing, but there are about fifty yards of piping from the furnace and the water was never more than tepid. The second footman used to have to bring big cans of boiling water in the morning.'

'The Governors put in an electric heater for me,' said Miss Sparling, opening the bathroom door. 'And they kindly put a little electric cooker in that sort of lobby and partitioned it off from the passage, which makes a nice little kitchen if I want to be independent.'

Mr Belton saw, admired, and had a pang of envy for people who could afford these comforts. But he liked Miss Sparling and for her sake was willing to forgive the Hosiers their wealth.

The whole party then went along the covered arcade to the main building. In the hall a number of girls were talking or reading. Sounds as of ping-pong balls and a gramophone came from the drawing-room and morning-room. As the party came in, all the girls stood up.

'I have brought Mr and Mrs Belton, whose beautiful house you are living in, to see what we are doing,' said Miss Sparling, suddenly becoming quite a different person. 'This is our head prefect, Mrs Belton. She is sitting for a university scholarship and hopes to take up teaching. Miss Apperley, our games mistress; Miss Head, our literature mistress.'

She mentioned a few more names and dismissed the girls to their recreations with a graciousness that Elsa much admired and resolved to try to copy for the benefit of her juniors at the hush-hush job. Then she took Mrs Belton up to look at the bedrooms, leaving the rest of the party to their own devices.

It is the duty of a Captain in one of His Majesty's vessels of war to entertain at every port when cruising a number of people chiefly female whom he has never seen before, does not wish to see now and will probably never see again. But such is the discipline of the Royal Navy, that unless a Governor's wife or a highly race-conscious local potentate is coming aboard, the Captain orders the Commander to carry on, while he himself goes riding, or bathing, or sits on an old friend's veranda with long drinks.

So to Commander Belton a crowd of unknown women had no terrors and he chatted, as the Press so knowingly puts it, with mistresses and girls, bringing temporary devastation by his blue eyes and uniform and earning universal admiration by having lately had the head prefect's brother serving as a midshipman under him. Emboldened by this discovery, the head prefect asked him if he liked dancing, and led him to the morning-room where he obligingly partnered one young lady after another.

Mr Oriel begged Miss Holly to make his excuses to Miss Sparling and hurried off for the evening service. Charles, who despised dancing because he wouldn't learn to dance, stood about looking handsomely awkward and sulky till Miss Holly in her universal competence took pity on him and talked to him about himself till he felt sufficiently at ease to talk about himself to her.

Presently his mother and Miss Sparling came back from their tour and they all went into the morning-room to look at the dancing. A tall lumpish girl with a pasty face was standing by the gramophone, changing the records.

'I think I remember that girl by the gramophone after church this morning,' said Mrs Belton. 'Isn't she the one that dropped her prayer book?'

'It is Heather Adams,' said Miss Sparling. 'She has been having horrid boils, poor child. Dr Perry had to lance one for her and I am afraid she is starting another on her chin. Her father owns big works at Hogglestock and on the other side of Barchester and she is an only child. She is not a clever girl at most lessons but her mathematics are quite unusual.'

'Adams,' said Mr Belton in rather too loud a voice. 'That's the man I was telling you about who sits on the bench with me. The one that—'

But Mrs Belton, seeing that her husband was about to bring out some remark which might make the boil-afflicted Heather Adams uncomfortable, hurriedly spoke to her, saying she was so glad to see the girls dancing.

'We used to have balls in the long drawing-room,' she said, 'but that was when the children were little. Do you like dancing, Heather?'

Heather, upon whose unfortunate chin the next boil was beginning to be but too apparent, said she didn't mind it, but it was silly to dance with girls, and put on a fresh record.

Mrs Belton fully sympathized with her young friend, but did not add that there was to one of her generation something almost disgraceful in the spectacle of girls dancing together because there were no men.

'Charles isn't doing anything, my younger son that was at church with me this morning,' said Mrs Belton. 'He must dance with you. You have been putting on records for the others quite long enough. I'll get him.'

But Charles, having caught his mother's last words, took one look of terrified horror at Heather Adams and turning to Miss

54

Holly said, 'We might dance a bit. I'm not frightfully good, but it seems a pity not to.'

Miss Holly, who had for once not seen what was going on, owing to her attention being distracted by Isabella Ferdinand whose Sunday dress had split under one arm, did not realize the deliberate slight to Heather Adams, so remarking that it was his funeral, she seized Charles in her short but powerful arms and bounded away round the room with him like a hard indiarubber ball. Heather Adams's pasty face was suffused with a dull flush and Mrs Belton, for once quite at a loss, was annoyed with Charles's selfishness and sorry for Heather who though unattractive had not deserved the snub. Commander Belton who had been recovering from a round with the Captain of Hockey, whose idea of dancing appeared to be to hack her partner's shins with her feet as vigorously as she hacked her opponent's leggings with her hockey stick, saw the whole tragi-comedy and thanking the Captain of Hockey warmly for her company, he moved to Heather Adams's side and offering her his arm with a smile, for the noise of the gramophone and all the girls laughing and chattering made speech difficult, drew her into the dance. His kindness brought no particular reward. Heather Adams was a cumbrous armful, clumsy in her movements and so occupied by counting her steps under her breath that she was unable to answer the few polite remarks that her partner shouted into her ear.

Presently the gramophone ran down. Mrs Belton gave her family a mother's look to collect them. Commander Belton thanked Heather Adams, whose large face was now shiny as well as pasty, and rejoined his family. As they had left various coats and gloves and sticks in the West Pavilion, Miss Sparling said she would go back with them and let them out by her private door. Arrived in her apartment, she offered her guests some sherry in a very gentlemanly way. Mr Belton's admiration for her rose on finding that she had also a gentlemanly taste in wine and he congratulated her.

'I am glad it pleases you,' said Miss Sparling. 'It belonged to my father. He had a small cellar but a very good one.'

This unexpected sidelight on Miss Sparling's family made Mr Belton, for no apparent reason except to bring shame upon his family, ask which university her father was at.

'He wasn't at a university,' said Miss Sparling. 'He was a wine merchant, but only in quite a small way.'

'But he had very good taste,' said Mr Belton, vaguely feeling that by this tribute he could somehow make up to the late Mr Sparling the want of a university education. 'It's a sherry anyone might be glad to have in his cellar.'

What Mr Belton had set out to say was 'any gentleman', but had altered his phrase even as it left his mouth, though not quite so quickly but that Miss Sparling's ear caught the hesitation.

'He was a very good father,' she said simply, 'and devoted to my mother who was a clergyman's daughter. They died when I was fifteen and my grandfather made me get scholarships and left me all his books. It all helps me in my work.'

'Your library do you mean?' said Elsa, much impressed by a woman who had made a career for herself by her own efforts.

'That of course,' said Miss Sparling. 'But I really meant only being half a lady. You were asking about the girls here Mr Belton,' she continued, addressing Charles who felt and looked very sheepish. 'They are mostly much the same as I am, only they have wealthy families and not so many books. In London my girls came from good lower middle-class families, quite a lot of them well off in a quiet way. When we were evacuated down here and became a boarding school, the people who had got rich quickly in war business began to send their girls to us, like poor Heather Adams to whom Commander Belton was so kind.'

Commander Belton looked slightly confused. His mother mentally added another good mark to Miss Sparling's score for realizing the nobility of Freddy's behaviour. Mr Belton began to look at Miss Sparling's books, opening some and admiring their binding or their contents. It must be confessed that part of his interest was in the fly leaf, where he secretly hoped to find who Miss Sparling's grandfather was, but most of them had evidently been bought at sales, for the inscriptions or the labels with coats of arms were varied. So pleasantly was the time passing with books and talk and sherry that Mrs Belton almost jumped when she caught sight of the clock and realized that it was nearly seven. At that moment Dr Perry came in.

'Good evening, everybody,' he said cheerfully. 'I've just seen that Adams girl, Miss Sparling. I'm going to give her injections for those boils. Plaguey things they are. She looks better though. Not quite such a mass of gloom. Does she get enough exercise?'

'I can hardly say yet,' said Miss Sparling. 'You see she came as a day girl while we were in Barchester. Miss Pettinger, who took a kind interest in the Hosiers' Girls,' said Miss Sparling without any change in her voice or expression, 'often used to tell me that they had not enough of the team spirit, by which I think she meant that they didn't all play hockey. Certainly Heather didn't if she could possibly get out of it, but she is so clumsy, poor thing, that games were really a torture to her.'

'Well, that's neither here nor there,' said Dr Perry, who had the lowest opinion of organized games for girls. 'What else does she do? Does she go for walks?'

'I don't know what she did at home,' said Miss Sparling, 'but my games mistress is arranging walks and garden work and I will see that Heather gets out as much as possible.'

'Good,' said Dr Perry, looking at his watch. 'I must be off. Can I give any of you a lift, Mrs Belton? It's all quite legal, because I'm going home and can drop you at your door.'

Mrs Belton gratefully accepted, for she was rather tired. The rest of her family went off by the field path.

'Well, what do you think of your tenant?' said Dr Perry, whose curiosity about his friends was as boundless as his professional kindness and devotion. 'Nice woman. A bit long in the tooth, but a fine upstanding figure. Quite a good lot of girls too. Not exactly out of the top drawer, but that's all the better for them nowadays. Norman blood and all that doesn't get you anywhere now. I'm sorry myself. My people are the ordinary run, not a bit of blue blood, but I've lived long enough to see that breeding tells. That woman, Miss Sparling, has breeding somewhere all right. Interesting study too. I look forward to seeing more of her.'

Mrs Belton, who though humble had a secret pride in an unblemished Saxon ancestry as far as these things can be known, agreed with Dr Perry on general lines, and said she and her husband were dining with Mr Oriel on the following Saturday to meet Miss Sparling and understood that Dr and Mrs Perry were to be invited.

'Oh yes, I nearly killed Oriel outside the lychgate on my way up,' said Dr Perry. 'All his fault for not having those yews cut back. No one coming round the corner can see a thing. He told me about his dinner. I can't come I'm sorry to say. I've got to meet Sir Abel Fillgrave at Barchester that evening. But my wife is going.'

Mrs Belton was sorry to hear this. Not that she disliked Mrs Perry, but that lady was given to enthusiasms and causes and apt to talk of nothing but the cause of the moment. She had just had a severe bout of Mixo-Lydianism, during which she had plagued all her friends with demands that they should buy rather dirty peasant embroidery or subscribe to a translation of the Mixo-Lydian national epic *Gradkonski* (so called from the mythical national hero Gradko and written in an old Mixo-Lydian verse of extreme obscurity). So Mrs Belton said how nice it would be to see Mrs Perry and how were the boys.

Dr Perry said doing nicely. Bob was now House Physician at Knight's, Jim had got the Smallbones Anatomical Medal, and Gus was doing a refresher course on Leprosy and Allied Diseases.

"'Axis diseases, I hope, my boy,' I said,' said Dr Perry laughing heartily, so Mrs Belton laughed heartily too.

Her medical man then told her most indiscreetly, but he knew his hearer well, some gossip from the Barchester General Hospital, and while he did so Mrs Belton thanked her good fortune that the subject of Dr Perry's boys had dropped, for nice, hard-working boys as they were, she had always found it difficult to tell them apart as they seemed to have no distinguishing features and were practically all the same age, Bob being only fifteen months older than the twins, Jim and Gus. There had been a time, at the beginning of the war, when the fortunes of the Perry family had occupied the mind of Harefield to a considerable extent. All three boys had been destined by their father for a professional career, the word professional in his mind having no meaning but as applied to some branch of bodily healing. Bob had just finished his second year at Knight's Hospital when war broke out and his brothers their first year. All three boys very naturally wished to join the Navy, Army or Air Force and be killed at once, but the authorities were not favourable, their father, a martinet in his own family and almost a worshipper of his calling, commanded, reasoned, and even pleaded. The boys submitted, and after a brief period of rebellion very unpleasant to the harassed authorities at Knight's and to their parents when they came home, settled down and had done brilliantly. Jim and Gus were now full of hope of being sent abroad and Bob, after thinking the matter out, had decided that to be the youngest House Physician Knight's had ever had, nearly made up for not having been killed or wounded. One or other was often down for a weekend or a night, but from the vantage of Harefield Park Mrs Belton had been able to remain vague about their individuality. Now, an inhabitant of Harefield High Street, a tenant of her tenant, she must apply herself to memorizing somehow Bob's slightly darker hair, Jim's slightly longer nose and Gus's bushier eyebrows. She sighed.

'You need a rest and a change,' said Dr Perry, drawing up before Arcot House. 'You can't have either: no need to tell *me*. I'll tell Potter to send you up something. Don't forget to take it. Are you taking that glucose I told you to?'

'Yes,' said Mrs Belton with simple untruth, for that seemed the easier path.

'Where did you get it then?' said Dr Perry. 'I know for a fact that Potter slipped up on his last quota and was sold out the day it came in. Barchester?'

'Nowhere,' said Mrs Belton, reduced by her medical man's insistence to telling the truth. 'I haven't had any for three weeks. I said I had just to keep you quiet.'

'I knew you hadn't,' said Dr Perry, with a triumph that almost outweighed his annoyance with women who wouldn't look after themselves. 'Potter had his quota yesterday. I'll tell him to send you some with the tonic.'

'I lost your prescription,' said Mrs Belton meekly.

'No excuse,' said Dr Perry. 'Potter knows me well enough to give my patients what they ought to have first and get my prescription afterwards. He could retire any day on what he's made out of my patients and the lipstick trade. Good night.'

He drove away and Mrs Belton went into Arcot House. It felt small after the Park, but warm and friendly, and she gratefully went into the firelit drawing-room. A few moments later her husband came in.

'Nice afternoon,' he said. 'If we can't live at the Park, I'd sooner have those girls there than a lot of soldiers. Burn the house down as likely as not.'

With which unpatriotic but excusable remark he sat down and stretched his legs out to the blaze.

'Fred,' said his wife. 'You know Miss Sparling took me over the house while you were watching the girls dancing.'

'Well,' said her husband, as she paused.

'What do you think she has done, Fred? She has locked my bedroom and says no one shall use it and she will see that it is kept aired. And if I ever want to come for a night, she says, I can go straight into it. I don't suppose I'll ever want to, but I must say it is extremely nice to think that it isn't full of mistresses, or girls with boils.'

Before Mr Belton could answer, their children came in with a turning-on of lights and some cheerful noise, so Mrs Belton did not know what her husband would have said. He for his part was just as glad not to have to say anything, for though he would have loudly condemned his wife as sentimental, he was secretly much touched.

The visit of the Beltons was naturally the chief topic of conversation during supper at Harefield Park. Two parties had already formed. The one, headed by the head prefect whose brother had served under Commander Belton, could not sufficiently praise his eyes, his gold braid, his small-talk, and determined with one accord to marry him as soon as they left school. The other, which had for leader Miss Ferdinand, who had strong dramatic leanings and was a natural rebel, was already in a state of Byronic devotion to Charles, whose scowling manner and marked disinclination for their society had made an excellent effect.

At the mistresses' table it was agreed that Mrs Belton was charming; and, after a short pause, that Miss Belton was quite pretty, but rather vacant; this last adjective being the contribution of the science mistress who looked round proudly and almost cackled.

'Vacant? Pff!' said Miss Holly, suddenly charging into the conversation like a catapult. 'Miss Belton has any amount of brains. Any amount. Too many perhaps. When we've got too many, we don't marry.'

Her colleagues might have been tempted to find this remark offensive, but the tribute to their brains was flattering and they were used to Miss Holly's brusque ways, so the matter dropped.

Miss Sparling, presiding at the High Table, managed to agree with everyone or at any rate to give the impression of agreement, and Miss Holly, as she often did, admired her employer's gifts and wondered if anyone really knew her.

The case of Commander Belton *v.* Lieutenant Belton continued after supper and in the dormitories. In what had been the largest spare bedroom, Miss Ferdinand, in her pyjamas, with a green satin handkerchief sachet as a beret, gave a very good performance of Lieutenant Belton's scowl, followed by a spirited impersonation of Commander Belton dancing with Heather Adams, represented by a bolster, in the middle of which Heather Adams came back from having her bath. The performance suddenly collapsed, for though no one had any particular liking for Heather, she was quiet and inoffensive enough and they were on the whole a good-natured set of girls. Heather, apparently

62

unaware of what had been going on, brushed her scanty reddish hair and got into bed.

'If I was Commander Belton,' said a pretty, sharp-faced girl whose only claim to fame was that she had a schoolmaster brother who had been turned down medically for the Forces and loudly proclaimed himself a Conscientious Objector, 'I wouldn't stick at the Admiralty. I'd get sent to sea and *do* something; not have tea with typists.'

Her audience, taken aback by this sudden attack on their new idol, remained stupefied. Suddenly Heather Adams sat up in bed.

'As a matter of fact,' she said, 'he was wounded three times and blown up in his ship and then he rowed about a hundred miles with the men he had saved and got them all back to England. Didn't you see his ribbons?'

She then flounced down in her bed, turned over with her back to her friends and pulled the bedclothes over her head. The rest of the dormitory, silenced and impressed, went quickly to bed and were soon all asleep. Not so Heather, who after crying with silent rage under the blankets, presently came up to breathe. For at least half an hour after the others were asleep she lay awake thinking of Commander Belton. Her brief passion for Charles was utterly extinguished, killed by his brutality. Even the thought of a green beret, which between church and a quarter to six had given her a delightful feeling of going to be sick whenever it came to her mind, was now an idle dream. Its place was taken by a dark blue uniform, a kindly smile, a guiding arm, soothing conversation. That what she had told the girls was made up by her on the spur of the moment, in fact a lie, did not trouble her in the least. For his sake anything was excusable, and she would cheerfully do it again. If only she could die while saving Commander Belton's life, she would be perfectly happy. Or even better, make a will leaving him all the money that she would one day inherit, and then die. Or perhaps come into the money quite soon and buy back (for she was ignorant of the business arrangements of the Hosiers' Company) Harefield Park for him, give it to him on the day of his wedding to a very beautiful aristocrat, and then go into a nunnery and die. This arrangement, to be followed by her burial in Harefield church and periodical visits of Commander Belton and his beautiful wife to her humble tombstone, gave her such pleasure that she sleepily elaborated it till deep slumber claimed her for its own.

3

By eight o'clock on Monday morning all three young Beltons had left the house and returned to their respective jobs. Mr Belton had his usual local and county work to do, and as he had his estate office in the East Pavilion his life, apart from coming back to Arcot House to eat and sleep instead of to the Park, was not much changed. Mrs Belton, grimly and efficiently seconded by Wheeler, well-meaningly though temperamentally by the cook, and zealously though ineffectively by Florrie Wheeler, aged sixteen, very soon had her household organized. The Red Cross working party that used to meet once a week at Harefield Park now met at Arcot House, and Mrs Belton found that she enjoyed the various meetings at Plassey House, Clive's Corner, or Dowlah Cottage all the more that she could get home in a few minutes instead of having to walk or bicycle a mile uphill in all weathers. Dr Perry was, as indeed he always was, as good as his word and looked in on Potter the chemist the very next day and had a tonic and a tin of glucose sent to Arcot House. Mrs Belton, after the fashion of intelligent women, took some of each when she thought of it, and if she had forgotten it took a double dose of one or both for luck.

It will hardly surprise our readers to learn that the evening chosen with so much trouble for Mr Oriel's dinner party had to be altered after all, because his housekeeper had a slight attack of influenza. But a fresh date was settled for the first week in October which suited everybody, including Dr Perry. On the afternoon of this day (which was a Wednesday) Mrs Belton set out for Plassey House where Mrs Perry had a working party once a week, though no one ever quite knew what it was for. It had been begun, long before the war, to make children's underclothes for an East London Mission. At the outbreak of war all the children were sent to one of the midland counties and Mrs Perry turned her workers on to making pyjamas for the Barchester Infirmary. When this was amalgamated with the Barchester General Hospital who already had more pyjamas than they knew what to do with and in any case did not approve of the pattern used by the Infirmary, all the ladies switched onto sea-boot stockings for the Merchant Navy, but were headed off from this by an urgent appeal for nightgowns for expectant mothers evacuated from a bombed West-country town. This was followed by an interval of bandage-making during which every worker got her hair, eyes and nose full of particles of lint besides being mostly too stupid (though delightful intelligent women) to sew a many-tailed bandage together in the right way. So when Lady Pomfret, the head of the Barsetshire W.V.S., came to address the united Harefield Working Parties and told them that at the Barchester General the nurses hated and despised the elaborate many-tailed bandages and used them as dusters whenever the ward sister took her eye off them, the Plassey House party gave a sigh of relief. Mrs Perry put her ladies back on to knitting in which, as she truly said, it was impossible to waste quite so much material, as one could always unravel the ones that were knitted all wrong and knit them up again. Assisted by Mrs Belton she had embarked upon a process of elimination by which the good knitters made socks and gloves for the Barsetshire Regiment Comforts Fund, the less intelligent made Balaclava helmets if Mrs Perry would *just* be good enough to show them once more how one cast off for the hole for the face, and the real incompetents made scarves for the Mixo-Lydian refugees, whose cause, as we know, was very near to Mrs Perry's heart. Their work was not professional, in fact it was very bad, but as the Mixo-Lydians used the scarves as floor cloths on the rare occasions when they did any cleaning, it was not altogether wasted.

Plassey House was smaller than Arcot House and its sash windows less elegant, but it had a beautiful carved shell-shaped projection over the front door. Mrs Perry kept to the pleasant country practice of an open front door during the day, with a glass door inside it, through which people passing the house could see the long garden beyond and the big cedar tree, Dr Perry's pride, the biggest in that part of the county except those at the Palace. Patients went by the carriage-gate through the cobbled yard to the surgery which had once been a little orangery and was connected with the house by a short passage.

Mrs Belton came out of Arcot House with the intention of going straight to Plassey House and telling Mrs Perry that Mrs Updike, the solicitor's wife, must somehow be degraded from socks to Balaclavas as nothing would cure her of doing a peculiar variety of stitch that made the heels end in peaks instead of being rounded. She was always perfectly agreeable about it, and never minded undoing them again in the least, but her last pair had been such a Penelope's web that they appeared likely to last her till the end of the war.

It was a mysterious property of Harefield, as indeed it is of most villages, that it was practically impossible to go straight from one point to another because life, as Mrs Updike had said when a lorry carrying the trunks of several enormous trees came round a corner too sharply and crashed with its near front wheel into the wall of the almshouses while the tree trunks caught the laundry van full in the bonnet, was always going on to such an extent.

First Mrs Belton remembered that she had forgotten to post her husband's letters, so she had to go in the wrong direction to the post office. This was an uninteresting building, called by the knowing ones functional, but luckily tucked away round the corner where it did not spoil the High Street, and here she met Mrs Hoare from Dowlah Cottage, who was also going to the working party and was sending a parcel to her married daughter in Australia.

'Gladys has just had her fourth, Mrs Belton,' said Mrs Hoare. 'A dear little girl.'

Mrs Belton congratulated her and said a girl must be very nice.

'They did hope for a boy this time,' said Mrs Hoare. 'Four girls is quite a lot. But her husband is partly Dutch, you know, so I always thought they would have girls. It's something to do with Princess Juliana I always think, it seems to run in the blood. I'll come with you if you are going to Plassey House.'

Mrs Belton didn't really care if Mrs Hoare came with her or not, and the ladies left the post office together.

'It is very sad for you not being able to see your grandchildren,' she said, for want of anything better to say.

'I don't know,' said Mrs Hoare, who though she had always worn decent black since her husband's death a few years previously was a very active bustling woman, full of good works and always rush-ing off to nurse relations in impossible parts of England. 'I often

68

think it's just as well. If Gladys lived in England she would expect me to have all the children to stay and go off gallivanting herself. Besides, my family need me. Old Aunt Fanny in Derbyshire died in the summer and left me her Sheraton writing-table. Aunt Patience is weak in the intellect, but she does miss Aunt Fanny, and often says she would be glad to be Taken, but those mental cases always have very good constitutions. The house is left to me and Gladys, so I'll have to go up there soon and see that everything is all right. And Uncle Joe at Tregaskis is breaking up. Uncle Andrew, his brother, died last winter and left me all his Indian brasswork, and when Uncle Joe dies I am to have the house. When they have all Passed Over I hope Gladys will come back and she and the children could go and live at Morecambe with Cousin Harriet who needs someone in the house since she got so blind. But I really couldn't manage children at Dowlah Cottage.'

'I should have thought,' said Mrs Belton cautiously, not wishing to offend Mrs Hoare, who was an old acquaintance, 'that one would get rather fond of one's grandchildren. Of course I don't really know, as I haven't any, as none of my children are married.'

'All very well in peace-time,' said Mrs Hoare firmly, 'but not now. If I had four little girls at Dowlah Cottage and probably no nurse, for you know how impossible it is now and the wages they want, I would kill them all at once.'

'I suppose there is something in that,' said Mrs Belton, who was far too apt, from a distrust of her own powers of judgment, to give undue consideration to statements with which she disagreed. 'But one always might get a nurse. Alice Wicklow has one.'

'What does she pay her?' said Mrs Hoare.

'I never asked her,' said Mrs Belton, feeling even as the words left her mouth that they might sound rude, and remembering also that Mrs Hoare, as widow of the late agent to the Pomfret estate, naturally had a rather poor opinion of the wife of the present agent, though on perfectly good terms with her. 'But the nurse has curvature of the spine and something wrong with her eyes, so she mayn't lift either of the children and has to lie down every afternoon for two hours. Still,' she continued, feeling that she was not making out a very good case, 'it is another pair of hands in the house.'

Mrs Hoare looked at her with the interest a mental specialist might show in a hopeful borderline case, but made no comment. Just as they got to the chemist's shop a little pony-cart dashed up and a chorus of small voices shouted, 'Mrs Belton.'

'It's Lady Graham,' said Mrs Belton delightedly.

'I'll go on then,' said Mrs Hoare, looking at the cart full of children and dissociating herself from it. 'I'll see you again at the working party.'

Out of the pony-cart then tumbled three of the Graham children, followed by their mother, a charming dark-haired creature in what Mrs Belton wistfully recognized as the well-cut tweeds she could no longer afford, with a diamond and ruby clip on her jacket and a pearl necklace of exactly the right length for a country outing.

'Lucy!' said Lady Graham, embracing Mrs Belton in a soft impersonal way. 'How lovely to see you. John and Robert, say how do you do to Mrs Belton. Darling Edith, say how do you do to Mrs Belton. And here is Merry. We have all come in to buy our chocolate ration. Come and ask Mr Humble at the shop if he has some nice chocolate, darlings.'

Lady Graham and her flock went into J. Humble, General Supply Store, and Mrs Belton shook hands over the side of the pony-cart with Miss Merriman, the perfect secretary of Lady Emily Leslie, Lady Graham's mother.

'How are Lady Emily and Mr Leslie?' she said.

Miss Merriman said Mr Leslie's heart was always an anxiety, but he had been better this year. Lady Emily, she said, apart from her usual arthritis, was well and full of energy.

'We had a Wings for Victory week at Little Misfit,' said Miss Merriman, 'and General Graham lent the racquet court for a meeting. Lady Emily painted one of her lovely imaginative compositions of cherubim and seraphim with red and blue wings on the back wall of the racquet court behind the platform for the speakers and Sir Robert was really annoyed. Even Lady Graham noticed his annoyance.'

Mrs Belton laughed. Miss Merriman did not laugh, but she and Mrs Belton understood each other very well and both loved Miss Merriman's provoking, incalculable, enchanting employer. Miss Merriman asked after Mrs Belton's children; Lady Graham and her flock came back and got into the cart. With many wavings and hand kissings from the children the pony-cart went away towards Little Misfit.

'Whenever I see Lady Graham,' said a voice at Mrs Belton's elbow, 'I feel how entirely unnecessary intellect is in a woman. Are you going anywhere? I am going to see Updike.'

Mrs Belton turned and saw Mr Carton.

'Well, I am really going to Mrs Perry's working party,' said Mrs Belton, 'but I had to post some letters first and somehow it is always very difficult to get along the High Street.'

'More happens in this High Street than anywhere else in the world,' said Mr Carton, accommodating his long stride to her walk. 'I've been away with my mother, but I can assure you that Bognor was the Gobi Desert compared with Harefield. And here is Oriel. Much as I like and value Oriel, I sometimes feel that if I meet him more than five times a day in the High Street

I shall come to hate him. A delightful man, but he cannot see one without stopping to talk.'

They were now abreast of Clive's Corner, a long two-storeyed house in the angle formed by the High Street and Bodger's Lane. Mr Oriel was coming down the steps accompanied by Mr Updike the solicitor.

'Ha, Carton, we meet again,' said Mr Oriel, and took his hat off to Mrs Belton. Mr Updike with a friendly gesture disappeared into his office. 'A busy man,' said Mr Oriel, looking after him admiringly. 'You are the very man I wanted, Carton. I have a small favour to ask you.'

'Out with it,' said Mr Carton, mounting the first step. 'I am going in to see Updike about a bit of college property near here.'

Mrs Belton said she would leave them, as she was going to Mrs Perry's work party.

'I will accompany you if I may,' said Mr Oriel, 'as I have an errand in Madras Cottages. Just one word with Carton and I am at your service.'

Mrs Belton would have liked to say, 'All right, only do hurry up,' but courtesy forbade, so she smiled and stood waiting.

'On second thoughts it will keep,' said Mr Oriel to Mr Carton. 'I will look in on you on my way back to the Vicarage, for I must not detain Mrs Belton. It is extraordinary,' he continued, as he and Mrs Belton walked on, 'how one cannot help meeting people in the High Street. This meeting with Carton was fortunate, as I particularly wanted to ask him something; yet I sometimes feel that much as I like him I shall one day be tempted to cross the road to avoid him, so often do our steps cross each other during the day.'

Mrs Belton thought it was either very nice of Mr Oriel (as

showing that he didn't really dislike Mr Carton) or very silly of him (as wasting a good opportunity) not to have asked him whatever it was when he was there. But she had long ago decided within herself, though perhaps barely conscious of the decision, that it was better not to take any notice of what men said, because they didn't seem to have much sense.

Apart from a few friendly words with three friends whose names do not concern us and two shopkeepers who were taking the air at their doors, and nearly being run over by Miss Holly on her bicycle, there were no more interruptions. Mr Oriel left Mrs Belton at the door of Plassey House and pursued his way to Madras Cottages.

As it was by now half-past three, the working party was in full swing. Mrs Perry's comfortable and slightly over-furnished drawing-room looking out on the cedar was boiling over with nine or ten ladies, some winding wool on the back of a chair or on a friend's hands, some not being quite exactly sure how one did that other casting-on stitch, not the one where you go on knitting with two needles, my dear, but the one where you measure off ever so much more than you want and twist it round your left hand like this – no, like *this* – and keep on making a stitch with one needle, but I haven't quite exactly got it, don't look at me for a moment and I'm sure it will come back. Others again were knitting with such frenzied speed that, being also much occupied in conversation, they overshot their mark and had to take off all the stitches and unravel back to where they ought to have begun increasing and pick up all the stitches again except the one that always managed to escape, turning up sometimes as the end of a long ladder. And Mrs Updike, a tall, fair, thin woman looking ridiculously young for the mother of four children between fifteen and twenty-five, was sitting with her legs crossed, examining her knitting with an expression of bewildered friendliness.

School summer holidays were usually a close time for the Harefield working parties, as mothers were either away with their families or worn out by them. Mrs Perry's was the last to begin again and its members were all a little, though quite kindly, curious to see how Mrs Belton would behave now she was a villager and no longer living at Harefield Park. Mrs Belton, though she did not attach very much importance to the change in her life when everything was changing and so many old things uprooted, could not all the same help feeling that she came back to the working party slightly on approval as it were. But if she was at all nervous, the friendly murmur of greeting which met her was enough to make her feel quite comfortable. Knitting needles clashed on the floor as ladies half rose to offer her their seat, and the ball of wool that Mrs Hoare was winding sprang out of her hands, ran with incredible speed across the floor and went to earth under a Chinese cabinet.

'Oh, dear,' said Mrs Hoare, pulling at the wool.

'You'll only make it worse if you do that, Mrs Hoare,' said Mrs Perry. 'It's because the floor slants in that corner. A lot of our floors do. One moment and I'll poke it out.'

Seizing the hearth-brush she pushed it under the Chinese cabinet. The ball ran out, Mrs Perry picked it up, the wool caught round one of the clawed feet and broke.

'That's all right,' said Mrs Hoare. 'I'll tie the ends together.'

'Oh, Mrs Hoare, it will make a knot if you do,' said Mrs Updike. 'I believe one ought to lick one's fingers and roll the ends together.'

Mrs Perry's sister-in-law who was staying with her said licking was no use because the natural grease in the wool didn't give the lick a chance and she always threaded one end into a darning-needle and wove it in and out of the other end and if anything stuck out afterwards she cut it off. The wife of a Rear-Admiral who was in the Middle East said tie it by all means, but a reef knot. This led to several ladies showing each other how a reef knot was made, but owing to an uncertainty as to the second movement of the tying, all the knots came undone at once when pulled. Mrs Perry said she knew reef knots were all a matter of luck. Mrs Hoare, who had sat down again, took up the broken ends of her wool, tied them together in a knot with two tails sticking out of it and continued her work.

This enthralling episode being disposed of, Mrs Belton was put next to Mrs Perry's sister-in-law, took her knitting out of her bag and cast on for a glove. As soon as she was well settled into knit two, purl two, she cast her eye on Mrs Updike on her other side. That lady, who had not taken any part in the affair of the knot, was still looking at the knitting on her lap with a benign but dazed expression.

'It is quite extraordinary,' she said, 'how I can't do things. Do what I will these socks get the better of me. What do you think I have done, Mrs Belton?'

Mrs Belton examined the sock which would have been an excellent fit for anyone who had a conical back to his heel.

'I have done it four times, and each time it comes out differently,' said Mrs Updike. 'And I do exactly what it says in the book. I suppose I've got a sort of thing about it.' She laughed a very young, pretty laugh.

'I wonder if you would feel more comfortable with a different kind of knitting,' said Mrs Belton, seizing her chance.

'Oh, I'd love it,' said Mrs Updike, tearing all the needles out of her work and beginning to unravel and re-wind the wool. 'I always love doing anything new. I'm always making experiments with cooking and the family seem to like them. Look at my hands.'

With some pride she held them out. Mrs Belton had seen many women's hands, previously cherished, coarsened by all kinds of household or other work. Mrs Perry's were not improved by two days a week at camouflage netting, Mrs Hoare did part-time in a small factory from nine to one six days a week, Mrs Belton's own hands were the worse for a mixture of camouflage nets and gardening, but Mrs Updike's were more chipped, burnt, cut, rubbed, bruised and generally ill-treated than any she had seen.

'What *have* you done to yourself?' she asked.

'I can't think,' said Mrs Updike, with her gay laugh. 'I only do some housework and cooking and gardening and the family mending, but I must have a thing about getting knocked about. All those dirty lines,' she said, looking proudly at a network of grime on the forefinger of her right hand, 'aren't really dirt you know. I mean not dirt from not washing, but when I clean the gas stove it seems to get grimed in. That horrid red place is where the lid of the little boiler that heats the water fell on me when I was raking it out, and the children all say I am not fit to be trusted near a knife or a kettle,' said Mrs Updike, gazing with abstract interest at a very unpleasant cut on the top of one finger and the mark of what had evidently been a severe scald.

'But you really ought to take more care,' said Mrs Belton. 'Do you put anything on them after they have been in water?'

'Lots of things,' said Mrs Updike vaguely. 'I am always going into Potter's for hand cream, but it only gets all over my clothes and doesn't seem to make my hands any better.'

At the mention of Potter the whole room had pricked up

its ears and no sooner had Mrs Updike finished than seven or eight ladies began to speak at once, each lady recommending a different salve or unguent for war-worked hands, mostly with the rider that one couldn't get it now. All were genuinely shocked by Mrs Updike's hands, and none could quite understand how anyone could get herself into such a mess.

'It is partly being very clumsy,' said Mrs Updike, pleased at being the centre of so much kind attention. 'And then I don't see very well without my spectacles.'

Mrs Perry said she had never seen Mrs Updike wear spectacles.

'My husband always says I don't wear them because I am vain,' said Mrs Updike, laughing at the idea, 'but it really is because I often can't find them.'

'You ought to have two pairs,' said Mrs Hoare. 'My old Aunt Janet – the one who died last Christmas and left me all that silver,' she added to the company in general – 'always had a pair of spectacles for each room she used. Of course most of Durnford Grange had been shut since Uncle Henry's death, but she always had six pairs in use. That nice still life in my little hall was Uncle Henry's bequest to me and I value it very much. If he had been spared he was going to have it cleaned and find out what it was really meant to be.'

'I *love* still lifes,' said Mrs Updike. 'I've got a perfect thing about them. But I have got two pairs, Mrs Hoare, only I can't see with either of them and somehow I never seem to find time to go to Barchester. I know I ought to. But if I go to the oculist he is sure to make me have a new pair and it does seem such waste when I've got two pairs already, both quite useless.'

All the ladies began to recommend their favourite oculist, as they had before recommended their favourite hand cream, with the same drawback, that the oculists were as impossible to get as the cream, having all gone abroad or been sent to military hospitals. As no work at all was being done, it was just as well that tea came in at that moment.

Mrs Perry, owing to her husband being a doctor, was allowed to keep her faithful maid Ruth who was in any case above calling-up age and didn't hold with people going into factories and earning all that money. Most of Mrs Perry's friends were rather afraid of Ruth. She put the tea-tray down on the table and went out to fetch the cakes which her standard of living for the gentry caused her to provide whether her mistress liked it or not.

At this point a curious ritual took place which was repeated in every working party in Harefield, and for aught we know in the whole county. The majority of the ladies drew from their reticules bottles of varying sizes and shapes, from a large bottle of pleasing blue formerly the home of fluid magnesia (Mrs Hoare) to a smaller bottle whose stout and well-fitting cork proclaimed it unmistakably as the former abode of Eno's Fruit Salts (Mrs Belton). In these bottles the wise virgins – or in other words the patriotic and thoughtful members of the party – brought their portions of milk, for not only was milk officially rationed, but owing to a dry summer the local dairies had been obliged to cut down supplies especially to houses where there were no young children. These ladies having produced their bottles and set them up on the table, a piece of furniture now conveniently to hand, the improvident members of the party then exclaimed with apparent, and often with genuine surprise, that there now, they had forgotten their milk again, and would drink their tea without, just to remind themselves. To which the hostess, in this particular case Mrs Perry, would say it didn't matter in the least and there was quite enough milk in the house. The faithful Ruth, who kept a very sharp eye on 'the working ladies' as she called them, stood by the door, looking through her uncompromising steel-rimmed spectacles for possible backsliders.

Mrs Perry's sister-in-law who was staying with her was of course a member of the family for the time being and had an emergency card for her rations, though Ruth held it against her that two points, lawfully the property of the Perry household, had been done away with before the kitchen was able to use them. Mrs Updike, after a great deal of cheerful conversation aloud with herself, found in the bottom of her bag a very small aspirin bottle which she said was all the milk there was left over because she had let half a pint boil right away when she was making a custard for lunch and the dairy didn't come till three.

'I hadn't time to wash it out, so I expect I shall go off into a deep slumber,' she said, amused by the idea. 'I used the last aspirin last night for my toothache and of course it is Wednesday so I can't get any more.'

Every lady present except Mrs Perry's sister-in-law, who came from some outlandish place where Thursday was early closing, told her nearest neighbour what she had forgotten to get at the shops that morning and it was universally decided that Wednesday came at least twice as often as any other day. If the Rear-Admiral's wife and Mrs Hunter, who was not a Harefield native and had only been asked on approval, thought this discussion would enable them to escape the consequences of careless, and in the case of Mrs Hunter we fear deliberate forgetfulness, their fools' paradise did not last long. The faithful Ruth, advancing a step and planting herself before the tea-table, waited for a temporary lull and said to her mistress and her mistress's sister-in-law,

'That's all the milk there is. There's just enough for you two. Cook kept it back from the pudding she's making for the doctor's dinner.'

She then cowed the whole room with a glance and went away.

The Rear-Admiral's wife apologized; Mrs Belton said she had heaps for two and the ladies fell into naval talk, for Freddy Belton had been on a torpedo course at the beginning of the war under the Rear-Admiral. Mrs Hunter, on the other hand, not only omitted to apologize, but said with the voice of one crying economy in the wilderness that in *her* kitchen she never used anything but powdered milk for puddings, because her dear pussies needed the fresh milk.

There was a moment's tension which Mrs Belton relieved by saying how much she liked Miss Sparling and how glad she was that the Park would be in good hands. As none of the other ladies had yet met the headmistress of the Hosiers' Girls' Foundation School, Mrs Belton was plied with questions, those who had known the Park in former days being anxious to know exactly what changes had been made and who slept where.

Mrs Hunter, having made a pretence of looking in her bag which deceived nobody, said she knew sugar was a difficulty, but had anyone any saccharine as she had forgotten to bring hers.

'It was one of the things I meant to get at Potter's this morning,' said Mrs Updike. 'I used all mine to bottle apple pulp yesterday and most of it stuck to the pan while I was putting some sticking-plaster on my finger where it had burst out again. It is so stupid, but I've got a perfect thing about Wednesdays.'

Mrs Perry said with a cheerful smile which those who knew her best took at its face value that there was plenty of sugar for everyone and put two teaspoonfuls into Mrs Hunter's cup. That lady stirred it with loud clinkings and said sugar wasn't as sweet as it used to be; in which hour she sealed her own doom.

Tea and talk being over, which were partly the secret of the success of Mrs Perry's working parties, as what with homes and work and children and one thing and another the ladies sometimes hardly saw a friend, unless at the shops, from one Wednesday to the next, they began to pack up and go.

'It was so nice of you to come, Mrs Hunter,' said Mrs Perry. 'And if I have another working party after Christmas, perhaps you will be able to come.'

Mrs Hunter said she would like to so much. She had thought, she said, that it was a weekly fixture.

'Well, you know what it is,' said Mrs Perry. 'One means to do a thing regularly, but in war-time things do get out of control. And I am so frightfully busy with my Mixo-Lydian Refugee work that I can't ever be sure when I'll be free.'

'Mixo-Lydian?' said Mrs Hunter, looking at Mrs Perry as if she was a blackbeetle.

'A most gallant little people,' said Mrs Perry, with a slight edge on her voice. 'Such a fuss is made about Czechs and Poles that people forget the great, great sacrifice that Mixo-Lydia has made.'

'One sometimes wishes,' said Mrs Hunter, 'that they could have dispensed with sacrificing themselves to the extent they do.'

'Oh? How?' said Mrs Perry coldly.

'Coming here in millions and living in great comfort at our expense,' said Mrs Hunter, her voice trembling slightly. 'Of course no one who has not been in Slavo-Lydia knows the atrocities the Mixo-Lydians have committed. I cannot repeat to you the horrors the manager of the hotel in Slavo-Lydiapolis, a *most* intelligent Russian Jew, told me about the massacres of 1832. They have never been forgotten.'

Both ladies were now in a difficult position. Mrs Perry as hostess had to keep her temper; Mrs Hunter felt that this moment of triumph was the moment to go, but also felt a slight awkwardness about the manner of doing it.

Luckily Mrs Updike, who had just upset the remains of her bottle of milk into her lap and was wiping it off with Mrs Belton's assistance, looked up and said, '*Who* massacred the Russians?' which enabled Mrs Hunter to smile a pitying and all-forgiving smile, shake hands, and take her leave.

'I never know *anything*,' said Mrs Updike, 'because it's all so confusing, but the next thing will be millions of Russians coming over here like the Mixo-Lydians and then we shall wish we hadn't.'

'If I were you, I'd dip my handkerchief in the hot water if there is any left,' said Mrs Perry's sister-in-law, 'and just dab the front of your skirt. Don't rub; dab.'

'Hadn't what?' said the Rear-Admiral's wife, who liked conversation to be all taut and shipshape.

Everyone looked at Mrs Updike for an explanation, but she was now turning the hot-water jug upside down in vain.

'Hadn't what?' Mrs Updike repeated in a perplexed way.

'Well,' said Mrs Belton, who always had a protective feeling towards the solicitor's wife, 'when Mrs Hunter talked about the Mixo-Lydian massacres in Slavo-Lydia, you said we'd wish we hadn't.'

'Oh, *I* know,' said Mrs Updike, with the air of someone who for the first time that day had come to grips with a real fact. 'I mean Russia is so enormous, especially on that sort of map that makes the British Empire look so large, you know, the one where the North Pole is the same length as the Equator.'

The Rear-Admiral's wife said Mrs Updike must mean Mercator's Projection.

'Quite right,' said Mrs Updike, gratified by the last speaker's understanding. 'Only I can't do maps. I've got a sort of thing about them. I mean even on the map that was specially made to make us look big, Russia looks much bigger, so it stands to reason that it must be, because Mercator probably didn't know anything about it in those old days. Well, imagine the *millions* of people in Russia, all wanting to get out.'

'But why should they want to get out?' said Mrs Perry's sister-in-law.

'Everyone does,' said Mrs Updike vaguely. 'I mean they want to colonize and things; anything sooner than live at home, for which one can't blame them, poor things. Well, they can't get out on the right, can they?'

'You mean the east,' said Mrs Belton doubtfully.

'Well, the east is the right on the map, isn't it?' said Mrs Updike. 'And the Japs are somewhere there and the Russians are friends with the Japs, at least they intern American airmen who are their allies for flying over Japan which is, I suppose, International Law, so they don't want to go that way, so they'll have to go to the left. And if you ask me,' said Mrs Updike, suddenly assuming a most statesmanlike business voice, as of one in inner cabinets, 'if they once get as far as the Rhine which they are sure to do, at least everyone says they are so wonderful, so I suppose they'll simply have to go on advancing unless it rains, we shall have to spend the rest of our lives keeping them out of England, where they would all turn into refugees, because all foreigners do.'

As Mrs Updike, once launched, showed every symptom of going on for ever, Mrs Belton gently interrupted her and suggested that she might care to knit seaboot stockings, as the wool was beautifully greasy and might be good for her hands.

'My father used to say I had nice hands, like his grandmother,' said Mrs Updike, rising and dropping her bag mouth downwards.

At these words Mrs Belton and Mrs Perry, as they found on

comparing notes afterwards, nearly cried, and each confessed that while grabbling (as Mrs Belton said) or grubbling (as Mrs Perry preferred to say) among the legs of the table to collect the contents of Mrs Updike's bag, she had seized the chance of dashing her hand across her eyes and sniffing.

Mrs Updike then remembered that her husband had asked for dinner early and she was sure the rabbit wanted attending to, though she had done the potatoes and vegetables before she came out and made a cold pudding.

'But it is much more fun cooking in the holidays when the younger children are at home,' said Mrs Updike. 'It seems to give one more scope. I cut my hand so badly last holidays filleting some fish that I had to dash round to Dr Perry's surgery to be stitched up. When they are back at school, Phil and I feel almost old.'

When she had gone, Mrs Perry, Mrs Perry's sister-in-law, Mrs Hoare and Mrs Belton had a kind of committee meeting about Mrs Hunter. No harsh words passed, but it was understood that Mrs Hunter would not come to any more working parties.

'I think,' said Mrs Perry's sister-in-law, 'you ought not to try any more of those London refugee people, Maud. You remember there was that woman who put us all in a book, though I must say I didn't think the likenesses were very good.'

'I don't think you are quite fair,' said Mrs Perry. 'The whole of Little Misfit and Pomfret Madrigal are convinced they are the people in the book. So are a lot of people at Nutfield and even at Skeynes. But I certainly shan't have Mrs Hunter again. I will ask her to come to the next Bring and Buy sale for the Mixo-Lydians.'

Her sister-in-law said Mrs Hunter certainly wouldn't come, as she was too stingy to bring, too mean to buy, and didn't like

Mixo-Lydians, and Mrs Belton and Mrs Hoare went away rather quickly in case Mrs Perry should begin to get enthusiastic.

Mrs Belton had not in the least forgotten that she and her husband were dining with Mr Oriel, but it had gone rather far down into her mind during the working party, so it was with a slight shock that she heard the church clock melodiously chiming the half-hour.

'It can't be half-past six!' she exclaimed.

'It must be,' said Mrs Hoare, 'because it was a quarter past when we began to say good-bye. Not that the church clock is always right. I go by my French clock on the drawing-room mantelpiece. It belonged to my husband's old cousin Sarah Hoare whose mother was a Parisienne – but a good, worthy woman. She left it to me when she was Taken, which was only two months after my poor husband passed to Higher Service. You know, Mrs Belton, his chosen motto, though of course he never had a coat of arms, was 'For he had great estates.' Not that he had any land himself except the house in Hampstead that his Uncle Beecham left him which was let on a ninety-nine years' lease, but he had always looked after the Pomfret estates since he came as under-agent when he was thirty and he said those words meant much to him. And without punctuality you can accomplish nothing, he used to say, so he particularly valued Cousin Sarah's clock for being such a good timekeeper. Well, here I am at my own front door.'

Mrs Belton said good night and walked quickly up the street to Arcot House, where she found her husband in the hall.

'Who do you think has just rung me up, Lucy?' he said. 'Captain Hornby.'

His wife looked at him with a glazed eye.

'The old lady's nephew,' said her husband.

85

Her mind still occupied with the working party, with Mrs Updike's domestic misfortunes, and a top layer of Mrs Hoare's recital of legacies, she still stared at her husband.

'He wants to look at some things that are put away in that locked room,' said Mr Belton. 'Not tonight of course, because he is in London, but some time when he can get leave and it suits you. I said you'd settle it all with him. "I never meddle with anything to do with the house," I said. "You get onto my wife about it."'

'Oh, you mean Captain Hornby,' said Mrs Belton, pulling herself together. 'I'll write to him. Do you remember we are dining with Mr Oriel, Fred?'

'Of course I do,' said her husband. 'I've heard of nothing else all day. I was up at the estate office after lunch and ran across Miss Sparling in the grounds and she said she was looking forward to seeing us tonight. Nice woman she is. Then Wheeler wanted to know what I should be wearing.'

'You look very nice as you are,' said Mrs Belton. 'Or were you thinking of your blue suit, the other one I mean?'

'I wasn't thinking of anything,' said Mr Belton almost snappishly. 'If people go out to dinner they ought to be able to dress like gentlemen, not go in the clothes they've been wearing all day. I told Wheeler she could put out what she liked. I'll probably go as I am, I said.'

Mrs Belton felt very sorry for her husband. She didn't much care for going out to dinner herself in a day dress and groping her way back with a torch, but she knew that her husband minded much more and that there was nothing she could possibly do for him. So she murmured some consoling noises and went up to her room, quite confident that Wheeler would have put out the blue suit and that her husband would wear it.

*

All of which came to pass. For much as many of us loathe changes, and especially changes that imply a lowering of standards which we know can never be restored in our lifetime, if ever, the passing of time brings its soothing influence and we can at least pretend that it is rather fun to eat in the kitchen and all live in one sitting-room, and hang our tail coats and evening gowns in a bag with moth balls, thus fostering a pleasant delusion that we may one day put them on again.

'But most of us will be too thin,' said Mrs Belton aloud to herself as she put on a light woollen frock with high neck and long sleeves for Mr Oriel's party, and thinking of the number of times her coats and skirts had had to be taken in since the war; or to be exact since Munich, when the shadow fell darker and the nerves became more taut. In fact every time she took a suit to her tailor to be altered she had feared he would dismiss her as unworthy of his craft, for she knew that he still had many customers who could afford new suits and mysteriously had the coupons for them. Then she laughed at herself for being sentimental; and then she laughed again, because it made her think of Mrs Updike and her silly yet captivating way of deriding herself for her own carelessness. So that Mr Belton called from his dressing-room to ask what she was laughing at and when she said because she was always getting thinner, said it was time she let Perry give her a good overhaul.

As they left the house together they saw a fragile silver sickle in the sky, half-veiled in a dusty pink wisp of cloud. The west was cold, clear green, and away to the east a faint after-glow hung upon the rolling top of a great cloud bank.

'How *heavenly*,' said Mrs Belton.

'Must look nice from your sitting-room,' said Mr Belton, looking up the slope to where Harefield Park was silhouetted against the sky. 'One always got a good view of the sunset from that room. My mother chose it because of the view. Funny how you don't notice things at the time. I never understood why one sunset was better than another when I was a little boy. It was something the grown-ups talked about.'

'Never mind, we get a splendid view from the High Street,' said Mrs Belton. 'There is Miss Sparling, Fred, coming out of the lodge gates.'

They quickened their pace, met Miss Sparling and went up together to the Vicarage.

4

The great advantage of being a bachelor, as Mr Oriel was apt to say complacently, is that you can ask people to dinner without worrying. This general axiom was such a fallacy as left all his hearers indignant or gasping, according to their nature. But fate had so far been kind to the Vicar of Harefield that his bachelor life had been sheltered throughout. He had lived as a young clergyman in great harmony with his mother and elder sister. When his mother died his sister had continued to keep house for him with the assistance of two maids and an excellent cook. His sister had died just before the war, bequeathing him to Mrs Powlett the cook. Mr Oriel had mourned his sister most sincerely, but had long become reconciled to her loss. Mrs Powlett, daughter of a sexton and widow of a verger, had ruled him with firm kindness ever since, supplying him with good food, encouraging him to have old school and college friends, especially if in orders, for visits, mothering the nieces who came from time to time, and never presuming. Her one weakness was Barchester whose cathedral and shops shared her allegiance. As we know, her day out was of a very sacred nature, and her invariable treat was to go over by the eleven o'clock bus, look at all the shops, buy any little unrationed bit of food that she thought Mr Oriel would like, attend Evensong at three, have tea with the verger and his wife, and come back by the 7.25 bus in summer and the 5.25 in winter. Of the two maids, both over fifty, one had gone to look after an invalid sister-in-law, but Dorothy, the other one, remained, and apart from being a Plymouth Sister got on very well with Mrs Powlett. Friendly relations were the easier that the Plymouth Brethren had no place of worship nearer than Southbridge, so that for years Dorothy had attended divine worship at Harefield church, always reserving to herself the right to feel superior to the other worshippers and even, from 6.30 to 7.30 p.m. on Sundays only, to her employer.

'And mind you remember to serve Mrs Belton first, Dorothy,' said Mrs Powlett to her underling while taking a look at the dinner table to see that the girl (as she still naturally called the middle-aged Plymouth Sister) had got everything as it should be, 'for she must Feel it a good deal, having to come and live in the street just like anyone else.'

'Yes, Mrs Powlett,' said Dorothy, who had hardly ever been known to say anything else.

'If it was any other time, I'd say serve Miss Sparling first,' Mrs Powlett continued in her soft Barsetshire voice, 'as being the first time she has dined here. But we may say, Dorothy, that this is the first time Mrs Belton has dined here in a way, as she comes from Arcot House and not from the Park. And Mrs Perry last, Dorothy. Not but what as a married lady and the doctor's wife she should come before Miss Sparling in Etiquette, but we must remember, Dorothy, that Miss Sparling is dining here for the first time, which makes her more important than Mrs Perry just for this once. Of course, Dorothy, as I have often told you, any lady who dines out for the first time after her marriage is the chief lady for that once. And I dare say Miss Sparling will be getting married one of these days,' said Mrs Powlett, who had never set eyes on that lady except in church and knew nothing about her at all, but spoke from a kindly and hopeful nature.

'It says there's no marriages in heaven, Mrs Powlett,' said Dorothy, giving a final polish to the pudding spoons with a piece of washleather.

'I'm ashamed of you, Dorothy,' said Mrs Powlett, 'speaking of the Bible as "it". And don't tell me it's in the Bible, Dorothy, for that is a book we were never meant to understand. Now come along and give me a hand and don't leave the shammy on the Vicar's chair.'

So speaking she returned to the kitchen, followed by her underling in a state of complete imbecility and confusion about the question of precedence.

Shortly after this the front door bell rang and Dorothy admitted Mr and Mrs Belton and Miss Sparling. As the ladies took off their coats and other encumbrances in Mr Oriel's study, Miss Sparling emerged in a rather noble heliotrope dress with a bit of lace across its front, worn under a short black velvet cape. Looking at her with friendly, appraising eyes, Mrs Belton found the words, 'a dress which set off her matronly figure to the best advantage' rising to her mind, though whether a quotation or not, she could not say. There was something so imperceptibly wrong about Miss Sparling's choice of clothes, yet so absolutely right for her position, that Mrs Belton admired her more than ever and felt that she could never have dressed as a headmistress so well herself.

Mr Oriel received his guests with obvious pleasure and offered them sherry.

'My one piece of war hoarding,' he said. 'The cellars at the Vicarage are so large and airy that it seemed to me really flying in the face of Providence not to keep them well stocked. And I have a little change in our plans which I hope you will approve. You may possibly remember, Mrs Belton, how we met Mr Carton outside our friend Mr Updike's this afternoon and I told you I had something to ask him, but decided that it would do later.'

He paused for confirmation and Mrs Belton said she remembered perfectly and would be so much interested to hear what the plan was.

'Well, I saw Carton later and unfolded my plan to him,' said the Vicar, 'and I am glad to say he agreed.'

He then looked round for applause.

'And what was the plan, Mr Oriel?' said Miss Sparling, for which intervention Mrs Belton was grateful, feeling she had shown enough sympathy for the moment, especially as it had produced no really clear explanation.

'Aha! the plan,' said Mr Oriel.

Dorothy opened the door, announced Dr and Mrs Perry, and got in their way while they tried to come in. After a slight fracas they each got round one side of her and coalesced in the drawing-room as a couple. Dorothy looked surprised and went away.

Everyone was acquainted with everyone else, except for Miss Sparling and Mrs Perry. The two ladies were introduced. Mrs Perry, who liked her husband's patients on principle, thought she would also like Miss Sparling for herself. Short of having Miss Holly to interpret for us, we cannot say what Miss Sparling thought of Mrs Perry, but she also had trained herself to take all newcomers (which mostly meant parents) as friendly till they proved that they weren't. Then they all went in to dinner.

The conversation at first was general and chiefly about the fish, which was fried whiting. It is a sign of the changing times that Mrs Belton, who would certainly never have discussed a host's food before the war, unless asked to do so, expressed loud admiration of the freshness of the Vicarage fish.

'We get ours at Pratt's in the High Street,' she said, 'because we have always dealt there, but he is very unreliable, I find. Not that his fish is exactly bad, not smelling *really* nasty, I mean, but it is always tired.'

'Come, come, Lucy, we mustn't complain,' said Mr Belton, who was always the first to push his plate away and say this stuff was only fit for the dustbin. 'Fish is zoned, you know.'

'I know people say zoned,' said Mrs Belton with spirit, 'but I don't suppose they know what they mean when they say it any more than I do. If it means Pratt's shop smelling quite dreadful whenever one passes it, I wish they wouldn't.'

'And even when one doesn't pass it,' said Mrs Perry. 'I can hardly bear to go to church on Sundays the shop smells so frightful, even with the big shutters down.'

Mr Belton asked how she didn't pass it if she smelt it on her way to church.

'You know what I mean, perfectly,' said Mrs Perry, looking at him with as intense a gaze as if he were a Mixo-Lydian. 'When one says, "As I was passing the fishmonger today" one means one went in and got some fish, if there was any. You don't mean you passed it and didn't go in.'

Mr Oriel, a humane man, said it was dreadful to think of that smell being shut up in the shop all Sunday.

'Luckily Pilchards deliver twice a week at the School,' said Miss Sparling, 'though we never know exactly what we are going to get.'

'Then I suppose they'll be able to serve you here too,' said Mrs Belton.

'But they do serve us,' said Miss Sparling, perplexed. 'Twice a week.'

'How very stupid of me,' said Mrs Belton, looking confused, a thing which rarely happened. 'When you said the School, I was thinking of your school when it was in Barchester. I had forgotten that the Park is the School now. I am somehow used to its being the Park.'

She then felt uneasy, lest she should be seeming to reproach Miss Sparling, and through her the Hosiers' Company, for having taken over at a handsome rental a house her husband could no longer afford. Miss Sparling also felt uncomfortable. The place where the School was settled was to her naturally the School, and she had merely spoken a word which she used in speaking or writing dozens of times every day. With a quick turn of sympathy she realized how startling, even perhaps wounding, her use of the word might be to the Beltons. Mrs Belton's apology of somehow being used to thinking of her own house by its own name made her feel like a usurper, or a Norman baron in possession of a Saxon manor, while the former owner lodged with a faithful swineherd. But the dinner-table is not the place for such delicate explanations and she resolved to think no more of it till the right opportunity occurred. To do them justice, it did not occur to either lady that the other would be annoyed: there was merely an anxious hope that a stupid remark might not have been misunderstood.

But all these thoughts passed with the speed of lightning, as Mrs Perry said it was rather a horrid thing to say, but she positively knew that Pilchards kept back fish for some of their customers. On being pressed for details she said that several times when going down that little lane behind the High Street to get to the school children's communal dining-room where she worked, she had noticed people slinking away from Pilchards' backyard with suspicious parcels. She had not she admitted, ever seen the contents of one of these parcels, but the smell coming from them was exactly the same as the smell in the shop.

Miss Sparling, throwing a headmistress's caution to the winds, said her secretary, Miss Holly, bicycling that way to get half a dozen loaves, as the baker was allowed to bake but might not deliver more than twice a week, so if they ran short as they occasionally did someone had to go down and fetch it, had noticed the same phenomenon and commented to her upon it.

This led to some inconclusive talk about how something ought to be done, though as no one knew what, or who had the power to do it, and Dr Perry said they had better be careful or they might find themselves in trouble, it did not get the matter any further. But the whole episode, slight though it was, somehow gave Miss Sparling a status as one of the village, and Mrs Belton and Mrs Perry opened the ranks as it were and accepted her as a comrade: which meant that the rest of Harefield would do the same.

'And now,' said Mr Oriel, 'I have a little plan which I hope will please everyone. I have told Mrs Belton, who was kind enough to approve, so I will now tell it to my other friends.'

Mrs Belton tried to look as if she were the repository of a state secret, and quite used to such responsibility, but what Mr Oriel's plan was, she still had not the faintest idea. 'Talking of plans, Oriel,' said Mr Belton, 'I have got the large-scale map of the bit of glebe near the river that the W.A.E.G. want to have ploughed. Any fool knows that it is flooded at least every other year. You'd better come up and have a look at it.'

'Last year,' said Mr Oriel, 'the water came right up to the lower wall and a swan was stranded in my kitchen garden, as you may remember. It must have been carried down from your lake. We had great trouble in ejecting it.'

'Carried down!' said Mr Belton. 'It would take more than a rise in the river to take a swan where it didn't want to go. Interfering, selfish birds they are. I know that swan. One year when my man hadn't clipped their wings nearly enough, that swan went over to Pomfret's bit of water, simply to give trouble. If Hitler were a bird he'd certainly be a swan, barging about with his wings and trying to frighten people. Where do you get rabbit, Oriel? We haven't seen a rabbit on the place for weeks.'

'I am not supposed to know,' said Mr Oriel. 'But from what Mrs Powlett hasn't said, I think it is her nephew who works at that factory at Hogglestock. He was at home last weekend.'

'Well, so long as the local men do the poaching,' said Mr Belton, 'I suppose I can't complain. But if we get any foreigners on the place, my man will probably shoot them. I'd like to put an advertisement in the *Barsetshire Chronicle* to that effect. By the way, Mrs Powlett's nephew is a cousin of my man's now I come to think of it. That's all right then.'

Mr Oriel said he seemed a quiet enough lad, but the Army had turned him down as mentally defective, so he was earning from six to seven pounds a week at Adams's factory, sweeping and cleaning the workrooms.

'Poisonous fellow, Adams,' said Mr Belton. 'We had a couple of young louts up before the bench yesterday for stealing two sacks of potatoes and selling them from door to door, and he wanted to preach a sermon to them and let them go.'

'Did he?' asked Miss Sparling.

'He would have,' said Mr Belton. 'He talks all the older men down. But these lads had stolen the potatoes off the allotments, and when he heard they were robbing the poor, he gave in.'

'And were they robbing the poor?' asked Dr Perry.

'You know too much, Perry,' said Mr Belton. 'As a matter of fact that piece of the allotment was taken up by the wife of the manager of that big insurance company that was evacuated to Harefield Court. She has cultivated it for victory like a Trojan, and so have her children in the holidays. I told Adams afterwards and he was furious. 'You want one law for the people you think are rich and another law for the people you think are poor,' I said. 'Let me advise you to find out which are which before you make a fool of yourself.'

'Did you *really* say that, Mr Belton?' said Mrs Perry, earnestly.

'Adams,' said Miss Sparling, who felt pretty certain that Mr Belton had exaggerated his chastisement of Mr Adams and did not wish that nice Mrs Belton to be brought to shame. 'That must be the father of Heather Adams, one of our girls. I think you noticed her, Mrs Belton, when you came to tea with me. A big girl, not very healthy-looking. Your elder son was kind enough to ask her to dance. I was so glad, as she is not an attractive girl and is often left out of things.'

'She's quite intelligent though,' said Dr Perry. 'She reacts to those injections for boils remarkably well; better than ninety per cent of my patients.'

'She is almost a genius at mathematics,' said Miss Sparling, not wishing the dinner party to think that her pupils were only distinguished by responding well to Dr Parry's treatment for boils. 'She was third out of all England in the School Certificate examination.'

Having vindicated the honour of her school, she quitted the schoolmistress and lapsed into the role of very pleasant guest.

It was no part of Mr Oriel's plan to neglect his ladies, and as a rule he gave his men a very short interval in which to discuss whatever it is that men discuss when left together; high politics and dashing days in the hunting field, or the Odes of Horace, we would like to think, though finding ourselves unable to do so with conviction. But on this evening he had got up some rather special port and the conversation happening to turn on the Bishop of Barchester, who had made a very subversive speech in the House of Lords, saying that in his opinion no bishop should accept an ordinand unless the said ordinand had been to an elementary and secondary school and was entirely untainted by any knowledge of the classics, time passed unperceived, and not for at least twenty minutes did Mr Oriel think of his higher duties as a host.

Meanwhile the ladies, having reached that pleasant moment in a dinner party when, having dined and drunk in elegant sufficiency, they were at last free to talk as man to man and not feel obliged to humour the menfolk, were happily thrashing out the story of Pilchards and the backyard parcels of fish, digressing by easy degrees to Mrs Perry's three boys and Mrs Belton's two sons and one daughter. Miss Sparling was very sympathetic, so much so that Mrs Belton felt it was only fair to ask about the health and general well-being of her flock. Miss Sparling was able to report that everyone was well and seemed contented, but she was afraid she was going to have trouble at the end of each term now, because a number of her girls wished to go straight into the Forces or the Red Cross as soon as they were old enough, while their parents wanted them to go to a university and learn education, or get a job in a reserved occupation; while another section whose parents hoped to see them in uniform of some sort were determinedly bent on going on the stage and performing to the troops, or going to a physical culture college to learn to be Gym and Games mistresses.

'But the girls who are giving me the most anxiety,' said Miss

Sparling, 'are the ones who want to go into the Wrens because they like the hat.'

'It's an enchanting hat,' said Mrs Belton. 'If I were a young officer I'd take every Wren I met by her chin and lift up her face and kiss her. Charming little birds they are.'

'I quite agree,' said Miss Sparling. 'But nearly all my girls who want to be Wrens haven't the faintest chance of getting in, even if the Admiralty were taking new ones, which they aren't at present. And their parents will blame me. That girl Heather Adams is going to be another of my troubles. She is an only child and her father has great ambitions for her to go into his works and become a partner. She seemed very ready to do so and has a real interest in figures and factory management, but she came back this term wanting to join the A.T.S. They both have strong wills and I shall be the buffer. However, I'm used to that, and she is only just sixteen so the question is not pressing yet.'

At this moment the door was opened and Mr Carton came in, followed by Dorothy with coffee. Mrs Belton and Mrs Perry were pleased though surprised to see him.

'I don't think you have met Mr Carton,' said Mrs Belton to Miss Sparling.

Mr Carton said he hadn't and shook hands.

'I seem to have made a social blunder,' said Mr Carton. 'Oriel looked in before dinner to ask me to come round this evening. Dorothy was going into the drawing-room with coffee, so I followed her. Shall I go to the dining-room?'

'What is it, Dorothy?' said Mrs Belton, seeing Dorothy hovering with the coffee tray just out of everyone's reach.

'Mrs Powlett said to remember Miss Sparling isn't a married lady,' said Dorothy in a hoarse whisper, pushing the tray at Mrs Belton, 'not unless it was the first time she came here.'

'That's quite all right,' said Mrs Belton soothingly, for she knew through long experience that Dorothy's mind worked on slightly subnormal lines and was quite incapable of holding more than one idea, and that usually a totally wrong one, at a time. 'You can put the tray down, Dorothy, and tell Mr Oriel Mr Carton is here.'

Dorothy accordingly went to the dining-room, opened the door and said, 'Please, sir, Mrs Belton says the gentleman is come,' and fled for refuge to the kitchen, where Mrs Powlett put her through a severe cross-examination. But as that worthy woman gave her no space in which to reply, Dorothy was able to concentrate on thinking of nothing at all.

The Vicar hastened to the drawing-room, apologies were made, Mr Carton was invited to go to the dining-room, but he said he was very well where he was, so the Vicar fetched the other guests.

'And now, Mr Oriel,' said Mrs Perry, 'what was your surprise?'

The sentence somehow sounded unfinished and Mr Oriel looked at her.

'My surprise? At what?' he said. 'Oh, my little surprise for you all. I am afraid it isn't a surprise any longer. I had asked Carton to come in and join us, just a little plan of mine to make the evening more entertaining, but here he is, so I fear the surprise has failed.'

He looked so downcast that his hearers felt almost guilty till Mrs Belton, with great presence of mind, said they had been extremely surprised when Mr Carton came in, so everything was perfect. The Vicar's face cleared.

Mr Carton, owing as he often said to having to see a great deal of undergraduates who though delightful fellows were not of ripe vintage and were still so near the schoolboy as to feel obliged to do a great deal of their crude and valueless thinking aloud, often in colloquial and ill-chosen English, possessed in a high degree the power of talking and listening pleasantly to one person while studying another, or even following a train of thought in his own mind. Owing to this gift he was extremely popular with the wives of heads of colleges who found in him an old-world courtesy and a mature sympathy for which their beings craved. And as they never heard what he said about them afterwards to Mr Fanshawe, the Dean of Paul's and his great ally, it did not matter. So, now, Mr Carton was able to converse with Mrs Perry about the Bring and Buy Sale for Mixo-Lydian refugees (in whom he took no interest at all) and sympathize with her about her sons (whom he looked upon as undergraduates of an unusually boring kind whose only interest in the humanities was the Latin and Greek names for diseases) never all getting leave at the same time, while also quietly studying and appraising the headmistress of the Hosiers' Girls' Foundation School. In her he recognized, without disappointment for he had expected nothing else, the type, but too familiar to him, of the female don. A good specimen of the type, he admitted. Not the sort who when she had married a professor was far too apt to feed him on husks, keep all the doors and windows open, snub the undergraduates whom he asked to Sunday lunch, sing in the Bach Choir and wear a mackintosh to Encaenia garden parties; still less the bachelor type who shared a flat with a friend and was arch over coffee. But there was a something, a shade to which he could not as yet give its precise value, which told him whether truly or falsely that he would find little profit here. Whether it was her rather unfashionable stylishness, the contrast between it and her kind, intelligent face, her slight air of being an uncrowned queen, we cannot say. We can only state that having listened to her talking and looked at her as she talked, Mr Carton decided what he had already made up his mind to decide, that Miss Sparling was simply another of those school and college-educated women with no background at all, which to his mind was not education in the least.

Presently there was a shifting of chairs and Mr Oriel set Mr Carton beside Miss Sparling, saying that he knew they would have much in common. This introduction, besides making them form an immediate determination to show that they hadn't, at the same time united them in a strong sense of ingratitude to Mr Oriel who was happily engaged in parish talk with Mr Belton. Their conversation therefore ran on such ordinary topics as why radio announcers had to pronounce Italian and other place-names in so original, and should they say uneducated a way, the rearranging of Harefield Park as a school, how uncomfortable one always felt while Mr Churchill was away, the possible choice of a husband for the Heir to the Throne, how very kind the girl bus conductors and porters were, and why people in trains and hotels sniffed all the time.

'I often wish,' said Miss Sparling, permitting herself a quite human spark of hatred, 'that one could have No Sniffing carriages on the railway as well as No Smoking.'

'None of them can read, or want to read; and even if they can, the words convey nothing to them,' said Mr Carton. 'Besides if you label a carriage No Anything-at-all, people deliberately get in and do it.'

'I know,' said Miss Sparling. 'If you labelled a carriage, No Wooden Legs, you would find six a side and one standing.'

Mr Carton smiled his tight scholar's smile. The woman's remark had shown understanding, nay a certain mild wit: but he was not to be taken in by these toys. Even the wife of the Master of St Barabbas could be witty on occasion; but what a woman! doing folk dancing in a cotton frock before the war, and taking up Dr (Ph.) Professor Kropóv, that arch-impostor of a Mixo-Lydian refugee and getting a special chair of Romano-Lydian culture (which was in itself a gross contradiction in terms) created for his benefit. It would not surprise him in the least if Miss Sparling folk-danced among her girls. And what girls! He had seen them all coming out of church and catalogued them as the perfect type of future woman undergraduate, for undergraduette was a word whose existence he inwardly contemned and outwardly ignored.

'How *very* nice Mrs Updike is,' said Mrs Belton, during a slight pause in the conversation. 'I can't think how anyone can knock herself about as much as she does and remain so cheerful.'

'And so delightfully right about Russia,' said Mrs Perry. 'I only wish Mrs Hunter had heard what she said. I didn't like to contradict Mrs Hunter in my own house, but of course all that talk about Mixo-Lydians massacring Slavo-Lydians is quite ungrounded. It was the Slavo-Lydians, backed as usual by Russia, who massacred a number of Mixo-Lydian peasants in 1830. If the Mixo-Lydians did retaliate who can blame them?'

Everyone present took no interest at all in the past, or present, history of Mixo-Lydia, and wished Mrs Perry had not mentioned it, for once started it was very difficult to stop her. The word Russia is also a very powerful chemical agent to throw into conversation, stirring up as it does an amount of entirely uninformed and doctrinaire prejudice one way or another, which does no credit to anyone.

'I believe I am correct in stating,' said Mr Carton, who hated uninformed political talk of the present, but hated inaccuracy about the past even more, 'that the massacre to which Mrs Perry alludes was in 1829. The Slavo-Lydians of course still keep to the old calendar – mostly to spite the Pope, though I doubt if the Vatican knows or cares – but even so, as the massacre was in the early autumn, the year is not affected. I hold no brief for either side, for two more degraded and backward races do not exist in Europe, but the Slavo-Lydians had had great provocation. The Mixo-Lydian peasants on the frontier had already made armed demonstrations.'

'The Slavo-Lydians had stolen three cows!' said Mrs Perry, her eyes glistening.

Mr Oriel, terrified that a conflict might break out in his drawing-room, though he need not have feared this, for Mr Carton had no intention of arguing with Mrs Perry, made a hasty and ill-advised diversion by saying that the visit of the Archbishop of York to our Russian allies was a great step towards the reunion of the churches.

Mr Carton unkindly asked which churches.

Dr Perry said the Russians having a Patriarch again sounded quite like the Bible; quite like the old times he meant, fearing that an allusion to the Bible might not be quite tactful in the Vicarage.

Several people speaking at once said any sort of church, universal toleration, wasn't the Russian Church rather theatrical, how nice it was at the end of the first act of *Tosca* when that religious procession went by and they had never quite known what it was about; unless you counted Verdi, who really began quite a long time ago, what had a United Italy produced creatively; it was high time Italy and all Europe was divided into little states again, why did some people call it Renascence and some Renaissance, what a pity it was there were so few kings and queens left, one wondered if all the Royal Family had the same coupons that we do or special ones. Not that we wish it to be understood that all these trains of argument were followed simultaneously, but each followed so hard upon the other that the effect was as of a kaleidoscope.

In the first lull Miss Sparling, turning to Mr Belton, said in her equable voice that she believed he knew a Mr Adams slightly, the parent of a rather difficult pupil of hers, and she would be most grateful if he could tell her anything that would help her in assessing the child's-background, as she felt a certain responsibility for her.

Mr Belton, appealed to in a reasonable way by a good-looking, intelligent woman, who was also his tenant and as such entitled to his help and protection, showed his best side, the side that had made him considered and respected in the county. Far from indulging in abuse of Mr Adams as a rank outsider and unmitigated vulgarian, as he would certainly have done at home, he answered that he only knew him on the bench, where he perhaps put himself forward a little too much for a newcomer without experience of country conditions, but was regular in attendance and often quite willing to listen to what older magistrates had to say. He also believed, though on this he could only speak from hearsay and not from personal knowledge, that he had a good name for treating his factory hands well, while standing no nonsense.

'And that is not easy under present conditions,' he said, 'with high wages and a certain amount of what one can only call low business morality among the workers who are brought to Hogglestock from other parts and billeted in the villages. I'm sorry I can't tell you more.'

Miss Sparling thanked him and said she was glad to hear a reassuring account of Mr Adams.

'His daughter takes after him in many ways,' she said. 'She is extremely obstinate, but if you can once make her see reason she allows herself to be guided. I had an example of this not long ago. As I was saying, she was anxious to go in for factory management, but a few weeks ago she suddenly said she wanted to go into the A.T.S. as soon as possible. It was on that Sunday when I first had the pleasure of meeting Mrs Belton, and I remember it because Heather made herself quite troublesome about her new idea at lunch. I can't make out why she had this sudden passion for the A.T.S., unless it was something in Mr Oriel's sermon. She was so absent-minded after it that she dropped her prayer book in the churchyard while I was talking to Mrs Belton and your younger son, and the prefect on duty spoke to her rather sharply. I don't usually see the girls on Sundays, but I am sorry for Heather, so I made a point of giving her a few moments on Sunday evening and she was quite sensible and said she saw she was mistaken and did not think she would like to have anything to do with the Army. Girls are curious creatures.'

'Oriel!' said Mr Belton, who as a churchwarden felt he ought to get to the bottom of this.

Mr Oriel, who was talking to Dr Perry about the Pomfret otter-hounds which still occasionally had a kind of token meet, started and looked round.

'This is something in your line,' said Mr Belton.

Mr Oriel looked alarmed.

'No, not the Bishop,' said Mr Belton. 'But what did you say in church Sunday fortnight ago?'

'What did I say in church?' Mr Oriel repeated nervously.

'In church; in the pulpit; where you preach,' said Mr Belton kindly. 'Sermon. You know.'

'My sermon on the 13th Sunday after Trinity? Let me think.

It was – no – yes, I have it; it was on the materials and orna-ments of Aaron's priestly garments. I have given a good deal of attention to that subject. It was perhaps a selfish choice of text, but it may not have been wasted. I wish you had heard it,' said Mr Oriel, mildly dashed.

'I heard it all right. I was in my usual pew and read both the lessons,' said Mr Belton. 'I can't do more. But sometimes things escape one. You are sure there was nothing in it about the army? I mean that it was a bit rough, or didn't keep all the Commandments, or anything of that sort?'

'Certainly not,' said Mr Oriel decidedly. 'There is of course quite a distressing amount of small damage and petty theft whenever we have troops billeted here, and the married women with husbands serving are far too obliging. In fact Mrs Hoare tells me that there is a good deal of feeling among the young women in her Bible Class, because they say the married ones don't give them a chance, but I would certainly never mention it in public. But I did make what I considered a good point about Urim and Thummim, which you may remember.'

'Yes, yes; Urim,' said Mr Belton. 'And Thummim too,' he added hastily, not wishing the latter to feel slighted. 'Thanks, Oriel. Well, Miss Sparling, we don't seem to get much further about Adams's girl. I'm sorry for all these young people now. If we get a good frost you must bring your girls down to the lake to skate. Cheer them all up.'

Miss Sparling thanked him very much, but in a curiously abstracted way, as if a train of thought had been started in her mind and must be followed.

The telephone was heard in the distance. A moment later Mrs Powlett came in.

'Excuse me, sir, but I've sent Dorothy to bed,' said Mrs Powlett, who was speaking the literal truth and had sent her underling upstairs so that she herself might have an excuse for a good look at Miss Sparling when the guests left. The telephone was therefore a heaven-sent opportunity for entering the drawing-room and taking a preparatory survey of the newcomer. 'It's for Dr Perry. I think it's that Dr Morgan, sir, the lady doctor.'

'No peace for the wicked,' said Dr Perry, who always had the right comment for the situation, and he went across to the study. Mrs Powlett slowly collected the coffee cups, by which ruse she was able to study Miss Sparling in the round.

'Lady doctors!' said Dr Perry coming back. 'Morgan's in a jam as usual. One of her old panel patients throwing fits and she wants my opinion. Opinion! What she wants is for me to do the job. Dispensing for Potter is about all she's fit for. Why doesn't she try her psychology on the old lady? I'm sorry for you all when I take my holiday, as there's no one else to carry on at the moment. Did I put my bag in the car, Maud?'

His wife said he had.

'Don't wait for me,' said her husband. 'I'll come back if I can, but if I can't, I can't. I'll be coming up to give that girl of yours her last injection, Miss Sparling, and I hope she'll carry on through the winter without any more boils. If not, I'll have to send her to the Barchester General for some tests. Good night, Oriel, and thanks for the evening.'

He made a comprehensive farewell to the rest of the party, talked himself out of the room and was heard shutting the front door.

'Poor gentleman,' said Mrs Powlett, availing herself of her position as an old retainer.

'What about this Dr Morgan, Mrs Powlett?' said Mr Carton, who took great pleasure in a gossip with his friend's cook.

Mrs Powlett said she wouldn't like to say, but she didn't think it was the act of a lady putting such ideas into people's heads. Mr Carton pressed her as to the kind of idea, but she would not be drawn, and taking refuge behind a generality as to people having something better to do than talking about their dreams, and she had never dreamt in her life, having always had plenty to occupy her mind without such fancies, carried the coffee cups away.

'Dr Morgan is quite a nice woman,' said Mrs Perry, with a vague feeling that she ought to uphold the medical profession, 'but she will try psychology on the cottagers. It doesn't go down at all. The schoolmistress tells me some of the elder girls are asking her the meaning of some most peculiar words. You have her, don't you, Miss Sparling?'

Miss Sparling, trained by her profession to a guarded speech, said Dr Morgan had given one of her girls some injections when Dr Perry was too busy, but she had only met her once, for a few moments.

'I thought so,' said Mrs Perry, whose instinct as a doctor's wife had apparently extracted from this colourless statement all she wanted to know. 'Of course if she likes to ask the village girls what they dream about, anyone will tell her the answer. Soldiers of course. But I do wish she wouldn't despise my husband for not being a psycho-analyst and then ask him to do her difficult cases in the middle of the night.'

Half an hour or so passed agreeably in general talk, at the end of which time Mrs Perry said it was no use waiting for her husband and she would go home. The Beltons said they would see her safely into Plassey House; she protested, saying she had a torch and thought nothing of the blackout and it would be taking them out of their way; the Beltons counter-protested, saying that it was only a step from Arcot House on to Plassey

House and such a fine night, Mrs Belton adding that if they walked to Plassey House on the shop side of the High Street and back to Arcot House on their own side it would be no distance at all, a piece of fallacious reasoning which somehow carried entire conviction.

'Can I see you back to Harefield Park, Miss Sparling?' said Mr Carton, who though he did not care for her type thought it a long lonely walk at that hour on a moonless night. But Miss Sparling thanked him, saying that Mr Oriel had kindly ordered the taxi from the Nabob's Head and it ought to be here now. So the Beltons and Mrs Perry went away and Miss Sparling waited for the arrival of her taxi.

'May I say, Mr Oriel, how interesting I found your sermon about Aaron's vestments,' said Miss Sparling.

Mr Oriel expressed himself much honoured and said he was afraid vestments were hardly a lady's subject; that he did not mean to say that ladies were not great authorities on clothes in general, but the question of a High Priest's clothes was of course slightly different.

'I only happen to know a little about them because my grandfather was so much interested in the subject,' said Miss Sparling. 'I think I hear the taxi.'

A grinding of war-worn gears and a bang on the door confirmed her thought.

'Thank you for a most pleasant evening, Mr Oriel,' she said. 'I had better go at once, for Wheeler doesn't like to wait.'

The gentlemen accompanied her to the hall where Mrs Powlett was waiting with her coat and other wraps.

'By the way,' said Mr Oriel, while Miss Sparling was tying a scarf round her head, 'it is unusual to hear of anyone who has studied that subject of the High Priest's robes. Since old Canon

Horbury died I have not known anyone who was an authority.'

'He was my grandfather,' said Miss Sparling. 'I lived with him from when I was fifteen till I left college, when he died. I have his books if you would care to look at them.'

'My *dear* lady,' cried Mr Oriel, transported. 'I am even more delighted to have you among us than I was before. Horbury's granddaughter! A real scholar and an inspiring teacher. He was very kind to me when I was a young curate. You knew him of course, Carton.'

Mr Carton said he didn't, but had often heard his name.

'And that accounts for your library,' said Mr Oriel. 'A most interesting collection, Carton. I ought to have guessed, but I had no idea. I cannot tell you what pleasure this gives me.

'Grandpapa was always buying books,' said Miss Sparling, 'but he wouldn't put his name in them, so his friends were always borrowing them and forgetting to bring them back. He had a very good classical library as well as his theological books. Good night, Mr Oriel. Thank you again, and I am so glad you knew grandpapa.'

Mrs Powlett opened the front door. Mr Oriel put Miss Sparling into Wheeler's taxi with repeated expressions of pleasure and the taxi ground its way down the drive.

'Come into the study, Carton, and we'll finish the port as you didn't have any after dinner,' said Mr Oriel. 'Good night, Mrs Powlett. Dear, dear, what a strange thing. Canon Horbury's granddaughter. I never knew he had one. I thought his daughter had married someone queer and died. Port, Carton?'

Mr Carton did not say no. The port was finished, with some village and Oxford gossip, for Mr Oriel was an old Paul's man, and Mr Carton got up to go.

'I mustn't be too late,' he said. 'I'm correcting proofs of my new book and haven't much time as term begins next week. You haven't Slawkenbergius's edition of Fluvius Minucius, have you? Mine is in my rooms at Paul's. The Amsterdam 1594, I mean.'

Mr Oriel walked to a bookcase, got on a chair and looked on the top shelf.

'I know I have Slawkenbergius,' he said, 'but I haven't opened him for years. I must have had him soon after I was first ordained, for I remember Canon Horbury being very helpful about him. Here he is.'

He took down a calf-bound volume whose covers were gently powdering away in fine brown dust.

'There you are,' he said opening it. 'Amsterdam 1594. And what's this?'

A piece of paper was sticking out from among the pages. He took it out and looked at it.

'"Borrowed from Horbury, 2.ix.'02",' he read in accents of horror.

'Well, you *have* done it,' said Mr Carton, not unpleased by his friend's discomfiture. 'Miss Sparling said her grandfather's friends were always borrowing his books and not bringing them back.'

'But this is dreadful, dreadful,' said Mr Oriel. 'When I think what my own rage and despair would be if anyone borrowed a valuable book of mine and did not return it. What can I do?'

'Nothing,' said Mr Carton. 'If Canon Horbury had missed it he would have enquired. I always heard he was an absent-minded old fellow.'

'But that does not make my fault the less,' said Mr Oriel, looking at the book in agony. 'I do not know how to face Miss Sparling.'

'Then don't,' said Mr Carton unsympathetically. 'It has been away for forty-one years, and a few more days won't make any difference, especially as she doesn't know. Besides I want it. Hand it over, Oriel, and I'll take it back to her when I've done with it.'

So overcome with contrition was Mr Oriel that he gladly left the responsibility to Mr Carton, who walked off with his prize and much enjoyed himself in writing with its aid a few very acid and trenchant remarks about the present Master of Lazarus's edition of Fluvius Minucius before he went to bed.

Mr Oriel went upstairs to sleep off his shame. Mrs Powlett locked the doors of the living-rooms on the outside as was her custom, being a well-known recipe against burglars in her family, but extremely annoying to her master, as she always took the keys with her and if he suddenly wanted a book late at night, as he often did, being a great reader in bed, he couldn't get it. She then pursued her majestic progress to the second floor. Seeing a light under Dorothy's door, she went in.

'Time to go to sleep now, Dorothy,' she said. 'What do you want books in bed for? Our beds weren't given us for reading.'

'It's ever such a nice book,' said Dorothy. 'I got it at the two-penny libery, Mrs Powlett.'

'What's it about?' said Mrs Powlett.

'It's ever so nice,' said Dorothy, her face and spectacles gleaming with the romance that her negligible features and wisp of colourless hair would never bring her. 'It's a gentleman, Lord Victor he is, and he gives Lady Isabel a diamond necklace to seduke her.'

'You give me that book, my girl,' said Mrs Powlett. 'Who let you take it out?'

'Dr Morgan, Mrs Powlett,' said Dorothy, clasping the book to her flat chest.

'Don't you tell me lies, Dorothy,' said Mrs Powlett, not harshly, but as one whose mission it was to look after fools gladly. 'Dr Morgan's a doctor – if doctors you can call them, poor things, but we can't all get married – not a libery-lady.'

'Oh, Mrs Powlett, you know I don't tell lies,' said Dorothy.

'Well, take it as if I hadn't said it,' said Mrs Powlett magnanimously. 'I don't think you've got the wits to do it, Dorothy. Now, what's all this about Dr Morgan?' she said, sitting down on the one chair with its rather dilapidated cane seat.

'Please, Mrs Powlett, Dr Morgan was in the libery and I was looking for a nice book and Dr Morgan said what I needed was something to give me colour in my life.'

'I always did say you needed a tonic, Dorothy,' said Mrs Powlett. 'It didn't need Dr Morgan to tell you that. A bottle of Abdomo-Pep a week, that's what you need. It puts red blood into you.'

'And she said to read this, Mrs Powlett,' said Dorothy, who had by long practice stopped hearing most of what her overlady said.

'Well, Dorothy, I say don't,' said Mrs Powlett, removing the book from Dorothy's grasp. 'And next time you go to the libery, I'll come with you and see there's no nonsense. You did nicely this evening, Dorothy. I don't say this to puff you up but I always say don't grudge a kind word where a kind word is due. We gave Miss Sparling a nice evening.'

'Oh, yes, Mrs Powlett,' said Dorothy. 'I thought she was—' She paused to find in her limited vocabulary a word that would describe the guest of honour.

'You've got no call to think at all, Dorothy,' said Mrs Powlett. 'You just do as I tell you and don't forget to dust under the dining-room clock. Miss Sparling is a very nice lady. You know, Dorothy, that I have always said it was time Mr Oriel got married, for I can't live for ever not nowadays and I'm five years older than he is though thank God I have the use of all my legs and sleep well, but I'd like to see him settled.'

'Yes, Mrs Powlett,' said Dorothy, whose mind was still straying among the dreams of a diamond necklace and Lord Victor.

'So I shouldn't be surprised if it was a match,' said Mrs Powlett, looking at the ceiling. 'Made in heaven they say, though goodness knows what heaven was about when it let me marry Powlett, a poor thing if ever there was one and no loss except his wages when he died and he usually drank them by Saturday night. Mark my words, Dorothy, we'll have a mistress at the Vicarage before long.'

'But you're the mistress, Mrs Powlett,' said Dorothy.

'Don't you talk nonsense, my girl,' said Mrs Powlett, not displeased. 'I know my place and I hope I've taught you to know yours.'

'It would be ever so nice, Mrs Powlett,' said Dorothy, dimly apprehending romance. 'Perhaps Mr Oriel will give Miss Sparling a diamond necklace and seduke her. I *would* like to see it, Mrs Powlett.'

'Really, Dorothy!' said Mrs Powlett, rising in majestic indignation. 'That's quite enough and you go to sleep at once. And mind you don't repeat what I said about Miss Sparling. Good night.'

Turning out the light at the door she went to her own room where she tied up the offending book in a piece of brown paper. As it was clear that Dorothy had no idea of the implications of Lord Victor's gift beyond its general desirability, Mrs Powlett was not anxious for her. But she determined to accompany Dorothy to the twopenny library herself in future, or at any rate speak to Miss Faithful Humble who kept it as a branch line of a small tobacconist's, and warn her to supervise Dorothy's choice of books.

5

Mrs Belton, as she had promised, wrote to Captain Hornby and suggested that he should come down for a night or two and go through the things that were in the locked room upstairs. Captain Hornby gratefully accepted her offer and named a week-end when the Admiralty were giving him forty-eight hours off, which wouldn't be till the middle of November. So Mrs Belton noted the date in her engagement book and applied herself to her ordinary duties. All the working parties continued. Mrs Updike, except for the fortnight when she had her arm in a sling owing to falling off a ladder on which she was looking round her attic with a torch to see if she could see any of the mice who had been ravaging her emergency store cupboard, knitted the leg of a seaboot stocking very creditably. It was then taken away from her by Mrs Hoare who turned the heel and started the foot. At the last meeting it had been restored to Mrs Updike (now out of her sling, but having to wear one of her husband's shoes owing to a broken blister) who enthusiastically added fifteen inches to it before she was discovered and checked.

Mrs Belton was very glad to learn in a letter from her daughter Elsa, received on the Thursday before Captain Hornby was expected, that she also was getting leave from her hush-hush job and would be turning up some time on the Friday and not to bother. So Mrs Belton, having learned by experience that it was no good trying to find out when or where any of her children would arrive, even if she could get a taxi which she usually couldn't, laid in such unrationed food as she could procure and awaited the event. Vegetables and milk, as we know, she got from Harefield Park, eggs (as we may not have mentioned) she had from the Home Farm, but the man who looked after them had at the moment no cockerels old enough to be worth killing. Mrs Updike, who had been fattening cockerels for Christmas, said she could give her one if she could get it killed.

'Thank you so much,' said Mrs Belton, who had run across Mrs Updike at the post office. 'Fred will get one of the men to kill it. How do you manage, then?'

'I did mean to learn to kill them myself,' said Mrs Updike apologetically, 'but I am so dreadfully clumsy that I know I would wring their necks the wrong way round. Phil did shoot one when we had two of the children back for half-term last week, but it made such a noise and seemed rather cowardly. I mean, I think one ought to learn to do brave things, don't you?'

'One moment,' said Mrs Belton, seeing one of the two post office girls disengaged. 'A packet of stamped envelopes, please.'

'Sorry, they're rationed,' said the girl, who was Mrs Powlett's niece, Olive, and very kind as well as knowing her work backwards.

'Rationed?' said Mrs Belton.

'Only four to each customer,' said Olive.

'Four then, please,' said Mrs Belton. 'But what happens if I want to write more than four letters in a day?'

'You could always come in again,' said Olive. 'Or as often as you like, Mrs Belton.'

'But I'm afraid it's rather a trouble for you,' said Mrs Belton.

'That's all right,' said Olive, handing her the envelopes. 'A shilling, please.'

Mrs Belton took her envelopes, paid for them, looked perplexed, and returned to Mrs Updike.

'I'm so sorry, but I had to seize my chance,' she said to Mrs Updike. 'You were telling me about how to kill fowls.'

'Well, if one was on a desert island one would feel so silly not knowing how to kill a fowl,' said Mrs Updike. 'I suppose if one could catch it, one could cut its head off if one had an axe. But I'm sure I wouldn't have an axe. The only thing I can think of would be to work myself up into a great fit of rage and *stamp* on its head.'

In saying which ferocious words her pretty fine-drawn face beamed with gay enthusiasm.

'If you aren't doing anything, come back to tea,' said Mrs Updike. 'I made some rock cakes because a cousin in Australia sent me a tin of sultanas. We can look at the chickens first and you can choose which cockerel you like.'

Mrs Belton had nothing particular to do and it was nearly half-past four, so she walked with Mrs Updike to Clive's Corner and in by the old stable entrance. Beyond the stables was a small paddock, part of which was wired off for about twenty fowls who were pecking at the grass and at each other with equal viciousness. Some were of a matronly build and a rich chestnut colour, some were white and rather refined, some were speckled in various shades, but all looked extremely well and defiant, with ruby crests. Mrs Belton's attention was particularly drawn by a gang of cockerels who were strutting about, eyeing each other malevolently and seizing food from under each other's beaks without daring to come to a real fight about it.

'Which would you like, Mrs Belton?' said Mrs Updike. 'I'm afraid I don't know much about them. I only began keeping them two years ago for eggs and the cockerels were quite an after-thought. We had a white one, and he fed four of us. I steamed him and then made him into a sort of pilaf with rice and a few prunes and some paprika and anything handy, and except for scalding my arm over the steamer it was perfect.'

'I'm afraid I know nothing,' said Mrs Belton. 'You see they always kept our fowls down at the Home Farm and I never saw them much till they came to table. Which do you think looks ripest?'

Mrs Updike gazed with an abstracted eye upon her flock and said she thought the one with the black speckles round his neck was the best.

'He was the one we meant to shoot,' she said, 'but just as Phil aimed at him another one got in front of him, so Phil shot the other one because he didn't want to stay out any longer. Would you like to take him home with you?'

'Alive, do you mean?' asked Mrs Belton. 'I'm afraid I might hurt him.'

'You can't hurt fowls,' said Mrs Updike. 'It's the one thing I do know. I'll catch him for you. Wait a minute.'

She ran back to the stable and returned with a handful of barley which she scattered towards the doomed bird, crying, 'Chook, chook, chook.' At the sound of her voice the whole army of fowls hurled itself upon the barley, the cockerels with a great want of chivalry pecking and kicking at the hens in their own eagerness to gorge. Mrs Updike made several grabs at Mrs Belton's cockerel, but each time he escaped shrieking from her grasp and rushed back into the mêlée.

'If one threw a net over them, they couldn't get away,' said Mrs Belton.

Mrs Updike said she was afraid it would take all night to disentangle them. She looked so dejected that Mrs Belton was just about to beg her to come indoors and leave the hens till a man could come from the Home Farm and kill one, when her chosen bird, suddenly catching sight of an imaginary titbit in a corner of the run, made towards it at full tilt, striding like an ostrich, his neck stretched, his handsome white tail plumes waving like pennons in his wake. Mrs Updike with admirable promptitude gave chase, cornered him up against an old packing-case and, as Mrs Belton afterwards averred, knocked him down and picked him up by the legs. She then returned with the cock hanging head downwards and too surprised to complain.

'He'll suffocate!' cried Mrs Belton. 'Oh, do hold him the right way up!'

'You can't,' said Mrs Updike. 'They hit you with their wings and jab you with their beaks. Come in and I'll put him in a basket.'

She led the way through the kitchen where she took a large basket with a cover from a hook, pushed the cockerel unceremoniously in and fastened it down.

'Now we'll have tea,' she said, and lighted the gas under a kettle. 'I've got a thing about kettles,' said Mrs Updike, taking the lid off the kettle, putting her finger in and withdrawing it quickly, 'since the time I let the big kettle burn to death. Sometimes I nearly scald myself.'

'Couldn't you just tilt the kettle a little over the sink and see if any water comes out of it?' said Mrs Belton. 'It would save you scalding your fingers.'

'What a good idea,' said Mrs Updike. 'I am so stupidly clumsy. I wish you would go into the drawing-room and rest. I'll bring the tea in a minute.'

So Mrs Belton went into the drawing-room and looked out of the window on to the garden where a few yellow leaves were illumined in a dying golden light from the west, thinking, as she so often did, of the wider sunsets from her own room at Harefield Park. Then Mrs Updike came in with a tray, laid the little tea-table with hearty and rather dashing goodwill and exclaimed upon the chill of the room. Mrs Belton protested, with truth, that she was not at all cold as she had been walking, but with soft shrieks of hospitable despair, Mrs Updike knelt down and put a light to the paper and sticks in the fireplace. They burst into joyous flame, crackled, glowed and were gone.

'Oh dear,' said Mrs Updike, laughing at herself. 'That always happens the first time. I'll get some paper out of the salvage bag and start it again.'

She went away into the back regions and came back with sticks and logs and some dirty newspaper, which she stuffed into the grate.

'Do you think a little coal on the top?' said Mrs Belton. 'Then perhaps it won't go out so soon.'

'I always forget important things like that,' said Mrs Updike admiringly. 'Now it ought to be all right. I'll just wash my hands and call Phil. Would you mind opening the door for me? I've got a sort of thing about my hands. I always seem to get them dirtier than other people.'

Mrs Belton accordingly opened the door for her hostess, who went out, calling to her husband. No further contretemps occurred and in a few moments all three were having tea.

Mr Updike was a middle-aged man with grey hair, not so tall as his wife, with a quiet voice and manner. His family had been the Harefield solicitors ever since the Nabob began to make the local practice a lucrative one by his incessant quarrels with neighbours and his frequent purchases of land and cottages. The passion for lawsuits had luckily not survived in the family, but the Updikes had continued to handle its affairs and to them had gradually added those of several other large landowners and most of the wealthier inhabitants of the town, besides the local interests of Lord Pomfret. On all important matters, Mr Updike was discreet, but much enjoyed giving his older and more favoured clients scraps of information.

Conversation began with a great asking after each other's families. All the young Updikes were well, as indeed they always were, for there had never been a generation in which Updike sons had not done well at school, at college and in their profession, and Updike daughters married well into minor county families or London legal circles. This generation was no exception. The elder boy, whose law studies had been interrupted by the war, was already a young colonel, the elder girl was rushing up the ladder of the W.A.A.F. as fast as she could go, the younger girl doing well in school and the younger boy raking in scholarships, though his chance of using them at present appeared very slight. Mrs Belton contributed the latest news of her own family, perhaps slightly exaggerating Freddy's importance at the Admiralty, the indispensableness of Elsa in her hush-hush job and Charles's unusually brilliant career in the Artillery where he had lately performed the daring and uncommon deed of getting his second pip.

'I was thinking the other day,' said Mrs Updike, 'that the real difference between mothers and nurses used to be that the mothers praised each other's children out of politeness and the nurses praised their own children out of truth. Now we haven't got any nurses we have to praise our own children. I know I am quite dreadful about praising mine, Phil says I've quite a thing about it.'

'You must surprise people who don't know you when you praise your colonel,' said Mrs Belton, who had a pleasing, though sometimes disconcerting habit of saying nice things about people she liked to their faces, which, she said, would appreciate it much more than their backs would, 'because it is so ridiculous to think of you as a colonel's mother.'

'Oh, do you think so!' said Mrs Updike flushing. 'Ought I to look more dignified? I am always in such a hurry with the house and the cooking that I can't remember to be my age.'

'I don't mean that,' said Mrs Belton hastily. 'I mean you look so ridiculously and charmingly young. You really do.'

Both the Updikes looked pleased and Mr Updike, glancing at his wife with an agreeable mixture of pride and protection, said he was glad to hear that Elsa would be down for the weekend.

'And Mrs Ellangowan-Hornby's nephew is coming too,' said Mrs Belton. 'You know him, don't you? We've never met him, but he wrote very nicely about the house.'

Mr Updike said he had met him several times when the old lady was ill, and again over the will.

'A lucky young man,' he said. 'He had money of his own, I gather, and his aunt left him what even with death duties is almost a fortune. She was very shrewd about her affairs – her Scotch legal inheritance I presume. If he dies without heirs, and he isn't even married yet, the money goes to another distant cousin in Scotland.'

He fell silent and the ladies were silent too, for each was reflecting that a sailor who wasn't married now and who might be sent to sea again at any moment hadn't a very good chance of an heir; which equally applied to Commander Belton. And Mrs Belton also realized that the distant cousin in Scotland might wish to live in Arcot House, to which she was already much attached.

'No need for you to worry, Mrs Belton,' said her host, who usually knew what his clients were thinking before they knew themselves. 'Your lease is seven years, and by the time it is up I hope we shall see you back at the Park.'

'I don't see how we can ever live there now,' said Mrs Belton. 'Not unless Freddy marries an heiress. Now if Captain Hornby had been a girl I might have intrigued and caught her for Freddy. Only I'm sure I wouldn't intrigue well.'

'But much better than I would,' said Mrs Updike. 'I am so clumsy that I would spoil everything.'

In proof of which she put a log on the fire, which was doing quite well without it. The fire rejected the log which crashed on to the hearth, scattering sparks in all directions and singeing the fur hearth-rug. Mrs Belton said she must go, and hoped the Updikes would look in on Sunday afternoon. Mrs Updike fetched the basket, in which the cockerel had subsided in contemptuous sulks.

'By the way,' said Mr Updike, as he let his guest out. 'I have to thank your husband for a new client, a Mr Adams over at Hogglestock. He is buying some property round here and said if I acted for Mr Belton I'd be good enough for him.'

'I thought he and Fred didn't get on very well,' said Mrs Belton. 'At least Fred says he is rather awful on the bench.'

'I dare say he is,' said Mr Updike. 'He is not the sort of client we are used to, but one has to move with the times, and I can't let my eldest boy come back and find the office going downhill. But he seems to have a great respect for your husband, who, I gather, gave him a piece of his mind the other day. In fact Adams described him as a fine aristocratic old gentleman.'

He did not add that Mr Adams had qualified his praise by adding, 'And a conceited old stick-in-the-mud.'

'Well, doesn't that simply *show*,' said Mrs Belton, whose secret pride in her own Saxon descent did not include any illusions about the Belton family being more than county, and only of a hundred and fifty years' standing or so.

'Have you a torch?' said Mr Updike, for the street was now dark.

'Oh yes,' said Mrs Belton, feeling in her coat pocket. 'Oh dear, it is dead. I hoped it would last me till tomorrow, because of early closing today. But I'll manage.'

The customary argument then took place, ending in Mrs Belton's acceptance of a kind of policeman's lantern on a small scale guaranteed to shed a legal amount of light on the ground only. She was finally induced to take it by deciding that it would be easier to remember to return the basket if she knew she must remember to return the torch as well. She reached Arcot House in a few minutes, let herself in and rang the bell for Wheeler, to whom she confided the cockerel. Wheeler, who had a countrywoman's contempt for cockerels except as food, opened the basket and took out the bird whom she poked in what her mistress considered a very unfeeling manner.

'Oh, do take care, Wheeler,' she pleaded. 'He may be homesick and I'm sure he's hungry.'

'Hungry, madam! Not with a crop like that,' said Wheeler. 'I'll have my fine gentleman plucked and hanging up in the larder before I go to bed. He'll just be about right for Miss Elsa.'

'You won't hurt him, Wheeler, will you?' said her mistress.

Wheeler made no reply, but carried the cockerel off to the kitchen regions, never to be seen again in the flesh, or rather the feather, by mortal eye. And as she dexterously wrung his neck she thought what a pity it was Mrs Belton had to leave the Park, for at the Park such a thing would never have happened.

Mrs Belton, with an oppressive feeling of blood-guilt about the cockerel, put the torch in the basket to remind her to take it back, and the basket in the hall cupboard so as not to look untidy, by which means she successfully forgot about them both for three days.

After dinner, Mrs Belton was called to the telephone to speak to Miss Sparling.

'I am sorry to bother you, Mrs Belton,' said Miss Sparling's voice. 'You know this weekend is our half-term holiday. Most of our girls can't go home for so short a time because of transport difficulties, so we are having to arrange some treats for them. On Saturday, Mr Oriel has most kindly offered to conduct a small party over the church at two o'clock and I wondered if your husband would give us permission to see over the Garden House afterwards; and perhaps he would say a few words about it.'

Mrs Belton said she was sure her husband would give permission, but she could not answer for his addressing the girls as he usually spent Saturday afternoon with the keeper. 'And if it isn't too large a party we would love to give you tea,' she added. 'My daughter will be here and Captain Hornby whose aunt used to live here.'

A skirmish of politeness then took place, but when she realized that Mrs Belton had plenty of her own milk and was high on the list of people who were allowed to get cakes on Saturday from the Rajah Café, Miss Sparling accepted the invitation with no further argument.

It is well known that forty-eight hours' leave can be counted in many different ways. If the hours are counted from when you leave the office or the regiment or the ship to when you rejoin it, a bare minimum, the fault is usually not so much in your stars as in yourselves, for being underlings. But when you are a naval captain doing a responsible temporary job at the Admiralty, or a clever reliable young woman engaged on important secret work in a place you may not mention (not that you need to, for it is remarkable how many people always know it), you can usually arrange to get off some time on the Friday afternoon and report on the following Monday morning, which does not give you such a bad weekend.

Accordingly, Miss Belton and Captain Hornby, R.N., converging from their different places of employment, met at Barchester station on Friday afternoon, caught the local to Nutfield, and there were lucky enough to find one of the Pomfret Estate lorries going over to the other side of Harefield to fetch a couple of pigs. As Elsa knew most of the Pomfret men there was no difficulty about getting a lift, and dismounting at the crossroads they walked up the dark street, silent except for the unpleasant voice announcing the same thing with insufferable condescension from every house with a chink of window open.

Mrs Belton had often felt grateful that though her daughter Elsa was independent in her ways, she had never wanted to lead her own life, much preferring to live in her parents' house where without any trouble she had a delightful bedroom with a small sitting-room and a bathroom attached, good food, fires in winter, two motors, several horses, and could ask her friends whenever she liked and go to Scotland, or the Riviera, or India, or even once on a cruise to the Northern capitals which was rather marred by the number of lectures given by the Dean of Barchester, who was himself travelling free as a kind of superior bait or attraction, with his wife and three of the girls, first-class at second-class fares. Very soon after the war began one motor was put down, then horses were commandeered, rationing set in, all England was imprisoned within its sea wall; but Elsa still had her own horse and enjoyed the local work that had to be done. Shortly after that she got a job in the secret occupation where she now stood so high and was constantly in contact with people who almost knew what was really happening, and as time went on her home did feel more and more decaying, less and less comfortable and interesting.

When her father told her that he would probably have to give up Harefield Park, she had a moment's wild anger and despair.

'It's not as if it were going to be mine, or anything,' she said to Captain Hornby with whom she was lunching in town, some time before the opening of this story, 'and I must say the house is pretty depressing now, and anyway I'd hardly ever be there, but it does get me down having to see a school there. I don't know. If it were a lunatic asylum it would be worse, I suppose.'

Captain Hornby said he thought a good deal worse, and he would hate to see his house with iron bars on the windows and a padded room and warders: or even wardresses who he was certain always walked on their patients' feet in pattens and poked them in the ribs with a bunch of keys like Miss Miggs.

'What does really worry me is my father and mother,' said Elsa. 'I must say I don't often think about them, not in an unselfish way at least,' she added in a burst of self-examination, 'but I think it must be quite ghastly for them to have to turn out at their age. And where they'll go I can't think. There isn't a house for miles round and father would die if he couldn't go round the place every day. I can't think why nobody ever built a dower house. What a lovely dower house your aunt's house would have been. I simply adored it that time you took me over.'

They then talked of other things, but Captain Hornby had not forgotten the conversation. Arcot House was now his property, at least for the term of Mrs Ellangowan-Hornby's lease. He saw no chance of living in it till well after the war. He felt sorry for the Beltons, and he thought it would be not disagreeable to please Elsa's parents.

So he made an offer of the house, as we have already heard, through Mr Updike, which the Beltons gladly accepted. No act of charity was involved, for he asked a good though reasonable rent for so well appointed a residence, but he felt a mild glow of satisfaction at having got rid of an unwanted piece of property and eased the troubles of old people (for as such he vaguely thought of Mr and Mrs Belton) of his own class; and he vaguely hoped that Elsa would have the front bedroom that she had fallen in love with on their visit to Arcot House.

Mr and Mrs Belton were sitting in the drawing-room when they heard the front door opened and shut, and in came their daughter Elsa with Captain Hornby.

Captain Hornby was introduced and conventional greetings passed, but under the calm surface varying emotions were seething. Captain Hornby had for no particular reason formed to himself an image of Elsa's parents as a doddering old couple, he probably walking with a stick and deaf, she chair-ridden in a shawl, knitting, with a cap. Why he should have thought all this we cannot imagine, except that our preconceptions are among quite our silliest and most unreasoning thoughts. If he had reflected for one moment it would have occurred to him that most fathers and mothers of his friends were just like ordinary people; perhaps a little older, but he was forty himself and might have been a parent for years if he had ever met anyone he could bear to consider marrying. And now he was suddenly confronted with a gentleman, elderly it is true, but looking very well, rising actively from his chair to greet the newcomer, with clear eyes and skin and an upright, spare figure; and by a lady who bore no more signs of the ravages of old age and decay than her husband, a very good-looking woman in fact, one might say, as one's taste was no longer for debutantes, more attractive in some ways than her daughter, with a softer face, a manner that had more poise and less assurance.

Mrs Belton on her side, and her husband too when she managed to drag out of him later on his opinion of their guest, had vaguely been expecting a jolly tar: though why, when her son Commander Belton was quiet and studious, she should have expected all other naval officers to be young daredevils with a glass of rum in one hand and a telescope in the other, we are unable to explain. So it was with a considerable shock that she saw a tall man of dark complexion and quiet address who might more reasonably have been her younger brother than her son.

Any slight awkwardness that might have been felt as between a landlord who was his tenant's tenant and a tenant who was his landlord's landlord was quickly dissipated when it was ascertained in casual talk that Captain Hornby's mother had been related to General Graham who married Agnes Leslie, for the county still hangs together.

'I am so sorry, Captain Hornby, that I couldn't put you in your old room,' said Mrs Belton, who had made careful enquiries from the late Mrs Ellangowan-Hornby's charwoman in the village. 'Elsa is there. So I have put you in the room with the white panelling.'

Captain Hornby said that much as he admired the view from his old bedroom, he had so lively a recollection of his aunt coming in suddenly, before her stroke of course, in a purple quilted dressing-gown and her head tied up in a silk handker-chief to satisfy herself that he had everything he wanted, usually when he had been asleep for an hour or more and so frightening him out of his wits, that he was delighted to be in the white panelled room. So he was taken there, to make what is called by our older novelists some slight change in his attire before dinner; and why not change altogether, or else leave it alone, is what we should very much like to know. Captain Hornby's changes consisted in washing his hands and face and deciding that his collar would do, after which he went downstairs.

The dinner, which was very good, but did not include the cockerel who was waiting to be a *pièce de résistance* on the following night, passed agreeably. Elsa and her father talked estate matters, while Mrs Belton and Captain Hornby found some common acquaintance and he won his hostess's heart by speaking in praise of her elder son and work he had done in the Mediterranean. The talk in the drawing-room afterwards was much the same. Mrs Belton was so pleased to see her husband really enjoying himself with Elsa, who had been at home much more than her brothers and knew every corner of the estate and every man, woman and child on it, that she did not try to shuffle the company, but talked with her guest about people and books and life and let him do most of the talking, the result being that everyone was surprised to find that it was eleven o'clock.

'That is a lovely portrait of my great-great-grandmother,' said Captain Hornby, going to the other end of the drawing-room and standing, a glass of soda water and Lord Pomfret's whisky in his hand, before the ill-fated Lady Ellangowan. 'Why aren't women as beautiful as that now?'

'I could give you a dozen reasons, but they would all seem out of date,' said Mrs Belton who had accompanied him on his tour of inspection. 'For one thing, men had time to admire them. It does help you know.'

'And artists did like making a beautiful woman look beautiful instead of a three-cornered, lopsided horror,' said Captain Hornby. 'Some of them can do the quite young women. I can imagine Elsa making a very good modern portrait, but I can't think, if you don't mind my saying so, of anyone who could make a success of you.'

'One could always ask them to make one look particularly nice,' said Mrs Belton.

'But they wouldn't get your bones and your modelling,' said Captain Hornby. 'I paint a bit myself – very badly – and I know what I mean even if I can't express it.'

At which Mrs Belton, realizing that Captain Hornby considered her worth painting with her face, however tired or ravaged, just as it was, suddenly felt quite young inside and they passed on to the Raeburn.

'I like your friend Hornby,' said Mr Belton, who liked anyone that appreciated his wife, as Hornby obviously did. 'Lucky young man.'

'Arcot House, do you mean, Father?' said Elsa. 'But it's not much good to Christopher if he's always away and can't live there.'

'He could buy Arcot House a hundred times over and the Park at least three times over by what Updike told your mother,' said Mr Belton. 'Upon my word, Elsa, I sometimes think I'll have to sell outright, if Freddy agrees.'

'Father!' said Elsa, much perturbed.

'It's a fact, my dear,' said her father. 'Never you mind. It's no good worrying about it just yet. I'll have a talk to Freddy next time he comes down. No need to say anything to your mother.'

'But what would you and Mother do?' said Elsa, a cold sinking at her heart.

And then Mrs Belton and Captain Hornby came back and everyone went to bed. Mr Belton, perhaps regretting a little his outburst before Elsa, was rather quiet and thoughtful, which his wife, occupied by the remembrance of Captain Hornby's discernment, or flattery, she could not decide which, attributed to sleepiness. Captain Hornby in the white panelled room thought of a Latin quotation he had learnt at school about a beautiful daughter more beautiful than a beautiful mother, or a beautiful mother more beautiful than a beautiful daughter, he couldn't remember which; thought how horrid it must be not to be able to live in your own family home; congratulated himself warmly on the impossibility of his aunt's coming in to disturb him; and with a last drowsy thought that it was nice to think of Elsa so peaceful in his old room upstairs, was asleep in ten minutes.

But far from being peaceful Elsa was restless and unhappy. The change to Arcot House she had accepted as inevitable. She liked its sober beauty and comfort, she was glad to think that her parents would be warm and well cared for, and she was pleased that Harefield Park was to be lived in and properly kept up. In fact she had gone back to work from her last leave with a comfortable feeling that everything was all right, that the rent the Hosiers' Company paid would pay all their debts, and that as soon as the war was over they would all be back in their old home and Freddy would leave the Navy and settle down to his inheritance. Rather silly thoughts for an intelligent young woman, and now she had to admit to herself that she had very little ground for them and had wilfully taken what she wanted for what was going to happen. Probably the most they could hope was that Christopher would renew the lease of Arcot House, and if he wanted his aunt's belongings, they could furnish it from the Park and still make a home of it. And even so there would be the question of servants. Cook and Wheeler couldn't live for ever, and how could her father and mother run Arcot House on unreliable daily help from the village? Perhaps they could live in one of the smaller houses that belonged to them. Even in Dowlah Cottage, which might be quite nice if Mrs Hoare and all her possessions were gone. She and her brothers would have to remain in their jobs. But would the jobs want them? Freddy, a professional sailor, had the best chance if he wasn't killed. But as for Charles and herself, the war had snatched them from their own life; the peace would probably disgorge them into it again, three, five, ten years to the bad, if Charles hadn't been killed; and she herself might be killed. She suddenly thought of that unattractive Heather Adams with a rich father and his factories behind her and envied her. If only she weren't so dreadful, if only Father didn't dislike Mr Adams so much, Charles might marry her and retrieve the Belton fortunes. Oh why wasn't Christopher a woman, and then Freddy could marry him. 'If I were a proper heroine,' she thought angrily, 'I'd make Christopher fall in love with me.'

So her thoughts tossed and turned and thrashed about, till she too fell asleep.

On the following day a picked and slightly unwilling party of Hosiers' Girls, headed by Miss Holly, entered the churchyard. The party included the head prefect, Miss Isabella Ferdinand, and Heather Adams who was in the sulks. The reason for this state of mind, one not uncommon in her, was that she had intended to go home for the half-term holiday and put in a delightful half-day in the costing department on Saturday and a mentally stimulating whole day in the chief accountant's office on Monday, returning to her school in glory in her father's big works car. But her father, who though proud of his daughter did not much approve of her poking about the works, as he put it, had written to say she was to stay at school. Schools charged quite enough, he wrote, without getting rid of their pupils at half-term and in any case the Government did not let him have petrol to drive girls about the county. Perhaps if Mr Belton had known of Mr Adams's attitude about petrol it would have modified his dislike of that gentleman. So Heather was in a black and lumpish mood, to which however her fellow-students were so well accustomed that they hardly noticed any difference.

Mr Oriel was waiting for them in the porch and to him Miss Holly offered her employer's excuses. Miss Sparling, she said, was much disappointed at being unable to join the party, but was detained by business and feared she would not be able to get away in time.

Mr Oriel's face fell.

'And I may tell you that happens to be true,' said Miss Holly. 'It isn't always, you know. A couple of the Governors came down and she had to give them lunch and do the civil.'

So pleased was Mr Oriel to hear this that Miss Holly's compact round form appeared to him almost seraphic; for the theft of Canon Horbury's Fluvius Minucius lay heavy on his mind and he feared Miss Sparling might have heard of it and so taken a dislike to him. Though how she could have heard of it except through Mr Carton he could not conceive, and he knew Mr Carton, though rather free-thinking he feared, to be strictly honourable.

'We shall all feel the disappointment,' said Mr Oriel, benevolently scanning his flock of sightseers who did not care much whether their headmistress was there or not, or had a faint preference for her company rather than that of Miss Holly, because Miss Sparling out of school hours often had an obligingly blind eye and deaf ear, whereas Miss Holly, who took advanced mathematics as an occasional relaxation, was as sharp as a needle and apt to pounce. Indeed, Miss Ferdinand had already been in trouble on the way down for imitating too closely Mr Oriel's delivery in the pulpit.

'But,' he continued, 'I should much like to make the acquaintance of my young friends before we begin our little tour. Will you be so very kind as to introduce us? One or two faces are of course familiar to me from my confirmation classes, but you can imagine,' he added in an audible aside to Miss Holly, 'how with fresh young faces coming up so often for preparation I sometimes get a little confused. I know their faces are all quite different, for we are indeed a diversity of creatures, but they yet have a curious similarity. It is my fault, I know.'

'Not a bit,' said Miss Holly. 'There are only three or four types of schoolgirls, and as they all try to look exactly alike it doesn't help. Nor does a school uniform, though I must say,' she continued, looking dispassionately on the group of girls, 'that they look much worse out of it. This is our head prefect. She is going in for teaching.'

'A very fine profession,' said Mr Oriel, shaking hands with the head prefect. 'I did a good deal of coaching myself at one time. A dog's life.'

'Quite right,' said Miss Holly. 'And this is Isabella Ferdinand. She hopes to get on the stage and entertain the Forces.'

'Dear, dear,' said Mr Oriel, again shaking hands. 'I used to do a bit of amateur acting myself. Shakespeare of course.'

Miss Ferdinand was so obviously about to counter with some

136

unsuitable quotation from the Bard that Miss Holly hastily passed on to the next girl.

'And this,' she said, 'is Heather Adams. Mathematics are her subject and she wishes to go into her father's works. Mr Adams owns the rolling mills at Hogglestock.'

'To help your father. What a good decision,' said Mr Oriel.

Heather Adams, scowling at Mr Oriel who felt very guilty though he had done nothing to provoke her, said she was going to be a Wren.

'A fine body of young women,' said Mr Oriel, looking at Heather as if he were trying to find any common ground between her and the fine body in question, which made Miss Holly quickly introduce the next girl. The rest of the little party were soon named and Mr Oriel, after a brief survey of the interior of the building, proposed to take them up the tower.

Harefield church, the sole remains of Harefield Abbey, like so many Barsetshire churches had been built when the wool trade was at the height of its prosperity and was now far too large for the village. Its handsome square tower was a landmark up and down the Rising valley for many miles, its bells a peculiarly melodious company. Inside, it was almost a small cathedral, having a clerestory with a gallery round it and an ambulatory behind the altar, besides a crypt now disused and kept locked. The glass was not good. Most of it had been destroyed by the Puritans during the Civil Wars (Mr Oriel, a firm Cavalier, always maintained by Cromwell's personal orders and in his presence), and the Nabob, more we fear from motives of ostentation than piety, had presented several painted windows by not very eminent hands. The artists, who were more used to painting His Sacred Majesty King George II dressed as Mars in a wig and attended by Commerce, Prosperity, Lord Chatham and Britannia than sacred subjects, had not succeeded very well with Scriptural figures and no one really knew which of the Prophets were meant to be represented by the togaed and buskined figures who decorated the east and west ends. For many years a figure with particularly large calves and a kind of woolly horns on his head was accepted as Moses, but Mr Oriel's predecessor, an ardent student of the eighteenth century, had unsettled this belief by showing that a kind of wig rising to two peaks was in vogue at about that time, so that the figure might just as well be anyone else. However, as Mr Oriel said when war was looming, if it had been fifteenth-century stained glass they would have been put to the hustle and expense of having it all taken down, numbered, packed, stored, and then very probably blown up in its place of safety, whereas second-rate painted glass could take its chance.

The top of the tower was reached by the usual winding steps, approached by a low, heavily barred door in a dark corner. The joy of a steep corkscrew stair with uneven treads, lighted at rare intervals by high narrow lancet windows, full of echoes and dust, is a passion not shared by all. The head prefect, who had claustrophobia without knowing what it was, was so terrified by the darkness and the nearness of her friends' heels to her face above and their faces to her heels below, not to speak of feeling more and more giddy as they circled higher and higher, that she had to concentrate on the Honour of the School or she would have begun to cry. Luckily for her prestige Mr Oriel stopped on a little landing and unlocked a door. The girls crowded through after him and found themselves on a narrow balcony, stone-balustraded, which ran round the inside of the tower. The head prefect took one look at the floor of the church far below and retired to the landing, so that she missed the greater part of what Mr Oriel had to say. His lecture was short and to the point, and ably seconded by Miss Holly who offered such encouragement as, 'Fourteen eighty-five; remember that, girls,' 'English Transitional, you'd better write that down, girls,' 'Lepers' squint – Isabella, you are not at all funny,' this last being addressed to Miss Ferdinand who was giving so lively an impersonation of a leper with both eyes turned inwards, a gift much admired by her friends, as to distract their attention entirely from their kind guide.

As the party was about to continue its climb to the top of the tower, Miss Holly caught sight of the head prefect's face which was such a queer colour that she asked if she felt ill. The head prefect, playing up to the best Hosiers' traditions, said she wasn't and then relapsing into private life said the stairs made her feel funny. She then waited to be degraded and expelled.

'That's all right,' said Miss Holly calmly. 'You'd better stay here on the landing and I'll come down with you myself when we come back. I'll leave someone with you. Here, Heather,' she called to that young lady's heels which were vanishing round the next curve of the stair. The owner of the heels turned and came down.

'I want you to stay with her,' said Miss Holly briskly. 'She's got a bad head. I must go up and see that the others are all right on the tower.'

'I wish you wouldn't have headaches,' said Heather ungraciously to the head prefect. 'I was awfully keen to go on the tower.'

'It isn't a headache,' said the head prefect indignantly. 'I've got a rotten head for high places, they simply petrify me. I don't know how I'll ever get down that stair again.'

Heather looked at her as a mother may look at her child when nurse has asked for a whole day off to go about another place, and went through the door on to the tower gallery. The balustrade though solidly built was unusually low. The head prefect gave one sickened look towards her companion and said, 'Come back, Heather. You'll fall over.'

On hearing these words Heather scowled and deliberately walked round the four sides of the tower, pausing at short intervals to lean well over the balustrade and examine the carving on the outside. Having accomplished this tour she sat carelessly on the balustrade and leaning slightly outwards took a good look at the inside of the tower roof. She then returned to her charge, who had been following her progress with horrified fascination.

'I'll have to report you to Miss Holly,' said the head prefect, really shaking with nervous rage. 'You were on honour to look after me.'

'All right, report me,' said Heather, 'and I'll tread on your coat going down the stairs. How do you think people are sailors if they can't stand heights?'

'But I'm not a sailor,' said the head prefect, 'and nor are you.'

'I'm going to be a Wren anyway,' said Heather.

'You said you were going to be an AT the day you made such a fuss the day we had treacle pudding,' said the head prefect. 'And anyway you're going into your father's works; you said so.'

'Well, I'm going to be a Wren now,' said Heather, her large pasty face assuming an almost live expression. 'If it weren't for the Navy we'd all be killed or starved. I wonder if Wrens ever go to sea. Still, one could be an officer's servant on shore.'

At any other moment the head prefect might have been surprised not only by Heather's rapid change of plans but by her unusual confidences about herself, but she was still feeling far too frightened and sick to think of anyone but herself. Luckily the tramp of the returning party was heard from above. Miss Holly, seeing that the head prefect still looked queer, sent Heather and the other girls on ahead and escorted her unhappy pupil down the giddy spiral, going very slowly just in front of her which gave her much more confidence. Mr Oriel then offered to show them the crypt. Miss Holly, who in spite of her sturdy frame and robust mind was frightened of being underground, remained with the head prefect who soon recovered, becoming so much her usual self that she nearly reported Heather to Miss Holly. But Miss Holly, whose life was extremely busy from morning to night and whose standard of duty both to Miss Sparling and the girls rarely gave her time to think of herself at all, seized the opportunity to sit down in the old Lady Chapel where the head prefect could not well disturb her, and make her mind a blank.

Before long the sightseers returned, much exhilarated by some broken stone coffins, an empty leaden coffin with one side ripped open, several long ladders, a fire hose, the sexton's grave-digging and gardening tools and an old oaken chest bound with iron containing two brass taps, a tea pannikin and a crowbar.

'Well,' said Miss Holly, bringing her mind briskly back to the world again. 'Did you enjoy yourselves?'

'It was *lovely*,' said Miss Ferdinand. 'We did a bit of *Hamlet*. I was Hamlet, only there wasn't a skull so I had the sexton's gardening hat. And Mr Oriel was the grave-diggers.'

'I really do not know what you will think of us,' said Mr Oriel to Miss Holly, 'but my young friend is almost as great an admirer of Shakespeare as I am, and her enthusiasm carried me away. I trust we have not been too long.'

Miss Holly, who had so much enjoyed her brief period of being alone that she would have made no objection to Mr Oriel and Miss Ferdinand acting *Hamlet* without cuts, thanked the Vicar for giving up so much of his valuable time and said it was now almost three and they must hurry as they were to meet

Mr Belton at the Garden House where he had promised to tell them its history. Mr Oriel accompanied them to the end of the little lime avenue. As the last farewells were being exchanged Mr Oriel asked Miss Holly, with some diffidence, whether she thought Miss Sparling would consider the idea of some dramatic readings during the winter, either at the Vicarage or at the School, just as it suited her. Miss Holly said she would give Miss Sparling the message and it sounded an excellent plan. The party then set off for their next treat.

6

The Garden House, so called because it lay at some distance from Harefield Park and was not in the garden, was a species of pleasure-house or folly, built by the Nabob in his old age under the influence (we regret to say) of a French lady of great charm and beauty who was no better than she should be and found the market for this quality better in England than in Revolutionary France. It had also afforded scope for the undoubted gifts of the French architect and decorator who was the ultimate cause of her being dismissed from Harefield Park with a handsome present of bank notes (for the Nabob was, to tell the truth, heartily glad to get rid of her and her extravagance) and a large amount of jewellery whose absence was not discovered till she had gone.

An exotic among dog violets and daisies, a bird of paradise among barndoor fowls, its delicate fantastic rococo graces had looked homesick and out of place from the very beginning. It stood on a grassy knoll, lightly shaded in its early days, now heavily overshadowed, by two drooping willows; a *cottage orné* with a pagoda roof, approached by a small flight of stone steps with widely outcurving balustrades, its little terrace and a shell-roofed alcove at each end sprinkled with urns and statues. In default of a stream (for that part of Barsetshire is dry except in the water-meadow valleys) a very small artificial lake had been excavated and spanned by a Palladian covered bridge with a Chinese roof, and the lake so cunningly designed, its banks so cleverly planted, that any onlooker who divested his mind of the fact that he could almost have leapt the lake might think himself a thousand miles from his familiar Barsetshire. Until the Victorian era was well on its way all these elegancies had been kept up. The bells on the pagoda roof tinkled and shone, the seats and statues were kept free from moss, the terrace was gravelled, the lake was rilled by an elaborate system of pumping from the real lake with its ever-flowing spring, the rooms were heated in winter, their silks and velvets repaired, their lustres polished, and the little kitchen occasionally used for parties of pleasure. Thither the ladies would drive in the carriage of the period; thither the gentlemen would repair on horseback or on foot. That it was not more than a mile from the house added to the charm of these excursions which were not long enough to let anyone be bored.

Gradually with the change of taste and the decrease of ordered leisure the pretty toy had fallen into disuse. Mr Belton's grandfather had spent a good deal of money in putting it into repair in the last flare of gaiety at the end of the nineteenth century, but he would have done better to put his money back into the estate, and his grandson, going over old account books, had reason to wish his ancestor's holdings in Consols had been entailed as well as the land. By the time his family were growing up the Garden House had fallen back into complete disrepair. The rusted bells were tongueless, the stonework crumbling, the steps broken, the statues fallen or all aslant. The Sino-Palladian bridge spanned a reedy waste and had great holes in it. The pumping works down in the valley were rotted and useless, a place of attractive terror to the young Beltons who climbed among the wheels and beams against orders. The best of the furniture had been moved to the Park or sold, the lustres were like icicles in thaw, the mirrors, set in the wall, tarnished. High weeds and suckers of the willows forced the stones of the terrace and the steps apart year by year and in the little kitchen ovens and grills were rusty and broken. The Belton children used to take their tea there in nursery days, but no one visited it now and probably another twenty years of neglect would see it disintegrate altogether.

On the morning of this day Mrs Belton had reminded her husband at breakfast that a party from the school were coming to visit it that afternoon and he had promised to tell them something about it. On hearing this Mr Belton, with perfect truth, said he had promised nothing of the sort, that he had to go to Barchester and wouldn't be back to lunch, and would probably ride over to Pomfret Towers about the tractor when he got home. He then got up and went to the estate office.

'Look here, Mother,' said Elsa, 'I'll show them round and Christopher can help me. We did mean to go over to Little Misfit but it doesn't matter. It's a pity Freddy isn't here, he knows the stuff much better than I do. You haven't seen it, have you?' she added, to Captain Hornby.

Captain Hornby said he hadn't and would like to very much. And if Elsa would tell him what to say he would say it, and as no civilian ever seemed to know the difference between a petty officer and an admiral, let alone a commander and a captain, he would do his best to represent Freddy. This was a great relief to Mrs Belton and after inquiring if she could in any way further their plans for the morning and hearing that Elsa was going to help their guest to go through the things in the attic, she went off to her household duties and to fetch the cakes from the Rajah Café.

There were not really any attics at Arcot House, for it was far too self-respecting to do anything so out of its period, but the top storey was almost as inconvenient as if there were. The house was elegantly finished by a pierced stone parapet which ran right round the roof and concealed the sloping slates, which parapet also served the excellent purpose of preventing the servants who slept up there from seeing anything out of their windows. Originally, when women servants slept two in a bed, or three and four in a room, and the men servants in the basement, there had been only four large rooms, reached by a breakneck wooden staircase. Though large, they were not lofty, and their sash windows were longer than they were high, the upper part immovable, the lower usually requiring to be propped open with a stick. But at a later period when large mid-Victorian families needed more space and servants had the uppishness to expect at least a bed to themselves, three of these rooms had been subdivided, making a rather frightening rabbit-warren of little, low rooms, some of them having to share the light with their next-door neighbour; the partition, little more than a screen, coming up against the middle of the window. These had long been disused, but there was one large room left at the back and it was here that all such property of Mrs Ellangowan-Hornby had been stored as was not to go with the house, and to it Elsa and Captain Hornby repaired.

To go into a disused room full of one's own or even someone else's boxes, books, furniture, odds and ends, is never exhilarating, nor was it in this case. The air was musty, there was dust everywhere, the flooring, though sound enough, was far from level, the walls stained where pictures had hung or other furniture been placed. There was a general impression that though no rats, mice, cockroaches, bats, or spiders were visible, they had merely retired at the sound of feet on the stairs and were ready to come back the moment the visitors had gone, or even earlier. Also the mere fact of its being lighted only by one window about four feet long by two and a half high was in itself depressing.

Captain Hornby strode over and among the lumber to the window and tried to open it.

'It's no good trying the top half,' said Elsa sympathetically. 'It doesn't open.'

Captain Hornby tried the bottom half. At first it resisted his efforts, but suddenly it went up with a rush. He stood up and dusted himself. The window fell down again with a crash and a pane of glass fell shattered on the floor.

'Sash cord's gone on this side,' said Captain Hornby examining the wreckage, 'and I can't see the cord on the other.'

'I don't think these windows ever had more than one,' said Elsa. 'At least that's what Wheeler says her grandmother told her. The servants used to put a billet of wood to keep them up, she said.'

'And where the dickens am I to get a billet of wood?' asked Captain Hornby, angrily sucking a finger which had suddenly taken it into its head to bleed from an almost invisible cut. 'It was all very well in those days, but one doesn't keep billets in empty garrets. This'll do.'

He opened the window again with some difficulty and wedged it firmly with a black iron trivet.

'What extraordinary things do get into attics,' he said. 'I really haven't the faintest idea what is here. Where *do* I begin?'

He looked helplessly round at servants' washing-stands in cheap imitation-grained wood, a heap of bedroom jugs and basins, several very good chairs, a gigantic screen, a mahogany pedestal surmounted by a yellow marble basin with a pink marble dove of massive contour pretending to drink from it, four carved and gilded curtain rods with lotus flowers for knobs, hair trunks, leather trunks, two large washing baskets containing copper saucepans, a three-legged table with a marble top and a little brass railing, a library ladder that could be turned into a kind of chair, a spinning wheel, a pile of bound volumes of the *Strand Magazine* and a very hideous blue vase with a raised design of convolvulus on it containing coloured pampas grass.

'Good God!' said Captain Hornby, opening a large wardrobe.

A feather bed tied up with yards of plush ball-edging fell out into his arms, nearly knocking him over with its unwieldy bulk.

'I'll tell you what,' said Elsa when they had stopped laughing. 'I'll get some paper and we'll list the things. It's the only way.'

She ran downstairs and came back with a pad and a pen.

'Now, we'll begin at the door and simply *go* straight round the room,' she said, 'and if we've time we'll do the trunks and things afterwards. You tell me what you find and I'll put it down.'

She perched herself on an Indian chest painted red and studded with brass nails, and awaited her orders.

'Number one: large mahogany wardrobe with homicidal feather bed,' said Captain Hornby.

'Go on,' said Elsa.

'I was just waiting till you'd got that down,' said Captain Hornby.

'I have,' said Elsa.

Captain Hornby looked over her shoulder.

'I didn't know you could do shorthand,' he said admiringly.

'It's not really my job,' said Elsa. 'Of course I don't do it at the office or I'd lose caste. I have to dictate to my secretary. But I keep in practice. You never know when it will be useful. Carry on.'

Captain Hornby, much impressed by her capability, went round the room describing each article as well as he could and completed the circuit, winding up with a repoussé brass coal scuttle and a tantalus.

'And now the trunks,' said Elsa, getting off her box.

This was not so easy. Some were strapped and the rusty buckles had eaten into the leather which was stiff with age. Some were locked, and though Captain Hornby had all his aunt's keys, the locks were stiff with disuse. Elsa got Wheeler's sewing-machine oil and some pliers and presently the straps were unbuckled and the locks undone. The contents of the trunks were as varied as the articles already catalogued. Those containing papers were refastened for the present. Those containing dresses or materials were quickly examined. Mrs Ellangowan-Hornby appeared to have kept everything she had ever worn from babies' long dresses exquisitely worked with panelled fronts and puffed short sleeves by the old Ayrshire embroidresses, an art now lost, to the black silks and satins of her widowhood.

'What am I to do with all these?' said Captain Hornby hopelessly.

'Haven't you any relations or anyone who would like them?' said Elsa. 'You know what it is with coupons, and anyone would jump at the dresses and the materials. And the shawls. And the lace,' she continued, delving in a large trunk and holding up its contents to his view.

'There are some Scotch cousins,' said Captain Hornby. 'But my aunt never saw much of them, and I hardly know them.'

He went over to the window and looked out. The mists of a damp November morning had almost cleared away and a gentle autumnal sunshine lay on the park. Through a loophole in the parapet he could see Harefield Park, gaunt, distinguished, its long front with the pavilions and their connecting screens looking unreal, as if it were quite flat with no solid building behind it.

'Let's get out and have a look,' said Elsa.

With a rather undignified scramble she climbed through the narrow opening and Captain Hornby followed her. Side by side they leaned their elbows on the parapet and surveyed the view. The mild sun warmed them, beating back from the wall and roof behind, no breath stirred. Their elbows touched. And though Elsa felt no particular emotion at this contact, a vague unformed filament of thoughts, drifting like mist across her mind, informed her that Captain Hornby's elbow, even separated from her by a shirt and a heavy blue coat (his) and a woollen pullover and cardigan (hers), had about it something which separated it from the elbows of other men, exquisite, apart.

'Would you like to walk round?' said Captain Hornby.

The mist dispersed. Elsa said she adored roofs and one of her real regrets in leaving Harefield Park was that she couldn't go on the roof when she wanted to sulk.

'Freddy and I knew a lot of places that we could hide in,' said Elsa. 'Our great wish was to go down one of the chimneys like Tom in the *Water Babies* and we were quite sure that if we did we would find ourselves in a bedroom that we'd never seen before. Freddy did try to get down a very large chimneypot once, but I was so frightened that he came out again – he had only got one leg over anyway – and we were both simply filthy.'

Thus beguiling the time with anecdotes of her past Elsa preceded Captain Hornby along the narrow lead-covered path which went round the house below the servants' windows. Turning her back on Harefield Park she went widdershins about the house. First they paused to look towards the east, over all the long gardens, away to Plassey House and Dowlah Cottage,

Beyond them the High Street straggled away, past Madras Cottages, through a little village slum and then, crossing the Rising by a high arched bridge with elegant iron railings which bridge Mr Belton and other Harefield enthusiasts had repeatedly saved from widening and rebuilding, joined the main Barchester Road on the other side of the valley. Then, proceeding to the front of the house they again leaned upon the parapet to enjoy the view to the north. Here it was not so warm, for the sun did not reach that side at all in winter, but the prospect made amends. Below them lay the comfortable, red-brick street full of the bustle of Saturday morning. A number of pony-traps, governess carts and other small horse-drawn vehicles were going up and down and standing before the shops, usually with a child in charge. Old Lady Norton's brougham, an object of respectful dislike as announcing its owner's presence, was outside Potter the chemist, the old coachman sitting bolt upright with a cockaded hat, despising everyone. Young girls and boys on ponies clattered down to the blacksmith whose forge was working overtime all the week. On the other side of the street behind the shops and their gardens lay the water-meadows where a few cows and a donkey were grazing. The various channels of the Rising meandered gleaming down the valley and beyond rose the downs in their dull winter green with beech clumps in the hollows still bearing a few flaming leaves.

'Oh dear, oh *dear*!' said Elsa.

Moving on to the north-west corner they saw the High Street going up a gentle slope and hidden from view beyond the bend. The church on its rising ground, still with a faint mist round it that made it look like a vision, was soft gold in the sunshine. One deep note sounded from the belfry.

'One o'clock,' said Captain Hornby. 'Oughtn't we to go in?'

'Hush!' said Elsa.

A jangling carillon, which was yet exactly the right noise for the church to make, burst from the tower, playing 'Annie Laurie'. Having repeated the tune twice, it played the Old Hundredth three times, and died away in a sweet far-off dissonance.

'By Jove!' said Captain Hornby.

'Hadn't you ever heard it before?' Elsa asked. 'When your aunt was ill?'

'I don't think church bells were being allowed then,' said Captain Hornby. 'Why are all carillons out of tune? And why do they make one homesick at once? Not homesick exactly, because these made me think of the West India station and heaven knows I'm not a mulatto. Nostalgic, I suppose.'

'I think,' said Elsa, 'hearing bells play a tune always makes one think of places where one has been warm, where one has heard bells in the sun. I don't know. They sounded so clearly at the Park. Oh dear! Come on.'

Rightly interpreting these disjointed remarks as a sign of emotion upon which he did not wish to intrude, Captain Hornby followed Elsa to the west side. This commanded, from the south-west corner, a full view of the lake, fed by its spring, open and sedge-bordered at its far end, rather frighteningly overhung by tall trees at the end nearest the village. And away up on the hill beyond was Elsa's home, almost a silhouette now with the sun behind it, its great front like a screen of stone. On a piece of level ground at one side some girls were playing netball.

'Beasts!' said Elsa, with sudden violence. 'I HATE them. Sleeping in my room and turning Father and Mother out. I wish they were all dead.'

Captain Hornby put a large hand firmly over hers and pressed it.

'Thank you,' said Elsa.

Captain Hornby resumed possession of his hand. But not as if he felt he had been rejected; simply because he had seen a job that needed doing, had done it, and now was no longer required to stand by.

'I might as well hate you, Christopher, for being Father's landlord,' said Elsa penitently. 'Only I don't. We must go and get clean for lunch.'

They climbed into the attic again, removed the trivet (which Elsa methodically added to the catalogue) carefully, so that the window would not again fall with a bang, stuck some bits of cardboard over the broken pane and saw that everything was strapped and locked. As they left the room Captain Hornby locked the door and held out the key.

'Will you keep it?' he said. 'You know where everything is now, and if I want any papers or anything, perhaps you will be so kind as to find them for me.'

'Of course,' said Elsa. 'And I'll type the lists in triplicate and keep one here.'

'Surely two would be enough,' said Captain Hornby.

'You'd better send one to your lawyers,' said Elsa. 'You do move about a good deal, and then you could write to them about anything you want doing with the papers.'

Captain Hornby thought this a very sensible idea. He knew, and Elsa knew, that the unspoken thought underlying her suggestion was, 'If you are killed your lawyers will know what is here'; a thought which, spoken and unspoken, must underlie most people's arrangements now.

Miss Holly and her party, the head prefect being now perfectly recovered and her usual self, walked at a brisk pace away from

153

the church and through the lych gate, but instead of going up the drive to the Park they followed a public footpath which skirted the lake. Here there was a slight delay as Miss Ferdinand, seeing an old willow which grew out over the water, felt compelled to be Ophelia before she fell into the brook, and to this end climbed on to the tree trunk, stuck some rushes in her school hat and gave a lively impersonation of an escaped lunatic, singing some of her heroine's more full-blooded lyrics, till Miss Holly said, 'That's enough now, Isabella,' and they all moved on. They then struck slantingly across the field by another path which intersected the path from Arcot House to the Park, followed it over the gentle rise and dropped again to the hollow where the artificial lake had been, with the Garden House on the further side. As this part of the park was out of bounds none of the Hosiers' Girls had as yet visited it, being mostly good, ordinary, law-abiding creatures; and even the head prefect was faintly stirred by its decayed romantic beauty.

'It's exactly like *Lac des Cygnes*,' said a dull girl in the Upper Fifth who had a passion for ballet, 'only there isn't a lake and there aren't any swans and it's all different.'

'There ought to be a prince and a princess on the terrace,' said Heather Adams suddenly.

Miss Holly looked at her pupil with surprise. That the dull girl in the Upper Fifth, one of the mass worshippers of English-speaking ballet, should see theatre in the scene was understandable. But that Heather Adams should fall under its spell was so peculiar a phenomenon that Miss Holly almost wondered if she had heard aright. Still, there was no doubt about it; Heather had spoken these words and was looking with a faint gleam of romance in her apathetic face towards the deserted Garden House.

Even as she gazed, out of the house came Captain Hornby and Miss Belton, who had been rehearsing the little lecture on the spot, and walked across the terrace to the steps.

'That is quite enough, Isabella,' said Miss Holly, as the irrepressible Miss Ferdinand hitched up imaginary trousers, and performed a few steps of a hornpipe. Miss Ferdinand stopped, saying 'Ay, ay, miss,' under her breath, thus giving several of her friends the giggles and causing the head prefect to look coldly at this breach of the Honour of the School. Miss Holly led them down to the Palladian bridge, Heather Adams following in a kind of golden trance. Just as everything was horrible and instead of going home she had to stay at school, and instead of going up the church tower she had to stay with the head prefect who didn't know a logarithm from a cosine, or even the simplest way of making out a time-sheet, everything had suddenly turned to gold. There, as she looked down the perspective of the covered bridge, she saw, even with her short-sighted eyes, Commander Belton, the one who had been kind to her, whose naval image filled her waking thoughts though she had unfortunately been unable to dream of him at night, the hero upon whom her young heart intended to lavish all her father's money. She could hardly curb her impatience as the sightseers loitered on the bridge, and was only comforted by the sight of the head prefect nearly putting her foot through one of the holes and going quite green again as she looked at the dizzy drop of at least three feet below her. If only Commander Belton would put his foot through such a hole, how willingly would she exert her strength to pull him out, if she died in the attempt. If he fell on to the marshy ground beneath how happily would she stretch her body in the mud that he might walk over it dryshod. For after each of these episodes of heroism and sacrifice, would he not think with gratitude of

One who had Given Him All. And again she rapidly sketched a tombstone for herself, but this time in front of the Garden House where he could sit on a summer evening thinking of the days that were no more. Upon which reverie her eyes became so blinded with unshed tears of pure happiness that she nearly fell into the hole herself and Miss Holly said she really must remember to wear her spectacles and the vision vanished.

Miss Holly and Elsa shook hands. Captain Hornby was introduced to Miss Holly. Miss Holly explained that Miss Sparling had been detained but hoped to join them before long.

'Now, girls,' said Miss Holly, beckoning her charges to draw nearer. 'Miss Belton and Captain Hornby are going to take us over this pretty summer-house. You remember what we read in the guide-book yesterday. It is in the rococo style and the bridge' (here most of the girls turned round and looked at it) 'is specially worth attention' (on hearing which they all looked at Miss Holly again). 'So are the interior decorations, but Captain Hornby says they are badly out of repair. Never mind, we shall all enjoy it just the same. Now, Miss Belton, we are ready to follow our guide.'

During this uninteresting little speech, Heather Adams had experienced several severe shocks. To her myopic eyes the tall figure on the terrace was still Commander Belton, though she thought he had grown a little. When Miss Holly first mentioned Captain Hornby's name it was so unexpected that her ears heard it without sending any message to her brain. When Miss Holly repeated it, her brain suddenly remembered that it had received the impression a little while earlier that the ears were keeping something back from it and felt rather angrily that it couldn't be expected to do all the work itself. Still, it was its duty to get things clear, so it told its owner to go up the steps on to the terrace and look, with the certitude that the eyes would treat it more considerately. So Heather Adams, pushing rather roughly and ignoring the head prefect's remonstrances, got onto the steps among the first and looked up at the tall figure. Captain Hornby, waiting with Elsa for the party to collect, was aware that he was being stared at, and looking down he saw a large, plain-faced schoolgirl looking practically bald under the pudding-basin school hat, gazing at him at first with apprehension and then with horror. But before he could ask what the matter was the tide of girls had swept on to the terrace and the large schoolgirl had her back to him.

'Don't dawdle, Heather,' said Miss Holly. 'You'll miss the lecture.'

Dawdle, the very word was like a knell to Heather Adams as she followed the school into the Garden House. It was not Commander Belton; it was just a naval officer, and she hated him. She also hated Miss Holly and the head prefect and Isabella Ferdinand and the bridge and the steps and the terrace and the rotten, beastly old Garden House and everything: and she wished she were dead and everyone were dead and the school and the Garden House burnt. Tears welled in her eyes, sobs rose in her bosom, her throat was constricted, but so used were her friends and her teachers to seeing Heather in the grumps that no one paid the faintest attention to her.

Elsa and Captain Hornby, who were both accustomed to addressing all sorts of people in large and small numbers on their special subjects, had together concocted a kind of running commentary on the rooms with a short historic survey of rococo and anecdotes of the Nabob, whose eccentricities had become very pronounced towards the end of his life. This commentary was well received. All listened. Some even laughed. And Miss Holly kept a kind of scholastic grip upon it all, as she had in the church, by acting as chorus, recommending her girls to remember this date, or write down that word. We may add that when she inspected the notebooks later on, no one got full marks, because of such words as Boulle, marqueterie, Aubusson, which were perfect pitfalls to the young ladies and obviously written down in a frenzy of hopeful despair.

At first we must admit the sightseers were a little disappointed, having vaguely expected after the guide-book's recommendation to find something magnificent and exciting, but during the short tour the elegant melancholy decay of the house made an impression; the dull balletomane in the Upper Fifth going so far as to say that it was like the *Speckter Dellerose*, which it certainly wasn't. The little dining-room, the little saloon with its looking-glass doors and tattered faded silk hangings, the bedroom where a carved and lacquered Chinese bed stood gauntly tilting on three legs, were admired, or (in the case of most of the party) tolerated, till the kitchen was reached. This room the architect, with the logic and common sense which have been crystallized into an attribute of the Gallic nation by the acceptors of ready-made ideas, had conceived not as a piece of Chinoiserie or rococoterie, but as a kitchen. As a concession to the mode he had supported the roof on four pillars carved to represent bundles of bamboos and sprouting wrought-iron palm leaves at the top, which pillars got frightfully in the way and were roundly cursed by all the cooks and footmen, but in other respects the kitchen was, or had been in its time, severely practical. The ovens, the grill, the little furnace for heating water were all rusted and derelict, many of the windowpanes were broken and some were stuffed up with old cloths. To Heather Adams it was a reflection of the state of her heart at the moment and more than she could bear. Lingering behind the others she slipped unperceived into the saloon and wandered round it, looking absently at the blackened mirrors in their pretty gilded plaster frames decorated with flowers, musical instruments, scrolls, bearing fantastic candle-holders, trellised, railed. As she was examining one of them by the window the light of the western sun streamed in and illumined her face. In the mirror she saw a strangely dim and spotted version of herself, which as she gazed at it began to make faces expressive of an effort to keep back tears. This chance of self-pity was too good to miss, and Heather stood rooted to the spot enjoying her own torments in the glass.

Meanwhile in the kitchen Elsa had explained what was left to explain and told an incredulous audience how the Nabob used to have as many as six dozen partridges cooked at a time and only a slice from each side of the breastbone served, the rest being thrown away. The head prefect said that would never do in war-time, would it, in a self-righteous voice which somehow implied that the Belton family for many generations back were entirely responsible for the present state of affairs all over the world. Elsa might have made a sharp retort, which she would afterwards have regretted, when there was a sudden exclamation from Miss Ferdinand who had been opening doors and looking in, conveniently ignoring Miss Holly's disapproval. All the girls crowded round Miss Ferdinand, who pointed with the air of a successful conjurer to a large dead rat. Confused cries of 'Beastly thing,' 'Poor little thing,' 'Is it a mouse?' 'What a *darling*,' and similar expressions of silliness burst from a dozen or so throats. Captain Hornby was quite brave enough to pick the rat up and throw it out of the window, but was unable to penetrate the excited crowd. It was evident to Elsa that Miss Ferdinand had provided a treat far more sympathetic to her friends than any number of churches and rococo garden houses.

She was not surprised, having a lively remembrance of how she had hated visits to the Barchester Museum and the Old Guildhall, remains of foundations probably Saxon found when reinforcing the cellar floors in 1896 may be seen on application to the curator, when she was at the Barchester High School; and also having a poor opinion of schoolgirls taken in the lump. At any rate she and Christopher had said their piece and done their best to interest the Hosiers' girls, and if the Hosiers' girls preferred a dead rat (as she admitted that she and Freddy would have done at that or a slightly earlier age) they were more than welcome. She went into the little octagonal hall or lobby from which all the rooms opened, and from the saloon heard so loud a sniff, so violently repeated, that she thought she had better go and see who it was.

In the saloon she found one of the Hosiers' girls, standing alone before a mirror, apparently trying not to burst into tears. Practical help seemed the best thing.

'I've got two handkerchiefs,' she said, 'if you want one. One so often forgets to take one.'

The girl, without saying a word, put out her hand, seized the handkerchief and blew her nose violently.

'Thank you,' she said ungraciously.

Elsa was quite used to ungraciousness from her juniors, both in her office and in the world in general, but as the girl was at the Hosiers' School and so part of the estate, Elsa felt the responsibility.

'Anything wrong?' she said.

It was not said with any particular gentleness or sympathy, but Heather recognized in it the voice of someone who was used to dealing with other people's troubles and would not, in her own inelegant phrase, be sloppy. She turned round, showing to her benefactress a face made no less plain and unattractive by being now splotched and mottled with crying.

'I wanted to be alone,' she said. 'You can't ever be alone at school and nobody understands, not even Daddy.'

'School is pretty ghastly,' said Elsa, dropping into Heather's language. 'But you soon get out and get a proper job. What are you going to do when you leave school?'

'Wrens,' said Heather, giving a final convulsive sob and rubbing her eyes vigorously with the borrowed handkerchief.

The girl certainly did not look like a possible Wren, Elsa thought. Still, no need to depress her any further at the moment.

'I'm Elsa Belton,' she said. 'My brother Freddy is in the Navy and so is Captain Hornby who was telling you about rococo. It's a splendid service.'

'I thought Captain Hornby was your brother,' said Heather, her heart fluttering at the mere mention of Commander Belton, even in the unromantic role of somebody's brother.

'Lord! no,' said Elsa. 'He's just a friend.'

Such are the niceties of language and so little calculated was Heather Adams to grapple with them that she gave up any hope of trying to explain that it wasn't that she thought that Captain Hornby was a brother of Miss Belton's, but that she thought Captain Hornby was Commander Belton. The distinction is apparent, but takes a little considering. But it was just like Commander Belton to have a sister who had an extra pocket handkerchief, and to his greater glory. That Miss Belton had done anything kind in giving her handkerchief to an unknown schoolgirl who was crying about nothing at all, did not for a moment occur to her.

'They found a rat in the kitchen,' said Elsa, hoping to cheer her young friend.

'Has anyone killed it?' asked Heather with interest.

Elsa said it was dead, and she thought they were all too frightened to touch it.

At this Heather's inexpressive face assumed an unmistakable look of scorn. Pushing past Elsa she walked into the kitchen where the girls were still excitedly clustered round the cupboard, made a way for herself, picked the rat up and threw it out of one of the broken panes into the long grass and weeds. Miss Ferdinand remarked 'Dead for a ducat, dead,' and flicked the taint of an imaginary rat from her finger-tips with one of her gloves. The dull girl in the Upper Fifth said how could anyone bear to touch a rat. Heather looked contemptuously at her, hugging to herself the thought that when she and Commander Belton were on a raft together (a raft to which she had swum with his unconscious form from the torpedoed ship) and attacked by rats, she would shield him from their teeth, stamp on them and strangle them with her bare hands, nay, if necessary, allow them to eat her that he might live and weep over her neatly picked bones. This beautiful and practical thought put her into what was almost a good temper, and when the head prefect said rats carried bubonic plague she merely withered her with a glance.

As it was now four o'clock and getting chilly the whole party went back by the field-path, through the garden door, down the long garden to Arcot House, where they found Mrs Belton with Mr Carton who was at home for the weekend and Miss Sparling, who had escaped from her Governors and come across the park.

Tea was laid in the dining-room. The Rajah Café, on hearing that Mrs Belton was having some of the girls from the Park to tea, gave her, or rather allowed her to buy, an extra cake which they had not quite exactly promised to Mrs Hunter. Cook and Wheeler had performed wonders with oatcakes and scones, there was honey in the comb and mulberry jam and cream, and a large fruit cake sent by a naval friend of Commander Belton's from he wasn't allowed to say where, though as everyone knew he was at Washington and was in the habit of sending over anything from silk stockings to wrist watches by his other naval friends who were united to the Customs by the closest bonds of duty-free gin and whisky, the pretence of ignorance deceived no one in the least.

For a while the grown-ups had the conversation to themselves, with a ground bass of determined chewing from the younger members of the party. Grief had but sharpened Heather's appetite and she ate steadily through an amount of starchy food which cannot have done her pasty complexion any good. Miss Holly described their visit to the church, omitting the performance of *Hamlet* in the crypt.

'By the way,' she said to Miss Sparling, 'Mr Oriel wants to suggest some dramatic readings for the girls next term, if you think it would be a good thing. He would arrange them at the School or at the Vicarage to suit us. I said I'd tell you, and if you don't approve he won't say any more.'

'That is very nice of Mr Oriel,' said Miss Sparling, 'and I shall certainly think about it.'

'During the short and disagreeable period when I was a schoolmaster,' said Mr Carton, 'a period to which I can hardly refer without shuddering, I found that the play we acted at the end of the winter term brought the boys a stage nearer some kind of humanity than I could have believed. In fact by the time we had rehearsed *The Knight of the Burning Pestle* every Monday in the term in the hour which should have been given to the French lesson, I was almost reconciled to my lot. The boy who sang the drunken song was remarkably good. His father was an analytical chemist.'

As these emotions recollected in tranquillity were evidently addressed by the speaker more to himself than to the company, no one liked to be the first to comment.

'What happened about the boys' French?' said Miss Holly, at length, really interested in this point.

'Nothing,' Mr Carton replied. 'M. Grimier, like all other French masters, could not control small boys, and more ink was wasted in his lessons than in any others. They couldn't have learnt anything and I taught them all they needed in the week before the exams.'

'Didn't the French master mind?' said Mrs Belton.

'He was writing a life of Gambetta,' said Mr Carton, 'so it gave him more time. Poor fellow, I wonder where he is now.'

Miss Sparling asked if he was in occupied or unoccupied France, which led to so uninformed a discussion as to whether any of France was unoccupied now, each speaker having a different point of view, with only this in common, that not one of them had any ground for any statement made, that in the turmoil the luckless M. Grimier was quite forgotten.

'I don't think we could give up French for dramatic readings,' said Miss Sparling, 'but I might be able to arrange something. I must thank Mr Oriel and see what he suggests. Remind me, Miss Holly.'

Elsa said that when Charles acted in his school play he looked too handsome for words as a girl, to which Miss Holly added that when they did *She Stoops to Conquer* in her last term at school, two of the sixth-form girls made the most handsome young men she had ever seen, at which words her pupils paused for a moment in their meal, each seeing herself ravishing in a wig and knee breeches.

The head prefect asked what Miss Holly acted.

'Tony Lumpkin,' said Miss Holly with some pride.

'Oh, Miss Holly, how *gorgeous*,' said Miss Ferdinand. 'Oh, Miss Sparling, *do* let us have a play. Let's do *Romeo and Juliet*, I'd adore to act Romeo, or Mercutio, or Juliet, or the nurse, or—'

'I think you are more like Bottom,' said Miss Sparling, confident that her stage-struck pupil would at once take the cue. Miss Ferdinand after a panic-stricken second caught the meaning and good-humouredly accepted the rebuke. Mr Carton looked with interest on the headmistress. She was coming out. If only she didn't remind him of a don's wife he would be prepared to admit that she was not only good-looking, but quick-minded. And after all, she was old Horbury's granddaughter and must have some scholarship in her blood.

'By the way, Miss Sparling,' he said, 'I happened to borrow a book from Oriel on that evening when we dined at the Vicarage, and have found your grandfather's name in it. I wonder if you know it.'

Miss Sparling's face lighted and she was about to ask eagerly what book it was when Mr Belton came in, back from his ride to Pomfret Towers and in excellent spirits. He greeted Miss Sparling and Miss Holly and took a chair at the far end of the table.

'Well, young ladies, what have *you* been doing?' he asked, scraping the remains of the cream on to a scone and covering it with mulberry jam.

The head prefect said Mr Oriel had taken them round the church and up the tower.

'Well, that's more than I've done for many a day,' said Mr Belton, 'but it's worth going up for the view. Could you see Bolder's Knob?'

'She didn't go up,' said Heather Adams, suddenly seeing a

chance to settle old scores with the head prefect for preventing her going on the tower roof. 'She said the stairs made her feel sick.'

'You ought to get over that, young lady,' said Mr Belton, looking at the head prefect. 'I'll tell you a good plan. When you're going up, say to yourself at the time, "Now I'm one step nearer the top." And when you are coming down just go quietly, one step after the other you know, and say, "Now I'm one step nearer the bottom."'

'And then Miss Belton was kind enough to show us the Garden House before tea,' said Miss Holly, who saw that the head prefect was far from convinced by this sovereign remedy for giddiness.

'Ah well, it's a ruin now,' said Mr Belton. 'What did you all think of it?'

As he addressed the question to no one in particular and was at the moment engaged with the honeycomb, no one answered till Heather Adams, flown with her large tea, said,

'It was lovely. There was a dead rat and I threw it out of the window.'

'I knew there were rats there,' said Mr Belton. 'I have said there were rats there all along. I've been telling Humble so for weeks. How long had it been dead?'

'I don't know,' said Heather, 'but when I picked it up by its tail it didn't come off, so I shouldn't think it was long. It was a grandfather by the look of it.'

'You seem to be well up in rats, young lady,' said Mr Belton, whom the discovery of the rat had put into very good humour. 'Where did you learn all this? At school?'

'Father gets rats in his store-sheds and I like seeing the men get them out with their terriers,' said Heather, surprised to find herself talking so easily.

'And what does your father do? Farm?' said Mr Belton.

'Heather Adams's father owns those big rolling mills at Hogglestock,' said Miss Holly, who had been listening with interest.

'So you are Miss Adams, eh?' said Mr Belton. 'I know your father. He sits on the bench with me.'

'Well, I hope you'll send the boys to prison that stole Daddy's onions,' said Heather. 'He can't. They were just ready for storing and they stole them all in sacks, but our gardener heard them and rang up the police and they caught them.'

'Your father doesn't like sending people to prison who steal vegetables,' said Mr Belton, rather grimly.

'But it's his vegetables this time,' said Heather, at which Mr Belton laughed and began to talk to Elsa about putting a dog into the Garden House to deal with the rats. Miss Sparling then looked at Miss Holly who collected the girls and after good-byes and thanks took them into the hall to put their hats and coats on. Miss Sparling also made her farewells and went into the hall, followed by Mr Carton, who asked her if she would come to tea with him and see her grandfather's book, saying that he would ask a few friends to meet her. She accepted with pleasure and the school cavalcade went away in the dark.

The drawing-room seemed incredibly dignified and peaceful after the half-term tea party. The Beltons and Mr Carton, not much noticing the absence of Elsa and Captain Hornby, or if they did, thinking they preferred not to be hampered by their elders, sank into comfortable gossip before the fire.

'So that's Adams's girl. She certainly has a head on her shoulders,' said Mr Belton, who appeared to confuse brains with a knowledge of ratting. 'And a deuced plain one too,' he added.

'Perhaps she's only an ugly duckling,' said Mrs Belton.

'Not a chance,' said Mr Belton. 'She's the living image of

Adams. She'll need all the brains she's got if she's going to take an interest in his works. He must be worth a couple of hundred thousand by now. Still, the Government will keep an eye on that,' he added with some satisfaction. 'No wonder Charles had a shock when he went up to the Park by mistake and saw all those girls! No beauties! Still, they take their feed well.'

Mr Carton laughed his dry laugh.

'To pursue the comparison,' he said, 'your friend Adams's daughter might be called the Flanders Mare.'

'A bit heavy in the build, eh?' said Mr Belton, who privately thought that Mr Carton was going too far with a guest of Arcot House.

'I think Mr Carton meant Anne of Cleves, Fred,' said Mrs Belton.

'All right, all right,' said Mr Belton, who did not wish anyone to explain anything to him. 'That Miss Sparling is a good-looking woman. I wish you'd ask her to dinner here some time, Lucy. Might have a return party for Oriel.'

Mrs Belton said she would certainly try to arrange it, but everything would depend on the Nabob's taxi, as they couldn't expect her to walk to Arcot House and back in the dark cold night.

'And ask Carton too,' said Mr Belton, and went away to write letters.

'Will you dine with us to meet Miss Sparling,' said Mrs Belton.

'I'd like to,' said Mr Carton. 'That woman interests me. She is the perfect female don and yet there's a something. Did I tell you that Oriel discovered by chance that old Canon Horbury whom he knew in his young days was her grandfather? That sort of thing always tells.'

Mrs Belton, who had naturally never heard of Canon

Horbury, said how very interesting that was. And we must here state that Miss Sparling at once went up in her estimation. It may be snobbishness to think the better of a person because your Vicar has known her grandfather who was a Canon; but it lies deep at the roots of social life, and there is good reason for it.

'And yet,' continued Mr Carton thoughtfully, 'it's all just wrong. I can't quite explain, but I suppose as a headmistress she is perfect; yet the more perfect she is, the less satisfactory.'

Mrs Belton, with her usual kind tact, begged him to explain.

'You will correct me in what I am about to say,' Mr Carton began, this being his favourite method of undermining any adversary, who then felt that politeness forbade him to make the correction (except in the case of scholars of Mr Carton's standing who were quite oblivious of forms when, say, the enclitic *de* or the properly based *oun* was in question), 'and I know I am hardly qualified to speak of women's dress, but I feel she is dressed for the part too well; it is like a disguise.'

Mrs Belton again, with her eyes this time, expressed the liveliest interest and a wish to hear more.

'Now,' said Mr Carton, addressing an imaginary group of third-year men, 'I imagine that for the country in autumn a tweed coat and skirt, such as you and Elsa wear, or Mrs Perry, or Lady Graham, is as it were the uniform. I notice that Miss Sparling always wears what is, I believe, called a one-piece frock, usually with a V opening – correct me if I err – and some lace across it; and often with a touch of what I can only describe as a reminiscence of braces over the shoulders in some form of trimming. And over this a coat with what strikes me as an unfashionable kind of fur collar. And both a little longer than is the custom; which is quite unnecessary, for Miss Sparling has good ankles.'

Mrs Belton could not help being amused at Mr Carton's analysis of Miss Sparling's way of dressing and had to admit that it was pretty near the truth.

'And a felt hat which somehow reminds me more of the hats worn by elderly ladies in Edinburgh than what I see you and our other friends wearing,' said Mr Carton thoughtfully. 'And a necklace of greenish beads, just the wrong length. And yet she manages to convey an impression of being well dressed in her own right. Not that this in the least explains what I mean. Good-bye.'

Mrs Belton was used to Mr Carton's abrupt departures. When he had gone she lay back in her chair and thought how much more intelligent about the ordinary things of daily life he was than anyone who only met him over Latin and Greek would think. Perhaps his manner was also a disguise, a dressing for the part too well. Then she thought of her tea-party and how nice it was to see the girls eating so much, and what a mercy Fred had taken a liking to that poor Adams girl. And then she vaguely wondered where Captain Hornby and Elsa were and began to feel wistful. But this did not last long and she looked facts in the face with her accustomed aloofness and confessed that to have one's children in the room with one was delightful, but to have them not in the room, yet know that they were happy somewhere about the house was even better. Probably in the little upstairs sitting-room talking.

Elsa and Captain Hornby were certainly talking, but not in the little upstairs sitting-room. They had cleared away all the tea things and were washing up in the pantry. Wheeler had tried to prevent them, but Elsa, knowing that the Updikes were coming to dinner so that the men could discuss business, and that Wheeler and cook were pretty busy as well as having provided a large tea, and that Florrie was always more nuisance than help on Saturdays because of going to the cinema with 'the boys,' had taken no notice of her ex-nurse's protests and quietly packed the tea things on to a trolley. Wheeler had then followed them to the pantry to take offence, but she had a soft spot for the Navy, as being the home of her eldest nursling Freddy, and when Captain Hornby appealed to her to let him do the drying, on the grounds that he never remembered having a mother, she relented grimly and went away to tell young Florrie there were some that didn't know which side their bread was buttered on, that poor gentleman never having a mother and all.

Elsa rinsed, stacked and washed the tea things with her usual competence. Captain Hornby was an excellent drier-up and Elsa was secretly much impressed by his demanding a washleather to finish off the spoons. They discovered a further bond in their dislike of tea from a silver teapot and rejoiced that all the heavy silver had been put away.

'Do you really never remember a mother?' said Elsa, leaning against the pantry table while Captain Hornby washed his hands.

'Really not,' said Captain Hornby. 'She died when I was about a year old. But I dare say it was just as well. She mightn't have liked me; or I mightn't have liked her. Heaps of fellows don't seem to get on with their people. And it was nearly forty years ago.'

'I didn't know you were as old as that,' said Elsa. 'I'm twenty-five.'

Captain Hornby dried his hands on the roller towel behind the pantry door and thought twenty-five a very young age. Too young to be in a responsible position, to bear the sorrow, the mortification, the disappointment, whatever you liked to call it, of an alienated inheritance.

'When I saw those girls going back to the Park, I could have murdered them all, and the mistresses too,' said Elsa, staring at the glass cupboard. 'Chuck those tea-cloths over the hanger, Christopher.'

Captain Hornby, whose naval training had taught him to do things neatly, hung the damp tea-cloths on a kind of small aerial clothes-horse which could be raised and lowered by a rope and pulley and was apt to get stuck at an angle.

'I would do almost anything to get you back in your home,' he said, making a knot in the rope with meticulous care. 'I simply hate to see you worried.'

'Oh, that's all right,' said Elsa. 'Perhaps Freddy will pick up an heiress. It's time somebody did.'

'You know what I mean, Elsa,' said Captain Hornby, still busy with his knot. 'It seems coarse to mention it, but I'm extremely well off.'

Elsa put out her hand, touched his coat sleeve, and withdrew her hand.

'Does that mean anything?' said Captain Hornby.

'I don't know,' said Elsa.

'All right, we'll leave it like that,' said Captain Hornby.

7

On this vague and rather foolish footing matters remained. Captain Hornby and Elsa went back to their work on the following day and continued to meet a great deal in London whenever they could, but the subject of an engagement was not mentioned again. Each preferred the company of the other to that of any other friend or acquaintance, but neither seemed to wish to formalize their relationship. Elsa's parents knew nothing about it and London was far too busy to pay attention to them. Even that gossip Geoffrey Harvey, now happily back at the Ministry of Red Tape and Sealing Wax and sharing a flat with his friend Peter, got so used to seeing them about together that he stopped noticing them at all, and as for his sister, she was safely in the Censorship, though this will not really interest anyone.

The term went on. Examinations loomed, surged up and broke over the Hosiers' girls' heads and retreated. The head prefect only got A− or B+ for most of her subjects, but as Miss Holly remarked to Mrs Belton who was very sympathetic about the girls, it was character you needed in a prefect, and that was, as a rule, about all they had. Miss Ferdinand did excellently in Literature, History and Languages, but failed quite shockingly in Algebra and Physics. But, as she so truly said, Shakespeare didn't know Physics and if her reflection in the looking-glass was the wrong way round it didn't matter a bit. The dull girl in the Upper Fifth got 100 per cent for Scripture, and said it was just like her luck because Scripture didn't count in exams. As for Heather Adams, our readers will not be surprised to learn that she got A or A+ for all Mathematics and for Physics, remaining otherwise at an undistinguished level among the B minuses.

Then they all went home. But not as in pre-war years with a taxi to Barchester Central Station, or fetched by their parents in the Austin, or sent for by the Daimler with a chauffeur. George Potter, cousin to Potter the chemist, Furniture Removed and Stored, came with his large van, collected all the trunks and suit-cases and rug bundles and took them to Nutfield station whence they were dispatched by train to their various destinations. The Southbridge United Viator Passenger Company supplied two immense touring motor coaches which collected all the girls and most of the mistresses and deposited them at Barchester Central, whence they all got to their respective homes sooner or later. Miss Sparling and Miss Holly and the school matron remained behind for a couple of days to get various things in order.

Oxford was also down by now, so Mrs Belton obeyed her husband's wish, which coincided with her own leanings, and asked Miss Sparling and Mr Carton to dinner, also Dr and Mrs Perry, Mr Oriel, and Mrs Hoare who had to be asked once a year owing to her honorary position as relict of the late agent of the Pomfret estate. The evening had gone very well. Miss Sparling, who was labouring under the advantage of only hearing about Mrs Hoare's legacies for the first time, proved an excellent and appreciative listener in the drawing-room after dinner and on telling Mrs Hoare that her grandfather had left her his books, became almost a blood relative.

Mrs Belton asked Miss Sparling in a friendly way where she was going for her holidays. Miss Sparling said she was spending Christmas with an old college friend, now a librarian in the north, but would probably be coming back to the school after the New Year with Miss Holly as there were so many things to be done before term began.

'Why not come to us for a few days?' said Mrs Belton. 'I know how cold it will be up at the Park. You shall have the little upstairs sitting-room to yourself and do exactly as you please about seeing us or not.'

Miss Sparling, who in her exalted position did not look for kindness and, perhaps owing to that position, seldom was offered any, was almost confused and thanked Mrs Belton warmly, saying with the simplicity that lay under her headmistress's manner that she was hardly ever in a real home and would love it.

'I only hope I shan't get one of my dreadful colds then,' she said. 'I am so well as a rule, but I usually get one appalling cold in the winter term.'

'You'd better let me inoculate you, Miss Sparling,' said Dr Perry. 'Three shots and you'll not see a cold till Easter.'

Miss Sparling said she had always heard that injections were a great help and really must try some.

'We'll see about it,' said Dr Perry. 'But I'll be on holiday for a week after the New Year and you don't want to have Morgan. She gives an injection as if you were a rhinoceros, and there's no one else round here unless it's serious.'

The taxi from the Nabob, secured as a special favour for this occasion, then announced itself and took Mr Oriel, Mr Carton and Miss Sparling away, depositing them at their homes in that order. There was no intimate talk, as the Nabob's gears and also its springs made such a thing impossible. Good nights were shouted as loudly as good breeding permits, Mr Carton said Miss Sparling must come to tea and see his bachelor establishment when she returned, and the taxi carried her away.

Of the blight of Christmas we have spoken from the heart elsewhere and not once but several times. To our former descriptions of that odious and society-disrupting season we have nothing to add. Suffice it to say that the Beltons and the Updikes each ate a cockerel and that everyone was heartily glad when the wheels of life began to turn again and the New Year had begun.

'I don't know how it is,' said Mrs Updike to Mrs Belton, meeting her at the stop for the Nutfield-Barchester bus, 'but I've got a perfect thing about Christmas. I used to have it when the children were small, but now what with one getting leave and one not, and always wondering if the war will go on long enough to catch the younger ones, I simply loathe the Christmas holidays. Of course Christmas Day itself was a help because they all went to church and I could cook the dinner in peace. Though when I say peace I dropped the bottle of ammonia in the scullery and it nearly choked me. I couldn't help laughing at it. Are you going to Barchester?'

Mrs Belton said she was only waiting for the bus to arrive from Nutfield, as she was expecting Miss Sparling to stay with her.

'I *do* like her,' said Mrs Updike enthusiastically. 'I always hated all my schoolmistresses, because they would want me to learn things and I simply couldn't. But Miss Sparling hasn't got that dreadful thing about being educated. She is just like an ordinary nice person. Do you know, Mrs Belton, I secretly envy schoolmistresses now, because they are the one person that still has clean hands. I sometimes wish I were a schoolmistress, because even if the food was horrid, I wouldn't have cooked it, and then I can't help laughing at myself, because I couldn't be one if I tried. I was so stupid at school that they gave up trying to make me pass exams, and then I got married, which is *much* nicer.'

There would apparently have been no end to Mrs Updike's artless confidences, but just then the bus came up. Miss Holly, who was going on to the stop near the lodge gates, waved through the window, the bus disgorged Miss Sparling with a suitcase and took Mrs Updike away. There was the usual polite argument about carrying the suitcase, but most luckily the bread came past and said it was delivering on that side of the street and would take the luggage along. The evening was pleasant and Mrs Belton looked forward to a few agreeable, uneventful days with her guest. But on the following day Miss Sparling had a slight roughness in her throat which heralded, she knew but too well, one of her bad colds. In vain did she use every remedy that despair suggested. She had to apologize to her hostess and ask if she might go to bed as she knew she was not safe company for anyone. Mrs Belton was only too thankful to be warned, as her husband was apt to catch any colds that were about and endured his sufferings in a very uncontrolled way, and most luckily Wheeler considered anyone with a cold or minor ailment as an inmate of the nursery and under her charge. It was her boast, and no vain one, that in virtue of having been a children's nurse she never caught anything, so she forbade her mistress to go near Miss Sparling and looked after her herself. By the end of the second day Miss Sparling was so feverish that Mrs Belton felt she would be happier if a doctor saw the patient.

'Just as you like, madam,' said Wheeler. 'Of course you know Dr Perry's away and there's only that Dr Morgan. I wouldn't ever have a lady doctor in *my* nursery.'

Mrs Belton didn't much want one either, but her guest was a responsibility, so she rang up Dr Morgan who said she would come on the following morning. The news was broken by Wheeler to Miss Sparling, who was feeling so wretched that she didn't care who came to see her and was having a kind of mild delirium about the School Governors getting C minus in an examination and dismissing her because she hadn't told Mr Oriel that there was a rat in the Upper Dormitory.

Next morning however she felt so much better that she wished Mrs Belton had left ill alone, or that she had gone to the school where she could have been ill without fuss. A tap at the door made her pull herself together. Wheeler opened the door and announced, 'It's the lady doctor, miss.' At least this was what Miss Sparling knew she must have said, though it sounded uncommonly like 'that lady doctor'.

Miss Sparling had once or twice had occasion to meet Dr Morgan, who had treated pupils if Dr Perry was urgently engaged. Also Ellen Humble was one of her panel patients and, at her mother's command, threw any medicines prescribed for her anaemia down the sink, for, as Mrs Humble said, it stood to reason that Abdomo-Pep, or 'Doc' Heal-well's Revivo Blood Syrup was there long before that Dr Morgan was born. So it was without surprise, or indeed any emotion but weakly wishing Dr Morgan would go away, that Miss Sparling saw her temporary medical attendant who, as was her usual embarrassing custom, put a chair just far enough away to make the patient have to raise her voice, and sitting down looked at her as if she had paid sixpence for the privilege.

It must be said, in justice to Dr Morgan, that besides being of insignificant appearance and uncertain temper, she spent a good deal of her earnings on her clothes, of which she had a large wardrobe, nearly all unsuitable to her particular type of dowdiness and her honourable profession. For this reason she had a certain following among the younger women of the village who said she had style: though what the word meant to them, we cannot exactly say. In summer she much affected printed voile dresses with an all-over flower pattern, dripping at one side or at the back, and large hats which made her marmoset face look even smaller. In winter she had a variety of the one-piece frocks with V's and braces, so ably described by Mr Carton, worn under coats which were far too apt to have fur in the wrong places, such as a plastron across the front, or half a sleeve, or a band six inches from the bottom, and rather dashing little felt hats, three-cornered and worn at an angle, or almost flat with a loop of themselves sticking up behind and tilted well over the eyes. This particular hat she was wearing today to celebrate her entrance into Arcot House, where she had long wished to get a footing, but owing to Dr Perry's abominable good health had never succeeded during old Mrs Ellangowan-Hornby's lifetime.

Miss Sparling looked with a lacklustre eye at her physician, at her stockings slightly wrinkled round the ankle, at her feet in too high-heeled shoes slightly turned in, and having said 'How do you do, Dr Morgan,' waited for her to answer. But whether from inner shyness, or a determination to do something or other psychological by keeping silent, Dr Morgan uttered no word and continued to stare at her patient.

'It's only a bad cold,' said Miss Sparling at length, charitably breaking the ice, 'but Mrs Belton thought it would be better to have me looked at. I was going to have inoculations, but Dr Perry is away.'

'I could easily inoculate you myself,' said Dr Morgan without interest, 'but you'd probably be better without. Your type of cold is very common among over-educated women in a very feminine atmosphere. In co-educational schools you don't get them. I do not as yet attempt to explain this, but I have my theories.'

She then fell silent and staring.

'Perhaps you would like to examine my chest or take my temperature,' said Miss Sparling, annoyed, bored, and assuming something of her headmistress voice.

Dr Morgan seemed to think this was a good idea and took Miss Sparling's temperature which rather naturally was over normal, though nothing to worry about. The mere fact of having someone in the room and so having to exert herself had already done Miss Sparling good and she felt that if only Dr Morgan would get it over and go away she would be almost herself again.

'And what about my chest?' said Miss Sparling, determined to get through with it.

'You need not loosen anything,' said Dr Morgan coldly, thus making Miss Sparling, who was preparing to pull down her nightgown, feel she was being indelicate. 'I can manage without. I find it better from a psychological point of view.'

Miss Sparling wondered how she would manage from the point of view of her tilted hat, but with great skill Dr Morgan plugged the ends of her stethoscope into her ears and planted the little mouthpiece or whatever it is called at the other end firmly upon Miss Sparling's nightgown in several places.

'Nothing there,' she said.

'Perhaps you'd better listen to my back,' said Miss Sparling sitting up with surprising vigour.

Dr Morgan looked annoyed, but listened at various chosen spots and knocked double knocks with two bent fingers of her right hand upon two flat extended fingers of her left.

'Nothing there at all,' said Dr Morgan sitting down again, with the stethoscope still adorning her head and bosom.

'I knew there wasn't,' said Miss Sparling, and was at once privately ashamed of herself.

'Don't think too much about yourself,' said Dr Morgan, at which Miss Sparling nearly got out of bed and shook her. 'Women of your age do. I always find work is the best medicine. I will come in again tomorrow.'

'Thank you so much,' said Miss Sparling, 'but I feel ever so much better already and as I have a great deal to do at the School, I shall get up tomorrow.'

'I'd like to try some suggestion on you later,' said Dr Morgan, whose appearance with the stethoscope dangling below her tilted hat was in the highest degree impressive. 'I will just write you a prescription for a tonic. Please see that it is made up, and taken.'

'You will find my secretary, Miss Holly, downstairs,' said Miss Sparling in a cold fury and at the same time stifling a wish to giggle. 'She will see about it. Many thanks for your visit. Good-bye.'

Dr Morgan took off her stethoscope, set her hat at a more dashing angle by Miss Sparling's looking-glass, a proceeding which that lady bitterly resented, and went downstairs. In the hall she found Miss Holly lying in wait, who drew her into the study and asked how her employer was.

'Nothing wrong with her at all,' said Dr Morgan. 'I find that women in important jobs, or what they think important, especially dealing with other women and girls, are apt to dwell too much on their own health.'

'If you can make Miss Sparling dwell on her own health a little more you will be doing me a personal favour,' said Miss

Holly, who had never cared for Dr Morgan since she had seen her give Heather Adams one of her boil injections rather clumsily. 'This term is always a bad one and she won't spare herself.'

'That makes it worse,' said Dr Morgan. 'I must tell you, Miss Holly, that I doubt whether I can be of much use to Miss Sparling as yet. She has, as you will agree, a rather antagonistic attitude to modern methods. I won't say to psycho-analytic methods for that is entirely out of date, but to any attempt on the doctor's part to gain her confidence. Of course I shall break this down by degrees.'

'I don't think so,' said Miss Holly blandly. 'It was very good of you to give up some of your time, Dr Morgan. Will you be so kind as to send the account to me at the school.'

She then let Dr Morgan out of the house and went up to her employer's room where she and Miss Sparling had a refreshing hour over the Upper Fifth time-table and were quite surprised when Mrs Belton came in to say that a tray was coming up for Miss Sparling and she hoped Miss Holly would stay to lunch. This the secretary gladly did, for she liked Mrs Belton and thought Arcot House was a good and restful background for her employer to whom she was very much attached in a businesslike, unemotional way. The ladies said a few unappreciative words about Dr Morgan, and Miss Holly said what a bore it was to have a woman doctor at the school which was already quite feminine enough and how glad she was that Dr Perry would be back before term began. Then Mr Carton rang up to suggest Saturday next week for his tea-party, Miss Holly went up to tell Miss Sparling, the invitation was accepted and Dr Morgan comfortably forgotten.

Providence, which is notoriously and grossly partial to bachelors in comfortable circumstances, had seen to it many years ago that

Mr Carton should have an ex-scout from St Jude's and his wife to look after him, who were well above any kind of calling-up age, the husband also having a game leg from the last war and the wife being very deaf. The game leg did not prevent Wickens getting about his work in the house and the little garden, and Mrs Wickens's deafness had made her silent, though quite contented. When Mr Carton was at Harefield they looked after him excellently; when he was in his rooms at Oxford they gently sold such eggs, fruit and vegetables as would not be necessary for their own and incidentally his comfort, and kept the house very clean.

Mr Carton lived in a stone house, older than the red brick High Street. It had formerly been part of the Abbey property and could be found in old documents under the name of the Assay House, as having for a short period during prosperous days of the Barsetshire wool trade had a licence to stamp silver. This name the Nabob had by a pretty piece of fancy changed to Assaye House, and as no one noticed any difference, so it remained. It was a small house of two storeys with attics in the roof, a massive oak staircase and one large room, formerly a barn, entered through the dining-room. This large room Mr Carton used as his library, workroom, smoking-room, sitting-room and everything but bedroom. Here he spent much of the vacations compiling his history of the Abbey and Manor of Harefield which was when finished to include genealogical tables of all the older families and a number of photographs, those taken from the air plainly showing the site of Harefield Abbey in the fields next to the church.

Mr and Mrs Wickens quite approved of their master's dinner and lunch parties before the war, as affording them scope for the exercise of their peculiar talents, she as cook, he as waiter and general factotum. During the first year of the war Mr Carton had continued to give dinner and lunch to his friends; then what with petrol and food rationing things had become difficult and he had to confine himself to lunch and tea. Now, with all Barsetshire immobile, meat and cheese at a minimum, fish rare and what was worse in a distinctly tired condition, everything getting daily more difficult, he had been obliged to restrict his parties to tea only. But the tea itself, we mean the beverage, was good, for Mr Carton had discovered a small black market in China tea and hoarded it like anything, so all the ladies of Harefield and many of the gentlemen were delighted whenever a tea-drinking was announced.

'You know what Mrs Powlett said,' Mr Wickens remarked to his wife while they were getting the tea ready on Tuesday afternoon.

'What?' said Mrs Wickens.

Mr Wickens repeated his remark in a bellow. And as he chose to forget the fact of his wife's being deaf, or to take it as a personal slight which he preferred to ignore, this repetition took place nearly every time he spoke to her, but we shall not mention it again. Sometimes she heard him the second time, sometimes she didn't, but her even temper was quite unaffected for she knew all his subjects of conversation by heart and could mostly guess what he wanted to say.

'You mean about the Women's Institute jam,' said Mrs Wickens.

'No,' said her husband. 'About the Vicar.'

'That's right. The Vicar's coming to tea,' said Mrs Wickens.

'And Someone Else too,' said Mr Wickens.

'You mean from up there,' said his wife, giving herself a jerk more or less in the direction of Harefield Park. 'Mrs Powlett may say what she likes, but Mr Oriel is not a marrying man.'

'Nor was I till you married me,' said Mr Wickens.

'Mark my words,' said Mrs Wickens, unmoved by this gibe, 'we'll as soon see Someone Else here as we'll see her at the Vicarage. Not but what she's a nice lady, Ellen Humble says, and some lovely things. Linjery with vallenseens.'

'You don't know everything, Mother,' said Mr Wickens. 'Oxford gentlemen like Mr Carton don't marry. The sort they see at Oxford give them a fair sickener. Hurry up, there's Mr Oriel.'

Mrs Wickens went to her kitchen and Mr Wickens to the front door.

By half-past four Mr Oriel, Miss Sparling, Mrs Belton and Mrs Perry had arrived, the last two ladies bringing rather insincere promises from their husbands to look in later. They were shortly joined by Mr Updike, who brought a message from his wife to the effect that she was pickling some walnuts and would come as soon as she could, but they were doing something very peculiar.

Mr Carton, unmoved, said then they would have tea, which was in the dining-room, for he did not hold with food getting into the same room with his books, though he did not mind his books, children of his predilection, getting into the room with his food and habitually read at meals.

'I must thank you, Mr Oriel,' said Miss Sparling, 'for your kindness in taking the girls over the church. They did enjoy it so much. They had to write an essay on it last week and the literature mistress tells me the average was very high. One girl, I gather, was particularly interested in the crypt and made some really thoughtful references to Shakespeare.'

Mr Oriel looked pleased, yet nervous.

'The word Shakespeare,' he said, 'makes me think, perhaps with reason, of the drama. I wonder if Miss Holly happened to mention to you a little suggestion of mine that you might possibly care to consider of some dramatic readings next term. When I say dramatic, I do not of course mean anything violent; merely the reading aloud of selected scenes from our Shakespeare, or other suitable dramatists.'

Miss Sparling, feeling very unworthy of the careful deference paid to her by Mr Oriel, said she was ashamed not to have acknowledged his kind message sooner, but the end of term was always a very busy time.

'Some people would have said "hectic",' said Mr Carton, glaring at an imaginary class of low-vocabularied women undergraduates.

Miss Sparling acknowledged this rather pedagogic tribute with a little smile in his direction and continuing to address Mr Oriel, said she would talk the matter over with her secretary and Miss Head the literature mistress, and hoped to arrange a day once a week. If Mr Oriel felt equal to the walk, she added, it would be easier for her to have it at the school, where the big drawing-room, she said, with a deprecating yet grateful smile towards Mrs Belton, now a kind of common room for the senior girls, would make an excellent place for their meetings. So many fine shades were involved in her words that they almost escape us even as we write. To Miss Sparling Mr Oriel paid, as we have already noted, a well-bred attention as from one potentate to another, fully recognizing her status as the guide of so many future citizens without abrogating anything of his own position as pastor of all Harefield. To Mr Oriel Miss Sparling showed an equally well-bred attention as her spiritual guide, adding to this a touch of almost filial deference to an elderly man who had been a friend of her dearly loved grandfather; a deference which flattered Mr Oriel and yet caused him a slight, nameless uneasiness. And to Mrs Belton she had shown that not only did she realize that lady's prior claim, in the eyes of abstract justice, to her own drawing-room, but at the same time apologized to her for usurping it and thanked her for her friendly and generous attitude.

None of these shades were lost on Mr Carton, who was also clear-sighted enough to realize that Miss Sparling's smile of comprehension as of one initiate to another, though it met his full approval, also touched a chord in him responsive to flattery. He then told himself that he was a pedantic old don and smiled his peculiar sarcastic smile which consisted of a sudden stretching of his thin, tight-set lips, with no answering light in his eyes.

Mr Oriel, delighted at the thought of a little dramatic dissipation, eagerly plunged into Shakespeare with Miss Sparling and Mr Updike, who had been in his younger days an enthusiastic acting member of the Barchester Amateur Dramatic Society.

'I don't suppose you are thinking of real acting, Mr Oriel,' said Miss Sparling, 'for that, I fear, would take up too much time. Just readings.'

Mr Oriel was a little dashed, for under the innocent name of readings he had secretly hoped to coach the girls in a real play, or an act of a play, but if that was not to be, he would make the best of things.

'Also,' said Miss Sparling, giving her attention seriously to the subject in hand, as indeed she always did, which was partly why the Hosiers' Company valued her so highly, 'the question of clothes would be very difficult. One might manage somehow with bits of furniture stuff and borrowing for women's parts, but I fear the men's clothes would be extremely difficult for Shakespeare.'

'I don't know if I am betraying a confidence, Miss Sparling,' said the Vicar, 'but on the day your girls allowed me to show them the church, we had a conversation about acting at one point, and I gathered – I will not say I am certain of this, but I gathered – that one of them has some green tights. Now tights are always useful in Shakespeare.'

'I expect that is Isabella Ferdinand,' said Miss Sparling calmly. 'I know she has a yellow wig and a velvet cap with a feather in it, because she produced them when some of my girls took part in a pageant with the Barchester High School in aid of Comforts for the Mixo-Lydian Forces. Miss Pettinger thought the cap and wig unsuitable for one of Boadicea's attendants, which was what Isabella was cast for, so they were not used.'

'I don't see in the least why one of Boadicea's attendants shouldn't have a wig,' said Mrs Belton indignantly, 'or a cap either. Anything looks nice in a pageant. But that is so like Miss Pettinger.'

'Miss Pettinger doubtless had excellent historical reasons for her opinion,' said Miss Sparling impartially, 'and as I am not a historian I did not interfere. I was also Miss Pettinger's guest at the time.'

These simple words were well understood by all her hearers, every one of whom as mother of a pupil, or as having sat with that educationalist on committees, was more than ready to hear and believe anything against her.

'Where are the Mixo-Lydian Forces?' said Mr Oriel. 'One never seems to see any.'

Mr Carton said in a private way to himself and anyone who happened to be listening that they were on paper.

Mrs Perry said with an air of slight defiance that they were at 235 Grosvenor Gardens, and in splendid fettle, a word which much impressed her hearers.

Miss Sparling was not enough in touch with the cross currents of village life to know how careful one had to be about Mrs

Perry's Mixo-Lydian susceptibilities, but her long experience in receiving parents warned her that to speak of Mixo-Lydians was to trespass on uncertain ground, so she said she thought *As You Like It* might be a suitable play for the readings.

'A delightful choice,' said Mr Oriel. 'What do you think, Carton?'

Mr Carton said that if by delightful Mr Oriel meant that it was suitable for the Young Person in a Podsnappian sense, he supposed it was, though he himself, he added, always found it uncommon dull, perhaps because of its very flawlessness.

This depressed Mr Oriel, who already looked upon himself as spiritual sponsor of the play, a good deal.

'I am sure Miss Head will think it a very good choice,' said Miss Sparling, who could not bear to see her grandfather's old friend cast down. 'And if we did act a scene, I only say if, for I'm afraid it will hardly be practicable, Isabella's tights would do nicely for Rosalind, and whoever does Celia could have the wig and Orlando the cap with the feather.'

'And I saw among your girls one who would be quite admirable in the part of Audrey,' said Mr Oriel, much cheered. 'I do not know her name, but she must have a kindly nature, for I gather that she volunteered to remain with a friend who felt giddy on the tower staircase. A girl with, I would not be so harsh to any young creature as to say a face and general appearance that do not exercise the very highest degree of attraction, besides which Audrey must undoubtedly have had some charm if Touchstone wished to marry her, but, if I may so express myself, of unformed exterior, as one who is as yet, shall I say, slightly immature in the development of that bloom of youth which is such an added charm in the young. But perhaps I have but obscured my own meaning.'

'Not in the least, Mr Oriel,' said Miss Sparling, who from the very first had no doubt about the object of Mr Oriel's very guarded praise. 'It must be Heather Adams. She is very bad at literature, but there is always a chance that the dramatic side may wake her interest.'

'I do feel sorry for that girl,' said Mrs Belton, who, distinguished-looking herself and with good-looking children, could well afford it. 'She looks so apathetic and stodgy. But she did brighten up about the rat in the Garden House and my husband took quite a liking for her.'

'I fear,' said Miss Sparling, half-sighing, half-laughing, 'that the rat was the real success of the afternoon. Every single essay mentioned it. Miss Head tells me one half called it a darling little rat and the other half a horrible big rat. Heather's real interest is her father's factories and works. He is very proud of her.'

'Is that Adams's daughter that owns the Hogglestock rolling mills?' Mr Updike asked, breaking away from a conversation with Mrs Perry about fire-watching. 'We do a good deal for him one way and another. A remarkable man, Miss Sparling. He has no background and comes from nowhere, but he has a positive genius for guessing what kind of tenders the Government will be calling for six months ahead. We have elected him to the Barchester County Club, you know. A lot of members didn't want him, but he is extremely useful on committees.'

'One of our Conquerors,' said Mr Carton.

No one recognized his quotation, so he smiled his tight smile and added that if Mr Adams did not dress like a comedian's conception of a country gentleman he might pass as a successful commercial traveller anywhere.

'I think you are a little unkind, Mr Carton,' said Mrs Belton. 'Fred dislikes him very much, but he does struggle to see the best side of Mr Adams and sometimes he almost succeeds. He can't be quite horrid if he is so proud of anyone as flabby and depressing as that poor daughter of his.'

At this point an irruption took place of Mrs Updike and Dr Perry, who were warmly welcomed. Mr Carton sent for fresh tea and asked how the pickled walnuts were.

'All I can say is,' said Mrs Updike laughing, 'that I never knew how dreadful walnuts were. You know, Phil,' she said turning to her husband, 'that I told you they were being peculiar, and so they were. Most peculiar.'

She reached towards a cake, showing a bandage on her wrist.

'And what have you done now, Betty?' said Mr Updike, with less of anxiety than of resignation in his voice.

'It's all right, Updike; I've tied her up,' said Dr Perry. 'Nothing to worry about. Not like the time she broke that glass jug into her hand by drying it too hard. Your wife is a marvel,' said Dr Perry admiringly. 'If I sent in a bill every time I have to treat her for burns and cuts and bruises and putting drops in her eye without looking to see if the bottle is eye-lotion or embrocation, I'd be a rich man.'

'Not so rich as I'd be if I charged you for toning down your letters to the British Medical Association,' said Mr Updike.

'Oh, do be quiet, you two,' said Mrs Perry, 'and let Betty tell us what happened.'

'If you really want to know, I'll tell you,' said Mrs Updike, surprised and flattered by everyone's sympathetic interest. 'Well, you know what vinegar is. It's got a thing. It simply vanishes.'

'I didn't know,' said Mr Carton, 'and I still don't.'

'Yes, you do,' said Mrs Updike earnestly. 'It's so versatile, or whatever the word is when you all disappear on the slightest provocation, only because of turning the tap a shade more on.'

She crinkled her forehead and looked round, despairing of making herself understood, however clear her explanation.

Her husband suggested volatile.

'That's it,' said Mrs Updike, much relieved by finding herself understood. 'Well, I only turned the gas on a very little more and went to fetch a can that I'd left in the bathroom when I took some boiling water up there though why I can't remember, and when I got back to the kitchen, the vinegar was simply not there, except a very little of it and a lot of smoke, and I looked to see what had happened and I *immediately* understood exactly what people felt like in the Byzantine Empire.'

Satisfied that the whole affair was now explained, she drank her tea and took a hearty bite of cake.

'I have studied the Byzantine Empire in a modest way pretty thoroughly,' said Mr Carton, 'but have never yet felt quite sure how people felt. Gould you explain the sensation at all, Mrs Updike?'

'Well, you know the London Library,' said Mrs Updike, resuming her earnest air and voice.

Mr Carton said he did, and the number of new members who were foreigners and got in without an entrance fee and wore the staff out by asking questions and expecting to have their work done for them was a menace, besides forgetting to enter books and to return them. Also, he said angrily, the number of people in the Reading Room who apparently came there entirely to read tendentious weeklies. Thank God, he said, his father had taken out a Life Subscription for him when a Life Subscription *was* a Life Subscription and not on a sliding scale like an insurance policy. He then added that he was interrupting Mrs Updike.

'I know,' said Mrs Updike sympathetically. 'One always thinks of the thing one wants to say just when someone else is talking. I suppose it is because something they are saying reminds you of a thing you want to say, like suddenly remembering in the Litany that you can't remember what it was you meant to remember to remind yourself about. I've got a perfect thing about remembering things at the wrong moment.'

'My interruption was discourteous,' said Mr Carton, 'and,' he added proudly, 'ill timed. You will forgive me, Mrs Updike, and go on with what you were saying about the Byzantine Empire.'

'Well, I was reading a book from the London Library by a clergyman about the Byzantine Empire,' said Mrs Updike, who bore no ill-will, 'and when I say a clergyman I don't mean nowadays, but the kind of highly educated ones they kept in the middle of last century that wrote really learned books that are all crumbling away because of the leather bindings, and they used to blind people by putting some vinegar into a hot silver basin, I think, or was it some hot vinegar into an ordinary silver basin, which I must say always seemed waste to me, for why not just blind them without so much preparation. But when I looked into the saucepan to see what was happening, it was like History Come Alive,' said Mrs Updike, her delicate face lighting at the thought.

'To cut a long story short,' said Dr Perry, 'I came in by the back way to see if you and Betty had gone on to Assaye House, Updike, and found her choking and wiping her eyes over vinegar that had nearly all boiled away. And then she upset what was left and it went over her wrist, so I tied her up and we came along.'

By the time Mrs Updike's disquisition on the Byzantine Empire was finished her audience had lost touch with what they had been discussing, except for a vague remembrance of something about Shakespeare and Mr Adams at Hogglestock. As tea was now quite over, Mr Carton took his guests into the library, where they talked very comfortably round the fire and Miss Sparling quite forgot, a very rare occurrence with her, that she was a headmistress and thought she was just an ordinary person talking with other very nice, ordinary people. So had her grandfather's friends talked when not discussing clerical or theological subjects, and Miss Sparling thawed and opened in the easy friendly talk mixed with a little seriousness. Mr Oriel was pleased to see his kind old friend's handsome granddaughter so obviously enjoying herself and almost applauded aloud when she made a quick retort or threw the ball gracefully to Mr Carton, or Mr Updike, or Dr Perry, for the three other ladies, delighted to find the men for once doing their fair share of the talk and not having to be pushed and pulled along the road of conversation as dead weights, were having a little rest. Mrs Updike, it is true, made a few skirmishing entrances into the talk, but with such charming simplicity and goodwill that her interruptions, however imbecile, were always received with enthusiasm.

There seemed to be no particular reason for the party to end and it might have gone on even longer had not Mr Belton, rather to his wife's surprise, dropped in about six o'clock. Mr Carton, barely concealing his pride as a host, produced good sherry which gave his guests, unaccustomed now to such small luxuries, a delightful sense of wellbeing and content.

'It keeps on coming over,' said Mr Carton, 'but it's not the same thing. This is the real stuff. I bought it when the old Master of St Jude's died. He was a teetotaler himself, but he laid down good wine every year as one of his duties and gave excellent wines at his dinner parties. He was one of the old-fashioned clergymen who wore a loose white tie.'

'That reminds me,' said Mr Belton, who habitually used this phrase to introduce anything he wished to say, without attaching any particular meaning to it, 'that I met that fellow Adams at the Club today. I was next to him at lunch. I'd as soon dress like Punch as in what he calls tweeds – filthy light blue stuff like your coat and skirt, Lucy – but the fellow was polite enough. He thanked me for giving his daughter an interesting afternoon at the Garden House. "Well, Adams," I said, "your girl's no beauty, but she's got a good head on her shoulders. She tells me you're troubled with rats," I said.'

'Oh, Fred!' Mrs Belton exclaimed, for though she had quite understood that her husband's use of the opprobrious epithet filthy was applied solely to a blue suit when worn by Mr Adams and not in any sense to her own tailor-made, she did feel that in the matter of the rats he had perhaps gone too far.

'He said the rats were the deuce over at Hogglestock,' said Mr Belton, taking no notice of his wife, 'and he thinks the men put bits of food down to encourage them so that they can get some good ratting. They've all got terriers. So I said, "I'll give you a tip, Adams. Next time you have a holiday at the works, get old Bodger to come over from Starveacre Hatches. There isn't a rat that dares to show his whiskers on Pomfret's land, and Bodger and his father before him have always been the ratcatchers. Mind, you can't treat him as a workman," I said. "He's independent and the Bodgers have always been independent, since long before the Conquest. But if you treat him like a gentleman, he'll treat you like one."'

'I hope he will,' said Dr Perry. 'But Bodger has his own ideas of what a gentleman is. He wouldn't work for Sir Ogilvy Hibberd, you know, the man that tried to buy Pooker's Piece over near Skeynes and old Lord Pomfret got in first and gave the land to the National Trust. He told Hibberd he worked against rats and not for rats.'

'I'll have a word with Bodger myself,' said Mr Belton. 'He used to drink enough beer at the Park to drown all the rats he'd ever caught. Ah well, I suppose you've got no rats up there now, Miss Sparling.'

He heaved such a complacent sigh over the degeneracy of a ratless Harefield Park that Miss Sparling felt quite ashamed to disappoint him by telling him that they had had to put rat poison down in the old scullery and the laundry. This depressed Mr Belton a good deal, but he pulled himself together and said he supposed he'd have to get Bodger to come over.

'Don't you worry about it, Miss Sparling,' he said. 'I'll bring Bodger over one day. We'll make it a Saturday. Your girls will like to see a rat-hunt; cheer them up a bit. I often think living up at the Park must get you all down a bit. Nothing doing there now. Ah well!'

He heaved another sigh for times past, for horses and carriages in the stables, for motors at the door, for hunting, for hospitality, for balls, for all that was irrevocably gone. Miss Sparling felt so sorry for him that she felt it would be tactless to mention that far from living in an atmosphere of gloom, one of her chief preoccupations was to direct the bubbling good spirits of her young charges into suitable channels.

The party then began to dissipate itself. Miss Sparling apologized to her host for overstaying her welcome, but, she said, Miss Holly was having tea in the village and had promised to look in at Assaye House, so that they could walk up to the school together.

'I often think,' said Mr Oriel, who was the last to leave, 'of that long walk up the drive, Miss Sparling, and I do not like it for you. If at any time you wish for an escort, I beg you to look in at the Vicarage and it will be my pleasure to accompany you.

I do not like to think of my kind old friend's grandchild going through the park alone after dark.'

Miss Sparling, who had looked after herself for a great many years and was not at all nervous, was touched by the Vicar's kind anxiety for her and promised that if she ever felt at all nervous (which she was privately quite sure she wouldn't) she would certainly invoke his help. Mr Oriel looked extremely gratified.

'Well, Carton,' he said, 'I must be going. By the way, have you done with Slawkenbergius?' he added, in a voice so low that Miss Sparling could not hear.

'I'll keep him a little longer if you don't mind,' said Mr Carton. 'His scholarship may be out of date, but he throws more light on Fluvius Minucius than any later commentators. And you needn't worry,' he added, guessing that Mr Oriel feared he might betray the secret of the borrowing of the book from Canon Horbury and Mr Oriel's forgetting to return it.

Mr Oriel looked relieved, said good-bye and went away.

'Now,' said Mr Carton to Miss Sparling, 'we will go on drinking sherry till your Miss Holly comes,' and he poured out two more glasses.

'You said you had a book of my grandfather's, Mr Carton,' said Miss Sparling. 'Which is it?'

'An editio princeps of Slawkenbergius on Fluvius Minucius,' said Mr Carton, privately feeling that this was pearls before a very agreeable woman to put it mildly.

'I wonder – could it possibly be the one Grandpapa lost?' said Miss Sparling, evidently interested.

'I'll show it to you,' said Mr Carton. He tilted his chair backwards to the furthest angle of safety, reached out a long arm and took from a shelf a leather-bound volume which he handed lovingly to Miss Sparling.

'This looks like Grandpapa's,' said Miss Sparling, 'but he never would write his name in his books, and as he mostly picked them up second-hand they usually had other people's names in them. But the binding is in better condition.'

'It was in pretty poor condition when it came into my hands,' said Mr Carton, 'but I have been doctoring it. I made a corner in lanoline when I saw the war coming, and I keep all my old books well fed. There's nothing like lanoline, gently rubbed in with the finger-tips and the palm of the hand.'

'It might easily be Grandpapa's then,' said Miss Sparling, caressing the book in what Mr Carton thought an unusually intelligent way for a woman. 'He loved Fluvius Minucius. He often talked to me about him.'

'It's a queer thing,' said Mr Carton, who had a curious and unaccountable feeling that Miss Sparling had suddenly become a person he had never seen, a person who, if of the opposite sex, would not be amiss in a common-room, 'that no one has devoted much attention to Minucius since Slawkenbergius's time. Possibly your grandfather intended to work on him.'

'Indeed he did,' said Miss Sparling. 'We had made a great many notes. I used to be his secretary in the holidays.'

And that, Mr Carton thought, possibly accounts for your being so at home with an unknown late Latin poet.

'I can only recollect one serious contribution to the subject,' said Mr Carton, speaking as if to Mr Fanshawe of Paul's or any other intellectual equal. 'It was a long article in the *Journal of Fourth Century Latin Studies*. A most scholarly piece of writing. As you know, the contributions are only signed with initials. I meant to write to the Editor and ask who M.S. was. I shall do so now, if their papers haven't all been bombed and burnt.'

'I think,' said Miss Sparling, a little nervously, 'I could tell you.'

'I should be most grateful,' said Mr Carton.

'I'm very sorry, but they are mine,' said Miss Sparling in a small apologetic voice.

Mr Carton stared almost rudely.

'You mean that they are yours,' he said, half-incredulous.

'I really can't help it,' said Miss Sparling, taking no notice of his rather doubting attitude. 'Madeleine Sparling. My mother was Madeleine.'

'Then you wrote that article,' said Mr Carton, determined to get everything clear.

'Grandpapa was too ill to go on with his work,' said Miss Sparling, 'and he had always been so anxious to write about Minucius. He had been doing research on him for years, in Vienna and Lyons and Trèves and all sorts of places. He wasn't well off, but he used to take his holidays abroad with a bicycle till he got too old and spent them all in libraries and monasteries and places. When he died the Hosiers' Company were most thoughtful and gave me half a term off and I wrote the article. There is one more manuscript at Upsala, but I couldn't afford to go there and they wouldn't let me have a copy.'

'Beasts!' said Mr Carton. 'Devils! Neutrals! Do they call that being neutral?'

'It was long before the war,' said Miss Sparling.

'That makes no difference at all,' said Mr Carton vehemently. 'A nation that can refuse a copy of a manuscript to a real scholar is capable of anything.'

Miss Sparling, in spite of all her quiet assurance as the headmistress of a school belonging to one of the oldest and most important City Companies, was so overcome by the words 'a real scholar' that she sat blushing furiously and, if the truth must be told, gratified by Mr Carton's denunciation of the Swedes.

'I wish Canon Horbury could have read that article,' said Mr Carton. 'I can think of nothing that would give one greater pleasure than to know a relation one was fond of capable of a piece of such brilliant yet solid work. Miss Sparling, this is all most upsetting. I feel I have no right to work on Minucius at all. I was making use of your article to support some views of my own. You ought to be writing my book, not I.'

Miss Sparling, who had by now got herself in hand, thanked Mr Carton warmly for his praise and for his generous offer, but said she could never undertake such a work while she was at the Hosiers' Girls' Foundation School. It would not, she said, be fair to the Governors or the girls. And by the time she retired she might not be equal to the task, especially as there were very heavy years of reconstruction ahead when the school returned to London, or if, as the Hosiers had considered doing, the school were transferred permanently to the country and altogether reconstituted.

'It's your book, Mr Carton,' she said. 'But if I could be of any help, please let me know. Any knowledge that I have of my grandfather's methods is at your disposal, and I have some of his notebooks if you would care to see them. I think that is Miss Holly.'

And Miss Holly it was, quite Dickensishly rosy and warm with having walked briskly up the village street in the frosty evening, and quite ready for a glass of sherry. When she had drunk it, she pushed her hands violently into her gloves and told her employer they must be off.

'I shall be very busy for the next ten days,' said Miss Sparling, once more the headmistress, to her host. 'It is the beginning of term you know. But if you are still in Harefield and care to ring me up, we will talk over your book.'

Mr Carton said he would be going back to Oxford almost at once, but would write to her. Each wanted to say that it would be a privilege, nay an honour, to work with the other, but Miss Holly's capable prosaic presence was not conducive to the more exalted emotions, so they kept their own counsel, unless the word 'thank you,' escaping from each, with a slightly warmer handshake than usual, may be said to have expressed what was left unsaid.

'Remind me,' said Miss Sparling as she and her secretary walked in chill starlight up the drive, 'that we must fix the day for Shakespeare readings. Mr Oriel is very kindly coming up to the school. And as there are no bad exams this term and it is always a dull one with the blackout, I think we might manage to do a little acting. I must speak to Miss Head about it.'

Miss Holly gave it as her opinion that Miss Head would jump at it, but that Mademoiselle Michel would be furious, as she wanted her girls to do a scene from *L'Avare*.

'From that at least I can save them,' said Miss Sparling, 'and save the audience too. It has just occurred to me, Miss Holly, that if we can get the Shakespeare readings going, we might do one scene on Bobbin Day. A few of the Governors are very kindly coming, and if we have a little acting it will cut down the speeches. I must ask Miss Head what she thinks.'

It may here occur to the reader that Miss Holly may have felt some slight irritation at hearing Miss Head's name so frequently invoked when Miss Sparling had only to order a thing to be done and done it had to be. But Miss Holly, who was as near perfection as a secretary can be, combining devotion, competence and tact with a power of standing aside and watching her employer and the school as if it was all a puppet show, found it very suitable and showing a proper value of protocols and forms, that Miss

Head's feelings were to be consulted on a matter concerning English literature. Had the treat in question been an affair of logarithms and the binomial theorem (whatever that is, or to be perfectly open with our readers, whatever both of them are, for of logarithms no trace is left in our mind beyond a vague connection with a slide-rule and a conviction that you can do difficult sums by them if you happen to remember the formula like a parrot), Miss Holly would have bristled for her own right, just as Mademoiselle Michel would have bristled for hers in the case of *L'Avare*. So she applauded her employer's suggestion and said a little acting would do the girls a lot of good.

'I hope you had a nice tea-party,' she said, when the affair of the acting had been sufficiently discussed.

'Very nice indeed,' said Miss Sparling. 'Dear Mr Oriel is always so kind to me. Oh, remind me, Miss Holly, to look out my grandfather's notebooks. I think I put them in the big japanned box. Mr Carton thinks there may be some material there that will be of use to him, on Fluvius Minucius.'

'I remember docketing them for you,' said Miss Holly. 'I'll get them out whenever he wants them. Or perhaps you'd like to look through them first.'

Miss Sparling thought she would. Then they plunged up the darkness of the front steps, through the dimness of the front hall, into the big hall where a few of the girls who lived far away were already assembled, and the world of school engulfed them both.

8

Bobbin Day, so called by the statute of the Founders from the bobbin on which the yarn for weaving hose was wound, was an institution as old as the original Hosiers' Boys' School. It also, by a pretty conceit probably more appreciated in the sixteenth than the twentieth century, commemorated the first name of Robert Shuttleworth, Master of the Honourable Company of Hosiers from 1536 to 1539, during which time he managed to do so well for the Company in the way of abbey lands that they resolved to found a grammar school for boys whose parents lived within the bounds of St Hosius Without. The original purpose of the school had long been lost, and some forty years previously a girls' school had been endowed from some of the vast accumulated wealth of the Hosiers' Company, but some of the old names and customs still lingered, Bobbin Day being one. By statute this day was kept on the feast of St Hosius towards the end of February, a most inconvenient time, coming as it did right in the middle of the term. But, as Miss Sparling had remarked, the winter term was always a dull one and there were no exams that mattered and epidemics were usually flourishing, so the excitement of a visit from the Master and Wardens of the Hosiers' Company made a welcome break. Miss Sparling had for many years wished to diversify this ritual. Just as she had summoned her courage to approach the Governors with a suggestion of some changes, the war had broken out. The school had been evacuated to Barchester and with Miss Pettinger's star in the ascendant Miss Sparling had found it best to remain quiet. Now at last her own mistress again she decided to use Mr Oriel's dramatic reading class as a lever and let her girls act a scene from whatever play Mr Oriel and Miss Head chose.

Term was now begun and the school fell back into the routine of its own self-contained life. The weather was unseasonably warm and wet, the Rising overflowed the whole valley and almost came up to the arched bridge below Harefield, fields and paths were a quagmire. The village was swallowed up alive in a Fishbone Drive, a Pencil Stump Drive, three Bring and Buy Sales, at which the same hideous and useless articles changed hands till no one would buy them again, and a Mammoth Allied Gala Dance at the Nabob in aid of Comforts for the Barsetshire Regiment. Various young people came home on leave. Mrs Updike was always appearing with a son or a daughter whose not very much elder sister she could easily be. The Perry boys came down by one, two, and three and were perpetually being taken for each other. Mr Carton returned Slawkenbergius to Mr Oriel and disappeared into St Jude's. About half-way through February Elsa Belton rang up her parents to say that she and Captain Hornby were coming down that afternoon for two nights. As she did not say, and probably could not say, when they would be likely to arrive, Mrs Belton did not alter her plan for the afternoon, which was to go to tea with Mrs Hoare at Dowlah Cottage, a social duty which she performed about twice a year.

Dowlah Cottage as planned by its builder was quite a commodious little home with a wide hall running from front to back, four rooms downstairs and four up. When we say that the hall was wide, we speak in terms of measurement from wall to wall, but the impression made upon the visitor was one of plunging into a narrow underground passage, so was the hall darkened and crowded with the various pieces of furniture bequeathed to Mrs Hoare. A large black Jacobean dresser and two Cromwellian chairs flanked the front door, a great screen of Spanish leather and a fretwork Moorish arch blocked the bottom of the staircase, any light that came from the far end of the hall was obscured by a heavy velvet portière embroidered with embossed sunflowers, the work of an aunt of the late Mr Hoare's when under the influence of the aesthetic movement. Such wall space as was not taken up by Uncle Henry's Still Life (an interesting composition in thick varnish) and a number of china plates hung by wires, was occupied by a Dutch dresser displaying most of Uncle Andrew's brass.

Worming her way past a grandfather clock whose dial bore a sun and a moon both with faces, a seascape upon which a small sailing ship rocked to and fro with the oscillations of the pendulum and a kind of perpetual calendar which had not been in proper working order in the memory of man, Mrs Belton lifted the Indian curtain studded with little bits of looking-glass and went into the drawing-room, where Cousin Sarah Hoare's clock was ticking on the mantelpiece in an arrogant way and some of Aunt Janet's silver glittered on what Mrs Belton reverently recognized as an *étagère*. Here, rather to her annoyance she found Mrs Hunter. Not that she actively disliked that lady, with whom she was merely acquainted, but ever since the working party at Plassey House when Mrs Hunter had made herself so unpopular, she had been feeling guilty about her. Mrs Perry had been as good as her word and had not notified Mrs Hunter of any more working parties. But she had rashly asked her to a Bring and Buy Sale for Mixo-Lydians, where Mrs Hunter had not only brought some really good things but had bought generously, so that Mrs Perry, in council with Mrs Belton, had said she felt rather a beast and supposed she would have to ask her again some time. So far she had managed to evade any direct questioning, but a day of reckoning would undoubtedly come to one or another of the conspirators, and Mrs Belton felt uncomfortable.

Mrs Hunter however appeared perfectly at her ease, greeted Mrs Belton with affability and said how nice it was to feel the days drawing out though they always seemed to get shorter at about the time when they were getting longer, a profound truth with which Mrs Belton heartily concurred. The Rear-Admiral's wife then came in and Mrs Belton breathed again.

Mrs Hoare, who like most other people had now no help but a woman who came or didn't come three mornings a week, then went away to the kitchen to make the tea, so giving her guests an opportunity to look at her exquisite china tea-service, so delicate that it was almost transparent, a miraculous survival through generations of washing up. Mrs Hunter picked up a cup and looked at its mark.

'It must be foreign,' she said. 'I like good English china like those pretty Peasant Arts plates one used to get that chipped so easily. I always feel with foreign china you don't know what their hands were like. Especially from the Orient. Orientals have not our ideas of cleanliness and there are so many really dreadful diseases over there. I always feel with an Oriental cup that I might get leprosy.'

The Rear-Admiral's wife said she had visited the chief leper settlements when her husband was on the Indian station and could assure Mrs Hunter that she had not seen any sign of a china manufactory, besides which, she added, the missionaries of all faiths were doing remarkable work.

'Are you looking at my cups?' said Mrs Hoare, returning with a teapot and hot-water jug whose frail beauty nearly took Mrs Belton's breath away. 'They were left to my mother-in-law by a distant cousin who had travelled a great deal. They are from the Quin-Fang porcelain works, and the set is still quite whole. It is a very rare one.'

The Rear-Admiral's wife said she had visited the Quin-Fang works when her husband was on the China station, and had been much struck by the Jesuit orphanage and schools for exposed female children.

'I hear,' said Mrs Hunter, 'that there are to be great doings at Harefield Park, Mrs Belton.'

Mrs Belton's mind gave a jump, for she could not get quite used to her exile and imagined for a moment that she must have been arranging a sale, or an entertainment, or some other form of war activity and forgotten about it.

'Some acting, I understand,' said Mrs Hunter. 'My daily woman's niece works at the school and tells me they are getting up some scenes from *As You Like It*. So Shakespearean!'

The Rear-Admiral's wife said she and her husband had seen a most interesting performance of *As You Like It* by the girls in a missionary school in Zanzibar many years ago when her husband was on leave from Simonstown. It was of course, she added, a Church of England school.

'Of course it would be, with Shakespeare,' said Mrs Hunter thoughtfully.

'What I feel about Shakespeare,' said Mrs Hoare, 'is that in times like these he makes us all pull together. Duke's son, cook's son. England is a wonderful country.'

The majestic and universal nature of these remarks afflicted Mrs Belton with a kind of mental palsy, from which she was roused by Mrs Hunter's voice and at once knew that the worst had happened.

'Talking of all pulling together,' said Mrs Hunter to Mrs Belton, who said afterwards that she was quite certain the Rear-Admiral's wife would say 'All together, my hearties,' and lost consciousness from that point, 'talking of all pulling together, is our friend Mrs Perry still having her working parties? I have unfortunately been engaged nearly every Wednesday since our last meeting, but I am now quite free again. And how is that nice Mrs Updike?'

Mrs Belton, her mind searching wildly for means of escape, seeing the toils closing around her, said she thought so, but Wednesday was always such a difficult day that she never quite knew. She then enlarged obviously and idiotically on how well Mrs Updike was and how she had hurt her foot slightly by trying to tip the rain-water barrel in the garden over in order to clean out the mud and leaves that will always somehow get to the bottom.

'It was so kind of Mrs Perry to think of inviting me to her Mixo-Lydian Bring and Buy Sale,' said Mrs Hunter, 'and though I have very little sympathy for Mixo-Lydians, after all we are all Hitler's victims, are we not. And I want to interest her in a little drawing-room meeting in aid of Slavo-Lydia. A most interesting speaker has promised to come, a young Slavo-Lydian girl. She tells us such wonderful home truths and I am sure it does us good to hear them. She says we are doing nothing at all for the war and are a nation of land-grabbing money-grubbers. So true, alas.'

The Rear-Admiral's wife said, with a well-bred air of disgust, that she had once visited Slavo-Lydia with her husband when he was on leave from Malta, and found them quite uncivilized and very rude. The English chaplain at the hotel, she said, had told her that he wholly despaired of making any impression on a nation whose mind was entirely set on petty theft and blood feuds besides other unmentionable vices.

Mrs Belton looked anxiously at Mrs Hoare to see if she was going to control her own tea-party, but that lady, who did not believe in being idle, having switched on the lights, drawn the heavy window curtains and made all safe against hostile aircraft, had picked up a piece of old beadwork, evidently one of her legacies, and was carefully choosing tiny coloured glass beads from an inlaid ivory box (also a legacy) and repairing the ravages of time or a moth, and entirely absorbed in her work.

Most fortunately the noise of the front door being opened and shut as by someone coming in who had the entrée to the house was heard, and before either of the other ladies could draw her gun, in came Elsa, followed by Captain Hornby and, to Mrs Belton's intense delight, by Commander Belton.

Elsa, who had very nice manners, apologized to Mrs Hoare for bursting in without warning, but said they had caught an earlier train than they thought they could to Barchester and come out on one of the Pomfret estate lorries, and hearing from Wheeler that Mother was having tea with Mrs Hoare, they had come down to fetch her. Mrs Hoare, who had a weak spot for the young Beltons and had left them each a piece of Aunt Janet's silver in her will, was delighted to see Elsa and Freddy and offered them tea. But they had had some off a trolley at Barchester Central Station and declined. As always when any of her children came on leave, with Mrs Belton's joy in seeing them was mingled a chill apprehension. It was always possible that Elsa's hush-hush department might be sending her suddenly to Washington or to Algiers. It was always probable that Freddy's time at the Admiralty might have come to an end and that he was on leave before going to sea again. She tried to read in their faces if any such thing were about to happen, but could see nothing. Elsa looked even more handsome than usual, which seemed sinister to her mother's anxious mind; Freddy looked tired, which seemed to her equally full of portent. If she had been more interested in Captain Hornby it might have occurred to her that he had a slight air of exaltation from which she would have been quite capable of auguring the worst. But in a friend's drawing-room one cannot ask probing questions of one's children and their friends, so she talked to the Rear-Admiral's wife and smiled, and when Freddy joined them she told herself that she was very silly and there was nothing whatever to worry about. Mrs Hoare seized upon Captain Hornby as a fellow legatee and put him through a searching examination as to his aunt's portable property. This he bore very good-humouredly and said as everything was left to him he really hadn't bothered to look through it all, a point of view which profoundly shocked his hostess.

Mrs Hunter, one of those happy beings who cannot see a young man and a young woman in the same room without at once scenting romance, said she must not be a spoilsport and would get back to her own fireside. As she took her leave she issued a cordial invitation to everyone present to attend the drawing-room meeting for Slavo-Lydia. Mrs Belton and Mrs Hoare were profuse in untruthful protestations of how much they would like to and how terribly afraid they were they couldn't. The Rear-Admiral's wife, who had not lived at Admiralty House pretty well all over the world for nothing, said she could not go, but would send a guinea to the Merchant Navy instead, leaving Mrs Belton gasping with admiration and hoping to be strong-minded enough to do the same herself next time she was similarly approached. The Rear-Admiral's wife and Mrs Hunter then went away.

Mrs Belton was longing to get home and have her family to herself, but knowing how much Mrs Hoare enjoyed talking death duties with Captain Hornby did not like to hurry. And when a pause did come her kind nature would not let her leave until she had asked Mrs Hoare after the Pomfrets and their children. Not that she wanted news, or could not have got it by the simple method of ringing Lady Pomfret up for a talk, but she knew that Mrs Hoare still liked to feel herself a link between the Towers and humanity, so she did her duty and heard that everyone was well and dear Lord Pomfret very hard-worked as usual, and then they all escaped. But by this time it was so late that if everyone was to have baths they must hurry up, so she left all questionings till later, and went up to her room. Just as she had finished dressing, her daughter Elsa knocked at her door and came in, fiddled with her mother's dressing-table, looked at herself in the full-length mirror, made her face up a little more, opened her mouth and took a breath as if to speak, shut it again, stood awkwardly with one hip thrown out fingering the window curtains, and in general behaved in such an oafish and school-girlish way as surprised her mother a good deal. For Elsa had almost entirely escaped the awkward age and had been about so much and in such responsible positions since the beginning of the war that her mother sometimes felt a little abashed by her daughter's sophistication. It appeared to Mrs Belton that her child had something on her mind, though what it was she could not guess. Not bad news, she thought, or Elsa would not be look-ing so handsome. Perhaps, she then thought with a pang, good news from Elsa's point of view but not from her parents', being sent to Washington or Algiers. A cowardly wish not to hear the worst made her pretend not to notice. She put everything tidy as was her wont, turned out her dressing-table lights and went towards the door.

'Are you coming, darling?' she said, her hand on the switch of the other light.

'Oh, Mother—' said Elsa, and stopped short.

Mrs Belton waited, but Elsa had apparently said all she had to say.

'Come along, darling, you know Wheeler doesn't like to be kept waiting,' said Mrs Belton.

'I thought you'd like to know, Mother,' said Elsa reproachfully.

'I would,' said Mrs Belton, adding illogically, 'if I knew what it was.'

'It's Christopher,' said Elsa, speaking to the top shelf but one of the large tallboy. 'We wanted to tell you first.'

The mere mention of Captain Hornby's Christian name might not have made the matter clear to Mrs Belton, but her daughter's use of the word 'we' suddenly told her what had happened. Elsa, it is true, had had many men friends, and her mother was used to her free use of we and us in speaking of very temporary though amusing friendships. But it seemed to her that there was a faint caress in Elsa's voice, a lingering on the word, a kind of proud modesty as of a cat emerging from a hiding-place at the back of a shed, carrying her kittens one by one with proudly arched neck, which she had never heard before and which suddenly went to her heart from a creature so independent as her clever daughter.

'We didn't really mean to get engaged,' said Elsa, now addressing a pleasant but rather bad eighteenth-century engraving of Barchester cathedral which hung just to the right of her mother's head, 'but we somehow did. *Please* be pleased.'

Mrs Belton was indeed as pleased as her daughter could wish. We may add that her pleasedness was not because it was Captain Hornby, or even because Elsa would not now be an old maid which was one of her private fears, but because Elsa was, in spite of all her pretence of aloofness, so obviously happy and wanted her mother to share her happiness at once. She and Elsa had a quick, affectionate hug. Elsa asked her mother not to say anything about it at dinner as she and Christopher wanted to tell Father themselves and they hurried downstairs so that Wheeler might be pacified.

It is just possible that Mr Belton might have become aware of a kind of simmering atmosphere during dinner, but that he was full of the misdeeds of the Barsetshire War Agricultural Executive Committee who had as good as ordered him to put a field on the outskirts of his estate under wheat. It was well known to the whole county, he said, or at any rate to anyone who wasn't a conceited, jumped-up official who knew nothing about it, that Church Meadow would not carry wheat. His grandfather had tried it and his father had tried it and he wasn't going to try it himself. They only had to look, he said, at what that ass Norton had done, putting that bit of land along the Southbridge road under the plough. It was throwing money into the furrows. And Church Meadow lay right up against Norton's land, exactly the same soil. A set of damned fools was what they were, and what Church Meadow wanted was mangolds. Give it mangolds, he said, and it would show what it could do; but show it wheat and it turned sour at once. He couldn't account for it. Probably those scientific gentlemen, he said with elaborate sarcasm, from Whitehall knew Church Meadow better than he did. He dared to say they had tried wheat there themselves ever since 1853. Even a fool like Norton saw what a mistake he had made in trying wheat there.

'There's one thing though,' said Mr Belton, having pretty

well talked his subject dry through soup, fish, apple pie and a bit of cheese specially for himself, 'that man Adams isn't above learning from a man who knows the country. We were talking at the Club today and I told him it was monstrous to ask anyone to put Church Meadow under wheat and he quite agreed. I asked after that plain-faced girl of his. I think he was pleased. He said only a fool would think of trying to teach me my business. "I understand running my works, Mr Belton," he said – the fellow will mister me all the time, but I dare say that's the way now. I'm behind the times. In my young days we didn't mister. I said sir to my elders and Adams or whatever the fellow's name was to fellows of my own age. Not all this mistering. Where was I? Oh, yes – "I understand running my works," he said, "and you understand running your property." "Well," I said, "to be perfectly frank with you, Adams, I've lost money steadily on farming ever since I came into the place and so did my father before me. But these Whitehall meddlers," I said, "would lose double the amount." He was struck by that. "If I get meddlers in my place," he said, "I know how to deal with them." I didn't like to ask him what he meant. But it does one good to hear one of these tradesmen taking an intelligent interest in the land. Is that all we're having for dinner, Lucy?'

Mrs Belton, not mentioning that the sudden addition of a young woman and two young men to a rationed household meant a good deal of planning and did not produce legs of mutton or pounds of suet, said it was.

As they were moving to the drawing-room Commander Belton said that he had a nasty heel and was going to take it down to Dr Perry as the naval bloke didn't seem very intelligent about it. His mother, foreseeing blood-poisoning, delirium and death, at once begged to be allowed to see it. Her son said certainly not, and she wouldn't know what to do. Mrs Belton said to bathe it with boracic. Commander Belton laughed, kissed her, and left the house.

Now was the moment when Mrs Belton very much wished they had any port left; or to be truthful that she had thought of asking Wheeler to get one of the remaining half-dozen that they were keeping against emergencies, for a glass of port would have put her husband into a more mellow frame of mind. As it was he continued his battle with the Barsetshire W.A.E.C. in a really very boring way while Elsa and her mother exchanged long-suffering, conspiratorial glances. At last Elsa could wait no longer. Getting up from her chair she pulled a footstool beside Captain Hornby, sat down at his feet, took his hand to give herself courage and said,

'I'm sorry, Father, but we're engaged.'

Her father looked at her. In his experience of his children, at least of Elsa and Charles, they were quite ready to hold the hands of any friends they brought down. It wasn't the way he had gone on in his young days, but the children were all having a poor time now, a dull time, a hard time, and one couldn't interfere. If she and Hornby were going out – to the Nabob he supposed, all the young people did and perhaps they found it more amusing than sitting at home – let them go by all means.

'All right, dear,' he said, 'but I don't think you'll find much going on. They were out of everything but draught cider this afternoon, so Humble tells me.'

Elsa and her mother again exchanged glances in which exasperation got the upper hand of long-suffering.

'Father, do listen,' said Elsa. 'I'm engaged. To Christopher. I thought you'd like to know.'

'I wanted to tell you before, sir,' said Captain Hornby,

disentangling himself from his .betrothed and standing up, 'but Elsa wanted to wait till after dinner—'

'Because of Wheeler, Father,' said Elsa. 'She'd have been bound to hear and I don't want her to congratulate me. I mean,' she continued, rising to her feet, 'I want you and Mother to be pleased and then I don't mind *how* pleased other people are.'

She stopped, leaving an impression that she would have liked to go on. Captain Hornby had not looked at her, had made no sort of sign, yet Mrs Belton was as sure as she had ever been sure of anything that he had somehow checked her because he felt this was his business. And, as certainly, she knew that by the same occult means he had conveyed to her that she ought to get up and bring some touch of ceremonial into the proceeding.

'I know, sir,' said Captain Hornby, 'that Elsa is twenty-five, but all the same I would very much like your permission to marry her if you feel equal to it.'

Mr Belton, finding himself at a slight disadvantage in his armchair before the tall form of Captain Hornby, also got up and walked to the hearthrug. Mrs Belton had a fleeting impression, gathered from old novels, that he was going to marry the young couple out of hand, over the tongs or by consent before witnesses, but she knew this was nonsense and looked at her husband's face. What she saw reassured her.

'As you say, parents' permission isn't needed and what is more it doesn't seem to be wanted nowadays,' said Mr Belton, speaking with such gravity and honesty that his wife felt extremely proud of him. 'But you are doing the right thing in asking me. If you and Elsa know your own minds, I shall be perfectly content. We'll have a talk about business tomorrow.'

He then in a perfectly simple, unaffected way, held out his hand to Captain Hornby, who shook it.

'Now you'd better talk to my wife,' said Mr Belton, and returning to his chair he buried himself in the *Times* which he usually reserved for his evening treat.

'Elsa told me before dinner,' said Mrs Belton, looking an invitation to Captain Hornby to come and sit by her on the sofa. 'It's no good pretending that I'm not a little surprised, coming all of a sudden like this, but I am delighted. I am very glad indeed. It would have been quite dreadful if Elsa hadn't married.'

'Mother's nightmare,' said Elsa mockingly. Affectionately, but perhaps a trifle too mockingly Captain Hornby thought. Still, it was nice to see the friendly terms mother and daughter were on.

'I knew something must have happened,' said Mrs Belton, 'the minute you and Christopher came into Mrs Hoare's room, Elsa. You looked so happy that I thought you had got your transfer to Washington. And I expect Christopher looked happy too, but I was thinking about Freddy. Don't you think he looks tired, Captain Hornby.'

'I quite agree with you that Christopher three times in one breath would be excessive,' said Captain Hornby gravely. 'I shall go on calling you Mrs Belton if I may, but it means as much affection as if I said Mother or Mumsie or called you by your Christian name, which I will not do.'

Mrs Belton smiled, thinking that she and her son-in-law would get on very nicely, and also thinking, for we each have our small vanity, that though Elsa was in love with Captain Hornby and she wasn't, she would often catch his meaning before Elsa did. And this, she decided, was a thing to guard against.

'While I'm here, and as we are engaged,' said Captain Hornby, 'I think it would be a good thing to look at some of my aunt's jewels. The diamonds and the valuable stuff are at the bank of course, but she kept all her second-best trinkets here. I ought to have seen about it, but I haven't had much time since the valuers were here. Shall we look, Elsa?'

'I'm afraid the attic isn't blacked out,' said Elsa, 'and it's awfully cold up there. We'd better wait till tomorrow. You never told me they were there when we were listing the things.'

'It would have been a lie if I had,' said Captain Hornby, 'because they aren't up there. They are down here.'

Under the fascinated gaze of his future bride and future mother-in-law he got up, pulled a long serpent chain from his pocket and selected from it a small key. He then walked to the further end of the room where, over a blocked-up fireplace, a pleasant but undoubtedly spurious Watteau with a deeply carved frame ornamented the middle of a white panel. He put the little key in among the carved foliage, turned it, and the Watteau swung outwards on a hinge which the frame had concealed. Behind it was a small safe containing a number of leather cases.

Such loud exclamations broke from Mrs Belton and Elsa that Mr Belton looked up to see what was happening.

'Fred!' said his wife. 'It's a secret cupboard! And we never knew!'

'Secret cupboard?' said Mr Belton, looking towards the other end of the room. 'Just where you'd expect them to put one. Of course we never knew. It wouldn't have been a secret cupboard if we had. What's in it? Papers? If it had been port now, there'd have been some sense in it.'

'Some of my aunt's jewels, sir,' said Captain Hornby, making a clean sweep of the leather cases into a waste-paper basket and bringing them back to his audience. There was a large low stool with an embroidered seat before the fire. This he pulled up to Mrs Belton and seating himself beside her poured the boxes out of the basket.

The jewels were, as he said, only Mrs Ellangowan-Hornby's second-best, and a mixed lot, but there were some lovely things among them. At the worst they were gold lockets containing miniatures or hair and on being opened disclosed the name and date in fine writing on faded yellow paper, or massive brooches and bracelets set with cairngorms. At the best there were necklaces of Scotch pearls, sprays and rivières of old paste in delicate colours, fine Indian chains of pure gold, and some very lovely rings. One in particular, a glowing ruby surrounded by diamonds with a finely worked gold setting, roused Mrs Belton's admiration, for though she had not much jewellery she knew a good deal about it.

'It belonged to the beautiful Lady Ellangowan who died,' said Captain Hornby. 'It really ought to be at the bank with the good stuff.'

'May I try it on?' said Elsa.

She slipped it on to her engagement finger and held her hand this way and that to admire the depth of the ruby and the soft glitter of the diamonds.

'They are Brazilian diamonds. That's why they are so soft,' said Captain Hornby. 'Don't take it off unless you want to.'

'Do you mean to keep?' said Elsa.

'If you like it,' said Captain Hornby. 'It will do for an engagement ring until we can get a real one. Unless you mind someone else's ring who died.'

But Elsa, having a very reasonable mind in most things, said Lady Ellangowan would have been dead years ago by now anyway, even if she had lived to be a great-grandmother, and she did not want a shop ring in the least. And she again turned her hand this way and that to watch the glow in the heart of the ruby and the rainbow lights from the faceted diamonds.

'I may as well put all the rest back again,' said Captain Hornby.

'Or we could send it to be sold for the Red Cross,' said Elsa.

Mrs Belton, sometimes more sensitive to atmosphere than was pleasant to herself, felt a jar. To want to sell things for the benefit of the Red Cross was a laudable desire, and would be a generous one if the property were one's own. But Elsa was only just engaged, the jewellery was Captain Hornby's, not hers, and the 'we' which had reached Mrs Belton's ears a little earlier with a pretty, diffident pride, now suddenly had a possessive sound. It also sounded to her like an unnecessary slight on old Mrs Ellangowan-Hornby's trinkets, many of which might have had a family value for the Admiral's widow and though not in modern taste were not without a heavy handsomeness suitable to their period.

Captain Hornby may or may not have heard what Elsa said. In either case he took no notice and began storing the scattered brooches and rings and chains of gold and pearls in their cases again. The last case, a square box of faded red morocco leather, had contained a few odds and ends. A little crystal vinaigrette mounted in pale gold with a pierced design; a heavy clasp of some oriental enamel work; a clumsy true lovers' knot set with uninteresting turquoises and a couple of lockets.

'I hadn't looked at those,' said Elsa. 'Oh, Mother! I never knew people really had lockets like that, except in Dickens!'

She showed her mother a gold locket surrounded with seed pearls, containing the portrait of one human eye. Mrs Belton was equally overcome by the masterpiece and congratulated Captain Hornby warmly.

'By Jove, it is a remarkable affair,' said Captain Hornby thoughtfully. 'I shall give it to Mrs Hoare. She was always very nice to my aunt and the old lady would have liked her to have something.'

Mrs Belton applauded the idea, knowing that with Mrs Hoare the one-eyed locket would have a very happy and appreciative home.

'Oh, but I *must* have that one, Christopher,' said Elsa. 'It's the pick of the secret cupboard. Mrs Hoare can have the little snuff-box with the amethyst and silver thistle on it. She'd like it just as much.'

Captain Hornby said he thought not, and put the locket into his pocket. He then put the cases away in the secret cupboard and locked it, Elsa standing by him to see where the keyhole was concealed.

'I do think you might have given Mrs Hoare the snuff-box, Christopher,' she said. 'I adored that eye.'

'And I adore you,' said Captain Hornby, looking at her with deep affection. 'But the eye goes to Mrs Hoare.'

Elsa did not think it worth insisting. Her vanity felt a little hurt because Christopher had not at once given it to her, but as she looked up at him her being suddenly melted with pure love and she smiled enchantingly and stroked his coat sleeve, remarking that she simply could not help loving him.

And a very delightful, lover-like pair they made, thought Commander Belton coming in from the Perrys; and he went and sat down by his mother. Then Mr Belton emerged from the *Times*, kissed his daughter, said 'Tomorrow at half-past nine, Hornby, if that suits you,' and went off to his library.

'Did you know, darling, that Elsa and Captain Hornby were engaged?' said Mrs Belton to her elder son. 'And what did Dr Perry say about your heel? Is it bad?'

'In answer to your esteemed query No. 1, I hadn't been

told in so many words, but it was sticking out for yards,' said Commander Belton. 'And in answer to No. 2, Perry has tied me up nicely and given me some paint for it and all is well.'

'Are you pleased?' said Elsa coming to her brother.

'As pleased as the very dickens,' said her brother. 'It couldn't be nicer, Christopher, and I'll give you any of my service coupons you want to get married on. More I cannot do.'

He then hugged his sister and shook hands with his brother officer.

Mrs Belton felt the best thing she could do was to go to bed and leave the young people together, but Captain Hornby said if he might take the liberty of going to bed he would be very grateful, as he had been fire-watching for two nights to oblige some friends who were going to do his shift while he was at Harefield. Elsa said she was sleepy too, so they went off, and Mrs Belton was left alone with her son.

'Has it occurred to you, darling,' said Commander Belton when his mother had exhausted her raptures over the newly engaged couple, 'that Elsa is going to be extremely rich?'

'Dear me!' said Mrs Belton anxiously. 'No; it hadn't. Oh dear, I do hope it will be all right.'

'Of course it will,' said her son laughing at her. 'Christopher is a jolly good fellow and Elsa is a lucky girl. But isn't it like things that Elsa is marrying a fortune while poor Harefield is practically in the hands of the Jews? Poor Harefield.'

'It would be lovely,' said his mother, at once beginning to matchmake for Harefield, 'if you married a charming girl with a lot of money, darling, and then after the war you could live at the Park and your father and I could retire for good. When the lease of Arcot House is up, I think you and your father ought to make it into a permanent Dower House, by Act of Parliament, only even then you'd have to make a law to have slavery, or no one would ever be able to live here, on account of servants.'

'Jolly good thing, slavery,' said Commander Belton. 'The one drawback is that you have to support them in log cabins till they die and all their children and grandchildren. Still, if I get my Act of Parliament properly drawn up, I dare say I can get the country to pay for my old retainers.'

'It would be almost simpler to get it to pay for your father and mother,' said Mrs Belton, 'and their children and grandchildren. I do hope Elsa and Christopher will be sensible and have a nice family. I can't ever be a young grandmother,' she said with slight annoyance, 'owing to having you first, because boys always set one back in the grandmothers' world. And Elsa is nearly as bad, not getting married till she is twenty-five, that is if they get married before her next birthday. And Charles of course is hopeless.'

Commander Belton told his mother to cheer up. He was sure Elsa would provide her with a nice nurseryful of grandchildren and as for Charles, he said, half the young men he knew, the really young men, were marrying like anything and younger than Charles were happy fathers made.

'Still, Elsa's children won't help Harefield Park,' said Mrs Belton, 'and Charles's would only be a second string. Couldn't you possibly find a very nice heiress, darling? I would love her, even if it was Miss Swartz. And your father would be so pleased.'

Commander Belton said he would very much like to please his father, and his mother too, but he hadn't any heiress in view at the moment.

'You'll get over this matrimonial fever in a day or two, darling,' he said. 'It's just the sight of Elsa and Christopher. And I must say they look very happy and quite satisfactorily in love.'

Did his mother's apprehension catch a note in his voice as of one who was seeing a promised land which he could not enter?

'I do wish you had a *very* nice wife, Freddy,' she said. 'If I could find you one I would. And I wouldn't really mind if she didn't like me so long as she liked you.'

'Well, I haven't,' said Commander Belton patiently. 'And now leave my affairs alone, darling, and let us concentrate on Elsa's. I suppose she will have to be married in a white tablecloth with a veil of anti-splinter net. That's what we are coming to.'

'But I do wish there were someone for you,' said Mrs Belton, rather exasperatingly. 'Do you think you ever could find anyone?'

'Oh, Mother!' said her son, not exactly with impatience, but with a sudden look and voice as if everything were drab and hopeless beyond bearing.

His mother, to whom he had always been the most indulgent of sons, felt a chill at her heart for which she knew no cause.

'There is someone. There was someone,' said Commander Belton, looking towards the fire, his hands clasped round his knee.

'I think you would have liked her,' said Commander Belton. 'She was a Wren. Her father is an admiral. She was killed in an air raid on the East Coast in the summer.'

'Perhaps I will fall in love again,' said Commander Belton. 'It doesn't seem likely just at present, but one never knows. All sorts of things happen. And don't worry about me.'

To his mother's ears the last words also held the meaning, Please don't speak of this; I have had enough. Now she knew why Freddy looked so tired. He had kept his sorrow quiet within him. There seemed to be nothing she could do or say that would not be sentimental or jarring, but she could bear the weight of silence no longer, so she began to tidy the cushions and chair covers as she always did before going to bed.

'Poor Mamma,' said Commander Belton, getting up and giving his mother a hug with one arm. 'But it's all over now. Only don't tell Father or Elsa or anyone. They would only be sorry and ask questions.'

Mrs Belton promised, much relieved to find that her son had not suddenly gone grey, or become an old man in five minutes, or lost all his teeth, which varieties of shock had naturally occurred to her mind at once.

'Are you sure your heel is all right, darling?' she asked earnestly before going upstairs.

Commander Belton laughed and said it was doing splendidly. And they both knew that what Mrs Belton was really asking was whether her son's life was blighted for ever and that what her son was telling her was that he would rest a little while, then rise and fight again. So she went to bed, not happy it is true, but with a burden lifted, and the thought of Elsa to keep her mind busy. Commander Belton lit his pipe and went to his father in the library where they discussed county and estate matters and the question of some kind of settlement for Elsa.

On the following day Mr Belton and Captain Hornby met at half-past nine in the library, with Commander Belton as a kind of prisoner's friend, though he was never quite sure which side he was on. Mr Belton was clear enough about his own financial position and what he could do for Elsa which was ten thousand pounds, part of a trust fund established by his father for the benefit of his grandchildren. But the ten thousand pounds was mostly on paper and what she would really have to depend on was her three hundred pounds a year left to her by a wealthy Thorne relative, and everyone knew, said Mr Belton gloomily, what three hundred a year meant now.

Captain Hornby now took the field and said that owing to

no fault of his own he was extremely well off, even with income tax and super tax, and what he would like to do was to make a settlement upon Elsa and her children which would leave her quite independent. He then named a sum so staggering that Mr Belton began to protest.

'Calm yourself, Father,' said Commander Belton. 'It's only half that really, you know. As a matter of fact less than half.'

Cheered by this thought, Mr Belton agreed that this would be a possible basis for their respective lawyers to work on and it was decided that Mr Updike should be called into council and arrange with Captain Hornby's lawyers in London.

'And when do you young people think of getting married?' said Mr Belton rather to his future son-in-law's amusement, who did not think of himself as a young person. He answered that Elsa must decide, that he would of course like it to be soon, as his term at the Admiralty would be up in April and he didn't know where he might be sent.

'Well, that's that,' said Mr Belton, having comfortably shuffled all his responsibilities on to Mr Updike, as his father had done with Mr Updike's father and so back to the Nabob and the Updike of his day. 'I wish Freddy here would get married. A nice girl with some money. He ought to think of the place.'

Commander Belton said he would do his best and then there was a consultation about a notice in the *Times*, and perhaps the *Telegraph*, and various other bits of business and Mr Belton went off to see Humble about some timber, taking his son with him.

Captain Hornby went in search of Elsa, whom he had not seen for at least an hour, and found her hard at work in the garden.

'And what are those?' said Captain Hornby, pointing to the strong clusters of green shoots among which Elsa was weeding.

'Welsh onions,' said Elsa, tearing up handfuls of groundsel.

'Now I know why the Welsh Guards' badge looks like that,' said Captain Hornby examining the plants with interest. 'I knew leeks were the Welsh national flower but the thing the Guards have isn't a bit like a leek. Welsh onions. How interesting gardening is.'

'What *is* interesting,' said Elsa, still tearing at the groundsel, 'is that very venerable old men with beards used to make their living by selling this foul stuff at a penny a bunch in London for people's canaries. Yet I never see a bird eating it in the garden. They only eat important things like all the peas that have just been planted in a drill, or any seedlings that one values.'

Captain Hornby said he expected if she put some canaries in the garden they would eat her groundsel, and would Elsa like to wash her hands and come for a walk with him.

'Though I must say I adore you just as much when they are dirty,' he said.

So Elsa washed her hands and in Captain Hornby's company stepped down from Arcot House into the street.

'Christopher,' she said, as they turned towards the lower end of the town, 'shall we tell everyone we are engaged, or have it a secret?'

Captain Hornby said they probably both looked so idiotic that anyone could tell with half an eye what was the matter, but as he only had two days at Harefield, he would rather like to be incog. as it were, as if people knew they would undoubtedly want to talk about it and take up one's time. They would know quite soon enough, he added, if it was going to be in the *Times*; and apparently in the *Telegraph* too, as Mr Belton seemed to want it. Elsa said her father always used to take in the *Morning Post* and when the *Telegraph* absorbed it, he still clung to its shadow.

Besides, she said, quite an enormous number of people read the *Telegraph*, because it was so difficult to get the *Times*.

'Where shall we go?' said Elsa. 'Let's go into the park and see where the trees are being cut.'

'I have to go to Dowlah Cottage first,' said Captain Hornby, 'to give Mrs Hoare the locket. Then I will go wherever you like. Do you think anyone would notice if I stopped and kissed you?'

Elsa said she was quite certain they would all notice like anything, especially Mrs Hunter whom she saw bearing down upon them. Captain Hornby at once tacked to the opposite side of the street, cruised along in front of the newsagent and stationer's shop and the old furniture shop, put his helm hard over and had Elsa safely back on their own side of the road again before Mrs Hunter could turn her prow for a stern chase. This masterly piece of manoeuvring brought them up under the lee of Dowlah Cottage, so they went in, while Mrs Hunter went on her way morally certain that there was something between Miss Belton and that good-looking naval man.

Mrs Hoare was polishing some of Aunt Janet's silver in wash-leather gloves and delighted to see them. Elsa said she hoped they hadn't come at an inconvenient time, but Captain Hornby was staying with them for a day or two and particularly wanted to see her.

'Your poor aunt,' said Mrs Hoare. 'I used to go and read to her sometimes when her eyes were so bad – you know I used to read to Cousin Harriet at Morecambe for five or six hours every day. It was wonderful what pleasure it gave her; she didn't mind what I read so long as it was something. But now she has a wireless and keeps it on all the time. I think the wireless is quite wonderful for those who like something they needn't listen to.'

Captain Hornby said he knew his aunt had much appreciated

Mrs Hoare's kindness. She had, he said, left all her property to him (at which Mrs Hoare's eyes glistened, not in a predatory way, but with truly unselfish joy at the thought of legacies in general), but he knew that he would be doing what she would have wished if he asked Mrs Hoare to accept a small memento of her old friend, and taking a box from his pocket gave it to his hostess.

At the sight of the locket Mrs Hoare's joy and gratitude were unbounded.

'It is a very curious thing, Captain Hornby,' she said, 'that though there are dozens of these eye lockets about, a left eye is extremely rare. The artist who did most of them – for they are nearly all dated within the same thirty years or so – was quite celebrated. Glass was his name. His rivals called him Eye Glass, but he is better known as Monocle Glass from his habit of painting these single-eye lockets. I shall value this very much indeed.'

She went to a glass-topped table, opened its top and laid the locket on the faded velvet lining, among a varied collection of coins, medals and snuff-boxes.

'And now,' she said, 'tell me about yourself, Elsa. Dear Lady Pomfret came in to see me late yesterday and asked after you all and I said I had seen you for a moment in the afternoon, but did not know what you were doing.'

Elsa said she was still in her hush-hush job and told Mrs Hoare one or two unimportant details, as she knew her hostess dearly liked to feel in the know. But all the time, instead of the rapt attention that she usually received, she was conscious that Mrs Hoare could bear it no longer.

'Is that a new ring you have, Elsa?' she said. 'I've never seen it before.'

To her horror Elsa felt herself blushing, but her back was to the window and the room never very light owing to the amount of furniture and hangings. There were obviously only two courses open to her; one was to tell a lie, the other to say she and Captain Hornby were engaged. The Navy then came to her rescue.

'That ring belonged to my aunt, Mrs Hoare,' he said. 'It is a little legacy to Elsa. Do you admire it?'

This appeal to his hostess's connoisseurship gratified her and she begged to be allowed to examine it. Elsa took it off and gave it to Mrs Hoare who said it must be at least a hundred and fifty years old and she had seldom seen a more handsome setting, even, she added, among the late Lady Pomfret's jewels.

'It is so sad,' she continued, 'to think of that beautiful jewellery all in the bank. And even when things are settled again, I doubt whether Lady Pomfret will wear them. Diamonds are not every-one's jewels. You could wear them, Elsa. All my late husband's great-aunt Hoare's diamonds go to Gladys, but in Australia, with four little girls, what use are they to her?'

Elsa resumed her property, thankful that Mrs Hoare had been more interested in diamonds than in any implications of the ring, and said they must be going.

'By the way, Captain Hornby,' said Mrs Hoare as she took them into the hall, 'I know you like pictures. I want you to look at Uncle Henry's still life.'

Opening the front door wide, she let the daylight shine on the dark sepia mass touched up with a little dark red and shining with varnish which represented the late Uncle Henry's bequest. Captain Hornby looked at it.

'What it wants is cleaning,' he said. 'Have you any rainwater, Mrs Hoare?'

His hostess looked at him as if she politely thought he was mad.

'And some good soap flakes and some cotton wool?' Captain Hornby continued.

'You don't want to wash it, Captain Hornby!' said Mrs Hoare. 'Uncle Henry valued it very much and I wouldn't like any harm to come to it. Oughtn't it to go to a good picture restorer?'

'Just as you like,' said Captain Hornby. 'He'll charge you a stiff price and it might be bombed in London, or lost on the railway.'

'That Uncle Henry would not have liked,' said Mrs Hoare. 'Well, just a tiny corner of it then, to see if the paint runs.'

She went off to the kitchen in a good deal of excitement.

'Lord! what a picture!' said Captain Hornby, taking down the legacy. 'It might be a Titian or it might be a public-house sign. Impossible to guess with all this muck on it. Shut the front door, darling.'

'But, Christopher, our walk,' said Elsa. 'I want you to see where they are felling the timber.'

'All in good time, my girl,' said her betrothed. 'Now, we'll take this thing into the kitchen if there's any light there. One can't see a thing in Mrs Hoare's junk-shop. Down the passage? Right!'

Luckily the kitchen, looking on to the garden, was a cheerful little room and the pale February sun was beginning to slant in at the window. To Mrs Hoare's scandal, yet pleasurable excitement, Captain Hornby pulled a wooden chair to the light, stood the picture on it and took off his coat.

'Will you warm the water slightly, Mrs Hoare,' he said, 'and stir the soap flakes nicely. Splendid. Now the cotton wool. And another basin of clean water without any soap in it.'

Issuing these orders as from his quarter-deck, Captain Hornby began to wash Uncle Henry's picture with a delicacy of touch which his hostess much admired, being herself an adept handler of old and valuable things. Even Elsa, though annoyed at the postponement of her walk, could not help being struck by his quick, sure movements. Pad after pad of cotton wool brought away the encrusted dirt of many years. Bits of green and pink began to show, a touch of blue, a high light. The excitement grew, reaching its height when, after a careful washing of one part of the canvas, the head of an elderly man with a very repulsive expression stood clearly revealed.

'By Nelson and Bronte!' exclaimed Captain Hornby. 'It's going to be Susanna and the Elders.'

'Oh dear!' said Mrs Hoare. 'Do you think you'd better go on?'

Captain Hornby, swabbing away gently and industriously, said he felt certain that the relative who had bequeathed this picture would wish it to be properly appreciated. 'But Susanna seems to have had a scalding bath,' he observed, as quantities of red came into view. 'I'm afraid you are going to be disappointed, Mrs Hoare.'

After another breathless twenty minutes he had excavated a dish of boiled lobsters, a dead hare, a pewter flagon, half a loaf of bread, a large bunch of grapes and a cheese with a remarkably lifelike grub upon it; the whole surveyed by a bust of (apparently) Socrates.

'Your uncle was perfectly right, Mrs Hoare,' he said, standing up and stretching himself. 'A still life it is.'

Mrs Hoare was profuse in admiration and thanks. The picture was rehung, looked at as through a spy-glass from the foot of the stairs, squinted at from close quarters, and pronounced a masterpiece.

'And now,' said Captain Hornby as they left Dowlah Cottage, 'let us see the timber. It's not twelve yet.'

Elsa thought of standing on her dignity after being slighted for an old picture, but Captain Hornby appeared so entirely unconscious of any difference in her that she relapsed into a state of adoration which suited her very well. Captain Hornby's visits to his aunt had been, owing to his professional duties, at long intervals and seldom for more than a few days at a time and during the war naturally even less frequent, so that he knew little of Harefield Park and the surrounding country. He therefore listened with great interest to all Elsa told him as they walked across the park, remembering here an early ride to cubbing, here a nursery picnic with Freddy and Charles, there the stile where small Charles had fallen in the mud owing to disobeying nurse, or the field where Freddy and his puppy had chased the cows and been soundly thrashed by the justly irate cowman. After crossing the slope of the park they entered a pillared beech wood, prettily dappled by the sun through the bare branches. From hard by came the whine of a saw.

'That's the little saw mill that the tractor works,' said Elsa. 'I can't bear to see the trees being cut down. I expect Father is there.'

'They need thinning badly,' said Captain Hornby. 'There is a lot to be learned about forestry down here. In Scotland we are ahead of you.'

'I always forget about the Scotch part of you,' said Elsa. 'I suppose it is because I only see you in London or here.'

'I hope you'll love Scotland as much as I do,' said Captain Hornby. 'Aberdeathly is rather a grim place, but it has been taken over by a hospital, pepper-pot turrets and all. After the war I'd like to make some alterations in the factor's house and we could live there very comfortably. It's on the slopes of Ben Gaunt, just above Loch Gloom, and about ten miles by road from Inverdreary where the train stops twice a week. But if one goes by boat to Auchsteer one can get the express.'

All this was new to Elsa, but coming as she did of a land-owning family whose daughters were brought up to marry into other land-owning families and strike root firmly in new soil, the prospect sounded inviting to her, and she listened with eager attention to what her betrothed had to say.

The noise of the saw was by now deafening and they soon came upon the woodcutters' encampment with Mr Belton, a famous axeman in the county, helping to cut down a beech. The axe work was just over, wedges had been driven, and, as they watched, the tall tree began to slant, gathered momentum and fell through a wide arc crashing to the ground, its fall accompanied by the indignant shriek of birds, the crackling of broken branches and an undercurrent of scuttling in the bushes. The saw with a last falling whine came to rest and the men gathered for their midday meal. Mr Belton came up to them, axe in hand.

'It's heartbreaking to see these trees go,' he said. 'All my father's and my grandfather's planting. One of the worst things this war has done. Look at them. Government marks everywhere.'

Captain Hornby sympathized and encouraged his future father-in-law to talk, not saying very much himself, but what he said much to the point. Elsa listened and was rather amused to hear her father being gradually forced to admit that the woods needed thinning, that he was getting a decent price for the timber, that his ancestors' trees could not be expected to last for ever.

'Up at Aberdeathly we have been growing spruce and pine for the market for years,' said Captain Hornby, 'and replanting in sequence. That is on the Loch Gloom side of course. Down towards Inverdreary it is mostly bog and some good shooting. I'd like to drain a bit later on and get some good farmers in.'

At these words Mr Belton nearly fell on Captain Hornby's

neck, for he had in old days shared some fishing on the Dreary Water with friends and knew every turn of the river. Elsa thought, rather rebelliously, that it was to her that Captain Hornby was engaged and not to her father, but kept this thought to herself for the time being.

They walked together by the other edge of the wood, out into the grassland behind Harefield Park and skirted the house. Some girls were knocking a hockey-ball about before lunch on the playing-field. As they passed behind the goal posts the goalkeeper, shivering in her netted cage, turned to look at them. So many expressions of surprise, ecstasy, doubt and deep chagrin passed in turn across her unattractive face that Elsa could hardly believe her eyes.

'Aren't you Heather Adams?' she said.

The girl said sulkily that she was. A shout from the players made her turn; the ball rushed into the goal. A bell sounded from the Park, and the girls began to hurry towards their dinner.

'There's Freddy coming to meet us,' said Elsa, and Commander Belton, who had been to see Mr Oriel, came up the hill, cutting across the ploughland.

Heather Adams, who with the eyes of a secret passion had espied him from afar, paused and began to unbuckle her hockey pads, an attitude which showed off her clumsy figure and ugly legs to the very worst advantage.

'Have you had a nice game?' said Commander Belton kindly.

Heather looked up, her unhealthy face mottled by stooping, and muttered yes.

'You are Miss Adams, aren't you?' said Commander Belton, 'you came to see the Garden House and we had a dance together last term. We must have another some day.'

He passed on and joined his family and they all went back

to Arcot House by the field path. Heather stood up, wished she were dead and went indoors. But under the revivifying influence of fish pie and steamed pudding she thought better of things. True, she had experienced, not for the first time, a terrible shock in thinking it was Commander Belton when it was really only somebody else. But as if to console her, He had appeared and had said they must dance together again. This exquisite thought caused her to be so disagreeable that Miss Ferdinand put some bread in each cheek and scowled hideously, to imitate Heather's general demeanour, for which Miss Head, who was in charge of that table, spoke to her severely.

The rest of the time passed but too quickly. Elsa, in spite of her happiness, was depressed again by the sight of Harefield Park in alien hands.

'I loathe it, Christopher,' she said as they parted for the night. 'I can't bear to think of Harefield full of dreadful girls and Father not having his home. Father said you were making a settlement on me which sounds too wonderful, but I do wish we could spend the money on Harefield. Oh, Christopher, *do*.'

Captain Hornby said kindly but very firmly that Harefield was not his property, that it would be highly improper for him to interfere with what was Mr Belton's and Freddy's business and that he hoped Wheeler would call him punctually as they must get that early bus to Nutfield. He then embraced his betrothed in a delightfully suffocating way and went to bed.

Elsa also went to bed, her heart in a whirl of love, her head irritated that Christopher could be so hard and cold to her appeal. If she had listened to her head a little more carefully it might have found time to tell her that Captain Hornby, though a very generous man, was extremely just, and was not used to taking orders from his subordinates. But instead of listening to it she began to count the slights she had endured; her plan of giving Mrs Ellangowan-Hornby's old trinkets to the Red Cross deliberately ignored, her plea for the eye locket rejected, her walk postponed in favour of Mrs Hoare's still life, her appeal for the rescue of the estate rejected in a way that made her feel like a naughty schoolgirl. In fact Christopher had been so cold, unsympathetic and beastly that she thought of breaking off her engagement. But this very thought brought with it such an agony of love that she nearly got up to bang on his door and ask him if he were alive; for it would serve her right if he were dead. Calmer counsels, however, prevailed, and she composed herself to slumber. She had meant to sleep all night long with her ring pressed to her lips, but this was so uncomfortable and made her elbow feel so cold that she compromised by holding her left hand very tightly in her right hand till she slid into unconsciousness.

9

Mr Oriel's Shakespeare readings had succeeded beyond his hopes. Miss Head, at first faintly resentful of his intrusion, had been so captivated by his elderly charm that of her own accord she suggested a second evening in the week. So on Tuesdays and Thursdays Mr Oriel walked up to the school, often having tea with Miss Sparling first in her pavilion, and took his class through *As You Like It*. His one stipulation was that no girl should come unless she wished, but such was the enthusiasm in the Fifths and Sixths (for to these forms the treat was limited) that extra chairs had to be brought in from the Lower Second. The readings rapidly turned into a dramatic class. Saturday was added to the Shakespeare evenings and Mr Oriel and various girls in turn ranted, raved, joked and melted on an impromptu stage at one end of the big room. Mr Oriel's Jacques was a rousing success and it was with genuine sorrow that he faced the fact that he could not very well act in the play himself on Bobbin Day.

When we say the play, this was of course impossible in its entirety, but Mr Oriel and Mr Carton, who had surprised everyone by showing an interest in the readings and had attended several of them before Oxford went up, and on Saturdays, which he spent more often at Assaye House than was his usual custom in the winter, had by snipping, cutting and contriving made a very potted version of such part of the action as takes place in the Forest of Arden, with Miss Head holding a watching brief for the Rev. Mr Bowdler.

Rosalind, we need hardly say, was to be played by Miss Ferdinand who in her enthusiasm besought the play-potters so to arrange matters that she could double the part with Orlando, which was unfortunately found to be impracticable. The head prefect, who spoke well and had no sense of humour, was happy to do Jacques because she had 'done' *As You Like It* for the School Certificate the previous summer and had written an essay on 'Jacques: do we in this character have a clue to Shakespeare, the Thinker?' At Mr Oriel's earnest desire Heather Adams was cast for Audrey with most of her lines excised, and the other parts found suitable interpreters, the Captain of Hockey, whom no one had ever suspected of dramatic leanings, suddenly coming out strong as Touchstone. Perhaps the happiest actresses, if we except Miss Ferdinand who knew everyone's part by heart and rather hoped that they would all go down with flu on the day, so that she could give a one-man show doing every part in turn, were two girls from the Lower Fifth with pretty voices who were chosen to be the two pages and sing, and went about giving life-like imitations of the hawking and spitting which are mentioned in their script.

Miss Sparling had come to look forward to Tuesdays, Thursdays and Saturdays with very pleasurable anticipation, nay certainty, that she would have a talk with Mr Oriel about her grandfather or a talk with Mr Carton about Fluvius Minucius, a subject which was apt to boil over on to a variety of subjects quite unconnected with that prolix though elegant author.

Gradually Miss Sparling found herself telling Mr Carton about her own life, her happy childhood, the death of both parents, her kind grandfather and the work they did together, her fight to get through college on scholarships, her years as an assistant mistress and the great blow of her grandfather's death. And after that the war and her struggles to keep her evacuated school in some kind of order.

'I can't tell you how difficult it was for the first year,' said Miss Sparling to Mr Carton one Saturday, after they had spent the afternoon with Canon Horbury's notebooks. 'I was billeted with Miss Pettinger, so I suppose I was very lucky.'

'You weren't,' said Mr Carton angrily. 'Good God, when I think of that woman and her insufferable ignorance and insolence on the Barchester Classical Association Committee, I could burst. What you must have suffered under her roof no one will ever know. What you told me about her attitude to your use of the telephone is enough to damn her eternally.' From which it will appear that Mr Carton and Miss Sparling had become very confidential.

'Still I did have bed and breakfast – and supper if one can call it that,' said Miss Sparling. 'But it was my girls and my mistresses that were so badly off. They were billeted in Barchester and for miles about at first. I spent practically the whole of my first term going round in my little car, which I could run then, visiting them all and hearing their complaints and seeing what I could do to get them better fed, or any room to work in. Some of them hadn't even a table do to their prep on and had to sit on their beds and write on their knees. They were all very good and did their best but it was an uphill job. And I had to write to all the parents, who were dreadfully worried because most of the girls enjoyed writing home and making everything sound worse even than it was. My staff were splendid too, except for a few who, I am thankful to say, went to the B.B.C. or Chatham House. But the good ones stuck to me, and Miss Holly was perfectly splendid. When we were at Miss Pettinger's together she managed to get a little solid-fuel stove and used to make tea for me when I came in after a long day in the car. If she hadn't, I really think I would have given in. Then my Governors got those big houses in the Close as boarding-houses and things went better, but oh! the relief when they took Harefield Park and I could have a home of my own again.'

Mr Carton had listened kindly, attentively, to this account of her troubles, as he had so often listened to his pupils at Oxford, with this difference, that they came to him as a rule to be got out of holes and Miss Sparling was telling him how she got herself out of them. That she could look upon a Palladian mansion full of great gabbling girls as home struck him as a comment on a headmistress's life; a bitter one.

'Haven't you a real home then?' he asked.

'Only one old cousin that I stay with sometimes,' said Miss Sparling. 'If it hadn't been for the war I was just going to buy a cottage in Sussex and spend my weekends and holidays there.'

'It wouldn't have been good for you to be so much alone,' said Mr Carton, looking at her over his eyeglasses.

'I had thought of that,' said Miss Sparling. 'Miss Holly was going to live with me for the first year, but we decided not to look upon it as a permanent arrangement. Women living together are such a bore. Miss Holly felt just as I do.'

'Miss Holly is an unusually sensible woman,' said Mr Carton. 'But after that?'

'How inquisitional you are,' said Miss Sparling. 'I might have taken pupils to coach when I retired. I might have done lots of things. But the war came and here I am and glad to be here.'

'And when do you retire?' said Mr Carton.

'You know, that is exactly the same as asking me my age,' said Miss Sparling. 'I have six years more here. The Hosiers' Company insist, and probably for good reasons, on a comparatively early retiring age. If the war ever stops I shall be working on the reconstruction of the school and I hope I'll leave it in a good, solid position. My Governors are most sympathetic and I owe a great deal to them.'

'And they to you,' said Mr Carton. 'Well, thank you very much for bearing with me. I have an inconvenient habit of wanting to know all about my friends when I am fond of them. Now I ought to attend the rehearsal, I think. Are you coming?'

Miss Sparling said she had a few letters to write and would follow him soon.

In the drawing-room Mr Carton found the Forest of Arden in full swing. The dull girl in the Upper Fifth was sitting on a pouf near the fire with the prompt book; Miss Ferdinand in her gym dress had just fainted in a most realistic manner on seeing the bloody napkin whose qualification, much to Miss Head's relief, had by now been so often mentioned that it no longer produced giggles; a fair girl from the Lower Sixth was supporting her lifeless form as Celia, while a tall dark girl from the Upper Sixth was making the most of Oliver's part by giving every word and every syllable of every word exactly the same emphasis. Mr Oriel, whose spirit was for the moment so far broken that so long as the girls were word-perfect he was content, was hovering about the actors like a second in a prizefight, and Miss Holly was busily machining some material in a corner; which material bore a suspicious resemblance to an old pair of curtains from the Vicarage.

On seeing Mr Carton the players were overcome with self-consciousness and remained stuck in whatever position he had surprised them in.

'Go on, you idiot,' said Miss Ferdinand without opening her eyes. "Why, how now, Ganymede".'

'It's Mr Carton,' said Celia.

Miss Ferdinand opened her eyes, remarked, 'Aroint thee, witch!' and relapsed into her swoon.

'Why, how now, Ganymede,' said the dull girl in the Upper Fifth with the prompt book who, like Casablanca, had no more wits than to stick to the letter of her instructions.

'Pray proceed, ladies,' said Mr Carton and went over to the corner where Miss Holly was working.

'What a nice quiet little sewing machine,' he said admiringly. 'Most of them behave like an aeroplane being wound up.'

Miss Holly said it was an old chain-stitch machine belonging to Mrs Belton, delightfully easy to work and almost noiseless. Its only drawback, she said, was that if you didn't fasten it off perfectly, there was a thread hanging loose which no one could resist pulling, and if you pulled, you were entangled in yards of cotton like the Lady of Shalott and all your work to do again.

'My mother had one like that,' said Mr Carton. 'I vividly remember being allowed to pull that thread when my mother was letting down tucks in my sister's last-year summer frocks and petticoats. We had many simple pleasures, Miss Holly, which this generation has never known.'

Miss Holly, gently whirring the machine, agreed with him.

'You have heard of our good fortune, I suppose,' she said. 'Mrs Belton had a chest full of dress-up clothes that her children used to act in and has let us take what we want. And with Mr Oriel's kind gift of curtains we are getting on excellently. And Ellen

Humble, who works here, has taken her little nephew's reins from him and given us the bells off them for Touchstone's bauble. Miss Sparling thought it a little unkind, but Ellen said he had a tricycle. She also appears to have told him that she'd give him a clip over the ear if he told his mother.'

'Good,' said Mr Carton. 'Why children, a loathsome breed who should be kept under hatches or in monasteries till they have acquired some rudiments of manners and consideration for others, should be encouraged to think themselves of importance now, I do not know. The English as a race have always been sentimental about dogs, and draught horses in Italy where most of them have never been, but this wave of sentiment about children is a new and revolting outburst.'

'How right you are,' said Miss Holly. 'They have all the oranges and all the eggs and all the cod-liver oil and extra milk and free milk and cheap lunches and free education and a fuss is made in the House if they can't have new toys and white cot blankets, and all they do is to be discontented, lawless hooligans. Ellen Humble's nephew and his friends have been stoning the horse-chestnut trees in the drive – where I may say they had no business to be – and broken the branches off and hit one of the cows. Little beasts.'

'You are a woman after my own heart,' said Mr Carton admiringly. 'And when they have got the chestnuts down, do they know what to do with them? No! Not one of them knows how to thread his conker on a piece of string and do battle with his friends' conkers. All they care for is to mangle and massacre the trees and throw the chestnuts about. One quite sees what Herod meant.'

'Why, how now, Ganymede!' said the dull girl patiently, her eyes glued to the prompt book.

Miss Holly turned and saw the whole cast still immobilized

and listening with great interest to the conversation of their elders, regardless of the protests of Mr Oriel who had in consequence begun to read a copy of *Hosius and Hosier*, the School magazine, known among its intimates as Hoe's Hoe.

'I beg your pardon, Mr Oriel,' she said. 'We were interrupting you.'

'I fear I was listening to the latter part,' said Mr Oriel, 'and,' he added, his eyes glistening with dislike, 'I may say that when I think of the boys who threw mud at the window in the south aisle and the children who regularly scribble in the hymn-books or tear out the pages, I feel that Herod was all too mild.'

'It's a pity,' said Mr Carton reflectively, 'that we can't have a second Children's Crusade. Innocent the Third got rid of a lot of them by encouraging it. We can still learn much from the Church of Rome, Oriel.'

Mr Oriel looked frightened.

'I don't mean in your line,' said Mr Carton kindly, 'but in Social Security. A nice little crusade of a million children or so to East Prussia would leave England a better place for heroes to dwell in. I wonder if the Archbishop would consider it. The clergy could send all their own children to begin with.'

This direct attack on the property of the Church roused Mr Oriel to protest and the discussion would have gone on indefinitely had not Miss Sparling come in. This remarkable woman looked once round the room, smiled, and installed herself in a comfortable chair facing the actors. Miss Holly began to turn the handle of her machine, Mr Carton took a chair near Miss Sparling, Mr Oriel laid *Hosius and Hosier* down and Miss Ferdinand, who had remained in a syncope as to her body but raised her head to look, flumped back on the floor and closed her eyes.

'Now, Celia,' said Mr Oriel, who as he could never remember the names of any girls except of his little confirmation flock, called them by their stage names.

Celia looked wildly round.

'Why, how now, Ganymede,' said the dull girl in the Upper Fifth with the devoted persistence of Thomas à Becket's future mother.

Celia started.

'Why, how now, Ganymede!' she said.

'Go on. "Sweet Ganymede",' said the dull girl in the Upper Fifth.

'I am so very sorry to be late,' said Miss Head, coming in with an armful of gay clothes. 'I was going through Mrs Belton's chest of theatrical properties and never noticed the time. How good of you to carry on for me, Mr Oriel. How is it going, Miss Sparling?'

Miss Sparling said she had only just come in herself.

'Now, girls!' said Miss Head. 'Go straight on where you left off.'

There was dead silence.

'Why, how now, Ganymede,' said the dull girl, her eyes still fixed to the prompt book. 'Oh – "sweet Ganymede".'

'That's right,' said Miss Head cheerfully. 'Now, Oliver.'

'Many. Will. Swoon. When. They. Do. Look. On. Blood,' said the tall dark girl from the Upper Sixth.

'Splendid,' said Miss Head. 'Perhaps a little more expression. Oliver has seen the young boy faint and is anxious about him.'

'Many. WILL. Swoon. When. They. DO. Look. On. Blood,' said the tall dark girl.

'That's better,' said Miss Head. 'Go on.'

'That's all of my piece,' said the tall dark girl.

'Yes, dear. Celia's turn now,' said Miss Head.

'There is more in it, cousin Ganymede,' said the fair girl from the Lower Sixth.

'No, dear, not "Cousin Ganymede"; "Cousin! Ganymede!"' said Miss Head. 'You must remember that Celia naturally calls Rosalind cousin because she is her cousin, then she recollects their disguise and adds "Ganymede!" And you might lift Isabella a little while you say that line, if she isn't too heavy. Just support her in a reclining position. Very nice.'

'Yes, Miss Head,' said the fair girl.

'Look. He. Recovers,' said the tall dark girl.

Miss Ferdinand had been waiting, her whole being tuned and tense, for this cue. Raising her head feebly from the fair girl's supporting though awkward arm, she opened her handsome eyes and looked around in bewilderment, saying in the muted yet far-reaching voice of every dramatic and operatic heroine as death in one form or another approaches her, 'I would I were at home.'

Celia and Oliver spoke their lines. Miss Ferdinand followed, ending on a 'Heigh-ho' which compelled the admiration of all hearers, especially of Heather Adams, who thought how lovely it would be if Commander Belton were (very slightly) wounded, though preferably not by a lioness which often leads to blood-poisoning, and she could faint at the news and then – slightly improving on Shakespeare – revive to find her head pillowed not on that Lower Sixth girl's arm, but on HIS.

'Pay attention, Heather,' said Miss Head. 'A really keen actress should know every part, not only her own. Go on, girls.'

Oliver, Rosalind and again Oliver spoke their lines. There was a pause. Miss Ferdinand, perhaps owing to a *sotto voce* remark she had rashly made to the fair girl not to untidy her hair like that at the next rehearsal, had missed her cue. This was so unusual that the dull girl in the Upper Fifth was taken unawares.

'Prompter! Prompter!' said Miss Head.

'Oh, sorry. "So I do, but eye faith I should have been a woman by right,"' said the dull girl.

'Not "*Eye* faith", dear,' said Miss Head.

'It says it here,' said the dull girl.

'No, dear. "I' faith"; the "i" sounded as in "kiss",' said Miss Head.

'But it *says* Eye, Miss Head,' said the dull girl.

'Bring me the book,' said Miss Head. 'Now look. The "i" is followed by an apostrophe which means a letter is omitted in current speech. It stands for "in".'

The dull girl said there wasn't an 'in' there at all.

'Let me make it clear,' said Miss Head, this being a fine example of the triumph of hope over experience. 'Shakespeare was using the expression "In faith". But in ordinary speech, such as you and I and all of us use every day, the words were slurred and the "in" became "i".'

The head prefect, who was waiting for her scene with Audrey and William, said it would be funny if it said 'I" on the lodge gate instead of In. Or, said the fair girl in the Lower Sixth, if you knocked at the door of the mistresses' room and they said 'Come i'.'

'Now, we must get on with the rehearsal,' said Miss Head. 'Go back into your places. Prompt please.'

'So I do; but Eye faith, I should have been a woman by right,' said the dull girl.

Miss Ferdinand repeated the line correctly, with a glance of withering scorn towards the unconscious prompter. The scene came to an end and Miss Head said Very nice and she was sorry there wasn't time to do the next bit and they would start there on Tuesday.

'And all be word-perfect,' she continued. 'Only ten days to Bobbin Day. You can go now.'

The girls went off to get ready for their evening meal, bandying Shakespeare as they left the room.

'Of course,' said Miss Head, 'we shall now have a run of "i" for in. It will be "i' the Upper Fourth" and "i' the French lesson" till they get tired of it.'

'We shall get tired of it before they do,' said Miss Holly, shutting up the sewing-machine. 'I'll go and type those letters now, Miss Sparling.'

So she and Miss Head went away, leaving Miss Sparling and the two gentlemen.

'How you can bear being a headmistress, I don't know,' said Mr Carton.

'Would you believe me if I said I liked it very much?' said Miss Sparling. 'In fact I don't know how I'd bear *not* being one. But it has its trials. I've just had a severe one.'

'Do you mean this acting?' said Mr Carton.

'Much, much worse,' said Miss Sparling. 'You know Miss Pettinger.'

Mr Carton said Thank God not in private and all he knew of her in public was repellent in the highest degree. Mr Oriel expressed an opinion that Jezebel at her worst was not so brazen as that woman with her tired hair and her mincings and amblings and painted face.

'But I have my hair waved, Mr Oriel,' said Miss Sparling. 'At least it has a little natural wave and I have it set when it is washed. And I do use lipstick for parties. I had some at your delightful dinner party and Mr Carton's tea-party.'

'My dear Miss Sparling, could you possibly think of any comparison between that – that Big-footed Bertha – and yourself?' exclaimed Mr Oriel in a transport of anxiety.

'How lovely!' said Miss Sparling admiringly. 'I knew her name was Bertha, but I never put two and two together.'

She looked at her own elegant feet and preened herself as far as a headmistress may.

'But what has Big Bertha done?' said Mr Carton.

'Oh, I had forgotten about that,' said Miss Sparling. 'Miss Holly of course sent her an invitation to Bobbin Day and she never answered, so I hoped she despised us so much that she wouldn't come. But just now her secretary rang up to say she thought she could come and what was the date as she had lost the card. Mr Oriel, I know I'm quite odious and unchristian, but I cannot *bear* to be condescended to by that woman after living with her and being so very looked-down on all the time. I should like to put a public slight upon her. Please forgive me.'

'My poor child,' said Mr Oriel, 'if you will allow a friend of your dear grandfather's to call you so, I sympathize with you with all my heart. I once had to sit next to her at a party at the Deanery and if she had been the patron of twenty good livings she could not have been more patronizing. I wish the Dean's grandfather could have been in my place. He would very quickly have put her in hers and told her to mind her distaff.'

'And as for Christian,' said Mr Carton, who was rather well read in patristic literature, 'nothing could be more Christian than your behaviour. The whole of the early Church spent their time trying to put public slights upon each other. The Patriarchs of Antioch and Constantinople and Alexandria devoted a lifetime to it. And to take a later example, St Jerome and St Augustine managed to get on each other's nerves to a high degree, as far apart as Palestine and Tunisia. In wishing to mortify Miss Pettinger in public you are living up to the very highest standards. Am I not right, Oriel?'

Mr Oriel said he thought it was high time he was getting back to the Vicarage.

'You are so kind,' said Miss Sparling, taking Mr Oriel's hand. 'Will you add to your kindness by calling me Madeleine? There is no one who uses my Christian name now except my old cousin and some of the women I was at college with. It would remind me of Grandpapa.'

'It would gratify me very much,' said Mr Oriel, 'to call you Madeleine, my dear. I really cannot tell you how much it would gratify me. To see my kind old friend's granddaughter in such a position of trust and showing such affection to me is more gratifying than I can say. Bless you, my dear.'

If Mr Oriel had not been conscious of Mr Carton regarding him with what he felt to be cynical detachment spiced with amusement, he would have kissed Miss Sparling in a paternal way on the forehead. Though why paternal, when the forehead is not the usual place for a father to kiss his daughter, being more commonly any portion of the face that the daughter in question happens to push against his own, we cannot say.

The evening was moonless, the drive dark. Mr Oriel and Mr Carton, escorted by two wavering spots of light proceeding from their torches, walked briskly towards the village.

'What a charming name Madeleine is,' said Mr Oriel. 'It had never occurred to me that Miss Sparling had a Christian name at all.'

'Well, Oriel, it ought to occur to you of all people,' said Mr Carton.

'I didn't exactly mean that,' said Mr Oriel. 'Dear me, Carton, I fear my battery is dying.'

'Give it a good shake,' said Mr Carton.

Mr Oriel did so. The torch expired.

'Never mind,' said Mr Carton, 'I've got mine. But I hope we won't meet any A.R.P. people or the policeman, because I forgot to put two thicknesses of tissue paper over mine. And why the devil tissue paper, or two thicknesses? Why not one thickness of paper that is twice as thick as tissue paper?'

Mr Oriel said he thought that had been altered and you had to have some brown paper or something of the sort right over the glass and then make a hole in it of a certain size.

'It's all very well to say a certain size,' said Mr Carton, with a pettishness unusual in him, 'but what size? Why haven't we eyes like cats? If Providence forces us to live in darkness, it ought to do something about it.'

Mr Oriel said if people went about in the dark, not relying on torches, they would doubtless develop keener eyesight.

Mr Carton said they might; but if he knew anything about Nature it took her at least three million years to notice any change in our habits. Look at teeth, he said. Mankind had been living on a mixed diet quite long enough for Nature to tumble to it, instead of which she still provided us with a quantity of teeth we didn't need and made them all go bad the moment they came through. Bah! he added.

He then repented his fit of ill temper and took Mr Oriel back to the Vicarage with his torch.

'Just hold my torch while I find my latchkey, Carton,' said Mr Oriel, fumbling in all his pockets.

Mr Carton took it, and absently-mindedly pressed the switch. Both gentlemen were almost blinded by a shaft of brilliant light which glittered back at them from every window in the Vicarage.

'Good God!' said Mr Carton and switched it off again.

'Oh dear, I must have shaken it shut when I shook it,' said Mr Oriel, and immediately wished he had framed his explanation with more care. But Mr Carton appeared to understand perfectly, bade him good night and went back to Assaye House.

His library was waiting for him with a good fire. He knew Mrs Wickens would serve him a small but excellent evening meal very shortly. His books and papers, undisturbed by sacrilegious duster, were to hand.

'Bachelor's ideal home,' said Mr Carton, looking cynically round him. '*Old* bachelor's selfish, comfortable home. Bah!'

He had a brief though violent temptation to throw a book across the room, but the scholar's innate reverence for the printed word restrained him. His eye lighted on a copy of a book sent to him for review. *Caligula: The Man and the Statesman*, by a left-wing young gentleman residing for the duration of the war in the Argentine Republic (or whatever it is), written in slightly out-of-date slang to show that Mr Churchill was quite wrong; in fact, as its publisher observed in a blurb which he forced the not unwilling author to write as he was too lazy, though he saw money in the book, 'Factual and fictional, the writer is at no pains to spare us the blood, tears and sweat of a Fascist Decadence.'

Mr Carton counted ten very slowly. He then picked up the book and hurled it across the room. Its war binding cracked, its yellow-grey pages with hair mangled into them were scattered. Mr Carton lit his pipe and sat down to work at Fluvius Minucius till his supper was ready.

Since the School came to Harefield Park Miss Sparling had received much hospitality, the best that servantless rationed households could provide. As a small thank-offering she invited all her kind hosts and hostesses to be present at Bobbin Day. There were very few amusements that winter, so the invitations were gratefully accepted and several people asked if they might bring a boy or a girl home on leave, or a paying guest who was giving satisfaction, or dear old Miss Surd because she was so deaf but did love to see young people. So by the time Bobbin Day arrived it was evident that, unless there was a fog, the big hall would be quite full. The estate carpenter had rigged up a temporary platform which was to be used first for the speeches and then for the play. The speeches were to come first, followed by a slight refection in the drawing-room, with the aid of the tea-urns from the British Legion and the Women's Institute; this would be followed by the play, and the Southbridge United Viator Passenger Company (by kind permission of the Petrol Board) would fetch the visiting Hosiers in time to get the 6.5 to London.

Several of the mistresses went to Barchester by bus and bought utility non-crease (though they were neither) ready-made dresses of a kind of fine sacking in shades of puce, olive green, dirty tomato and depressing claret, with utility short sleeves and altogether rather too youthful; which dresses immediately sagged behind to that extent that nothing could be done about it as there wasn't time. Miss Sparling, who knew exactly what was due to her position as an honoured servant of the Hosiers' Company, found a good dressmaker in Barchester through Lady Graham and from a length that she had by her (a technical expression which our female readers, if any, will understand) caused to be confected a very handsome afternoon dress, combining the dignified with the practical, but, as the dressmaker said, almost with tears, making moddom look her age, which moddom did not look at all, and what about a nice draped neck. But Miss

254

Sparling, steadfast in purpose, insisted on the V front and the bit of lace, for behind them she felt safe.

Miss Holly, who knew her limitations, stuck to her usual coat and skirt and thus showed her great good sense.

Mr Oriel lent Mrs Powlett and Dorothy, Mr Carton lent Mr and Mrs Wickens, and Wheeler informed Mrs Belton that she was going to help at the school and she supposed Mrs Belton would be going too, so it wouldn't matter about tea and if Mr Belton wanted his, cook would get it when she came back from the Baptist Chapel Working Party at five. Just as Mrs Belton was wondering if she had better stay at home, as Fred did so hate being alone for tea, Elsa rang up to say that she and Captain Hornby were coming down for a couple of nights. On hearing about Bobbin Day she said she would hate to go more than anything in the world, to see those great gawky girls all over Harefield Park, so she would stay with her father and go and inspect the new bit of ploughland and give him his tea and Mother could take Christopher to the bun-fight. All this did not sound very loverlike, but it was all different now and Mrs Belton agreed to anything Elsa wanted.

'Have you heard from Charles?' said Elsa.

Mrs Belton's heart thudded, as she said she heard about a week ago, and he didn't say where he was but the postmark was York.

'Oh, that's all right,' said Elsa. 'He only didn't say because of letters being censored. He probably posted it in the train. I thought he might be getting leave when I was down, that's all.'

This may have meant to be reassuring, but Mrs Belton at once felt the unreasoning fears against which no amount of common sense can avail. In a few moments she had transported Charles, from whom she had a letter posted in York less than a week ago, to the farthest East and arranged for him to be a wounded and malarial prisoner of war in Japanese hands. One cannot do much about these thoughts. The more improbable, nay impossible, one's self-made imaginings, the more difficult to subdue.

Accordingly on the evening before Bobbin Day the engaged couple arrived, looking well and handsome. Mrs Belton was ashamed to let her daughter know her fears, so she took the opportunity of asking Captain Hornby when they were alone if he knew anything about Charles. Captain Hornby said he was in Scotland. Elsa had had a letter from him the day before and there was no harm in mentioning it to her, but the authorities would probably have stopped Charles's letter if he had told her where he was.

'As a matter of fact he got a day's shooting at Aberdeathly,' said Captain Hornby. 'I told him to let the old factor know if he was up there.'

'Kind Christopher,' said Mrs Belton.

Since the announcement of their engagement, presents had been arriving, not in spate as they would have done before the war it is true, but in gratifying numbers. A great many took the form of cheques, for there is really very little to give now but money, and though we all say it isn't worth anything now, it still has a purchasing power if one can find anything to buy. Several of Elsa's special friends had contributed from their own coupons, a truly generous deed. An old Thorne cousin had sent a roll of soft ivory white satin long put away and one of Mr Belton's aunts a cloud of old lace.

Elsa had empowered her mother to open all parcels that looked like presents, so Mrs Belton had really had much more fun out of them than her daughter who was not only very hard worked at her hush-hush place, but when she was at home much preferred going about the park and the farm with her father to thinking about a wedding dress that she would only wear once and presents which she would have little opportunity of using. But Mrs Belton had for once been firm, and each time Elsa had a night at home she provided her with a new list of people who must be thanked, and Elsa, who had a pretty clear idea of her duties to society, sat down and wrote letters with a very good grace, thus further winning the approval of her betrothed.

The wedding was to be at the end of March or early in April, according to the leave the contracting parties could get. They were to go to Aberdeathly for a week. Then Elsa would go back to her job and Captain Hornby whithersoever glory and their Lordships of the Admiralty sent him.

At dinner and during the evening Mrs Belton covertly observed her daughter and her future son-in-law. Both were unashamedly in love and Mrs Belton was amused and touched to see Elsa the independent deferring to Captain Hornby's judgment and opinions in a very pretty and becoming way. This gave her pleasure, for she had not been altogether easy about the effect of a man as resolute and experienced as Captain Hornby upon her clever, self-willed and (she must confess it to her own shame) spoilt girl. Small clashes occurred during the evening, but Elsa far from arguing in the rather high-pitched voice she used in discussion with her equals, or letting her quick temper fly, curtsied, dived, outstripped and laughed at her conversationally slower-witted lover, wove a circle round him thrice and was gone again. Only for a moment did a storm threaten, when Elsa after dinner spoke rather pettishly and ungratefully (to her mother's mind) of a large cocktail party that Lady Ellangowan had offered to give to introduce her cousin Christopher's future wife to the family and a number of friends, mostly high up in the services.

'I hate to be on show,' she said not very courteously. 'Besides it means losing practically two days of my work, as I'll have to spend the night in London. It seems frightful waste in war-time.'

Captain Hornby without showing any annoyance said it was a pity he was a captain. If Elsa could have started as a lieutenant's wife, he said, she would have been properly trained. A naval officer's wife had to go to parties as part of her duty; and as he would probably be an admiral soon if he wasn't killed, it would be a good thing to practise now.

'Besides,' he added, 'Catriona Ellangowan is a charming woman. I nearly married her myself once, but she very rightly turned me down for Ellangowan who is a first-rate fellow.'

Mrs Belton was a little anxious over this difference of opinion and slightly ashamed of her daughter's incivility, though she knew it sprang largely from the nervous state that an engagement can put the most level-headed young woman into, but she could not help being secretly amused by Elsa's unconcealed surprise and mortification that Captain Hornby, who was considerably her senior and had been about a great deal, should have so far forgotten himself as to prefer any woman to her before he had met her.

'But it was just as well,' Captain Hornby continued, 'for if I'd married her, I'd have left her for you the moment I saw you.'

Elsa had the grace to look slightly ashamed. Captain Hornby smiled at her and held out his hand. Elsa pulled a footstool near his chair as she had done before and occupied herself by tracing the braid on his cuff with her forefinger, wondering how to retreat with least loss of dignity. But the subject was not again mentioned till they were going to bed when Captain Hornby asked her if she had accepted Lady Ellangowan's invitation yet.

'No, but I will tomorrow,' said the independent, spoilt Miss Belton. 'Oh, Christopher, I do ADORE you.'

*

On the following day Harefield Park was in a state of seething excitement only to be paralleled by the French Revolution or the roads to Rome at the approach of Lars Porsena. Among it all Miss Sparling moved unperturbed, Miss Holly by her side or in her wake.

At one o'clock the S.U.V.P. Coy's motor coach brought the Master of the Hosiers' Company, the Remembrancer, the Almoner, six Free Hosiers, four Indentured Prentice Hosiers and the Hosiers' Wardmote Bailiff, with all their various chains and badges of office in a suitcase carried by the Master's Apparitor of Worship. They were received by Miss Sparling, who then made known to the Master and the Remembrancer Mr Oriel and Mr Carton, who had been invited to the lunch partly in thanks for lending their servants, without whom they would have lunched in some discomfort, and partly because they had become such good friends to Miss Sparling that it gave her pleasure to have them.

Lunch for the Hosiers, Miss Sparling, her guests and the senior staff was in the library, where Mr Wickens had taken charge. There was every danger of a clash between that excellent servant and the Apparitor of Worship, whose peculiar privilege it was to wait upon the Master and all Free Hosiers at any public lunch or dinner. But most luckily the Apparitor, Simnet by name, turned out to be a brother of the butler at Southbridge School, formerly a scout at Lazarus; and the two functionaries, united by the bond of a common university connection, served the meal with deftness and dispatch, aided by Mrs Wickens and Mrs Powlett. Lunch being over, Miss Sparling and her staff retired to prepare for the fray, leaving the Hosiers to smoke and to drink in moderation, for the Master, to commemorate this visit, had taken the precaution of bringing four bottles of liqueur brandy from the Company's cellars, which we are thankful to say had not suffered in the London air raids and were remarkably well stocked.

'You are very lucky in your headmistress,' said Mr Carton to the Master, Sir Hosea Weaver, who though a Cambridge man (more through his father's fault than his own), had the root of the matter in him and had lately put the Bishop of Barchester down in an argument at the Megatherium Club about a quotation from Milton which he had happened to see in the *Times* crossword puzzle, while waiting for Lady Weaver to come in from her Red Cross work on the previous day. 'A very remarkable woman and a fine scholar.'

'Of scholarship I fear I am no judge,' said Sir Hosea with a misleading air of modesty, for he had put himself through a grammar school and college on his own brains and taken the highest kind of degree that the other place can give in Political Economy and seldom forgot it, 'but I quite agree with you. We owe her an enormous debt for her help during the very trying evacuation period and the general disorganization that followed. Have some more brandy.'

'If you will too,' said Mr Carton. 'Thanks. How much longer will she be here?'

'Till she retires, I hope,' said Sir Hosea. 'Nice brandy this.'

'First-rate,' said Mr Carton. 'Are you going to keep the school down here after the war?'

'It depends,' said Sir Hosea. 'Not in this house of course. We have it by the year and Mr Bolton—'

'Belton,' said Mr Carton.

'Belton, thank you,' said Sir Hosea, 'will want it back I presume. We would like to build. We shall have the senior and junior schools in separate buildings. But this is boring for you.'

'Not at all,' said Mr Carton.

'We are marking the occasion of this Bobbin Day by a public recognition of Miss Sparling's services,' said Sir Hosea, 'in a way that I hope she will appreciate.'

Mr Carton said he was delighted to hear it and then one of the Free Hosiers and the Wardmote Bailiff joined in the talk and the subject of Miss Sparling was dropped. At the same moment Mr Oriel made the delightful discovery that the Hosiers' Almoner, who was really the Company's official Chaplain, had been caned by him for smoking in the Lower Dormitory at their public school some fifty-odd years previously, which led at once to one of those enthusiastic friendships between people who are not likely to meet again and so can afford to let themselves go.

The junior staff and the girls had their lunch in the school dining-hall rather earlier, which was fine fun for the girls, but not such fun for the mistresses who found it more politic to give up any pretence at control over their excited charges. Most of the actors for the afternoon's play were already in states varying from wild spirits (Miss Ferdinand) through nervous apprehension (the head prefect) to complete apathy (Heather Adams who thought the whole thing very silly and waste of time).

The sight of the motor coach full of Hosiers passing the windows roused all spirits to the highest pitch. Miss Ferdinand drank a glass of water the wrong way, choked, went red in the face and had to be led out crowing and whooping by the junior science mistress. The head prefect said she felt sick and was frowned at by the Upper Third mistress. Heather Adams, who knew her words and had no nerves about acting, ate a great deal of steamed pudding and ruminated on a play in which she would act so movingly as to cause Commander Belton to wait at the stage door with a large Rolls-Royce and carry her away to a life of bliss.

By a great stroke of good luck the school cook, who came in by the day, was a niece of Mrs Powlett, so she was kind to the helpers and arranged a very handsome meal for them. Having two gentlemen present, said the school cook, looking proudly at Mr Wickens and the Apparitor as if she had laid a double-yolked egg, was quite an event. Dorothy, who had never eaten in such magnificence, thought of Lady Mabel and Lord Victor to whom, she decided, the Apparitor bore a striking resemblance, though beyond the fact that Lord Victor was six foot high and the Adonis of the Guards and Mr Simnet weedy and spectacled, they would have seemed to an impartial observer to have little in common. Mr Simnet, in virtue of his official connection with the Hosiers' Company, had managed to abstract a bottle of port, dismissed by the Bailiff as corked at the last wardmote. The port, it is true, was not, after several hours' journey by train and motor coach, in that state of perfect repose desirable for the best vintages, but Mr Simnet assured the ladies that the dregs gave body to the wine. Mr Wickens, who as an ex-scout knew better, merely smiled a superior smile and did not refuse to have his glass filled.

'Well, Sarah,' said Mrs Powlett to the cook, 'it's all gone off very nicely so far. The gentlemen made a very hearty luncheon. I do like to see gentlemen eat.'

'You should see our girls, auntie,' said the cook, who being an independent woman, mother of an illegitimate son who played about the kitchen and got under people's feet in her own right, was not going to call them young ladies. 'You'd think they'd nothing but their stomachs to think of. That Heather Adams eats for two as the saying is.'

'It's not for you to talk about eating for two, Sarah,' said Mrs Powlett with dignity. 'You've done that once too often, my girl. This is a nice tasty soup. What did you put in it?'

The cook, quite unabashed by her aunt's rebuke, said there was a lot going on at the meat's back door that it was as well not to talk about. And at the fish's too, said Mrs Wickens to whom her husband had kindly bellowed the gist of the cook's conversation.

'I was down the lane behind the shops day before yesterday was it,' said the cook, 'and there was the butcher's man at the yard gate, so I passed the remark we was having company in the kitchen today. All right, he says. Open your mouth and shut your eyes And you may get a nice surprise. So he took me in the wash-house where they do the fat down and gave me a lovely bundle of scraps. There was pigs' trotters and a nice bit of liver and a lot of pork trimmings and bones and I don't know what. So I got my bones on straight away and put the rest through the mincer and made some lovely rissles.'

'I do like rissles, cook,' said Dorothy, who so far had not uttered a word, being overcome by her surroundings and the charms of Mr Simnet.

'That's enough, Dorothy,' said Mrs Powlett. 'Anyone'd think you'd been brought up quite common. I made some nice rissles for the Vicar last Thursday,' she continued to the company at large, 'and there was one over so I let Dorothy have it for her supper. You'd think I'd never given her anything good to eat before. She's been talking about it ever since. Now then, Sarah, let's see your rissles.'

The cook fetched a large dish of excellent rissoles from the oven where they had been keeping hot and the company fell to.

'So you like rissles, miss,' said Mr Simnet, who had been much struck by Dorothy's appearance. 'So do I. My late wife was a great hand at them. Let me press you to just a drop of Our port, miss.'

Dorothy looked anxiously towards her mistress, but Mrs Powlett was engaged in talk with her niece about points and did not hear. Being the last drop in the bottle it was of a muddy nature, but Dorothy's simple and grateful palate found no fault with it.

'Well,' said Mrs Powlett when they were all well embarked on the rissoles, 'now Miss Belton is engaged we don't know who it'll be next.'

This her hearers rightly interpreted as being not so much surprise at Miss Belton's being engaged at all as a generalization on the theme of one marriage bringing on another. Cook said it was high time young Mr Belton that was in the Navy got married or the Government would take Harefield Park, so they said. Mr Wickens said darkly that he hoped Mr Charles Belton would marry a nice young lady, but these young men couldn't be trusted. Mr Simnet said yes indeed, and there was the Honourable Mr Norris that had lived on his brother's staircase at Lazarus College and nearly got entangled with a young lady if you could call her so at the Devorguilla Arms, who was really married to someone else all the time, but subsequently married a nice young lady, the Honourable Eleanor Purvis.

This anecdote, though proving nothing in particular, was well received as giving tone to the conversation.

Mrs Powlett coughed.

'Mr Oriel thinks the world of Miss Sparling,' she said, 'as we are all friends here, Mr Simnet. What Mr Oriel thinks is no concern of mine, he being a gentleman that *is* a gentleman, but he is as nice a gentleman as you would wish to meet and no one would ever take him for seventy. I dare say I shan't last much longer,' said Mrs Powlett, who had very good health, never worried, and came of a long-lived family, 'and I would like to see him settled before I go, dear gentleman.'

'That Ellen Humble,' said cook, 'says it's Mr Carton. He's always up at the Pavilion with his books and things.'

Mrs Wickens, who had the semi-deaf's annoying quality of suddenly hearing when it was least convenient, said she had always said the Vicar was not a marrying man and nor was Mr Carton, though a very nice gentleman, the marrying sort. Still, there was never any knowing and Miss Sparling was a very nice lady and not like some headmistresses she could name.

'If you mean That One at Barchester, Mrs Wickens,' said Mrs Powlett at the top of her voice, 'I had a cousin there as temporary once and what she told me—!'

Cook said, Well, they'd better be hurrying up if they wanted to get the things washed and see the entertainment, so the large steamed pudding was dispatched, the gentlemen sent away, and the ladies set to on the dishes.

'Mr Simnet's a lovely man,' said cook. 'He had a repeat help of pudding.'

On hearing these romantic words Dorothy broke a plate.

'Well, Dorothy, as it's a school plate it doesn't matter,' said Mrs Powlett mildly, 'but you'd better do the saucepans. See? And then if you're good you can stand at the back and see the feet.'

Rightly interpreting this as an invitation to participate in the fête or entertainment about to begin, Dorothy bestirred herself with such good will that she dropped an enamel saucepan with a resounding bang on the stone floor and the enamel flew about in a thousand small chips.

'Ulcerated stomachs, that's what we'll be getting now if I cook in that,' said the cook, putting the saucepan back in the rack.

IO

Mrs Belton and Captain Hornby, walking by the field path, were among the first to arrive at the school. The big central hall was lit from a skylight which had to be entirely blacked out. There was a certain amount of light from a large window on the staircase and through the entrance hall, but for all occasions it had to be artificially illuminated. On a chill raw February day this was no disadvantage and Mrs Belton was quite glad to find the large electric chandeliers burning and the central heating on. If she felt wistful, thinking of the last two winters when they could not get enough coal to heat the house except during the few weeks of frost, and had to huddle round a log fire in the small drawing-room and go to bed shivering, she made no mention of it.

'I've never been in Harefield Park, you know,' said Captain Hornby looking round.

'I wish we had known you when you used to come and visit your aunt,' said Mrs Belton. 'But she was such an invalid that we hardly knew her at all and you only came and went. It's a pity you couldn't have seen the Park in my father-in-law's time. It was delightful then, so well kept and happy.'

'And in your time too, I am certain,' said Captain Hornby. 'Where shall we sit?'

The first four rows of chairs were reserved for the Hosiers, the Lord Lieutenant (Lord Pomfret) and any other dignitaries who might attend. Mrs Belton was cheerfully preparing to sit somewhere in the middle of the hall when Miss Holly, who forgot nothing, came out of a side door and conducted her and Captain Hornby to a seat in the middle of the second row. This was, as Mrs Belton remarked, very gratifying, but it meant turning round all the time if one wanted to see who was there, which was such bad manners. However she supposed she would see everybody afterwards.

The seats behind them rapidly filled, and by the time the people disgorged by the Barchester bus had arrived the hall was pretty full. A slight commotion at the back made Mrs Belton turn her head in spite of her good resolutions and she saw Mrs Perry with a small dark wiry-haired woman in a leopardskin coat followed by a man huddled in a sheepskin coat and wearing a beret from beneath which his dark miserable eyes roamed in a terrified way round the hall.

'Oh dear,' said Mrs Belton. 'Mrs Perry must have brought some of her Mixo-Lydian refugees from Southbridge. I'm sure they weren't asked.'

Mrs Updike then drifted vaguely in wearing one glove and carrying the other in a bandaged hand. She saw Mrs Perry and made for her.

'Come by us, there is plenty of room,' said Mrs Perry with a malevolent glance at Mrs Hunter who was sitting on a chair and a half.

'Oh, I'm dreadfully sorry if you were sitting on them both,' said Mrs Updike. 'One does so *want* two chairs sometimes.'

'I had been hoping,' said Mrs Hunter, 'that my delightful Slavo-Lydian friend, the girl I told you about, would be coming.

She was to be in Barchester today. But evidently she has missed the bus.'

So speaking she moved herself and her bag wholly on to one chair.

'Oh, how kind of you,' said Mrs Updike. 'Those buses are dreadful, aren't they. I've a perfect thing about catching them; one never knows if one is early or late when one gets to the stop until finally the bus does or doesn't come.'

'Slavo-Lydie,' said the small woman in the leopardskin coat from the other side of Mrs Perry. 'Tas de cochons! Hein, Gogo? Ces Slavo-Lydiens c'est un tas de cochons, quoi?'

Her companion, huddling into his sheepskin coat, cast a frightened look towards Mrs Hunter and said nothing.

The Dean of Barchester's wife then came in and seeing Mrs Belton asked if she could sit by her. Mrs Belton introduced Captain Hornby.

'Dear Elsa. The Dean and I were so delighted to see the announcement,' said Mrs Crawley. 'I thought of you so much, Mrs Belton. It is *such* a comfort to have one's family off one's hands.'

As Mrs Crawley had eight children, six of them girls, Mrs Belton could understand her pleasure in having them all safely married, but the thought of losing her only girl, though to a man whom she liked and trusted, was not quite so alluring. She inquired after Octavia, the Crawleys' youngest daughter who had lately married her father's former chaplain Mr Needham.

'She is very well indeed,' said Mrs Crawley. 'The Vicarage is charming and so easy to run and dear Tommy manages wonderfully with his right arm. You know he lost the other in Tunisia.'

Mrs Belton made suitable noises.

'And she is expecting her first baby in the summer,' said

Mrs Crawley. 'She thought of going to the Barchester General Hospital where she nursed for so long, but the petrol was the difficulty, so she is going to the Cottage Hospital at Marling where her friend Lucy Marling works. Your goddaughter, isn't she? Lucy is such a charming name.'

Mrs Belton hoped Octavia was keeping well.

'Very well indeed,' said Mrs Crawley, 'and doing wonders with her Moral Welfare Committee in Lambton and Worsted. But what do you think, Mrs Belton, we have had to do. Josiah was furious, but one is quite helpless. You know the Bishop was to have been here today, but of course the Palace let us down. It always does. So Miss Sparling, whom we liked so much when she was in Barchester, appealed to Josiah and of course we said we would come.'

Mrs Belton said with heartfelt conviction that nothing could have been nicer and the Bishop would have ruined the afternoon.

'But I haven't told you the worst,' said Mrs Crawley. 'We are allowed some petrol for my husband's necessary journeys, and who do you think has forced herself upon us? Miss Pettinger.'

Mrs Belton would have thrown up the whites of her eyes if she had known how to do it.

'She said she was to have come out with the Palace people,' said Mrs Crawley, managing to convey inexpressible scorn into the words, 'and we couldn't very well refuse. So here am I; and she has gone into the headmistress's room hanging onto Josiah's coat tails.'

Before Mrs Belton could do more than begin to sympathize the side door opened and out came the Hosiers in all their glory, the Master in chain and badge, the Remembrancer in a sort of wig and gown, the Almoner with his ribbons from the last war, all the other Hosiers with their proper insignia. With them came Lord and Lady Pomfret, Miss Sparling in her M.A. gown, the Dean of Barchester, and, to the disgust of all who knew her, Miss Pettinger.

Miss Sparling, the Master of the Hosiers' Company, the Remembrancer, the Almoner and the Dean mounted the platform. Lord and Lady Pomfret were put in the middle of the front row, Lady Pomfret somehow contriving to have Mr Oriel on her other side, who would, she knew, be far too modest to come up higher without an invitation. Miss Pettinger tried to squash herself next to Lord Pomfret but was set aside by a stout elderly Free Hosier to all her ill-wishers' joy. Mr Carton slipped in beside Mrs Crawley.

This Bobbin Day, the first that had been held with such cer-mony since the outbreak of war, was a considerable event in the life of the School. Miss Sparling and most of the senior staff looked back wistfully to the gigantic champagne lunch (brought down in cars from Hosiers' Hall), the red baize, the banked flowers, the band of the Worshipful Company of Gunners, the girls in their unbecoming white Bobbin Day dresses, the parents who so often looked like nothing on earth with a good income, the magnificent tea afterwards, the excitement, the applause. Some of the eldest pupils remembered these things, now small and undistinguishable, like far-off mountains turned into clouds; some of the slightly younger ones had been brought up on the tradition, though to be truthful it seemed no more to them than the fierce vexation of a dream; but the greater number knew nothing about it at all and were wildly excited, which enabled their more instructed fellows to look down upon them with great satisfaction. Miss Holly placed herself at the end of the front row where Miss Sparling could catch her eye in case of need.

The ceremony opened, as always, with a brief prayer said by the Almoner, which privilege he had gracefully offered to the Dean and the Dean as gracefully declined, saying Every man to his own vineyard.

The Remembrancer then called upon Miss Sparling to read a report of the school year. This was dreadfully dull, including as it did the names of all those who had passed their School Certificate and the number of Credits obtained; the loss of Miss Marks and Miss Measel who had gone the one into the Board of Trade, the other to nurse a very old mother who couldn't get any servants; the death at ninety-seven of an ex-headmistress whom no one present had ever heard of; and finally a number of university and war distinctions gained by old Hosiers' girls reflecting great credit on the school.

As Miss Sparling sat down amid decorous applause there was a slight disturbance in the row behind Mrs Belton owing to a late-comer who had seen one empty seat and was edging his way into it. Mrs Belton looked round and saw a man of middle height and powerful appearance making his way along in front of the other occupants. He was dressed in rather loud tweeds with a good deal of orange-brown in them and a sky-blue pull-over, above which a yellow sports shirt and a blue foulard tie could be seen. He was clean-shaven with a fleshy but firm face, his hair was sandy and brushed very smooth, and Mrs Belton noticed with faint distaste that the back of the hand which he laid on a chair to steady himself was covered with dark hair. The newcomer sat himself solidly in the empty seat and all became quiet again.

Those girls who had gained scholarships inside the school or to universities then went onto the platform, shook hands with the Master and were congratulated, each receiving a round of applause, especially from the junior school, who found this a good way of getting rid of their high spirits.

There was then a pause while Mr Wickens and Mr Simnet, in his official position as Apparitor, pushed an upright piano into position from a corner. Miss Griffiths, the music mistress, struck up the opening bars of the School Song and the girls rose to their feet. Such is the power of mass suggestion that the audience did likewise, most of them dropping bags, gloves, umbrellas, parcels and scarves as they did so. Miss Griffiths, having played through the tune, crashed a loud chord with the pedal well down. Those near her could see her lips move and even hear her say, 'One and two and, *three* and four and.' On the last 'and' a number of shrill young voices burst into the well-known words, followed very shortly by those who had not been attending, or were too stupid to know one beat from another. The three verses were sung with equal and uninspired want of fervour and Mrs Powlett at the back of the hall wiped her eyes, saying it reminded her of how Mr Powlett used to sing when he'd had a drop too much.

In case anyone would like to have a copy of the School Song (obtainable, paper shortage permitting, at Hosiers' Hall, twenty-five copies for one shilling, postage fivepence) we subjoin the first stanza.

mf.	The Hosiers in the days of old
cresc.	Were valiant men and true.
f.	In freedom's cause they aye were bold,
pp.	As we would wish to do.
mf	To tyrants they'd not bow the knee,
cresc.	And though but girls, no more will we,
cresc. and ff.	For Hosiers, Hosiers, Hosiers, Hosiers,
rall. fff.	Hosiers ever will be free.

The tune is very bad indeed, and this verse is on the whole a more favourable specimen than the two which follow.

The Remembrancer, appealing to Lord Pomfret, the Very Reverend the Dean of Barchester, ladies and gentlemen, begged for silence for the Master of the Worshipful Company of Hosiers.

The woman in the leopardskin coat, who had shown an ostentatious want of interest in the proceedings, turned to Mrs Perry.

'What eeze it, Hosiers, which he says?' she demanded sharply. 'Dieu! quel baragouinage que votre langue!'

'Il est le maître des Hosiers,' said Mrs Perry. 'Les Hosiers sont une très ancienne compagnie, fabricants de hose. Hose est un vieux mot anglais qui—'

'Bien, bien, je comprends,' said the leopardskin woman. 'Il fabrique des tuyaux d'arrosage celui-là et il en a bien l'air. En Mixo-Lydie par exemple on n'a pas besoin de tuyaux d'arrosage. Nous avons partout des ruisseaux, des étangs, des fontaines, hein, Gogo?'

The miserable-eyed man next to her, thus appealed to, shuddered.

'Tu sais combien je déteste l'eau fraîche,' he said reproachfully and shrank further into his sheepskin coat.

Several people in the neighbourhood said Hush.

The Master of the Hosiers' Company then rose, greeted with loud clapping by the school, as it was well known that his presence always meant at least an extra half-holiday. He was a tall, imposing man who set off his robes and chain of office to excellent advantage, his voice from long practice at board meetings was of good carrying power and he spoke without any wearisome hesitations.

It afforded him and his fellow Hosiers, he said, the greatest pleasure to be present in the School's new home, expressing for himself and his brethren the gratification afforded to them by the presence of Mrs Belton whose hospitable roof now gave them shelter; at which Mrs Belton tried to look as if she were not there and felt she ought to mention aloud what a very handsome rent the Hosiers were paying.

It was also a great pleasure, the Master continued, to see among them the Earl of Pomfret, Lord Lieutenant of Barsetshire, and the Countess of Pomfret, the moving spirit in so many of the women's admirable war organizations; at which Lord Pomfret, who was only an earl because he couldn't help it, tried to look like a baron, and Lady Pomfret who watched over him with tireless devotion hoped Gillie wasn't in for one of his nasty chills.

The Bishop of Barchester, the Master went on to say, had promised to be among them, but his lordship had been prevented by a subsequent engagement and had been gracious enough to inform him, by the hand of his secretary, that he would be with them in spirit, a concession of which the Master appeared to have the lowest opinion. Smothered applause broke out here and there in the hall. The Dean smiled grimly, uncrossed his legs and recrossed them the other way round.

It was, however, with the greatest satisfaction, said the Master, that they welcomed among them today the Dean of Barchester. He himself, said the Master, was a professed member, however unworthy, of the Congregational Church, but in the Dean he recognized one in whom faith and works were united to a remarkable degree, and then wondered if he knew what he meant.

'Congregational Church?' said the leopardskin woman in a loud aside to Mrs Perry. 'He is of the Congregation?'

'It is not exactly the Church of England, but very Good, Worthy People,' whispered Mrs Perry. 'Very Devoted and Religious.'

'Ah, je comprends. Il est jésuite,' said the leopardskin woman. 'Vois-tu, Gogo,' she added to her companion, 'il est jésuite, celui qui fabrique les tuyaux d'arrosage. Te rappelles-tu, Gogo, comme on a chassé les pères jésuites de la Mixo-Lydie en mil neuf cent treize? Et pour cause!'

Several people said Hush.

Having completed these preliminaries the Master gave his audience a brief summary of the Hosiers' Girls' Foundation School, of the splendid way in which the Headmistress had carried it through the evacuation period, of the plans which the Hosiers' Company were already making for a large new school in the country as soon as building became possible again, and of their hope that this would be soon enough for Miss Sparling to be able to add to her good work for the school the labour of reconstructing it as an up-to-date boarding school with a senior and a junior house, equipped in every way to hold its own with any other school in England. Peace, he said, with the air of having hit on a wholly original idea, had her victories no less renowned than war, and the refounding of the Hosiers' Girls' Foundation School would be one of them.

Having allowed the dutiful applause to subside, he grasped his robe with both hands, hitched it forward on his shoulders, and continued. The Hosiers' Company, he said, could never sufficiently acknowledge their debt to their Headmistress, but had determined, in a specially convoked Wardmote, to make an innovation unprecedented in the history of the Company. Where, he said in an aside, was Mr Bailiff? Oh, yes. Had Mr Bailiff the box?

The Bailiff of the Wardmote lifted from beside his chair a polished wooden box which he placed on the table by the Master.

He would now, said the Master, have the pleasure, in the name of the Worshipful Company of Hosiers, of conferring upon their Headmistress, Miss Sparling, the Freedom of the Company, whereby she would become the first and probably the only Woman Freeman of one of London's oldest and most honourable bodies. Had Mr Bailiff the key?

The Bailiff handed him a key. He opened the box and drew out a roll of paper and a glittering badge suspended on a red ribbon.

'Miss Sparling,' he said, very kindly.

Miss Sparling got up and came to the table. Having passed during the last few moments through every degree of gratification, embarrassment, apprehension, satisfaction and a general feeling that she was not there at all, she had attained a state of stupefied acquiescence in anything that might occur. To the beholder she appeared her usual unruffled self. Her step was unfaltering, her demeanour composed. But inside herself she felt like a volcano of ice whose cold slopes might at any moment be consumed by an outburst of liquid fire. And even yet deeper inside herself she knew that this eruption would not occur and that Miss Sparling, Headmistress of the Hosiers' Girls' Foundation School, first Woman Freeman of the Worshipful Company of Hosiers, would never publicly fail in the decorum and self-command that her situation demanded.

The Master hung the badge round her neck and presented her with her charter of admission, sealed with the Company's Broad Seal. Miss Holly, suddenly materializing on the platform behind her employer, relieved her of the scroll and retired, leaving Miss Sparling to express her thanks, which she did briefly, sufficiently and with a very becoming dignity.

As Miss Sparling finished speaking, the head prefect found Miss Holly at her side, who under cover of the applause said something to her and returned to her seat at the end of the front row.

The head prefect got up.

'Sit down, dear,' said Miss Head from behind her.

But this was the head prefect's hour and power. 'Three cheers—' she began; but a fresh outburst of clapping drowned her voice. Looking scornfully at the backs of the audience in front of her, she waited for a pause and began again, 'Three cheers for Miss Sparling.'

The dreadful shrill, ragged, childish noise which is a number of girls trying to cheer burst from the Hosiers' girls and was echoed in a shamefaced way by part of the audience, who also banged on the floor with their sticks and umbrellas and clapped their hands. Miss Holly spoke to the music mistress who began playing 'For he's a jolly good fellow,' which was joyfully taken up by everyone, including the Master and all Hosiers present, Lord and Lady Pomfret and the Dean.

Miss Sparling wondered if one fainted or went mad when one was too happy and surprised, but at that moment her eye fell on Miss Pettinger in the front row. The headmistress of the Barchester High School was joining in the chorus with the air of Coriolanus trying to be friendly with the plebeians. But it was not so much her ungracious air which struck Miss Sparling as her general appearance, which hitherto she had been too much occupied to consider. Miss Pettinger, wearing her pre-war silver fox, now getting rather thin in places, over a claret-coloured coat with a band of monkey fur round the bottom edge, was a sight common enough not to attract special attention; nor was her tight new permanent wave any novelty to her acquaintance.

But upon the wave she was wearing a new hat, obviously destined for the final obliteration and destruction of Miss Sparling; a kind of Robin Hood hat of green felt with one long brown quill stuck jauntily through the high crown. A rather meagre piece of brown veiling was tied loosely round the crown and its end floated limply over her shoulders. Well did Miss Sparling know that nothing could shake Miss Pettinger's good opinion of herself, but her bosom was filled with content as she looked at her persecutor and knew that she, Miss Sparling, a member of a great City Company, was dressed exactly as in her position she should be dressed, even down to the V opening and the piece of lace. Steadied by this thought she was able to say the few words requisite to thank the Hosiers' Company in a firm voice.

There was an almost imperceptible pause. Miss Holly who had been holding a small piece of paper in her hand passed it up to the Remembrancer. He in his turn said something to the Master, who rose again and addressing Miss Sparling said that it was always the duty and privilege of the year's Master to ask for a half-holiday. On this unusual occasion, he said, he would ask Miss Sparling if she would grant a whole day's holiday. This Miss Sparling said she would be delighted to do as her first official act in the capacity of a Freeman.

The Remembrancer looked as if he were going to ask for more speeches, but it was now a quarter to four and tea and the play were yet to come, so Miss Holly, whose attention to detail was perfect, made a sign to the music mistress, the music mistress banged a chord, God Save the King was sung and that part of the proceedings terminated.

Miss Sparling, accompanied by the Master, led the way into the big drawing-room and took up her position between the two doors, so that the visitors could stream through unimpeded. Mrs

Wickens and Mrs Powlett were already behind the long trestle table with the tea-urns; Mr Wickens and Mr Simnet were ready with trays to hand tea to the more favoured visitors and Dorothy had orders to go between the drawing-room and the kitchen with kettles of hot water or crockery to be washed.

The first to congratulate Miss Sparling were the Pomfrets who had to get back as soon as possible for a Red Cross meeting at the Towers. They were followed by Mrs Belton who said very prettily how proud she was to have a Freeman of a City Company living at the Park, and then came Dr and Mrs Crawley.

'My warmest congratulations,' said the Dean shaking Miss Sparling's hand. 'If anything could add to the pleasure that we both feel at your well-deserved honour, Miss Sparling, it is the thought of how annoyed our friend will be. She wants to go as soon as tea is over, but I am determined to stay and see the girls act. If she likes to go in the motor bus she may, but out of this school we will not go till we have seen your play.'

'Here comes our friend,' said Mrs Crawley to her husband and at the same time drawing him away to let other guests follow on.

Miss Sparling, looking to her right, saw the Robin Hood hat approach. Her attention was claimed by the Rear-Admiral's wife, and when she looked again the hat was almost in the forefront of her guests, but the person underneath it was not Miss Pettinger, but Dr Morgan. It was quite obvious that both ladies had been to the same modiste in Barchester, and Miss Sparling in the middle of her triumph felt quite sorry for them. Then Mr Oriel, almost in tears with pride and joy, came forward with a kind of affectionate benediction, and other friends followed hard upon.

Tea was circulated industriously by Mr Wickens and Mr Simnet. Dorothy, overcome by having seen a lord, dropped a plateful of sandwiches on the carpet and trod on two of them.

The people who had to catch the motor bus back to Barchester took their leave and the party assumed more manageable proportions.

It was with a distinct sense of pleasure that Miss Sparling found Mr Carton by her side. She had not been conscious of thinking of him, but when she saw him she was glad.

'I wish Fluvius Minucius could have been here,' he said, 'or better still your grandfather. How extraordinarily pleased he would have been. Even more pleased than I am.'

Miss Sparling smiled.

'I wish Grandpapa could have been here too,' she said earnestly. 'But you will do quite as well as Minucius. And, Mr Carton, I do not wish to be unkind to anyone, least of all to you, but *could* you very kindly go and talk to Miss Pettinger. She seems to be quite alone.'

Mr Carton said he was in Christian charity with all the world at the moment and went towards Miss Pettinger, who by the ill luck which that day had dogged her (and not undeserved many people will think), had been hemmed into a corner by the stout Free Hosier and the man in the loud tweeds, who were arguing about the time the Simplon Express left Paris before the war. Much struck by her hat, of which he caught glimpses over the people between them, he forged through the press towards her and had almost reached her when a voice at his elbow said, 'How do you do, Mr Carton. I don't suppose you remember me. I am Dr Morgan.'

One very rarely does remember the people who say one doesn't remember them, but one would sooner die than admit it, and also would like to kill them for the insulting assumption that one is deficient in social qualities. Mr Carton did remember that he had once met Dr Morgan at the Perrys' and hoped not to meet her often again. But what interested him at the moment, so much that he quite forgot how deeply he disliked her, was her hat; a kind of Robin Hood hat of green felt with one long quill stuck jauntily through the crown, a rather meagre piece of brown veiling tied round it, its ends floating limply upon her shoulders.

'Of course I remember you, Dr Morgan,' he said, 'and I do so want you to meet another very distinguished lady. Miss Pettinger,' he continued, bursting with a slight apology through the crowd, 'it is a pleasure to see you here. I much want to make you acquainted with another lady very distinguished in her profession, Dr Morgan.'

Having performed which kind and thoughtful action he left the two Robin Hood ladies to make the best of themselves and their hats, and fell into talk with the Master of the Hosiers' Company.

It was now half-past four, the Barchester bus contingent had gone, and the Hosiers were to leave at half-past five. Miss Sparling invited the company to return to the hall, where the estate carpenter and his nephew back on leave had during tea prepared the stage, hung the curtains, and put the chairs in order.

The audience, now reduced in numbers by the departure of the Barchester visitors and such people as were bicycling or driving in pony-traps and did not wish to be out after dusk, settled itself more comfortably. Mrs Belton with Captain Hornby and the Crawleys sat together in the middle of the hall. Mrs Updike and Mrs Perry with her foreign guests sat in front of them, joined by Mr Updike and Dr Perry who had just arrived, so they were able to talk at their ease till the play began.

'Oh, Mrs Belton,' said Mrs Perry in rather a loud voice,

turning round, '*such* good news. We are hoping to get all the three boys here at once in March. We haven't had them all together for ages.'

Mrs Belton, who fully sympathized with any parents who got their offspring all under their wing at the same time, was just beginning to express her pleasure, when she felt a tap on her shoulder. No one likes to be touched suddenly by an unknown hand, and to those who have read too many novels a tap on the shoulder is unpleasantly associated with the Inquisition, Bow Street Runners, Sbirri and Scotland Yard. Mrs Belton turned, startled, and found the man in the loud tweeds leaning forward from behind her.

'Pardon me, Mrs Belton,' said the man, 'but you are Mrs Belton, aren't you? I heard that lady say Mrs Belton so I thought I'd presume.'

Even the best-bred are confronted with situations that for the moment they hardly know how to handle. Mrs Belton's first impulse was to say 'Unhand me, sir,' her second to pretend she was not herself. Her third and visible reaction was to say politely that she was Mrs Belton, with a questioning inflexion in her voice, clearly showing that she would like to know who was addressing her.

Whether the man understood the inflexion or not, we cannot say.

'I'm pleased to meet you, Mrs Belton,' he said, putting his strong heavy hand over the back of Mrs Belton's chair, so that she had to shake it in a most uncomfortable and contorted way. 'My little girl's told me about you. Adams is my name.'

'Oh – how do you do, Mr Adams,' said Mrs Belton, her politeness running ahead of her other faculties, for at the moment the name conveyed nothing to her at all.

'I dare say Mr Belton has mentioned my name,' Mr Adams continued. 'We've had one or two turn-ups on the bench – I'm Adams J.P. you know – but it's always a fair go and a ding-dong go and no malice borne.'

Mrs Belton, with a great gush of gratitude to Providence for explaining who her new acquaintance was, said of *course* her husband had *often* mentioned Mr Adams and told her how very helpful he had been.

'That's right,' said Mr Adams, gratified. 'The old gentleman was quite wrought up as they say about the War Agricultural Executive Committee. "If anyone tried to tell me how to do *my* work," I said to him, "I'd tan the skin off his backside," I said, if you'll pardon the expression.'

Mrs Belton said she *absolutely* agreed. At the same moment her sixth, or social, sense informed her that Mr Adams's little girl was that very large, pasty-faced girl who had got on so well with her husband on the subject of rats.

'Your daughter came to tea with us after the school had been visiting the Garden House,' she said, 'and my husband and she got on very well. She knew all about rats.'

'You've hit it in one, Mrs Belton,' said Mr Adams. 'She's a good girl, my little Heth, if a bit self-willed at times. But then she takes after her dad. Self-willed I may be, Heth, I said to her, but don't forget I'm self-made too and that's more than you'll ever be, thanks to your old dad's hard work.'

As he spoke he put his large face so far forward that Mrs Belton, who was already having to talk with her neck wrung as he was directly behind her, almost drew back in alarm. Also, for which she blamed herself, she was fastidiously irritated by his pet name for Heather, which he pronounced by dropping the last syllable and keeping the soft 'th'.

'Well, pleased to have met you, I'm sure,' said Mr Adams, sitting back again.

To Mrs Belton's relief the lights in the hall were now put out and the curtains drawn apart. As all amateur theatricals are exclusively for the benefit of the actors with no reference to the wishes or tastes of the audience, we will not attempt to describe these in any detail. The head prefect, swollen with Miss Sparling's honour in which she dimly felt she shared as having started the cheering, made a creditable Jacques. The Captain of Hockey, holding the bauble decorated with the bells off Ellen Humble's nephew's reins, came out even stronger as Touchstone than she had in rehearsals. The fair girl in the Lower Sixth was a very pretty Celia and brought the house down by her emphasis on the words 'doublet and HOSE'. The tall dark girl in the Upper Sixth remembered to put expression into her lines, doing so chiefly by emphasizing such words as to and for: by, with and from. Duke (in Miss Ferdinand's velvet cap with the feather), courtiers, foresters made appropriate gestures. The two girls in the Lower Fifth, one of them wearing Miss Ferdinand's yellow wig, sang their song very sweetly, accompanied from behind the scenes by Miss Ferdinand with ravishing divisions on a ukulele.

The real stars of the day, as our readers hardly need us to tell them, were Miss Ferdinand, dashing, timorous, mocking and love-sick in her green tights, and Heather Adams who, in a shapeless dress made by Miss Holly from old sacks, her scanty pale hair loose, word-perfect and entirely without enthusiasm for her part, was as good an Audrey as you would wish to see.

By half-past five the entertainment was over. The Viator motor coach took the Hosiers away to Barchester, and such of the audience as were personal friends of Miss Sparling's retired with her to the drawing-room for a few final words of congratulation. Mrs Perry asked leave to introduce two friends to Miss Sparling.

'Monsieur and Madame Brownscu,' she said, 'from South-bridge. Madame Brownscu was telling me about the theatre in Mixo-Lydia.'

Miss Sparling said how glad she was they had enjoyed the play.

'Enjoyed I do not say,' said Mme Brownscu, 'for to see acting en amateur repugnates me. In Mixo-Lydia we have a Company Repertorczy which you say Repertory, giving the plays of our greatest dramaturges for ever; over all the plays of Prsvb, intel-lectual of the first run which is dead at the age of twenty years, tout ce qu'il y a de plus moderne, pas comme Shakespeare dont on ne s'occupe plus. Tu te rappelles la Compagnie Repertorczy, Gogo?' she said to her companion.

'Czy pròvka, pròvka, pròvka,' said Mr Brownscu, huddling deeper into his sheepskin coat at the thought of Repertory.

'He says, "No, never, never, never,"' Madame Brownscu kindly translated for the benefit of her hearers.

Mrs Hunter who, so everyone considered, had no business to linger as if she were an old friend, said that in Slavo-Lydia Shakespeare's plays were acted regularly and the schoolchildren were forced to attend them all.

'In Slavo-Lydia that does not astonish me,' said Madame Brownscu in a frightening though obscure way.

'It has been a most pleasant afternoon, Miss Sparling,' said Mrs Hunter graciously. 'Quite a treat. I so much regret that my friend has not turned up. She would have enjoyed meeting you and might have been helpful to your girls. You must let me bring her to talk to them some day.'

Miss Sparling, with her usual pleasant manner, asked what the friend's subject was.

'Slavo-Lydia,' said Mrs Hunter. 'She is a charming girl. She was to be in Barchester today and had promised to come out to the school, but I fear she has been detained. She has to go and speak at a factory somewhere.'

Madame Brownscu, addressing an unknown deity on the cornice, said there existed no Slavo-Lydian which was charming. God willed it so.

'This young lady now,' said Mr Adams, to the surprise of all present. 'A short young lady, was she, by any chance? Not much in the way of looks? Foreign-looking, if you know what I mean?'

Mrs Hunter said she was certainly not very tall, but was of a very old Slavo-Lydian family and highly educated. She was on a mission to England to tell the workers how lazy and ignorant they were, and to encourage brotherly love between the nations.

Most of those present, who had all felt the same about their servants, gardeners, workmen, day labourers, nearly burst with rage on hearing these aspersions on the British working class.

'I think I can give you news of the young lady, madam,' said Mr Adams. 'She came over to Hogglestock today and asked to see me. Now I'm a self-made man and I believe in a fair deal, but only up to a certain point if you take my meaning. So I said to Miss Hooper, my seckertary that is, to bring her along and I'd see if it was worth wasting my time, because I was out in the yard looking at some of our new machine tools and bushes, a very pretty job too, to a thousandth of an inch, and I was a bit dirty for the office. So out comes your young lady and says she wants to talk to the hands in the lunch hour. Well, what about, I said. My chaps don't mind a good talk on something they know about, like precision work or the use of the micrometer, or the blast furnace, but they won't stand for any highbrow stuff. So my young lady says she wants to tell them that they are slaves and don't work half hard enough, and they are capittleists and are sweated by their employer, and in Slavo-Lydia all the hands work eighteen hours a day for twopence an hour and they must have a revolution and destroy the army and the navy and the air force and send a big expeditionary force to fight all Slavo-Lydia's enemies on six fronts. So I said the last fellow that tried to tell them that nearly got chucked in the rolling-mill. Well then, she says, what about giving us some money? Who, us? I said. The Anglo-Slavo-Lydian Red Cross Fund, she said. All right, miss, I said. You go back to Piccadilly Circus and I'll send a cheque for twenty pounds to the Red Cross by the afternoon post. So I shook hands with her and off she went.'

'You have shake her hand, cette espèce de chameau?' said Madame Brownscu advancing angrily.

'You wait a moment, madam,' said Mr Adams. 'If you'd been handling a lot of machine tools your hands might be a bit oily. So might my men's hands in the machine-shop be a bit oily. So I said they could all shake hands. And, believe me, that oil takes some washing off,' said Mr Adams meditatively.

Mrs Hunter, who had only just seized the point of this story, drew herself up and said she thought it a most heartless piece of anti-Slavo-Lydian feeling and hoped that he had at least sent the cheque.

'Now, you just wait a moment, madam, the way I said. You've only to ask anywhere in Barchester and you'll hear that Sam Adams's word is as good as his bond,' said Mr Adams. 'I sent a cheque for twenty pounds to the Red Cross this afternoon, same as I said. I did *not* say the Slavo-Lydian Red Cross to the young lady. I sent it to the British Red Cross and told them to earmark it for our prisoners of war.'

'Aha! you see me this one, he has treeked Slavo-Lydia,' said

Madame Brownscu. 'Comprends tu, Gogo? Ce type a triché ces sales Slavo-Lydiens, which massacre us in 1830.'

Mrs Updike, with her gay laugh, said she never could remember which was which of Mixo-Lydians and Slavo-Lydians, and anyway had a perfect thing about all those countries that kept on changing their names and making geography all wrong.

Mrs Hunter said as it was getting so dark she would be going. No one appeared to wish to accompany her, so she went.

'And we must be going too, Josiah,' said Mrs Crawley to the Dean. 'Is Miss Pettinger there? Oh, Miss Pettinger, if you are ready we really ought to be starting. Good-bye, Miss Sparling, and all our congratulations again.'

The Dean also bade good-bye to his hostess, emphasizing his pleasure in her new honour in a way calculated to inflame Miss Pettinger's spirit.

The headmistress of the Barchester High School then approached the Headmistress of the Hosiers' Girls' Foundation School, the woman whom she had so pinpricked and even bullied for so long.

'I cannot tell you,' said Miss Sparling to her late persecutor, gulping down at one gulp all the feelings of resentment and dislike that had sometimes nearly overwhelmed her and caused her many unhappy heart-searchings, 'how very much I appreciate your presence here today, Miss Pettinger. When I think of your hospitality to the School and to me and Miss Holly, I feel we all owe you a very great debt. And I feel that no one but you can realize how difficult it has all been. Thank you from us all for sparing time to come to our Bobbin Day.'

So challenged, Miss Pettinger, forcing herself to think of the honour of the Headmistresses' Association of which she was a Past President, shook hands with Miss Sparling and with a real effort said that she congratulated her most warmly on her well-deserved honour and on the delightful entertainment provided by the girls and further expressed the wish that the two schools might meet upon the hockey field at no distant date. She then went away with the Crawleys. And though her temper was not improved by hearing the Dean and Mrs Crawley sing Miss Sparling's praises all the way back, she did feel the better for having been civil to Miss Sparling and magnanimously resolved to forgive her rival the injuries she, Miss Pettinger, had done her, and to concentrate her whole dislike upon Dr Morgan and her Robin Hood hat.

As the Deanery party left, the actresses, now back in their hideous white Bobbin Day frocks, came into the drawing-room with Miss Head to be congratulated. Heather Adams made for her father who was talking to Captain Hornby.

'And here's my little Heth,' said Mr Adams, giving his daughter a hearty kiss. 'I suppose you'll be wanting to go on the stage now, Heth. This little girl of mine wants to be a Wren. What do you think of that?'

Captain Hornby thought nobly of the Wrens and in no way approved Miss Adams's ambition, but he did not like to put it in those words, so he said it was a splendid service, and congratulated Heather upon her acting. Heather, who had seen Captain Hornby when he first entered the hall with Mrs Belton and had not this time taken him for Commander Belton, looked faintly pleased.

'Wrens are all very well,' said Mr Adams, 'and Heth would look a treat in one of those little hats, but she's going to be my little partner, aren't you, Heth? Ever since Mrs Adams left Heth and I, when Heth was a toddler, we've been each other's best pals, haven't we, Heth? She knows any amount about my works,

Captain I-didn't-catch-the-name, as would surprise you. It's in the blood. My grandfather was in the Crewe railway shops and my father was in the naval line and finished up as chief engineer in H.M.S. *Carraway.*'

'She was my father's flagship at one time,' said Captain Hornby. 'Admiral Hornby.'

'Many's the time I've heard my father speak of the Admiral,' said Mr Adams admiringly. 'Pleased to have met you, Captain Hornby. I understand you are the fiancé of Mrs Belton's young lady. If she's as nice a lady as her mother, you'll do well. And Mr Belton's a nice old gentleman, but he doesn't understand how to look after Number One. He lets all those jacks-in-office at the War Agricultural Committee put it over him. Well, I must be pushing back. Is my journey really necessary, you may say. Well as regards that the answer is Yes, when I'm coming to see my Heth. How she made herself look like that in the play quite passes the comprehension as they say. It didn't seem feasible that Audrey being my little Heth.'

Shaking hands with Captain Hornby he went over to Miss Sparling.

'Excuse me, but that's a nice bit of work,' he said, indicating the badge of the Hosiers which reposed upon Miss Sparling's bosom, 'and believe me I know something about metals. Well, thanks for the invite. My little Heth came out surprisingly. It really didn't seem feasible her looking like that. Well, I must say good-bye. Pleased to meet all your friends. You must bring some of the girls down to the works one day. We'll take them round the machine shops and the rolling mills.'

Miss Sparling said, with truth, that they would enjoy it very much and, she was sure, learn a great deal, upon which Mr Adams, much gratified, went away, having issued a general invitation to everyone present to come and see the next big casting. The rest of the company dispersed, Mrs Belton and Captain Hornby going with their friends by the drive, for it was too dark to go comfortably by the field path.

To crown the exciting day Miss Sparling had her evening meal with the girls, wearing her badge; congratulated every girl who had taken part in the performance separately, said a tactful and kind word to each mistress and thanked every one for their help.

'You won't want me tonight,' said Miss Holly, who had accompanied her superior to the West Pavilion.

'I would if I weren't so sleepy,' said Miss Sparling, taking off the badge. 'We'll do those letters tomorrow. Thank you very much for your help. If you hadn't reminded us about the extra holiday, we should all have forgotten. You could run this place just as well as I can. Better perhaps. I do feel tired sometimes.'

'I don't say that I couldn't run it,' said Miss Holly, who had a very just estimate of her own powers, 'but not just yet. It all went very well. If there's nothing I can do for you I'm going to bed.'

There was only one thing wanting, Miss Sparling thought as she settled comfortably to read in bed; her grandfather to talk to. How proud and pleased he would have been. Or even dear old Mr Oriel, who treated her like a daughter and was, she knew, the only person to whom she didn't seem a competent, self-sufficing and entirely grown-up person. Or Mr Carton who, though he was sometimes rather dry and donnish, did understand her feelings for Fluvius Minucius.

Then sleep fell upon the West Pavilion and upon the whole school.

*

Only one other piece of conversation is worth recording. In the Vicarage kitchen Mrs Powlett was entertaining Mr and Mrs Wickens to a late collation after the dining-room had been cleared away (a phrase misleading to the reason but perfectly plain to the intelligence).

'Miss Sparling looked quite queenly,' said Mrs Powlett. 'And that gentleman in his robes and things. I shouldn't wonder if they made a match of it. She'll be looking high now.'

Mr Wickens repeated this remark to his wife.

'That's all right, Wickens, no need to break my eardrum,' said his wife placidly. 'What I say is you never know with gentlemen, and they do say sitting together and reading out of the same book has often Brought Things About.'

'It's letters you must be careful of,' said Mrs Powlett. 'They say if once you sign your name to a letter you're as good as engaged.'

'"Do right and fear no man; don't write and fear no woman,"' said Mr Wickens, not very gallantly.

'Mrs Powlett,' said Dorothy.

'Well?' said Mrs Powlett.

'How long does it take to get a letter from London?'

The company, including Mrs Wickens who had suddenly heard quite plainly, laid down their knives and forks and stared at Dorothy.

'It's all according,' said Mrs Powlett. 'And what do you want to know for, my girl?'

'Mr Simnet said Valentine's Day was past and gone, but he'd send me a nice picture card to remember him by,' said Dorothy.

'Now, look here, Dorothy,' said the outraged Mrs Powlett. 'Just you finish up what's on your plate and wash up those few things in the scullery and go to bed. You won't see *me* taking you to the play again if that's the kind of goings-on. Don't dawdle.'

Dorothy finished her supper quickly and silently and went off to break a plate or two in the scullery under the influence of Romance.

'Picture cards!' said Mrs Wickens darkly.

Mr Wickens said you couldn't be young but the once and they must be getting home now.

Up till the present time the weather had been mild and open for the time of the year, but now, seeing a good prospect of lambs and swelling twig-buds, it began to get colder and colder. By the last week in February the ground was hard, the winter grass brittle, and by the first week in March the ponds were frozen, birds lying dead on their backs with clenched claws, all garden-ing suspended. The great question, looming above the war and even above the Help for Mixo-Lydia week (which would have been a failure in any case), was Would the ice hold? First the sedges round the lake in Harefield Park were held in the frozen water; then the icy film spread; Humble and some of his friends kept guard as over a holy relic and gave a sound thrashing to a few Barchester louts who came over and threw stones onto the virgin expanse, in the certainty that if the case came before the magistrates, the law would wink. Finally at the end of the week even the slight troubling of the water over the spring that fed the lake was stilled, and though the spring continued to flow it was imprisoned till it got below the sluices. The lake was then formally declared open for skating by Mr Belton. The A.R.P. volunteered to keep order among the crowd, the N.F.S. to bring ropes and ladders to rescue anyone who got drowned, and the

W.V.S. under Lady Pomfret and Mrs Perry to run a coffee stall for the skaters. The crowds were not so great as in former winters, for the bus service between Harefield and Barchester was bad; the coffee though hot tasted of powdered milk; the sandwiches were tainted with indigestible health-giving vitamins; but there were enough people from the neighbourhood to keep the pond cheerful till the warmthless sun went down like a thin disc of pale gold in a hard, clear emerald sky.

Miss Sparling had not forgotten the Master's request, and when the ice had been tested, and the weather promised to hold, she announced that the next day but one would be Hosiers' Holyday (pronounced holiday). All girls who had skates would be allowed to skate, within the limits marked by Humble who knew the lake better than any man alive. All those who could not skate would be allowed to slide if they liked, and if they didn't there would be a Nature Ramble at a good brisk pace in Lord Pomfret's grounds with a private view of the sheeted state rooms and tea in the hall.

Whether the Admiralty and the hush-hush jobs took any special cognizance of their employees' engagements we do not know, but Elsa and Captain Hornby again got leave at the same time, and owing to an understanding between Room 149 and a very secret person called X47, whom everyone knew to be Mr Fanshawe, the Dean of Paul's, seconded for the duration while his wife ran an important bit of motor transport, Commander Belton was also let loose for a few days.

Mrs Belton, going down the street to see what the butcher could do about a bit of something off the ration, saw Mrs Perry with her three sons who, as we do or do not remember, were all getting leave at the same time. To see three young men not in uniform was so peculiar that Mrs Belton stopped to stare.

Mrs Perry, who always forgot entirely about her Mixo-Lydian activities when any of her sons were about, looked delightfully proud. Mrs Belton quite sympathized with her, merely reserving the right to be sorry for anyone who hadn't got a daughter.

'How is the shop?' she said to the young Perrys, having learnt that this question seemed to cover everything.

'Oh, just about the same old usual,' said one of the young men.

'You're doing Leprosy, aren't you?' said Mrs Belton.

'Wrong in one, Mrs Belton,' said the young man, who had a rather long nose. 'I'm Jim – the Sawbones, you know. It's Gus that does those foul skin troubles.'

'How stupid of me,' said Mrs Belton, wishing she could say, 'but you have all grown so much,' which she couldn't very well do to young men who had (it is to be hoped) stopped growing some years ago. 'And you are House Physician now, aren't you, Bob?' she continued to one of the young men who had bushy eyebrows.

'That's Bob,' said the young man. 'I'm Gus. Skin affections. All except warts. It's a queer thing, but it still takes an old woman in a cottage to cure warts. I dare say we'll find out why some day. Even Buckston can't account for it.'

Here both his brothers raised their right hands, remarking 'Heil Buckston.'

'You must excuse Gus,' said the third young Perry, who had sleek dark hair and already wore the manner which is going to take him very far in Harley Street if he and Harley Street are spared. 'He's got Buckston on the brain. A very good man, but we don't encourage Führer worship.'

The three Perrys then attacked each other joyfully. Their mother said they had better fight it out on the ice that afternoon and Mrs Belton went on her way feeling that Bob Sawyer and Ben Allen though being dead yet lived.

The butcher was most obliging with some liver and an oxtail, and on hearing that Mr Freddy was at home said in a jocular way that he'd a few scraps for a cat and pressed into Mrs Belton's basket a parcel which was found later to contain three chops and a kidney.

She then took her place in the fish queue, which luckily was only a short one that morning, for though there was not much wind what there was was keen and the sun was quite obviously a substitute for itself. Here she was joined by Mrs Updike, who in spite of a piece of sticking-plaster on her chin was looking more absurdly young and gay than ever, with four very tall boys and girls hanging on to her, two in His Majesty's uniform, two in obvious school clothes.

'Isn't it lovely, I've got them all at home,' said Mrs Updike. 'I knew the big ones were getting leave, but I'd no idea the little ones would be here. There was chickenpox at school and they hadn't enough nurses, so the ones that were out of quarantine were sent home and probably caught it in the train or the bus on the way. I think quarantine is all rubbish. I've a kind of thing about infectious diseases; you either get them or you don't, so why worry. And now we are hunting for our dinner, because as you can see by my chin I've been so stupid again.'

Mrs Belton said she had noticed the sticking-plaster and hoped it wasn't serious.

'Oh, not a bit,' said Mrs Updike, 'but I did mean to be out much earlier to get some fish, only I was dusting Phil's study and I tripped over the electric light wire and the table lamp came crashing down, so I tried to save it but somehow we all fell into Phil's big chair together and the electric bulb broke itself on my chin and it wouldn't stop bleeding. But I managed to stanch or staunch it, I never know which,' Mrs Updike continued joyously, 'and so here we are. Smoked mackerel. I've got a sort of thing about smoked fish, because I always think if it had been *really* fresh they wouldn't have smoked it, except kippers which one feels were practically born smoked. Oh, and herrings and that peculiar fish that looks grey inside like people with heart trouble.'

By this time Mrs Belton had bought some cod and said good-bye to the Updikes. All the young Updikes smiled at her in a very friendly way which was all she expected, for what with taking after their father who was a silent man except when he had to talk on business, and their mother's carefree flow of talk, they were hardly ever known to say anything, though on the best terms with their parents and each other. Whether in the regimental mess, the W.A.A.F. hostel, the fifth-form room at Southbridge School or the dormitory at St Perdita's School evacuated from St Leonards to Abergobblyn, the four young Updikes communicated with their co-workers, we shall never know.

'Are you coming to the lake?' she inquired, as she left the shop.

Mrs Updike said the children were going to skate all the afternoon and the whole of the next day, and she would be helping at the W.V.S. coffee stall.

'I was going to try to skate,' she said laughing, 'but Phil has a thing about it and says he won't have one peaceful moment if I'm on the ice. Not that I can skate, but I simply adore sliding. I did try to skate once, but I fell down and managed to cut my right arm with my left skate. Do you remember, chicks?'

Three of the young Updikes nodded gravely. The younger Master Updike, he who was at Southbridge School, was suddenly moved to laughter at the remembrance of his mother's misfortune, but vengeance at once overtook him and his voice cracked in the middle, at which he blushed furiously and Mrs Belton left the whole family laughing at each other and everything.

About lunch time Captain Hornby and Commander Belton arrived. Mrs Belton had, for no particular reason, expected Elsa to be with them, and felt an unreasonable chill, and told herself how very silly she was. Directly after tea Mr Updike came by appointment to talk business with Mr Belton and Captain Hornby. When these gentlemen had gone to the study, Mrs Belton sat with her elder son and they talked very comfortably of births, deaths and marriages among their friends, though all the time at the back of her mind she was ill at ease. Suddenly there was an unusually loud ring at the front door, followed by a good deal of noise which Mrs Belton with a mother's fine instinct at once recognized as her younger son, and in a moment Charles came in, looking broader and taller than ever.

'Totally unexpected arrival of Lost Hero,' said Charles. 'Hullo, Freddy! I say, Mother, I don't know what you give girls for their weddings now everything's rationed, but I hope this is all right.'

He pulled from a haversack with some difficulty a large, dirty, shapeless parcel. This he undid and took from it the largest, most delicate, most exquisite Shetland shawl Mrs Belton had ever seen.

'Oh, Charles, how lovely!' exclaimed Mrs Belton. 'What a heavenly shawl.'

'I'd rather give it to you than to Elsa,' said Charles, with a younger brother's frankness, 'but if you think it's all right she can have it. Oh, and if you like this it's for you,' he added, producing from the dirty parcel an incredibly soft, dark blue muffler and handing it to his elder brother.

'Thank you very much indeed,' said Commander Belton. 'If I may guess, I should say you've been somewhere north of London.'

'Having a splendid time, all among your blokes,' said Charles. 'And one could get anything off the locals for rum. That's how I got these. No coupons and by the time we had talked a bit they would have given me these for nothing. I say, Mother, I must show you my new beret.'

He dashed into the hall and crashed back with a beret made of red and white checks proudly on one side of his head. 'I can't tell you what this is,' he said, 'but it's the latest. The simply super-latest. What do you think of it?'

His mother privately thought, as she had thought about the pale green beret, that if there was one thing on earth that could spoil her younger son's good looks, it was the hat he was wearing. So she expressed her admiration of it and Charles, after having a good look at himself in the mirror over the mantelpiece, said he liked it. It was, he said, a good sort of hat. Charles chattered away, talking to his brother about naval men he had been meeting and to his mother about the clothes he needed washing and mending, the amount of food and sleep he proposed to have, the urgency for a hair-cut in Barchester, the tobacco he wanted. But all in such an agreeable and debonair way that his mother felt she would not be presuming too far if she asked how long he could stay.

'Oh, all today and most of tomorrow,' said Charles. 'I expect I'll get the 6.5 from Barchester to London and catch a train from there. My employers don't give me much time.'

Mrs Belton was sorry that his visit was to be so short, but glad that he had come and thought it very good of him to make the journey when there was so little to amuse him at home now.

'You know they are skating,' she said.

'Oh, goody-goody,' said Charles. 'Where are my skates?'

The skates were of course in the bottom of a trunk in one of the attic rooms where there was only a very perfunctory black-out curtain, as the room was never used. In spite of his mother's

300

fears and pleadings Charles said he would manage with his torch so long as the beastly thing wasn't locked and fled upstairs two steps at a time.

Hardly had the noise of his boots on the uncarpeted attic stairs died away when Elsa arrived, delighted to find her elder brother there, but apparently missing something.

'Isn't Christopher here, Mother?' she said. 'I wanted him to wait and come down with me, but he wouldn't wait. I did think he might have waited for me.'

Mrs Belton said he was in the study with Mr Belton and Mr Updike.

'I must say,' said Elsa, 'it seems a frightful waste of time to make settlements and things. I wish one could just get married without all this fuss. It would be much more sensible if all the money could be spent on Harefield and we could all go back there again.'

'I don't suppose Christopher would exactly see the point of your living at Harefield,' said Commander Belton.

'You know what I mean,' said Elsa impatiently. 'Of course we'll have to live in Scotland sometimes, but I want Christopher to buy a place somewhere round here after the war and then I could help Father with Harefield. Or Christopher might build a house on a bit of Father's land and pay him rent for it. It would all help. Father can't run it alone.'

'I expect I'll be here after the war,' said Commander Belton. 'I'm just about in the position where one gets axed.'

'That would be perfect, Freddy,' said his sister. 'There's such a lot that ought to be done if Harefield is to go on. Christopher could easily spare some money.'

If Commander Belton was not exactly enamoured of the plan that his sister and her husband should practically take charge of Harefield while the present owner and his heir were alive, he did not mention it, and what is more tried to keep a silence that would not seem reproachful, though whether his sister was capable of realizing such fine shades at the moment we cannot say. Mrs Belton, the chill again at her heart as Elsa's voice became hard and impatient, drew her attention to Charles's shawl. To her mother's relief Elsa at once became satisfactorily feminine. Charles burst back into the drawing-room with his skates and was delighted by Elsa's joyful praise of his present. The men came in from the study and Charles was warmly welcomed.

'Oh, I say, Father,' said Charles diving yet again into the filthy parcel and producing another soft muffler, of misty grey-brown, 'you needn't have this if you don't like it.'

'A very fine muffler, my boy,' said Mr Belton, secretly bursting with pride and gratitude; and seeing that his remark had not given offence to Charles, he felt more grateful still.

Mr Updike then said good-bye and Charles accompanied him to the front door, being so long absent that had it not been for his skates on the floor and the dirty parcel on a chair his mother would almost have thought that his presence was a delusion. He returned safely after about a quarter of an hour, but again filled his mother's heart with concern by removing the skates and parcel to his bedroom. As his normal course would have been to leave them about till he needed them, or even to clean and grease his skating boots on the drawing-room carpet, all mothers will realize Mrs Belton's anxiety and her secret wish to take his temperature. Encouraged by his bonhomie she almost suggested it, but she wisely decided that this might be going too far and left him alone.

The evening passed peacefully on the whole. Elsa appeared to have got over her outburst of impatience and her mother hoped that she would not worry her father with her plans, for she knew he would resent the interference and might lose his temper; a thing he seldom did.

People on leave usually enjoy sleeping, and all the visitors went to bed early, as did Mr Belton who had been out all day till tea time superintending the skating and occasionally making an excursion on to the ice with a broom to sweep stones and sticks away. Mrs Belton, who was nearly always a little in arrears with her large correspondence, for she was a kind of family clearing-house for a large circle of relations, remained in the drawing-room and settled down to her letters. As she finished the sixth letter and licked the so-called economy label that was to take the envelope back to its sender, her son Charles came in, apparently for no better reason than to pay her a call. Like a fowler who sees the bird almost in his net, she remained as quiet as possible, writing her letters with an occasional smile at Charles, hoping not to scare this rare bird. The bird, whose hair was very rumpled and who was to his mother's eye quite devastatingly good-looking in his old camel-hair dressing-gown, seemed quite content to sit by the fire and warm his knees until his mother had licked her last label and shut her bureau.

'I say, Mother,' said Charles, trying to keep a sense of great importance out of his voice, 'what do you think I've done?'

'Either you're going to be made a captain or you've got engaged,' said Mrs Belton. 'And either would be quite agreeable to me.'

'Well, it wouldn't to me,' said Charles. 'At least getting engaged wouldn't. Not to the sort of girls they keep nowadays. I've made a will.'

'Good gracious, why, darling?' said Mrs Belton idiotically.

'Well, one ought to,' said Charles. 'After all I'm over

twenty-one and if I die intestate the Government gets some, doesn't it? I mean even more than it gets anyway. So I told Mr Updike I wanted a kind of easy will and he made one in the study. And what is more, I'm going to sign it tomorrow, with a witness,' said Charles proudly. 'I must say it will look awfully well, "Charles Thorne Belton".'

'It sounds quite a sensible thing to do,' said his mother.

'As a matter of fact I left it all to you,' said Charles.

'Oh, darling!' said his mother.

'There isn't much,' said Charles reflectively. 'There's that two hundred pounds that old Aunt Mary left me in Government Bonds and a bit of my twenty-firster tips and a bit of my pay that I've saved. Anyway you're very welcome to it.'

Mrs Belton was not one of those people who feel that to make a will means instant death to the testator. Wills to her were, on the whole, things that everyone made and in many cases (notably in that of Aunt Mary) altered at least once a year through a long and quarrelsome life. Therefore Charles's announcement did not unduly discompose her and she merely wondered vaguely why no one had ever thought of his making a will before. But she was touched by his kind thought of her and thanked him very much indeed, though not presuming to kiss him.

'It's not for ever, you know,' said Charles with the air of a K.C. browbeating a reluctant witness. 'It's only for your life. And then it all gets divided up among my nephews and nieces if I have any. I mean if I had any because I'll be dead then. Do you think that sounds all right?' he asked, suddenly anxious.

His mother said it sounded splendid and she hoped she and all Charles's nephews and nieces would never get it.

'I did think of Father,' said Charles, warming to his subject, 'but I know he's in a bit of a hole with the taxes and everything, so I thought a little bit of money like that would be no use to him, so I thought you'd better have it all so that you could spend it on something.'

This very intelligent way of looking at his property impressed Charles's mother very much. It was quite true, alas, that two or three hundred pounds would be of little or no use to Fred with the estate encumbered as it was, whereas she could do a hundred things with such a sum for the house and for herself. Then she pulled herself up with a jerk, for it was Charles she wanted and not the pounds.

'Well, that's about all,' said Charles yawning. 'I'm off to bed. I've got to go down to Mr Updike's office tomorrow morning and then I'll skate. Oh, this is for you.'

Mrs Belton stood over him while he extracted from a pocket of his dressing-gown a Shetland woollen jumper of a feathery design, knitted in a misty blue wool that matched his mother's eyes.

'The last they had,' he said. 'I hope it's all right.'

He then allowed his mother to kiss the top of his head and went yawning to bed.

Mrs Belton remained by the fire, holding the soft wool that would almost have gone through a wedding ring, feeling Charles's rumpled hair against her cheek, till the growing chill made her turn out the lights and go to bed.

On the following morning Charles with the visit to his lawyer in view shaved with more than usual care, thus keeping his sister Elsa out of the bathroom, so that her day began badly. He then ate a very large breakfast, gave his belt and boots a final shine, touched up his buttons, put on his hideous beret and walked to Clive's Corner, the cynosure of every eye, causing the fish queue nearly to twist its head off. At Clive's Corner he signed his will, which to his immense pride was witnessed by Mr Updike's elderly clerk, and was then fallen upon by all the silent young Updikes who were off to the lake. From Plassey House the three Perry boys avalanched down on them carrying hockey sticks. A noisy contingent from Madras Cottages, bent on sliding, attached itself to the group with offers (not disinterested) to carry their skates. A brief halt was made at Arcot House while Charles fetched his skates and an extra scarf, and the procession moved on again with a good deal of noise (chiefly proceeding from Plassey House and Madras Cottages) up past the church, in at the lodge gates, sharp to the left, along the edge of the lake to where, at its tree-shadowed upper end, the W.V.S. were getting their coffee stall ready.

When we say coffee stall, it was one of those curious cars made of pale yellow varnished wood with seats in front and a kind of little van behind. This the ingenuity of Lord Pomfret's carpenter had converted into a tiny canteen with an urn, shelves, cupboards and a spirit stove which so far had not set anything on fire. Coffee, being unrationed, flowed freely and small quantities of (powdered) milk were added which did not make it appreciably nastier; buns and sandwiches had been laid in, warranted to stay the stoutest stomach; meat pies made of vitamin pastry and corned meat were to arrive as soon as they came out of the Rajah Café's oven.

Forty or fifty people had already assembled and were skating, or sliding, or looking on, but the real crowd was not expected till the afternoon. The Perry boys, who regarded the world as a large hospital with strong athletic tendencies, at once organized ice hockey. Emissaries sped back to the village to collect old hockey sticks or any kind of heavy stick with a curved handle.

Old Major Hargreaves from 'Chandernagore' appeared wheeling a garden basket with four croquet mallets in it and was received with cheers. Humble reported that the ice was bearing splendidly and so long as no perishing fools didn't try to crack her over the spring a-purpose, same as like when young Job Potter who'd a-been ninety-two if he'd lived till today was drowned, all would be well. Charles, feeling responsible for the lake in his father's and elder brother's absence, skated over the spring and assured himself that Humble was right. However, to be on the safe side, he routed about with one of the young Perrys in the old pumping house and got out, rather the worse for wear, the old notice board on a stand which said DANGER. DO NOT PASS THIS BOARD, and put it by the edge of the lake in case of need. Ice hockey then reigned supreme till lunch time.

'I shall be very glad,' said Miss Sparling to Miss Holly, 'when Hosiers' Holyday is safely over. I know it is all right, because Mr Belton promised me that he would let me know if there was the least danger, but I am always quite certain that several girls will be drowned. I suppose it's because I can't skate myself.'

Miss Holly said she did not think Miss Sparling need worry, as Humble had told her that the water was nowhere more than three feet deep except just round the spring, but to be on the safe side she thought Miss Sparling might tell the games mistress to keep the girls down at the lower end where it was absolutely safe and beyond getting wet and having pneumonia nothing could possibly happen.

So to the fury of the few girls who could skate well, they were sternly kept away from the ice hockey. It is true that they had a large expanse of ice with a small artificial island in it for their use, but naturally everyone wished to go where she was forbidden. A small body of malcontents led by Miss Ferdinand, who almost had the sulks on account of her fervent plea to be allowed to skate in her green tights having been rejected, did think of refusing to go to the lake at all, just to show, but when the dull girl in the Upper Fifth said if they didn't go to the lake she supposed they couldn't skate, they resigned themselves to tyranny and to judge by the noise they made were doing pretty well under the tyrant's rule. Miss Ferdinand made a fine gesture by wearing the black velvet cap with the feather, a red pullover and her own black flared skating skirt, and was told by the shocked head prefect that she would have to report her. This Miss Ferdinand, who was at the moment being Hamlet's father and smiting the sledded Polack on the ice, so much resented that she cut a figure of eight round the head prefect, thus causing that worthy creature to feel much alarm for the safety of her toes, and said she'd do it again and then fall down on top of her if she didn't shut up. And at the same moment the games mistress, seeing the head prefect apparently doing nothing, spoke a few serious words to her about her duty as a Leader, while Miss Ferdinand made a hideous face at the head prefect behind the games mistress's back.

But though Miss Ferdinand was a brilliant if slightly erratic skater, the star of the morning was Heather Adams. Ungainly as she was in daily life and on the hockey field, no sooner did she get onto skates than her feet were winged. She was skating in the ordinary school coat and skirt, her legs were hideous and her face not improved by the healthy and rather shining glow of outdoor exercise, but every movement was certain and her footwork such as to compel the admiration of all beholders as knew anything about the matter. We may say that though her fellow students envied her ease no one of them, unless it were Miss Ferdinand, realized what art lay behind that effortless swoop and twirl.

The games mistress, who had lugged a lumpy and unwilling Heather through physical drill, over the horse, between the parallel bars, but never up the rope because Heather simply stood flumpily at the bottom clawing ineffectively from time to time, but too heavy and sullen for anyone to push, was astounded, and thought poorly of herself for not having realized that Heather had it in her. But she was too busy keeping an eye on the smaller girls to comment on Heather's skill, and her exhibition skating might have been entirely wasted had not Mr Belton and his elder son come walking along by the lake looking at the skaters.

Heather's heart bounded. Angry with it, for had it not cheated her by bounding at least twice when it was only Captain Hornby, she darted away to the far side, swooped round the island and looked again. It was He. So she allowed her heart to do what it liked and drew up level with the walkers.

'Well, young lady,' said Mr Belton, who liked to see good skating though he had never been much good at it and had given it up years ago. 'You're Miss Adams, aren't you? The one that knows all about rats. How do you come to skate so well?'

'It's Daddy,' said Heather, happy to coast slowly along the ice so near the adored object. 'He's a frightfully good skater and he took me to the Barchester Glaciarium when I was quite little. We used to go an awful lot till the war and they turned it into a drill hall. I simply love it.'

'We were going to have another dance,' said Commander Belton, 'but as there don't seem to be any dances, will you skate with me after lunch? We might even waltz, only I'm afraid I'm not good enough for you.'

Heather heard her own voice saying thank you. Mr Belton asked after her father; the walkers said good-bye and struck up the hill. The games mistress asked Heather if she would help some of the beginners, and such is the power of Love that instead of looking as sullen as a badly cooked pudding and muttering under her breath, she took six Fourth Form girls in turn and by a kind of rough goodwill had them her devoted slaves in half an hour. The games mistress by virtue of her profession merely thought how much good a little exercise had done Heather and that perhaps a little more responsibility among the younger children would be good for her. But Heather knew, as we are privileged to know, that whoever had exchanged a word with Commander Belton, R.N., was a different girl from that hour and that in future all would be joy and rapture, that is if she lived till the afternoon; for knowing what Providence was capable of she thought it quite likely that she might die of pure bliss before the afternoon and so miss the treat. She hoped at the same time, so contrary are the hopes and aspirations of human nature, that if she was spared till the afternoon it would only be that she might die in Commander Belton's arms, or save him from drowning and be drowned herself and haunt his memory for ever after, so that between him and his wife and children would rise at odd moments the ghost of a sweet, pale face with dripping locks, and eyes closed by friendly death.

Mr Belton and his elder son pursued their way up the hill towards the Garden House where Humble and some friends were putting a terrier under the boards in case any rats had evaded the last hunt.

'I had a letter this morning,' said Mr Belton, 'from Updike. I don't know why he had to post it. He might have saved himself twopence-halfpenny by dropping it in the letterbox, but these lawyers are all alike.'

Commander Belton said possibly Updike was after six and eightpence.

'Nonsense,' said his father, veering rapidly. 'Updike's not a shark. But that's neither here nor there. What I wanted to talk to you about was what Updike said in his letter. It seems the people who own that school, the Graziers or whatever they call themselves,' said Mr Belton, very ungratefully, considering the amount of rent that the Hosiers paid him, 'are thinking of building an up-to-date school after the war. They like this neighbourhood, and Updike thinks they would buy Church Meadow and the land adjoining. It's on the Southbridge road, convenient for getting at, and the water and gas and all that are laid along the road. What do you think?'

Commander Belton said it depended very much on whether his father wanted to sell.

'Well, you know how we stand,' said Mr Belton ruefully. 'I can't afford to keep up the place and there'll be very little for you and the others. Your mother's all right. All her Thorne money is in trust. Not a fortune, but she'll be all right. It's you and the others and your children that I'm thinking of.'

Commander Belton said that Elsa was the only one who seemed likely to have any children at present, and she would be well provided for.

'Hornby has been generous, very generous,' said his father. 'But that doesn't affect Harefield, and I must get that ten thousand pounds of Elsa's. It's there all right, but it's damnably tied up in securities that aren't on the market at present. I suppose I'll have to go to the bank again. If the Glaziers or whatever their name is did buy all the land they want I'd be perfectly straight again, but now there's the War Agricultural Committee and they want me to plough; and which comes first, or if I'll be allowed to sell when they want me to plough, or if I can sell and make the Braziers responsible to the W.A.E.C. I don't know. And if they want to begin surveying and doing a bit of digging as Updike says they would, they can't grow wheat. I don't know, Freddy, I really don't know what to do and it's worrying me terribly.'

Commander Belton was as kind as he could be to his distracted father who was famous for getting into difficulties and making the very worst of them, and so far soothed him that he said he would get Updike to come to dinner and talk it over.

'Only you'd better do it soon, Father,' he said. 'I'm at the Admiralty now, but I might be moved abroad at any moment. If there is likely to be anything for me to sign, Updike had better let me know as soon as possible. It sounds as if Humble's terrier had got something.'

They went round to the back whence an excited yapping could be heard, and found Humble with a couple of friends and five or six demented terriers, one of whom was invisible and evidently in the death-throes of a battle. In a moment the dog emerged from under the house, dirty and rather bloody, but carrying a large rat which he laid tenderly at his master's feet.

'She won't have no more rattens, she won't,' said old Humble chuckling malevolently. 'The gentleman and Miss Elsa they're inside, where I took the board up. I gave the gentleman my nice knobby stick to break her back if she come out. But she didn't come out, she were carried out, weren't you, my lady.'

By this time Captain Hornby and Elsa had emerged from the kitchen and as the whole party were a little frightened by old Humble's atavistic outburst, which had evidently taken him back to the Battle of Brunanburh, or further still, they congratulated him and his friends and walked on.

Mr Belton who was not a believer in keeping one's troubles to oneself, poured out his perplexities about Church Meadow and the War Agricultural Executive Committee and the Hosiers' offer to his new audience. Captain Hornby listened attentively but did not make much comment. Elsa, full of indignation that her father and Harefield should be so scandalously treated, burst into an angry tirade against everyone involved. Her affianced, seeing her so handsome in her indignation, hearing her voice so shrill and uncontrolled, felt deeply sorry for her in more than one way.

'Do look at it sensibly for a moment,' said her elder brother. 'After all, the old Hosiers are paying Father a good rent; it isn't as if he were out of pocket by them. And if they did buy Church Meadow it wouldn't be at all a bad job.'

Elsa said she supposed Freddy wanted the family estate all to go to strangers.

'I can't say that I particularly do,' said Commander Belton, 'as it's our home. But we aren't the first and shan't be the last. The Nabob only came here about a hundred and fifty years ago. I wonder what happened to the people before him.'

'The Milburds?' said Mr Belton. 'Ruined in the South Sea Bubble. They hung on here for a bit. The father committed suicide some years later and the son shut the house and lived in the lodge. That's how the Nabob got it so cheap.'

'By Jove, Father, I never knew that,' said Commander Belton.

Silence fell on the party. But not, as the reader may think, a silence pregnant with moral reflections. Mr Belton was wondering if he had better get old Bodger over to see about finally clearing out those rats. Commander Belton was wondering where on earth he had put his penknife whose absence from its accustomed pocket he had just discovered. Captain Hornby was thinking his own thoughts, grimly remembering the many comparisons that have been made between a ship and a woman. Only Elsa had taken the story of the Milburds as a parable and in her over-eager, undisciplined mind already saw her father with his throat cut, Freddy in rags in the lodge among the evacuees who lived rather disgustingly there, and Charles and herself thrown upon the world. Her mother's fate she did not consider; for like most of us, though she was very fond of her mother she thought of her on the whole as in the beginning, now, and for ever, self-contained and needing no particular consideration.

This silence lasted except for a few unnecessary remarks till they got back, when lunch was ready and Charles so full of the morning's exploits that he talked for the whole party till they had finished their pudding. When coffee had been put on the table, Elsa, who had for some time been looking to her mother's eyes like a saucepan of milk just coming to the boil, suddenly said:

'Well, now we're all here I do think we ought to look things in the face.'

Charles said he was all against that and his second name was McOstrich. Elsa glared at him.

'We *can't* go on like this,' said Elsa. 'It's all very well for you and Freddy not to worry, Charles, but I do. I care for Harefield more than anything in the world and I can't stand those giggling girls there, and Father being under a kind of obligation to all those Hosiers. I *hate* it.'

Charles looked uncomfortable, as a man may well look when his sister is making a fool of herself in public. His elder brother remarked that he cared for Harefield too and hoped to be able to live there some day in the very distant future, so he naturally thought a good deal about it, but the best thing he could do at present was to follow their father's wishes, and what about skating that afternoon.

'Oh, *don't* try to put me off,' said Elsa. 'If you want to help Harefield, Freddy, why don't you *do* something about it?'

'I would if I knew what to do,' said Commander Belton, keeping his temper very well. 'Come along, Elsa. It will be frightfully cold later.'

'Oh, Father!' said Elsa, making one more effort to force her menfolk to do something, though she didn't quite know what, '*do* be sensible. Let Christopher lend you enough money to get things right. He easily could, and you could pay him interest or something and we could all go back to Harefield. Please, Father!'

Mr Belton had heard his daughter with an unmoved face, but inwardly he was seething with anger. He liked Captain Hornby, who had been more than generous about Elsa's settlement, and respected him. To be suddenly forced by Elsa into the position of begging his future son-in-law to support a property in which he had no interest was intolerable to him and he felt more acutely than anyone, except possibly his elder son, was aware, the indignity for both Captain Hornby and himself of being told how to manage their affairs by an over-excited, spoilt young woman.

'You don't understand what you are talking about, Elsa,' he said, controlling himself very well. 'Hornby, I apologize for what Elsa said, which has given me no pleasure at all. We won't talk about it again.'

On hearing these words Elsa got up and went out of the room, shutting the door with an ostentatious care which her family quite realized to be the equivalent of slamming it. Mrs Belton made as if to follow her, but Captain Hornby was at the door first.

'I'll tackle this,' he said. 'I'm going to marry her, and it's my business,' and went out of the room.

The rest of the family, overcome with shame or annoyance

315

according to the way each one looked at the events just described, exchanged resigned looks and Charles suddenly began to laugh, which brought everything back to normal.

'It's being engaged,' said Mrs Belton. 'When I was engaged to you, Fred, I was perfectly *horrible* to my father and mother. I can't think why, for they liked you and liked the marriage, but I think one gets very wrought up and says silly things. I remember being so nasty and ungrateful about the present Aunt Mary sent me, which was a very large, heavy mahogany tray, that I made Mother cry. And the tray came in very useful afterwards for dinner parties when we had a footman. How odious I was.'

'I dare say you were, my dear,' said Mr Belton, in no humour for excuses, 'but you didn't try to force your father to borrow money from me. I shan't come down to the lake this afternoon. I'm going to see some timber.'

It was recognized in Mr Belton's family that to look at timber was his way of whistling Lilliburlero, so no comment was made and he went away. Charles, who didn't see why everyone should be upset because of Elsa, said he was going back to skate.

'When do you have to go, darling?' said his mother.

'A fellow said he'd pick me up in a jeep at half-past four,' said Charles. 'He's going to London and it will save me going by train. No, I don't want sandwiches, filthy things, nor a thermos, nor an eiderdown, nor a rabbitskin to wrap the Baby Bunting in, Mother. See you again.'

'And you go and lie down with a hot bottle, Mother,' said Commander Belton. 'And don't worry about Elsa. She has met her match.'

So Mrs Belton had her hot bottle and lay down, slightly shaken and expecting to hear recriminations, oaths, a woman's shriek, a dull thud and see a slowly widening red patch on the ceiling above her; but before any of these agreeable things could occur, she was asleep. Nor would she have seen or heard any acts of violence if she had remained awake. Captain Hornby had overtaken his betrothed on the stairs, and told her to get her things on and come for a walk. Elsa, rather ashamed and frightened of what she had been doing, obeyed without a murmur and they set off. Both were good walkers. Elsa's nervous anger abated in the cold air, with their quick movement, but her stiffnecked pride was still strong within her and she determined not to speak, a vow which she kept for exactly fourteen minutes, when she heard a faint noise proceeding apparently from the whole universe so did it throb and fill the circum- and superambient air. This noise turned out to be no less a sight than three flights of aeroplanes heading south-east, infinitely high, infinitely small, looking as light as silver feathers in the frosty blue. In each of these flights her keen eyes could count at least seventy machines and she was faintly appalled by their steady ominous beat, their unearthly drumming through the empyrean. Captain Hornby, looking at them with a more professional eye, told her what they probably were, whither probably bound.

'Invention of the devil,' he said. 'Now we've found them we've got to use them and to build them better and stronger and faster than the other fellows. But it seems like the end of all peace and quiet to have the sky full of noise as long as we are alive.'

Elsa said as long as he was alive she didn't mind twice as much noise, and they had a delightful walk till Captain Hornby said they ought to go back, as Charles had told him he was leaving at half-past four. Elsa had by now almost forgotten her outburst at lunch, but Captain Hornby had not. As they approached the door in the lane behind Arcot House he stopped and said,

'Elsa, I must ask you not to try to arrange money matters for

317

your father and myself. It is very uncomfortable, even mortifying for us both and we are quite capable of managing our own affairs. I feel very much for your father, but if any business is to be done, we shall do it ourselves.'

At these perhaps slightly old-fashioned but perfectly justifiable remarks, all Elsa's irritation flared up again and without trying to control herself she let loose a flood of angry words, which appeared to have little or no effect upon her betrothed. Stung by his indifference and thoroughly overwrought by an accumulation of such things as the war, the work which she did so well that her superiors were always giving her more and harder tasks, the wrench of leaving a home she loved and was an integral part of, and the nervous excitement of her engagement, she allowed herself to work off a considerable accumulation of exasperation, rapidly reaching the point at which she had to go on scolding whether she wanted to or not. Captain Hornby, deeply fond of her, did not enjoy her railing, but he had faced battle and tempest for a good many years and had not the faintest intention of being bullied or frightened. If they had been out of human view he would probably have given her a hearty hug and so directed her thoughts into other channels, but the lane, commanded by every back window of the High Street, did not seem a suitable place. So they walked down the garden in silence to the house. As he held the garden door open for her to go in, Elsa said in what she recognized herself to be the voice of one who was not only creating but enjoying a dramatic scene, 'All right, Christopher, we'd better break it off.' To which Captain Hornby replied in an equable manner that she could break it off on her side till she was black in the face, but he adored her and was not going to be put off by a little thing like that. So she burst into tears, scrubbed her eyes violently with her handkerchief and flung into the hall where her mother and Charles were standing with the front door open and a little car making a frightful noise outside.

The crowd beside and upon the lake that afternoon presented a gay and varied scene, reminding Mrs Updike, as she said to Mrs Perry, of one of those Flemish pictures of people enjoying themselves on the ice, except that no one was roasting a pig, or getting drunk, or being sick, which deficiencies she appeared to deplore. Mrs Updike had trundled along with her one of those garden baskets on two wheels, like Major Hargreaves's, and had managed somehow to balance in and on it, rather precariously, a kitchen chair.

'Is that to sit on?' said Mrs Perry.

The question may have sounded stupid, but Mrs Updike evidently did not think it so.

'Oh *no*,' she said, as if that were the last use to which one would put a chair, 'it's to push. You see I can't really skate and Phil has quite a thing about my falling down and hurting myself which seems to happen to me much more than to other people, so I thought if I had a chair to push about it would keep me steady like people in old pictures of Christmas. Of course it really ought to be on runners and I did think of tying Phil's old skis on to it, but I can't make knots, at least not the sort that stay done up, so I brought it along just as it is. Of course one *could* sit on it if one wanted to,' said Mrs Updike reflectively.

Mrs Hoare now approached them, decently and warmly clad in an unusually long sealskin coat and black spats on her bony ankles.

'This is like old times,' she said. 'Old Mr Belton used to have great braziers on the edge of the lake and hot beer in a kitchen

319

copper for the tenants. But of course it was really cold in those days.'

'Oh, I couldn't have *borne* that,' said Mrs Updike. 'I do so hate the cold and I've a perfect thing about chilblains. Just look at my hands.'

Pulling off one of her gloves she exhibited a hand which aroused both pity and a slight feeling of repulsion in her audience. Mrs Hoare said that her husband's stepmother had chilblains quite dreadfully on her fingers, toes and ears, adding as a kind of burden that of course it was really cold then.

Mrs Updike got her chair out of the basket and took it on to the pond, where she was surrounded by her silent brood who appeared to look upon her as a very charming half-wit who had somehow got into the family and must be cherished. We are glad to be able to state that although her escapes from death or maiming for life were continuous and hair-raising, she enjoyed her afternoon deeply and did not once fall down.

Mrs Hoare, in virtue of her position as the late Pomfret agent's widow, held a kind of court and had the pleasure of showing the Cyclops locket which she was wearing on a purple ribbon to a number of friends. She also described to anyone who was good enough to listen the cleaning of her still life, and everyone agreed how nice Captain Hornby was and what a handsome couple he and dear Elsa made. Mrs Perry looked about her and said she hadn't seen them and why weren't they skating. Mrs Hoare, with decent archness, said she had seen them from her back window going across the park. Everyone said 'Ah' in a very knowing way, so true it is that all the world not only loves a lover, but feels itself entitled to overlook and discuss every movement of these marked beings. Then Mr Oriel joined them with Mr Carton, who won the admiration of all by wearing black closely fitting breeches and high boots, a relic of his younger days when he had been a considerable frequenter of Swiss winter resorts. It was his secret pride that his figure had not changed for the last forty years, which he attributed to reading too much, writing too much, skating and walking too much and doing nothing at all too much, just as it suited him, and eating and drinking whatever he liked. He then sped away on to the ice where he could be seen like an industrious water-spider, travelling about at tremendous speed with no particular aim.

Soon afterwards a rather disagreeable incident took place, which was the arrival, packed on to each other's motor-bicycles, for which they mysteriously had enough petrol, of a number of louts and gawks from Barchester who had got their mates to clock in for them and come out to make themselves as offensive as possible. Luckily the Hosiers' girls, down at the far end, were of no interest to them, but they were already making themselves extremely objectionable at the upper end by rowdy behaviour, barging into people on purpose, collecting handfuls of small stones and gravel from the edge of the lake which they threw about on the smooth surface and jumping in concert on the ice hoping to have the pleasure of cracking it.

A kind of Watch Committee or Vehm Gericht, including Commander Belton and his brother, the three Perrys, the two Updike boys, Mr Carton, the Madras Cottages contingent, and one or two of the men off the estate, was rapidly formed. Armed with hockey sticks, Major Hargreaves's croquet mallets, walking-sticks and other weapons, led by the Perry boys, they formed a half-moon and bore down upon the intruders, with the rallying-cry, by kind permission of the Perrys, of 'Knight's! Knight's! Tackle 'em low.' As the House Physician of Knight's, Dr Robert Perry, afterwards remarked, he wished they had stayed long enough to get the medicine they needed. But they were a lily-livered lot and after using some very objectionable language and throwing a few stones they fled ignominiously and were seen going away on their motor bicycles.

The enthusiasm on shore was tremendous. All the ladies shrieked applause, Major Hargreaves came out with a number of oaths learnt in the Indian Army, Mrs Updike who had just been reading *Barnaby Rudge* aloud to the two younger Updikes was heard shouting 'Ally Looyer, good gentlemen,' Mrs Hoare shook hands with old Humble, and Mrs Perry said, and none of her friends thought her capable of inventing it, that she had distinctly heard Mr Oriel exclaim, 'The sword of the Lord and of Gideon.'

Jim Perry then reported that owing to enemy action there was a slight seepage on the lake just about over the spring. He didn't think there was any danger, but with all the kids about one had better be careful. So he and Commander Belton carried the old board marked DANGER and set it up, also warning by word of mouth all parents and guardians that they met.

The more ardent spirits, including the Perrys and the elder Updikes, then went down to the lower end and played a kind of glorified Peep-Bo round the island, the object being to rush round and cannon into your brother or any other acquaintance before he could cannon into you.

Commander Belton, coasting down the lake, suddenly remembered his pledge to that Adams girl. So he approached the mistress in charge, who happened to be Miss Holly at the time, and asked if he might take Heather to waltz on the ice.

'Do,' said Miss Holly. 'She deserves a treat. She has been helping the beginners nearly all afternoon. Bring her back when you've done with her, as I'm responsible.'

So beautiful is the power of faith that although the cold afternoon was passing it had never occurred to Heather Adams that Commander Belton would betray her. In fact she was in a way pleased that he had not yet come, as the treat was still in store. Had he come earlier the treat would be now but a golden dream, and as Heather knew she would have to live on her dream for a very long time, she was quite content in its postponement. Then, as naturally as anything, she found Commander Belton at her side, the pleasure of her hand was requested and away they went in a cold ecstasy. Commander Belton skated quite well, but he had to exert himself to do justice to his partner who appeared to weigh nothing and be in a curiously intimate relation with the ice.

After twenty minutes or so he slowed her down at the upper end where Charles had taken off his skates and was preparing to go.

'Oh, good-bye, Freddy,' said Charles. 'That man's coming for me at half-past four. I say, if you are in Jermyn Street will you pay my tobacconist and I'll pay you back. Good luck and all that and I'll write to Mother when I know where I am. Tell Gus I've taken his bicycle. He'll find it in the hall.'

He then recognized Heather.

'Hullo,' he said. 'Sorry I can't skate with you, but I've got to hurry to catch my bus.'

The fury of a woman scorned is proverbial and mostly misquoted. Heather, seething with indignation against that horrid Mr Belton who had been so beastly to her the day Commander Belton was so nice to her, was for a moment bereft of speech. Just as Charles was riding off she recovered her voice and shouted, 'I wouldn't if you asked me. You don't skate well enough.'

Charles heard the noise but attached no meaning to it, turned from the saddle, waved, and was gone.

'I *hate* your brother,' said Heather passionately, knowing too that the treat was now over and that there would be an aching gap till she could get the afternoon's memories into good working order. She then swung out towards the middle of the lake.

It has long been obvious to the meanest of our readers – we allude to the one who asked the young lady at the libery for a nice book and now wishes she had got something different, something *really* nice if you know what I mean – that an author does not invent a lake with a spring under it and bring a band of hooligans out from Barchester at great waste of the country's petrol to try to crack the ice without intending to make someone fall in. This moment, as has been all too patent for some time, nor have we attempted to mislead the reader, or to conceal it in any way, has now arrived. Heather Adams, skating furiously, her sight blurred by tears, circled the DANGER board violently in narrowing circles. A crack appeared, the water began to flood the ice which broke up into lumps and splinters, her skate caught, she fell, tried to get up, slid, grasped at the edge of the ice and disappeared.

It will long be a subject for angry recriminations between the W.V.S. canteen and the A.R.P. and N.F.S. why nothing was done in time; the W.V.S. maintaining that if the A.R.P. and N.F.S. had put their ladders and life-saving tackle nearer the pond and not spent their whole afternoon having cups of coffee and cigarettes, they could have had all the glory of saving a real life; the A.R.P. and N.F.S. countercharging that if the W.V.S. hadn't got the canteen facing away from the lake, whether to avoid the wind or not they did not wish to discuss, and hadn't served the coffee so hot that no one could drink it and been so long over change for those cigarettes, they would have been on the spot at once.

But, to go back to our story, the A.R.P. and N.F.S. were at the moment screened from the lake by the canteen. Commander Belton called to Humble who ran to the N.F.S. dump, seized a ladder and pushed it over the ice to where his young master, on his stomach, was holding the hands of a very cross, frightened girl, hatless and soaked. With a great deal of pushing and heaving Heather was got up and dragged to the bank, a miserable and unattractive spectacle.

'Can you walk, or better still run in your stocking feet?' said Commander Belton, as he stooped to undo her skating boots.

Heather nodded, her teeth chattering.

'Then you'd better be Mr Pickwick,' said Commander Belton grimly. 'Take your jacket off.'

Heather did as she was told, Commander Belton put his jacket on her, thanking heaven that he had a woollen pullover under it, told Humble to tell the schoolmistress that Miss Adams was all right and he had taken her to Arcot House, and said to Heather, 'Now, run.'

It was not far by the back way from the upper end of the lake. Along the lane, through the door in the wall, down the garden, through the back door, up the passage, and they were in the hall, which seemed to be quite full of people and noise.

Charles, leaving his brother and Heather Adams on the lake, bicycled swiftly back to Arcot House by the road, came in by the front door and left his, or rather Gus Perry's, bicycle in the hall while he rushed upstairs to collect his kit, which involved pulling everything he had on to the floor and making hay of it. As he rammed a sponge-bag and a pair of socks into his already overfull suitcase he heard from the street a shattering noise which he at once recognized as his friend with the jeep. With his arms full of overcoat, suitcase, gloves and scarf he ran downstairs, opened the front door and threw his things into the little car which was throbbing as if it would burst and drowning the noise of a convoy of tanks that was speeding towards Barchester.

'Half a minute,' yelled Charles. 'I've got to say good-bye to my mother.'

The friend appeared to think this reasonable and pulled out a little handle which made the car so furious that it danced with rage, causing the friend to dither in his seat. Charles looked into the drawing-room and found his mother in her blue jumper writing letters.

'Oh, I've come to say good-bye,' he said. 'Good-bye, Mother, and thanks awfully for all the food and the bed and everything. Give Father my love and Elsa and Wheeler.'

'Oh, dear,' said Mrs Belton. 'It's all so sudden and so noisy. It's been lovely to have you, darling. I'll write and tell you about the skating and everything.'

'You needn't write just yet, and don't forward my letters,' said Charles. 'I'll write to you as soon as I've got an address.'

'Are they moving you again then?' said his mother.

'I hope so,' said Charles. 'We're all sick of being at home so long.'

His mother did not go white, nor did her voice tremble. But how white and trembling she felt inside, only she knew.

'Do you mean this is embarkation leave?' she said.

'Well, strictly speaking, we aren't getting any,' said Charles, 'but I thought you'd like it if I got a day or two. I'm awfully glad you liked the pullover. Don't worry about me. I'm going to have a whale of a time and kill everyone.'

'Well, don't get killed yourself,' said Mrs Belton, 'because I'd loathe it. And don't be missing and don't be a prisoner whatever you do, darling.'

'I'm all with you there,' said Charles. 'I say, I must go.'

In the hall he turned and not only allowed his mother to kiss him, but so far forgot himself as to give her a violent hug. As he was doing this his sister Elsa burst into the hall followed by Captain Hornby. Charles called a good-bye to them, hugged his mother once more and sprang down the steps into the car.

'Mother!' said Elsa, her face angry and flushed with tears, 'I'm not going to be married. Christopher can explain if he likes, but I never want to see him again. I only wanted him to help Father and he was *horrible*. I don't care what anyone thinks and I'm glad it's over.'

In proof of which she laughed in a most unconvincing way and began to cry.

'Oh dear,' said Mrs Belton, conscious that she must try not to think about Charles for the present. 'Christopher, are you really not engaged?'

'Personally I am as engaged as ever I was,' said Captain Hornby, 'and I mean to marry Elsa even if she doesn't marry me. But that isn't very important at the moment. I am very sorry we weren't back in time to see Charles properly. Was it embarkation leave?'

Mrs Belton, almost relieved by his matter-of-fact tone, said it was, and then looked anxiously at her daughter. All the time the friend's little car had been making the most hideous noises, just as Copper's motor bicycle had done a few months ago, and the conversation had to be carried on in a kind of agonized bellow.

'Never mind Elsa,' shouted the unchivalrous Captain Hornby to his future mother-in-law. 'Come into the drawing-room, or you'll catch cold.'

But even as he laid his hand on the knob of the drawing-room door, Commander Belton came in from the garden leading the unlucky Heather Adams. The car with a final outburst of noise leapt away up the street, and Commander Belton, now able to hear his own voice said, 'Oh, Mother, Heather Adams fell into the lake. You'd better put her to bed at once. I've told the school.'

From this point Mrs Belton felt that with Charles's departure she had fallen into a nightmare which might go on for ever, and comforted by the thought that she wasn't really there at all and might easily wake up in her own bed, or in a perfectly strange place, began to devote herself to her two remaining children and their troubles. The first thing to do, obviously, was to get Heather dry and warm. She rang the bell, told Wheeler briefly what had happened and asked her to get hot bottles at once, light the gas fire in the spare room and take the sheets off the bed. She then asked her elder son to ring up the Perrys' house, and Captain Hornby to catch Mr Belton if possible when he came back from seeing his timber and explain all that had happened.

'And you take Heather up at once, Elsa,' she said, 'and see that she has a boiling bath. I'll ring up the school and then come upstairs.'

Stimulated by the hope of tragedy, Florrie performed marvels with hot bottles, Wheeler had the sheets off in a twinkling and the blankets heating in front of the gas fire, while cook prepared a jorum of scalding rum and water laced with honey. Within ten minutes Heather had had her hot bath, put on one of the Viyella nightgowns which Mrs Belton always forgot to wear because she hated them, been thrust between warm blankets with three hot bottles to keep her company and was drinking the hot rum, in a dazed and slightly hysterical condition. While she was sipping it Mrs Belton came in.

'That's better,' she said. 'Thank you, Elsa, that's very nice. Now you might go down and give your father his tea. He has just come in. And don't bother him. Tell him Charles left his love.'

'Mother—' Elsa began, but seeing that her mother was not going to show any sympathy she went downstairs, rather sulkily and with a growing conviction that she had been behaving like a very silly, spoilt child, and not in the least like Miss Belton of Department ZQY 83.

'Now I'm going down to telephone to Miss Sparling,' said Mrs Belton to the patient as Wheeler came into the room with more blankets and pillows. 'Wheeler will stay with you. She used to be our nannie. And I'd better ring up your father. I'll tell him you are quite all right and spending the night with us.'

Heather smiled in an almost grateful way.

'The young lady's had a nasty turn, falling into the lake,' said Wheeler, quite deliberately willing the patient to feel faint and if possible have a heart attack. 'If it had been the sea, that's different. Salt water never did no one any harm. It's this nasty fresh water that leads to kidney troubles and all sorts of things. Still, we must hope.'

Mrs Belton glanced anxiously at Heather to see if this woeful prophesying was causing her any alarm, but as the child was obviously three parts asleep with the warmth and the rum, she left her with a mind at ease on that score and went downstairs.

Miss Sparling, to whom Miss Holly, telling the head prefect to bring the other girls back at once while she went on ahead, had

330

given a brief and not too alarming account of what Humble had reported, of course tried to ring up Mrs Belton, who was at the same moment trying to ring up Miss Sparling, and this might have gone on all night but for the masterly action of Gertie Pilson at the exchange, who already knew more about the accident than either of these ladies. Mindful of Mrs Belton's position as former Lady of the Manor, Miss Pilson ordered Miss Sparling to put her receiver back and wait till the bell rang.

'It's all right now, Mrs Belton,' she said. 'I'll put you straight through to the Hall. It's funny the way people get on the line at the identically same moment. I hope the young lady's all right. My cousin's young lady that does the dispensing was down there and she said it made her feel like nothing on earth, seeing the young lady fall in and the idear of her being drowned, so she put her fingers in her ears and shut her eyes. Here you are, Mrs Belton.'

Mrs Belton thanked Miss Pilson, said that everything was quite all right and turned her attention to Miss Sparling, who was glad to be reassured. Not that she had been unduly alarmed, for Humble and Miss Holly were exact in mind and not given to exaggerating. Still, a motherless pupil in several feet of icy cold spring water is a responsibility and the head-mistress felt it. So she was glad to hear from Mrs Belton that Heather had only been in the water for a few moments, had been made to run to Arcot House, and was now in a warm bed with hot rum, a medical comfort of which Miss Sparling highly approved. Also that Dr Perry had been sent for. Mrs Belton said she would ring her up again after the doctor had been, and should she ring up Mr Adams, or would Miss Sparling prefer to do it herself.

'I think if you would first, if you don't mind,' said Miss

Sparling, 'and I will later, when we have the doctor's report. Mr Adams likes you and your husband so much and I believe he would be pleased by the attention.'

'Are you a bit frightened of him?' asked Mrs Belton, sympathetically.

'Oh no,' said Miss Sparling, apparently not at all ruffled by this questioning of her courage. 'A headmistress can't be frightened, you know. My Governors would not like it.'

Another job done, Mrs Belton said to herself, and as she was downstairs she thought she might as well see if her husband was back. She found him and the two naval gentlemen peacefully having tea in the drawing-room and gladly had a cup of tea herself after the recent excitements.

Mr Belton said it was an extraordinary thing that girl falling in the lake. A girl like that, he said, a girl with a head on her shoulders, he wouldn't have thought that a girl like Adams's girl would have done such a damfool thing. It might have given Humble the rheumatics again, he said, getting his feet wet on the ice like that. And he did not, he added, know what girls were coming to. There was Elsa in a devil of a temper about an engagement or something and who had taken his *Times*.

'It's on the little table beside you, Father, where you put it,' said Commander Belton. 'I got on to Plassey House, Mother, but Perry is out and won't be back till late, so Dr Morgan is coming. They'll give her the message as soon as she gets back to the surgery.'

'What a nuisance,' said Mrs Belton ungratefully. And then she remembered Mr Adams and went back to the telephone. If, she thought, Mr Adams's works were as well run as his office, no wonder he was a successful man. Her call was answered by a competent female voice which said it was Mr Adams's secretary, heard Mrs Belton's name, repeated it correctly, asked Mrs Belton to hold on, came back with the news that Mr Adams was not on the premises and could she take a message. Much soothed by the voice, Mrs Belton asked it to tell Mr Adams that his daughter had fallen into the lake while skating, but had been got out at once and was in bed in her, Mrs Belton's house; that the doctor had been sent for and the school notified; that Mr Adams was not to worry as Miss Adams was quite all right and sent her father her love. The voice, which had apparently been taking down this message in shorthand, then read its précis aloud. Mrs Belton thanked it.

'Of course he will worry, like anything,' said the voice, 'but I'll do my best for you, Mrs Belton. I don't know when he'll get back, but he asked me to wait for him at the office till he did. Thank you so much. *Good* night.'

Thanking heaven for people like Miss Sparling and the voice, who could say what had to be said clearly and understood one when one talked, Mrs Belton returned to her family in the drawing-room and asked where Elsa was. Her affianced said in the sulks, he thought, and if her mother didn't mind leaving her there he would see about them later on.

'I'm sorry I didn't see old Charles,' said Commander Belton. 'He had told me he was probably going abroad, Mother, but he didn't want me to tell you.'

'And I'm very glad you didn't,' said Mrs Belton stoutly, 'because I'd only have worried about the time going so quickly, or wished I hadn't asked him to clean his nails. Oh, dear, I must go back to Heather Adams. Wheeler will be wanting to lay dinner.'

As she crossed the hall the door-bell rang. Calling to cook that she needn't bother, Mrs Belton opened the front door and let in Dr Morgan who with great courage was still wearing the

Robin Hood hat and with even greater, though unconscious courage, a brand-new utility suit of olive green. And why utility, thought Mrs Belton, one cannot tell, unless a reticence in the chest, a tightness across the back of the skirt causing it to bag like the knees of old trousers, a skimpiness of pleats and pockets which made of both an ungraceful adornment rather than a help to the wearer, are evidences of helping to win the war. And that the turnings of the seams should be so narrow (and neither pinked nor overcast at that) that they had already broken away from the stitching here and there did not add to the general unattractiveness and high unusefulness of the suit.

Dr Morgan having shed her coat and emerged in the full depression of the utility suit, was taken up to see the patient. Wheeler with a glance in which hostility and contempt were thinly veiled, though not recognized as such by their object, went away to lay dinner. Heather, who had been in a pleasant and mildly inebriated doze, woke up as Dr Morgan switched on the centre light which shone painfully into her eyes.

'Thank you, Mrs Belton,' said Dr Morgan. 'I will let you know when I come downstairs. I think it would be best for me to see Heather ALONE.'

The emphasis which she laid on this word so frightened Mrs Belton that she went out of the room without a word, leaving Heather to the mercies of her medical attendant.

The medical attendant, pulling a chair towards the bed, sat down with her toes slightly turned in and looked steadily at the patient for some minutes.

'I expect,' said Dr Morgan, 'that you don't like to think of what happened today.'

As Heather had been thinking of little else, letting her fancy play with the thought of Commander Belton rescuing her and how she could best – short of dying at his feet – show her eternal gratitude and devotion, she merely stared.

'I know it is difficult,' said Dr Morgan, looking earnestly at the patient, 'but we must bring all these ugly things out into the open and call them by their true names. What did you think of as you went down?'

'Went down where?' said Heather.

'Into the Cold Water,' said Dr Morgan.

'You mean when I fell in,' said Heather. 'Nothing particular, except I was awfully cross, else I wouldn't have fallen down.'

'Now we are beginning to remember,' said Dr Morgan. 'Now, Heather, dig. Dig deep into your mind. You say you were cross. Was there any reason to be cross?'

'Well, you must have something to be cross about before you're cross,' said Heather. 'If someone who had been perfectly beastly to you asked you to skate, *you'd* be cross. Can you skate?'

Dr Morgan, who was used to being the inquisitor rather than the racked victim, was so much taken aback that she said she couldn't before she could stop herself.

'Then you wouldn't understand,' said Heather. 'I say, I expect I've got a temperature. Would you like to take it?'

Hypnotized by her unusual patient Dr Morgan opened her bag, took out her thermometer, gave it a professional flick and put it into Heather's mouth. While it was maturing she went and looked out of the window, taking advantage of the dressing-table being in front of it to settle her Robin Hood hat at an equally unbecoming angle.

'Just ninety-eight,' said a satisfied voice behind her.

Dr Morgan turned and saw her patient twiddling the thermometer to the right position for seeing what is going on inside it.

'You must not do that,' she said, wrenching it carefully from Heather and examining it herself. As she did so her hand shook slightly with annoyance. Feeling the thermometer slipping, she grasped it more tightly and of course snapped it in two. Infinitesimal globules of quicksilver ran about on the floor. Dr Morgan looked at the patient whose heavy face betrayed an entire want of interest, dropped the bits of thermometer in the waste-paper basket, and smiled with all her teeth.

'We must not get temperature-minded,' she remarked, with odious brightness. 'All you have to do now is to keep your thoughts off the Cold Dark Water and your Crossness. Think of something you like. Flowers, singing birds, someone you are fond of and all the ugly thoughts will vanish. Good night, Heather. I shall tell Mrs Belton what to do for you.'

Heather's lips formed the words 'Old Beast' and she relapsed into the comfortable coma from which Dr Morgan's visit had roused her. Telling a person to think of flowers and birds! she thought with lazy contempt. To think of someone one was fond of was different. No need for that beast Dr Morgan to tell her that. Did she ever – with the exception of eating, sleeping, doing her lessons and her prep, and unwillingly going for walks – think of anything but One whom she was fond of; One who at the risk of his own life had saved hers; One who had lent her his own jacket, his bosom (except for a pullover and a shirt and probably a vest under it) bared to the icy blast. She drifted warmly and comfortably into her usual daydreams, tinged this evening by an unusual amount of self-pity, doubtless induced by the really trying experiences of the afternoon. As she relived the waltz on the lake, her angry rebuff to Charles, her foolish bravado on the dangerous ice, her struggle in the cold spring water, her rescue, the kindness of Arcot House, she became more and more sorry for herself. Her eyes and nose began to prickle, her throat to constrict and before she knew where she was, she was crying helplessly. And what made it the more dreadful was that though she despised herself, she couldn't stop. So that when Mrs Belton, after having been told by Dr Morgan that Heather, though not very amenable to suggestion, had no temperature to speak of and could get up during the following day, came upstairs to see how the invalid was, she found her in the lowest spirits.

'What is the matter, Heather?' she said very kindly. 'Is anything hurting you?'

Heather shook her head and blew her nose.

'Your father's secretary is going to tell him as soon as he comes in,' said Mrs Belton, hoping to cheer her patient, 'and he is sure to ring up.'

At this Heather, feeling sympathy in the air, cried more than ever and with gulps and chokes said, 'Commander Belton.'

'Don't worry about him,' said his mother. 'He wasn't really wet and he is quite all right and wants to know how you are. Would you like him to come up and see you?'

Heather nodded violently, her speech much impeded by chokes and strangulation.

'Stop crying then, my dear, and I'll send him up,' said Mrs Belton. 'And you'd better have another handkerchief.'

She fetched two large clean handkerchiefs from her husband's dressing-room, placed them beside Heather and went downstairs to tell her son he was wanted. Commander Belton had no particular desire to go and sit with Heather Adams, but he felt sorry for her and had a kind nature, so he went up to her room.

'Well, Heather,' he said, sitting where Dr Morgan had so lately sat, but with his toes turned neither out nor in, and looking very calm and reliable. 'My mother says that Dr Morgan is quite pleased with you, and you can get up tomorrow and go back to the Park.'

Heather was heard to mumble that she hated the Park.

'I'm sorry. I rather like it,' said Commander Belton. 'But then I've always lived there.'

'That's why I hate it,' said Heather, sitting up violently, her face blotched with crying and her scanty dull hair even more lifeless than usual. 'I mean I hate us being there when it's your house. I hate you not being able to live in your own house and I wish I was dead. I wish I'd been drowned.'

'I wouldn't wish that,' said Commander Belton, wondering how long courtesy bade him stay with this exhausting schoolgirl.

'But I do,' said Heather. 'Because I've made a will that if I die you can have all my money that Father is going to leave me and then you can buy back Harefield and live there. And I thought if I'd been drowned everything would have been all right, and now it isn't.'

After which artless and embarrassing words she uttered a kind of despairing bellow and buried her face in one of the clean handkerchiefs.

'My dear Heather,' said Commander Belton, touched, amused, irritated, but in a far from unkindly voice, 'you mustn't talk like that. I should simply hate you to die. And I couldn't possibly take your money, or your father's. But I think it was one of the kindest and nicest thoughts anyone could have.'

Heather removed the handkerchief and looked at him with tear-bunged eyes.

'I wanted to do something for you more than anything in the world,' she said, 'because you were so kind to me when your brother was so beastly. I didn't mean to tell you, but as I'm not dead it's all no use now and I can't ever, ever do anything for you, and I do want to help you so *dreadfully*. Oh please, please.'

She then relapsed into the handkerchief.

Commander Belton was acutely uncomfortable. It was appall-ingly clear that this unattractive, rather pathetic schoolgirl had been idealizing him; one of the most embarrassing things that can happen to a man. He vastly wished that he had not been good-natured enough to come up and see her. Then he felt real compassion for her and her plan of leaving him her father's money, and her apparent faith that her father would take the faintest notice of such a wish. Heather was still muffled in the handkerchief and something must be done.

'I want to thank you very, very much, Heather,' he said, 'for thinking of me. And now we won't talk about it again. Your father will be ringing up and I want to tell him you are quite well and happy here. Now stop crying.'

'I would if I could,' said a creaky voice. 'But it's so *awful*. I do think about you all the time.'

Commander Belton then did a most heroic deed.

'I want to tell you something, Heather,' he said. 'I was going to marry a Wren and she was killed in an air raid. Nobody knows except my mother. I want you to know because I'm sure she would have thanked you for thinking of me.'

Heather stopped crying and looked at him awestruck.

'And you will never forget her,' she said.

'Never!' said Commander Belton, knowing that time or the chances of war would probably heal this pain with many others.

'Oh!' said Heather, overwhelmed by being the confidante of so tremendous a secret, of such heart-searing romance. 'I say, I'm most *awfully* sorry.'

'So am I,' said Commander Belton, and fell silent.

'I'll never tell anyone,' said Heather, in a glow of gratitude at being treated as a really grown-up person. 'And thanks most awfully for skating and for getting me out of the lake.'

'Then that's all right,' said Commander Belton. 'And, I say,' he continued, falling into his young friend's manner of speech, 'you might tear up that will. I don't think your father would like it much.'

'All right,' said Heather.

'Then shake hands,' said Commander Belton. 'By Jove, it's after seven. I must go and wash. Do you feel like some food?'

'Rather,' she said, holding out her hand.

Commander Belton exchanged a companionable handshake with her and left the room. Once outside the door he uttered the exclamation known as 'Phew,' and turning his mind resolutely from his loss, spoken of to help a silly schoolgirl, now to be buried again with all dead things, went down to find his family.

When Mrs Belton rang up the School and reported that Dr Morgan was quite satisfied with Heather, but Mr Adams could not at present be reached, Miss Sparling felt that she ought to see her pupil herself, so that she might be in a position to reassure Mr Adams if necessary.

'No luck,' said Miss Holly, who had been telephoning to try to get a taxi. 'The Nabob's car is out and the other taxi says it is very sorry it can't take passengers at night unless it's an emergency. I'd better walk down with you.'

So Miss Sparling and her secretary, as soon as they thought the Beltons would have finished dinner, walked down to Arcot House, where they were warmly welcomed. Not only was Mrs Belton glad to have someone with whom she could share the responsibility for Heather Adams, but at the moment almost any outsider would have been gratefully received as Elsa's sulks, though ignored by her betrothed, were having a depressing effect on the rest of her family. That Charles had gone was a thought so depressing that his mother, almost unconsciously, and burdened as she was at the moment with her husband's money troubles, her daughter's unusual ill-temper, Heather's damp arrival, and the irritation produced by Dr Morgan who had taken an unconscionable time to say that Heather was all right but needed some suggestion, had put it right at the back of her mind and smothered it. She took Miss Sparling upstairs to see the invalid, who had just eaten a large dinner and, surrounded by kind attention, her secret adoration for Commander Belton transmuted to a delightful and flattering sense of being his trusted friend and the only person except his mother who really understood him, was in a warm and comfortable state of physical well-being and lazy mental content. Yet another miracle occurred when her headmistress, sitting where Dr Morgan had so lately sat, but upright, dignified, and quite uninquisitive, turned out to be a nice ordinary person who could talk about really interesting things like the costing department at the works.

After a short visit Miss Sparling said she must get back to the school and would ask Mrs Belton to telephone next day. If Heather felt all right, she could come back to the school in the morning or after lunch, just as it suited Mrs Belton.

'Oh, Miss Sparling,' said Heather.

Miss Sparling waited, with no sign of impatience.

'You know about me going to be a Wren,' said Heather. 'Well, I'm not. I'm going to have a job in Father's works and learn everything. Do you think that's war-work?'

Miss Sparling said she thought it was. 'And I forgot to say,' she added, 'that Isabella Ferdinand sent you her love and wants to know if you will give her some skating lessons if the frost holds.'

Leaving Heather in a state as near pure bliss as this world

can provide she said good night. On the landing she found Mrs Belton who escorted her to the drawing-room where Commander Belton was entertaining, and we may say being entertained by, Miss Holly, while Mr Belton was in a condition of coma with the *Times*. Mrs Belton said Miss Sparling must have some hot coffee before she left, and went to find Wheeler. As she crossed the hall the front door bell rang even more loudly and janglingly than usual, so she opened the door. Something like a furry packing-case came in. Mrs Belton shut the door and saw that it was Mr Adams, looking more thickset than ever in a thick Teddy Bear coat of orange-brown hue, a huge scarf round his neck, a vivid check cap pulled well down on his head and leather gloves with fur backs like a bear's paws. Rapidly shedding all these, he extended his hand to Mrs Belton.

'How's my Heth?' he said.

Mrs Belton said the doctor had been and said she could get up next day, and she looked very warm and comfortable and would he like to go up.

'One moment, Mrs Belton,' said Mr Adams. 'I only got back to the office an hour ago. My seckertary gave me your message, so I said, "Take these two letters, Miss Poynter" – that's my seckertary – "take these two letters," I said, "and then I'll go straight out to Harefield." You may say, Mrs Belton, is my journey really necessary, but when it's for my little Heth it definitely is. She's all I've got since Mrs Adams left me, and if Mother had been here she'd have said, "You go straight to Harefield, Sam" – that's my name, Sam Adams. That's what she'd have said.'

Mrs Belton said she was quite sure Mrs Adams would have wanted him to go, and would he come upstairs.

'You're sure it won't give her a shock or anything,' said Mr Adams. 'I could wait, you know. I told my seckertary to ring up the Nabob here and say they must find a bed for me if I wanted it, if it cost me a cool tenner.'

Mrs Belton assured him that if he wanted to stay the night it must be at Arcot House, as her husband and herself would be very unhappy if he refused, and took him up to Heather's room. It occurred to her as she came down again that her daughter Elsa and Captain Hornby had been missing since dinner time, but considering that on the whole they were old enough to look after themselves, she dismissed that particular trouble for the time being and returned to the drawing-room, where Miss Sparling and Miss Holly were drinking their coffee. She told Miss Sparling that her pupil's father had just come, and much admired the way in which she took it; showing neither relief at this sharing of responsibility nor annoyance at what some might have thought an unnecessary intrusion, accepting what had occurred and ready to make the best of it.

After they had talked for a quarter of an hour or so there was a knock on the drawing-room door, so unusual a phenomenon that Mrs Belton wondered if it was a ghost, though she had never heard of one at Arcot House, and thinking vaguely that it might be Florrie, who found the gentry's habit of expecting you to knock at the bedroom door but not at the dining-room or drawing-room door quite beyond her powers of apprehension, said, 'Come in.'

'Pardon me intruding,' said Mr Adams.

Mrs Belton, who did not know etiquette well enough to be quite sure of the answer to this, begged Mr Adams to come in. Mr Belton, emerging from his *Times* coma with the air of a dazed bull suddenly let loose in the ring, greeted Mr Adams warmly, and said something about the bench, though it was quite obvious to his wife and his elder son that he was at the moment uncertain whether Mr Adams had sat with him or been brought before him. Miss Sparling said how do you do and introduced Miss Holly.

'Will you have some coffee, Mr Adams?' said Mrs Belton. 'And how did you find Heather?'

Mr Adams said he didn't mind if he did and Mrs Belton poured out the coffee which had been keeping hot on a brass trivet, only it was a quadrivet, inside the fender.

'I don't know what to say,' said Mr Adams after gulping some coffee. 'I don't mind telling you all now that when my seckertary gave me the 'phone message, I saw red. There's my little Heth, I said to myself, with me paying a good round sum for her schooling and they let her fall into the lake. She's all I've got since Mother left us,' he added apologetically, 'and the best of little pals. I don't mind saying, Miss Sparling, that I was fairly beside myself and at that moment I'd have put the whole school and the Hosiers too into our biggest blast furnace, or through the rolling mill, with the greatest pleasure in life. But what my Heth tells me puts a totally different face on things. By what my Heth says, it was all her own doing. This lady, Miss Holly, gave her permission to skate with young Mr Belton – that's you, sir, isn't it – and instead of going back to Miss Holly like a good girl she skated off on her own where it said danger. Is that right?'

Commander Belton said Miss Adams was a first-rate skater and there would have been no danger at all if some young men from Barchester had not deliberately tried to break the ice over the spring.

'I'm going to make some inquiries,' said Mr Adams grimly, 'and if any of those young Huns are in my works, or any of my friends' works, they'll get a lesson they won't forget. I might have lost my little Heth, if you hadn't saved her, sir. I don't know what to say, I really don't. My little girl is all the chick and child I've got, and I don't know what to say or how to say it.'

His gratitude and his sincere emotion touched his audience very much, and on comparing notes later Mrs Belton and Miss Sparling found that they had both been divided between wanting to cry and feeling that at any moment they might giggle, accompanied in Mrs Belton's case by a firm conviction that Mr Adams, even if he did not stay the night, was going to talk for at least two hours without stopping.

'And there's another thing,' said Mr Adams, setting down his coffee cup, 'no, not a drop more, Mrs Belton, I've done very nicely if it's all the same to you, and though it's not strictly in order perhaps at the moment there's nothing like taking time by the horns. You know, Miss Sparling, my little Heth was as keen as mustard to go into her dad's works, and then she got it into her head she wanted to be a Wren. Well, when Mother died, she said to me, before she died you know, "Sam," she said, "you must study Heth and Heth must study you." And Mrs Adams, I may tell you,' said Mr Adams, looking into the fire, 'made her lifework, as you might say, of studying me. My second self you might say. Well, well, we won't discuss that now,' he added suddenly, looking round at his audience with a slightly challenging air, though none of them wished to discuss the late Mrs Adams whom none of them had seen and most of them not even heard of, 'but it brings me to my point, which is that my little Heth has been studying her dad. I didn't try to check her, Mrs Belton, about this idear of being a Wren. I knew Mother would have said, "Sam," she'd have said, "don't you check our Heth. You wait and be patient." So I did, to the best of my powers, and now this very evening Heth tells me she's going into the works, and the way she spoke I know it's not a passing fancy. S. and

H. Adams Limited; that's what we'll be some day. S. and H. Adams. It'll look well on the firm's letters and in adverts and on the packing-cases.'

He paused for a moment. Mr Belton, though secretly wishing that his fellow J. P. would go away and leave him in peace, said he was glad to hear it and she was a nice girl with a head on her shoulders.

'That's right,' said Mr Adams, gratified. 'And if you'd like to know who I thank for all this, well I make no bones about saying it, Miss Sparling. My little Heth said to me, "Dad," she said, "I arst Miss Sparling if the works was war-work and she said yes." I'm only a plain man,' said Mr Adams, getting rather red in the face, 'and I say things in a plain way but if Mrs Adams was here she would join me in a very hearty acknowledgement of your kindness to my Heth. You wouldn't think my Heth hadn't a mother, not to look at her,' said Mr Adams meditatively, as if girls bereft of a female parent bore some visible mark of Cain, 'but she hasn't, not since she was seven, and what I went through with housekeepers as they call themselves you wouldn't hardly credit not if I was to talk till tomorrow.'

By this time his well-wishing but exhausted hearers felt that it probably was tomorrow by now, or that eternity had begun, but they dutifully began to utter suitable words or sounds.

'Just one more word,' said Mr Adams, getting up and apparently addressing a board meeting. 'I'd like to shake hands with you, Miss Sparling. And with Miss Holly, the lady my naughty little Heth didn't listen to what she said; and with Mrs Belton, I don't know how to thank you for your kindness to my Heth, Mrs Belton; and with Mr Belton, my little Heth thinks the world of you, Mr Belton; and with you, Captain Belton, is it? oh, Commander, well with you, sir, and God bless you for saving my little Heth and if Mrs Adams was here she'd say the same. Well, that's all.'

By this time his whole audience had stood up, submitted to a most cordial and painful handshake and were in a state of tongue-tied embarrassment which even Miss Sparling with many years' headmistressing behind her and Mrs Belton with a lifetime of social intercourse as her inheritance, could not deal with.

'Well, Timon Tide waits for no man, as they say,' remarked Mr Adams, looking at his watch, 'and the works are the same. Miss Sparling, I'd like to drive you and Miss Holly back to the school if convenient. I know the way you feel about my Heth and I dare say you've been as upset as I have and ready to get a good night's rest. And we can have a talk about Heth on the way back. With her brains she'll get a good scholarship at Oxford or one of those colleges and polish up her mathematics and then we'll see about her starting in the works. And if anyone says was this journey really necessary,' said Mr Adams, looking round him for possible criticism, 'Sam Adams says it WAS.'

Miss Sparling, truly thankful to be spared the walk uphill in the dark, accepted Mr Adams's offer for herself and Miss Holly. Mr Belton accompanied them to the door.

'A nice girl of yours, Adams,' he said. 'Knows about rats too. I'll tell you what. If you really want to get rid of your rats I'll send old Bodger over to Hogglestock. He's been ratcatcher on Lord Pomfret's place for fifty years and what he doesn't know about rats isn't worth knowing.'

'Much obliged, I'm sure,' said Mr Adams gratified. 'And I'll be seeing a friend on the W.A.E.C. tomorrow, Mr Belton. Mind, no promises, but Sam Adams doesn't forget a kindness.'

347

Leaving his host quite dumbfounded by the length of his stay, the flow of his conversation and his final remark about the War Agricultural Executive Committee, Mr Adams shepherded Miss Sparling and Miss Holly into his car and drove away. Just as Mr Belton was shutting the front door Captain Hornby came up the steps.

'Didn't know you had been out,' said Mr Belton. 'Come in, Hornby, come in. I'm going up to bed. You'll find my wife in the drawing-room.'

Captain Hornby betook himself to the drawing-room where he found Mrs Belton and her elder son repairing some of the ravages of their unexpected party. So much occupied had Mrs Belton been with the events of the evening that she had temporarily forgotten about her daughter's affairs, but the entrance of her future son-in-law brought them crashing into her mind again.

'Oh, it's you, Christopher,' she said, looking up startled. 'Where is Elsa?'

'In bed, I hope,' said Captain Hornby. 'I have been round to the Updikes. What a delightful woman Mrs Updike is. I spent a little time with her till Updike came in. She had just dropped the electric iron on her foot when I arrived and I am afraid it is rather bruised. Of course when the flex pulled out of the iron all the downstairs lights fused, but one of the children found some fuse wire and we put it in.'

While Captain Hornby spoke, Mrs Belton knew, fatally, that he had been to the family solicitor to cancel all arrangements for the marriage settlement owing to her daughter Elsa's bad behaviour. Her alarm must have shown itself very clearly, for Captain Hornby said,

'I had business to do with Updike. Some quite private matters, nothing to do with Elsa and myself. It's no good asking you not to worry, Mrs Belton, but I would like to say again that I have every intention of marrying Elsa whether she likes it or not.'

'What she needs is a good beating,' said her mother, much to Captain Hornby's surprise. 'I'm ashamed of her.'

'And Christopher's the man to do it,' said Commander Belton unexpectedly.

'I would like to beat her; very much indeed,' said Captain Hornby dispassionately. 'But I can't stop to do it now. I've got to go back early tomorrow morning. Mrs Belton, if you can possibly not worry, do; or do I mean don't? In fact, don't worry. I shall see Elsa soon in London and I give you my word of honour that I shall come and marry her even if I come like Petruchio. If you will excuse my interfering I've told Wheeler about a cup of tea. I shan't want breakfast. I'll get that at Barchester. I love Elsa very much indeed.'

So saying he kissed his future mother-in-law affectionately and saying 'See you tomorrow morning,' to Commander Belton, went upstairs.

Commander Belton then helped his mother to clear away the remains of the feast and leave the drawing-room self-respecting, and escorted her up to her room.

'All right, darling?' he said.

Mrs Belton said a little tired but quite all right, so her son kissed her and went to bed. But Mrs Belton, though indeed tired, did not feel much like bed. So much had happened since the morning that she wanted to sort things a little and calm the restlessness which, she knew, was going to keep her awake. There was Charles: but no need to think of that yet: there would be time enough and to spare as weeks and months went on. There was Heather's accident; Dr Morgan, Miss Sparling, Miss Holly,

Mr Adams, and on the top of it Elsa's quite hysterical outburst. And this reminded her of her duties as hostess and mother, so putting on her soft bedroom slippers she went to Heather's room and listened, then opened the door very softly. The room was dark except for the glow of the gas fire turned low and everything peaceful. Heather was evidently all right and would be able to go back to school next day. Then she went to Elsa's door. This she did not dare to open, when a loud sneeze overcame her fear and she went in. Her daughter Elsa was sitting up in bed, looking very puffy about the eyes and sneezing her head off.

'I'm all right, Mother,' said Elsa rather crossly. 'It's only a beastly cold.'

Without a word Mrs Belton went back to her room, got a thermometer, came back and stuck it into her daughter's mouth, who made no particular resistance. It was a hundred and one when she took it out.

'You will have to stay in bed, Elsa, I'm afraid,' she said. 'I'll ring up your office tomorrow and explain and I'll get Dr Perry to come round.'

'Oh, all right, Mother, so long as it isn't that Morgan woman,' said Elsa dully. 'It's nothing really. I expect I got cold going that long walk with Christopher.'

Her mother said nothing, but fetched a hot bottle, one of the survivors from the rubber period, boiled water on the little gas ring by Elsa's fire, filled the bottle and put it in the bed. She then got aspirin and a little of her store of rum which she kept in the medicine cupboard, gave Elsa a hot drink, kissed her and left her. During all these proceedings Elsa looked as if she were going to burst, but whether with her cold, or with something she wanted to say, her mother could not decide. And if it was something Elsa wanted to say, she felt it could wait, as she had given them all quite enough trouble lately. She may have heard a noise as of someone trying rather ostentatiously to suppress a desire to speak, but she was now too tired to care very much. Elsa was warm and full of aspirin and would go to sleep and Dr Perry would come next day.

Just as she was shutting Elsa's door her eye caught a line of light under Charles's door. For a wild moment she thought all the day had been a horrid dream and that Charles was back in his room; but she knew it was really only Florrie who had done the blackout and left the light on, as she had twenty times been told not to do. She opened the door. In his precipitate departure Charles had left the bed, the chairs, the floor littered with his belongings. Drawers were open and spilling collars, pullovers, braces; cupboards ajar with coats and trousers lying in huddled heaps, and everything in indescribable confusion. Mrs Belton shut the door and began quietly to tidy things. The room struck cold to her. Too tired and stupid to light the gas fire when it was only for herself, she put on Charles's dressing-gown. In its comfortable warmth she smelt the nearness of Charles, as he was when a little boy and she could kiss him unchecked, as he was when a schoolboy and she used to kiss his rumpled hair when he tolerated it, as he was when a soldier and she liked to rub her face against his uniform, as he had been but a few hours ago when he had hugged her of his own free will. She looked at the clothes strewn on the floor and suddenly thought how when Porthos's death was known the faithful Mousqueton collected all the glorious clothes, his master's bequest, and embracing them died of grief.

'I could bear anything, if it didn't smell of Charles,' she said, hardly conscious that she had spoken aloud what she felt. Then she angrily brushed the stinging tears from her eyes with the back of her hand, put the scattered clothes into some kind of order, turned out the light and went downstairs to her own room where she muffled her face in Charles's dressing-gown and let it receive the tears she could no longer suppress, till she could control herself again and go to bed and at last to sleep.

13

Next day Dr Perry came to see Elsa, said she had the flu germ that was going about, commanded her to stay in bed, promised her a certificate to tell her employers she had not been malinger-ing and said he would send in a nurse he knew who was staying in the village for a few days, just to wash the patient and tidy the room morning and night. On hearing this the patient was very cross, but felt so unwell that she did not enter any formal protest, contenting herself with enduring Nurse Chiffinch's ministrations in an ungrateful spirit. Dr Perry then looked in on Heather Adams who had eaten a large breakfast and looked quite revoltingly plain in the boudoir cap and green woollen dressing-jacket that Mrs Belton had lent her.

'Well, young lady,' said Dr Perry sitting down. 'You've been giving a lot of trouble. My boy Bob hasn't forgiven you yet.'

Heather looked startled.

'He may be House Physician at Knight's,' said Dr Perry, who never lost an opportunity of boasting indirectly about his sons, 'but he has never had a drowning case yet. Of course they throw themselves into the Thames,' said Dr Perry thoughtfully, 'and get fished up and brought in, but it's always to the mortuary. If Bob hadn't been down at the other end of the lake, or you had stayed under a couple of minutes longer, he'd have had a perfect holiday. He's gone back to town now. Tongue. Pulse. I suppose Dr Morgan told you to stay in bed, eh?'

'Dr Morgan told me a lot of psycho-analysis,' said Heather scornfully, 'so I didn't listen. I say, Dr Perry, I'm going into Daddy's works when I leave school. I'm going right through all the departments.'

Rather to Heather's mortification Dr Perry roared with laughter. He then told her she could get up and go back to the school whenever she liked and left her. Downstairs he found Mrs Belton alone in the drawing-room.

'Well, what's wrong?' he said looking at her.

Mrs Belton said nothing.

'That's all right,' said Dr Perry. 'And now you've said your piece what is it? Elsa looks pretty sulky. That it?'

Mrs Belton said Elsa had been very troublesome lately.

'Selfish young woman,' said Dr Perry. 'It's high time she got married and had something to do.'

Mrs Belton thought of being indignant on her daughter's behalf, but Dr Perry was such an old friend that she decided to confide in him, as his quick curious mind would probably get at the truth, or quite near enough to the truth, in any case. So she said an engagement was always an upsetting time and she remembered having been very difficult herself, and it had made Elsa very nervy, and she was very hard worked at her office.

'Hard worked!' said Dr Perry unsympathetically. 'She's as strong as a mule and not a nerve in her body. But being in love plays the very deuce with these tough young women. Don't you let her play fast and loose with Captain Hornby. He's not a man to stand that sort of thing. Get her married whatever she says. She'll be all right with Hornby.'

Mrs Belton said, ruefully laughing at herself, that Dr Perry well knew she had no influence on Elsa at all, and then described to him Captain Hornby's matter-of-fact determination to marry her daughter, willing or unwilling. Dr Perry roared with laughter, said it was the best news he had heard for a long time, and took his leave.

'Charles told my boys this was embarkation leave,' he said on the doorstep. 'I'm sorry.'

'I'm not,' said Mrs Belton, who was looking all her age and more after the events of the previous day. 'I mean I can't bear to think that I'll probably never see him again, but it must be quite dreadful to go on being in England when all your friends are abroad and always training for a job and not being allowed to do it. In fact I think it does all the ones who haven't gone abroad great credit that they haven't gone mad.'

'I expect you are right,' said Dr Perry. 'Well, I needn't come again. They are calling up all the young doctors now like anything,' he added irrelevantly, and went away.

The winter term was now simmering towards its end. There had been so much mild influenza that the examinations were delightfully disorganized and not even the head prefect felt that the Honour of the School really depended on them. Heather Adams suddenly blossomed out as a personality in an almost alarming way, and for the first time in her life tasted, in a mild form, the sweets of popularity.

'I must say,' said Miss Head, who was in Miss Sparling's office going over form lists, 'I never thought Heather would develop the team spirit. The Games people,' said Miss Head with the tolerance of one who can afford to condescend, 'say it is hockey that did it, but I think there is no doubt that it was the Play. So often acting just gives a girl that little increase of self-confidence that makes all the difference.'

Miss Sparling agreed that this often occurred.

'She certainly came out well in the play,' said Miss Holly, 'but I think it was the skating myself. It was the first time she had done something the other girls couldn't do. And when Isabella Ferdinand asked for skating lessons it made a great impression.'

Miss Sparling quite agreed that the skating had been an eye-opener to Heather's fellow-students and that where Isabella led others were apt to follow.

'But I think myself,' said Miss Sparling, 'that she had been worrying about war-work. As soon as she decided for herself that she could do useful work by going into her father's firm, she seemed a new girl.'

Both Miss Holly and Miss Head agreed that there was something to be said for this suggestion, and then all three ladies fell to on the lists again. But only Commander Belton could have given them the real clue, and Commander Belton had quite other things to think about.

When the work was done Miss Sparling went down to the village to have tea with Mr Oriel, a treat which she always enjoyed. She was by now on so friendly a footing at the Vicarage that Mrs Powlett had graciously bestowed the freedom of the front door upon her, cordially pressing her to walk in whenever she felt like it. Miss Sparling had fallen into the habit of dropping in at the Vicarage at least twice a week and was even allowed by Mr Oriel to dust and rearrange some of his books, which lived in helpless confusion, overflowing on to chairs, sofas and windowsills and all over the study floor.

'You are looking tired, my dear,' said Mr Oriel when his guest came into the study.

'End of term,' said Miss Sparling. 'But we break up tomorrow and when I have tidied everything I am going to Devonshire with Miss Holly who has been lent a cottage. We don't get on each other's nerves and I believe there will be an egg or two and possibly extra butter as it is next to a farm. And I am looking forward to a great treat. Mr Carton, as you know, has been working on my grandfather's friend, Fluvius Minucius, and he is going to let me read his proofs while I am away.'

'Regarded as a treat, my dear, it seems more suitable to my age than to yours,' said Mr Oriel. 'But you are a very unusual woman. I will ring for tea.'

He did so, and in so doing knocked an untidy heap of papers off the corner of a bookcase. Miss Sparling came to his assistance, picked them up and began sorting them.

'How curious,' she said suddenly. 'Look, Mr Oriel, here is my grandfather's name.'

She held out to him the slip of paper on which he had, some forty-odd years ago, written the words 'Borrowed from Horbury. 2.ix.'02.'

Mr Oriel went hot and cold. His sin had found him out. Bitterly did he repent having listened to the serpent words of Mr Carton. Had he confessed at once to Miss Sparling that he had borrowed Slawkenbergius in nineteen-two and gone on forgetting to return him ever since, his grey hair would not now be bowed in dishonour. So unhappy did he look that Miss Sparling was alarmed, fearing that her old friend might be ill.

'Madeleine!' Mr Oriel said, almost groaning. 'I hardly know where to begin. There is something I have wanted to tell you for a very long time, but I feared your disapproval. May I tell you now?'

Neither Mr Oriel nor his guest had noticed that the study

door was being pushed open by a foot. Dorothy, carrying a tray with the preliminary outfit for tea upon it, saw her employer and Miss Sparling standing close together and heard Mr Oriel's words. Her dramatic sense told her to drop the tray, but most luckily whatever common sense she had told her that Mrs Powlett would not take this kindly, so after staring madly for a few seconds, she backed silently out, put the tray down on a chair in the hall and fled into the kitchen.

'He's Spoken, Mrs Powlett!' said Dorothy.

'I sometimes think, Dorothy, that your poor mother, if anyone knew who she was, would be downright ashamed of you,' said Mrs Powlett. 'Coming shouting into the kitchen like that. Who's spoken?'

'Mr Oriel, Mrs Powlett,' said Dorothy. 'Him and Miss Sparling were standing by the fire, just like Lord Victor and Lady Isabel, and I heard him say there was something he'd wanted to tell her for a long time. Do you think Miss Sparling will say Yes, Mrs Powlett?'

'Really, Dorothy!' said her outraged mistress, 'how you can stand there and tell such stories I can't think. And what have you done with that tray? I told you to put the tea things on the little table and bring it back.'

'Please, Mrs Powlett, I put it on a chair in the hall,' said Dorothy, who though conscious that she was telling the truth began to wonder if she wasn't.

'I'll see to it Myself,' said Mrs Powlett majestically. 'And you go upstairs, Dorothy, and do the blackout in the bedrooms. It won't hurt to get it done early. And don't let me hear you tell any more stories, Dorothy, or I'll have to say you're a wicked girl.'

Accordingly Dorothy went upstairs and Mrs Powlett set the tea things in the study, where she found Mr Oriel and Miss Sparling talking about books or something and Mr Oriel said he did ought to have given a book or something back a long time ago and Miss Sparling said not to commence to worry and any time would do and Mr Oriel said something about Mr Carton had the book or something, but Mrs Powlett never was one to concern herself with other people's affairs so she went back to the kitchen where the kettle was just on the boil and made the tea and took it in. Mr and Mrs Wickens then came in, by appointment, and Mrs Powlett poured out tea for everyone, including Dorothy, though how that girl could take as long over the blackout as she did was past believing and if her tea got cold she'd only herself to blame.

Mr Carton was also free of the Vicarage door. He had finished with Slawkenbergius and thought he might as well take him back to Mr Oriel. Fluvius Minucius was at last ready for the Oxbridge Press and Mr Carton hoped to see him in print by the autumn, the German Chancellor and the paper supply permitting. Whether he had noticed Miss Sparling go towards the Vicarage we cannot say: we think not. Coincidences do occur in real life, so why not in fiction? So, Slawkenbergius in hand, he opened the Vicarage door and went in. As he advanced by the dim hall light, he met Dorothy coming down from doing the blackout upstairs.

'Is Mr Oriel in, Dorothy?' said Mr Carton.

'Oh yes, Mr Carton,' said Dorothy. 'And he's Spoken, Mr Carton.'

'We all do,' said Mr Carton. 'What has he spoken about?'

'It's like Lord Victor and Lady Isabel,' said the fiction-besotted Dorothy, forgetting her terror of the gentry in what she had to impart.

'I'm sure it is,' said Mr Carton, 'though I haven't the honour of their acquaintance. Is he in the study?'

'Yes, Mr Carton. But he's Spoken to Miss Sparling,' said

Dorothy, standing with Mr Oriel's hot-water bottle which she had brought down to be filled when he went to bed right across Mr Carton's way. 'He said he had been waiting to tell her something for a very long time and he was as close to her, Mr Carton! Do you think Miss Sparling will say Yes, Mr Carton? Perhaps he'll give her a diamond necklace, but Mrs Powlett said not to talk like that, but I would like to see it, Mr Carton. Lady Isabel had a pink neglije, Mr Carton, it said so.'

If Mr Carton had not had a way of listening with what was apparently courteous attention to anyone who addressed him, a habit formed from long intercourse with undergraduates and meaning very little, he would have brushed Dorothy aside and gone into the study, where he would, as we know from Mrs Powlett, have found Mr Oriel and Miss Sparling talking about a book or something in a friendly and unemotional way. But his habit of appearing to listen kept him standing while Dorothy poured out her romantic tale. He did not like the tale. He knew that Dorothy was as near a halfwit as needs be, he knew that she had no business to stop and speak to him in the hall, he knew that he was very foolish to pay the faintest attention to what she said. But as her besotted prattle poured over him like a waterfall, he felt a growing unease. There was no reason why Mr Oriel should not, in Dorothy's phrase, Speak to Miss Sparling if he wished to: oh, no reason in the world. But Mr Carton suddenly felt old and cross and outcast. When Dorothy stopped talking he could hear through the study door a murmur of voices which struck him as of a very intimate, domestic nature. Thrusting Slawkenbergius into Dorothy's hand he told her to give it to Mr Oriel and went back to Assaye House, while Dorothy fled to the kitchen.

'What have you been so long upstairs about, Dorothy?' said Mrs Powlett. 'And what's that book doing? That's one of the study books. How often have I told you, Dorothy, never to touch the study books. I don't know what Mr and Mrs Wickens will think!'

'Mr Carton gave it me, Mrs Powlett,' said Dorothy.

'If you tell any more stories, Dorothy, you know what I said,' said Mrs Powlett. 'Really, Mrs Wickens, I don't know what's come over Dorothy. It's all these libery books. Thank goodness I've enough to do without reading. It only puts ideas into people's heads.'

'But Mr Carton did give it to me, Mrs Powlett,' said Dorothy. 'He was in the hall and he said was Mr Oriel in and I said Yes, he was Speaking to Miss Sparling, and Mr Carton said to give Mr Oriel the book and he went away. Oh, I do hope Miss Sparling will say Yes, Mrs Powlett. It's like that book Miss Humble gave me at the libery called *A Good Man's Love*.' And Dorothy, overcome by romance, began to cry.

'You've got above yourself, Dorothy,' said Mrs Powlett. 'Sit down and drink your tea and don't speak till you're spoken to. If she weren't almost a natural,' said Mrs Powlett at the top of her voice to Mrs Wickens, 'I'd never keep my temper. But there's no harm in her, poor thing, and she's better here than she would be in most places.'

Mrs Wickens, looking darkly but not unkindly on Dorothy, said she was one of those as Got Taken Advantage Of, and the three elders indulged in an orgy of prophecy about girls who took the wrong turning and were landed with a packet, this last contribution coming from Mr Wickens.

'Well, Wickens, I'm surprised at you,' said Mrs Wickens, whose deafness had improved under the stimulus of horrors. 'Before someone that shall be nameless too. Really, Mrs Powlett, I sometimes wonder how I came to marry Wickens.'

But Dorothy, who had not heard Mr Wickens's remark and certainly would not have understood it if she had, suddenly stopped crying, and coming out of a trance asked Mrs Powlett what time the buses went to Barchester on Thursdays.

'Same time as usual,' said Mrs Powlett. 'And don't you ask such silly questions, Dorothy.'

'But, Mrs Powlett, I want to go to Barchester on my Thursday afternoon off,' said Dorothy.

At this subversive remark the whole company turned and stared.

'I got a letter from Mr Simnet,' said Dorothy. 'He's getting his holiday at Easter and he says he's coming to Barchester to stay with his mother and he says old Mrs Simnet invites me to tea. Oh, Mrs Powlett, *please* can I go?'

There was a horrified silence. Then Mrs Powlett, rising to the height of her kindly nature and remembering that to Dorothy she represented Justice and Mercy, spoke.

'A hundred years ago, Dorothy,' she said, 'you'd have been put in a dark room on bread and water. But seeing there's a war on, and as you're a good girl if a bit wanting, I'll let you go. But I'm coming with you, mind. I know my duty if no one else does.'

'Oh! Mrs Powlett!' said Dorothy, overcome with gratitude.

'We might all go,' said Mrs Wickens. 'I want to do a bit of shopping and I dare say Wickens would like to see Mr Simnet, being as he knows his brother.'

'Oh! Mrs Wickens!' said Dorothy, even more overcome by the thought of these festivities. 'Oh thank you, Mrs Powlett. You *are* good. I suppose I couldn't kiss you, Mrs Powlett?'

'Certainly not, Dorothy,' said Mrs Powlett, getting up. 'Now you take the tea things away. I'll go and get the study tea things and then you can wash up.'

As Mrs Powlett came into the study she found Miss Sparling just going.

'Well, good-bye, dear Mr Oriel,' said Miss Sparling, kissing her old friend. 'I'll write to you from Devonshire and next term we all look forward to some more Shakespeare.'

'I beg your pardon, sir, but Mr Carton left this book for you,' said Mrs Powlett.

'Slawkenbergius, the very man we were talking about,' said Mr Oriel. 'Would you like to have him, Madeleine?'

But Miss Sparling said she knew her grandfather would like Mr Oriel to keep him.

'I wonder why Carton didn't come in,' said Mr Oriel. 'Well, good-bye, my dear, and have a happy holiday.'

He saw her out and came back to the study where he plunged into his work. Mrs Powlett took the tea things away and was able to report to Mr and Mrs Wickens that there was Nothing In It, and it was just one of Dorothy's ideas she got into her head. A crash from the scullery announced that Dorothy had broken something, so Mr and Mrs Wickens tactfully said good-bye, arranging to meet Mrs Powlett and Dorothy on the Thursday in Easter week at the Barchester bus stop. In the scullery Mrs Powlett found Dorothy contemplating the ruins of Mr Oriel's stone hot-water bottle on the floor.

'I didn't mean to, Mrs Powlett,' said Dorothy, 'It just happened.'

'I always said as that Hitler was up to no good, taking all the rubber hot bottles,' said Mrs Powlett, 'or the Russians, it's all the same. Never mind, Dorothy. I'll tell you what though, I'll let you wear that brown coat of mine with the bit of fur round the collar when we go and see Mrs Simnet. I wouldn't let everybody wear my coat, but I know you will be properly grateful, Dorothy, for being such a lucky girl.'

'Oh, I *am* lucky, Mrs Powlett,' said Dorothy. And what is more she truly meant it.

Mrs Updike, not without bruising and scratching herself more than seemed humanly possible, had been turning out her store-cupboard. In common with millions of other housewives she had, in the early days of the war, industriously bought and put away several weeks' supply of tinned and dry foods. Some of these she had packed in a tin regimental suitcase, formerly the property of an uncle of Mr Updike, and buried it in the vegetable garden against the invasion. In the course of three or four years, during which the cabbages which originally decked its resting-place had been succeeded by root vegetables, scarlet runners and celery, its whereabouts had been lost, and not till Mr Updike, driving a stake into the ground for a young fruit tree, had hit on something that jarred his arm with unbearable anguish, was it rediscovered. But unfortunately it had been pierced in several places by the prong of the gardener's large fork and everything not in tins had gone bad. So the fowls benefited by quantities of mouldy rice, lentils and other cereals, and Mrs Updike brought the tins indoors to re-store them in her cupboard. During the turnout she found a tin of candied peel and a tin of sultanas and decided to lay violent hands on her family's fat ration and make some fruit cakes. Of the three cakes she made, two were unfortunately rather burnt, owing to her going upstairs to lie down for half an hour to get rid of the giddy feeling caused by a saucepan falling off its rack on to her head, and going to sleep by mistake; but the third survived, and when she had pared away a good deal of the other two and anointed them with a kind of paste made from tinned milk and cocoa (also from the invasion store), she was so delighted that she at once asked several friends to tea. Accordingly, on the day following the events we have just narrated, the society of Harefield began to converge on Clive's Corner about tea time.

The first to come were Mrs Belton and Elsa, who was to go back to work the next day but still looked rather washed out. No more had been said about her engagement. Her mother was for the moment too busy and too tired to ask any questions, so Elsa was able to add her mother's silence to her sense of injury. How miserable she had been with influenza depression and her increasing consciousness of having behaved badly to Captain Hornby, only she knew. She had heard once from Captain Hornby, to say that he would be away for ten days and could not write. It was an affectionate letter, and she knew he was often on jobs where letters were forbidden, but she was able to torment herself with every kind of imagining that he did not wish to see her again after her behaviour, or had now returned his affections to Lady Ellangowan. And being no fool, though sometimes very silly, she quite realized that all her unhappiness was her own doing, which was no comfort at all.

As soon as Mrs Belton and Elsa arrived, the two younger Updike children silently seized Elsa and took her away to look at some white mice that they were keeping at the far end of the drawing-room. Mrs Belton and Mrs Updike sat by the fire, and before long Mr Updike and Mr Belton came in. They had been talking business in the office and it was obvious to Mrs Belton that her husband would burst unless he could tell someone about it, so to ease his path she asked him, generally, how things were going.

'I am afraid,' said Mr Updike, 'that I had several shocks for your husband, Mrs Belton. But quite agreeable ones. I think I am safe in saying that he will be able to accept the Hosiers' offer for Church Meadow and the adjoining land. And a very good offer it is.'

'I *am* glad,' said Mrs Belton, more relieved than she could express. 'But what about the War Agricultural? I thought they insisted on that land being ploughed.'

'I really don't know what happened there,' said Mr Updike, 'or I'd tell you. All I know is that I had a letter this morning from Mr Adams at Hogglestock—'

'You know Adams, my dear,' said Mr Belton, anxious to tell his own story, 'the father of that girl that knows all about rats. The one that's on the bench with me. A bit of an outsider, but I always said he was a decent fellow.'

'Indeed you didn't, Fred,' said his wife mildly. 'You said he was a bounder.'

'Well, well, that's neither here nor there,' said Mr Belton, dismissing the matter. 'But to make a long story short, Adams seems to have some kind of pull with the W.A.E.C. and he wrote to Updike to say there would be no more trouble.'

'Of course,' said Mr Updike, 'I could not take Mr Adams's letter as expressing the War Agricultural's views, but by the afternoon's post I had an official letter from them to say that on consideration they would not press the question of my client's ploughing Church Meadow, as their wheat expert had reported the land unsuitable.'

'And why the deuce they couldn't say so in the first place, I don't know,' said Mr Belton. 'I have an idea myself that Adams spoke to Norton. You know Norton ploughed that field of his that marches with Church Meadow, along the Southbridge road, and they got the finest crop of weeds and stones I've seen since I began farming. Mind you I know nothing, but that's my idea.'

Mrs Updike said the Government seemed to have a perfect

thing about ploughing, but it didn't make the bread any nicer.

'And one thing more, Lucy,' said Mr Belton, who was in that state of letting off steam that he would have taken the whole Albert Hall into his confidence sooner than keep silence. 'I didn't tell you this before, but Updike had a letter from Hornby. A most considerate and friendly letter. He said he would be willing to advance me a large sum of money if it would help me with the place, but on a business footing, as he did not want to make a personal matter of it. Ten thousand pounds, he said. Thank heaven that won't be necessary now, but I feel his kindness very much. No one knows about this of course, except ourselves. I feel it very much indeed.'

The ladies murmured sympathy. Mrs Belton was thankful past words that her husband's affairs would no longer weigh so heavily on him. It would be sad to see Church Meadow with a school in it: yet, to be truthful, when they still lived at the Park she sometimes did not go by Church Meadow for five or six months together, and as it lay some two miles from the house on the further side of a rise in the ground, there would be no question of seeing anything built there unless it had a clock tower or a factory chimney, both of which contingencies seemed to her improbable. As for Captain Hornby's offer, it was just like what one might have expected from his kindness, and thank goodness Elsa's very silly interference and almost rudeness had not had any bad results. Elsa was still at the end of the drawing-room, looking at the white mice, and made no sign of having heard anything. Just as well.

Now had the two younger Updike children been ordinary children, their talk would certainly have prevented any conversation from the far end of a long drawing-room reaching Elsa's ears. But as we know, the young Updikes were a silent family, and while they proudly exhibited the mice's bedroom, communicating with an adjacent sitting-room by a hole with a kind of portcullis which could be raised and lowered, and the arrangements for their food and water, the talk by the fire began to reach Elsa's ears. When she heard Captain Hornby's name, it was quite impossible not to listen and when her father went on to describe Captain Hornby's offer she was overcome by such mingled feelings of shame and admiration that she found it difficult to concentrate on the white mice. But she did her best and was rewarded by being allowed to look through a trapdoor in the roof and see the baby white mice which were too like primeval life for her taste, but she lied nobly and said how nice they were.

Now Miss Sparling arrived, and Mr Carton and Mrs Hoare. The two youngest Updikes silently left the room and after a few moments one of them looked in at the door and said 'Ready,' which was the signal for everyone to go into the dining-room and have tea. The sight of three cakes provoked loud exclamations from the party and for some time nothing but food was discussed. This was just as well, for Mr and Mrs Belton were still a little overcome by the solution, temporary at any rate, of their money difficulties. Mr Belton, rather late, was wondering if he ought to have talked about his affairs so freely before his hostess, and under cover of Mrs Hoare's account of a curry, the recipe for which was a legacy from her husband's old uncle who had been Political Adviser to a small rajah, he managed to say to his wife, 'I hope it was all right to mention the Hosiers and Hornby. After all Updike knows all my affairs.'

Mrs Belton smiled Yes at him, for it was well known that Mrs Updike, with all her agreeable feather-patedness and her habit of uttering every irrelevancy that came into her head, had some kind of saving instinct. And though she had more than once brought her very affectionate husband to the verge of shame by her kaleidoscopic view of life and her *obiter dicta* on the subject, she had never by the least hint shown that she knew anything about his clients and their business. So Mr Belton, now quite at ease, fell into a county conversation with Mrs Hoare who said she had never really quite understood the ramifications of old Lady Pomfret's family, and Mr Carton was of course drawn into this talk. Just as the exact relationship of the late countess to the now extinct branch of the Thornes of Ullathorne was being run to earth, Mrs Updike picked up the hot-water jug to refill her teapot. The lid fell off the jug into the open teapot and upset it. Mrs Updike, with a gentle, helpless shriek, dropped the hot-water jug on to her lap and everything became a sodden mass of watery tea.

The young Updikes rose as one man, went to the kitchen and returning with cloths and dusters silently groomed their mother, swabbed the tea-tray and took away the teapot and jug.

'I knew something would happen,' said Mrs Updike triumphantly. 'It's that jug. It has got a perfect thing about its lid. It's always falling off.'

'Are you sure you are all right?' said Mrs Belton. 'I mean all that hot water falling on you.'

'Of *course*,' said Mrs Updike, gazing into space as if she saw a vision, 'I ought to have been scalded. How stupid of me. But I've just thought what it was. I always get so wet when I wash up, so I put a rubber apron on. I suppose I ought to give it to salvage, oughtn't I?'

'The Council will only burn it if you do,' said Mr Carton with grim satisfaction. 'You know all those tins that we have been taking to their dump for the last two years. They say now they don't know what to do with them, so they are paying four men to dig a pit up by the allotments and bury them.'

'But you haven't got your apron on,' said Miss Sparling to Mrs Updike.

Mrs Updike looked down at her lap. Mild surprise, followed by indignation were visible in her pretty, fine-drawn face. Suddenly she laughed.

'Of *course*,' she said, again with triumph. 'There's a sort of thing about this dress that I always manage to spill something on it, so when I had washed up the lunch things I didn't take my apron off, to remind me not to forget to put it on when I changed into this dress. I meant to take it off and put it on again – *over* this dress not under it of course, but just as I had got my working dress off I was thinking about an electric light bulb that I had put somewhere and couldn't remember where it was and I simply put the apron on, so that I would be *sure* to have it on and then I suppose I put my dress over it. Yes,' she added proudly, after lifting the edge of her skirt and looking under it, 'here it is. I *do* do such silly things.'

She laughed so gaily that not one of her guests could help laughing with her.

'Excuse me,' said Mrs Hoare, 'but it has just occurred to me that what I thought was a bell must have been a bell, because there it still is.'

Her hearers then also became conscious that what had vaguely struck them as being the sound of a bell had been going on at intervals ever since Mrs Updike upset the hot water, but there had been so much noise, and so enthralled were they all by the drama which was unfolded that it had not occurred to anyone to do anything about it. The bell, having given one last shrill ring of despair, was silent.

'Well, whoever it was has given it up,' said Mrs Belton. 'What a good cake, Mrs Updike. I haven't had a cake like this since all these vitamins got into the flour.'

'I *am* glad you like it,' said Mrs Updike earnestly. 'I love making cakes. I could make them for ever, only something always happens. Oh, thank you, my pet.'

These last words were spoken to one of the young Updikes who came in with a kettle of boiling water which it placed on the hearth, and remarking to the company in general, 'Safer for Mother,' resumed its place at the table. The other young Updike then appeared, carrying a teapot, and held the door open for Captain Hornby.

'I am sorry to appear like the Demon King,' said Captain Hornby. 'I couldn't let anyone know I was coming, and when I went to Arcot House, Wheeler told me Mrs Belton was here, and I came along. I rang and rang and couldn't make anyone hear, so I went round the house and heard your young people in the kitchen and they let me in.'

There was a friendly hubbub of welcome. The young Updikes silently pulled Captain Hornby to a place between them, Mrs Updike laughed at nothing, all three cakes were eaten to the last crumb, everyone had fresh tea, and sat on at the table in pleasant idle talk.

Presently Mrs Belton said they must be going.

'You are coming for the night, Christopher, I hope,' she said.

Captain Hornby thanked her and said he would like to stay two or three nights if it suited her, as he had a few days' leave. To Elsa he said nothing. He did not ignore her pointedly, but appeared to take her rather as a matter of course. Elsa, still shattered by what she had overheard in the drawing-room, felt shy and uncomfortable, and at the same time felt how dreadful it would be if her stupid and odious behaviour had made Christopher stop loving her. Some chance there would be, there must be, of seeing him alone, but she felt too stupid to think when or how. Her growing impatience was not soothed when Mrs Hoare said she must be going too and would walk with them part of the way, and she could have shot or stabbed her parents and Captain Hornby for accepting the situation with such calm, nay with such apparent pleasure. But she was well brought up, so she concealed her nervous impatience and walked up the street, talking to her father about Church Meadow. At Dowlah Cottage Mrs Hoare stopped.

'Seeing Captain Hornby reminds me of the picture he cleaned so beautifully for me,' she said. 'Mrs Belton, you haven't seen it. Won't you and Mr Belton come in and look at it. It is really quite a masterpiece now and I have hung it in the back hall where it shows to greater advantage. I dare say Captain Hornby will look after our dear Elsa.'

The Beltons, always glad to please an old neighbour, went into Dowlah Cottage with her.

'Mr Carton and Miss Sparling are coming up the street behind us,' said Captain Hornby. 'I like them both immensely, but I see no reason why they should overtake us.'

He took Elsa's arm and crossing the street plunged into the little crooked lane that ran down behind the shops towards the river. Once safely round the first corner he stopped, released Elsa, and stood looking at her. Elsa could bear it no longer. Regardless of the back door of the fish shop, the yard of the bicycle shop, the garage where the N.F.S. personnel were lounging about, and the little local factory which was making a quite deafening noise like a circular saw talking to a motor bicycle, she found herself, to her great surprise but to her entire contentment, folded in a manly embrace. It only lasted for a moment, but in that time she knew that she had lost nothing, that all her self-tormentings had been folly.

'That's more like it,' said Captain Hornby, retreating a pace to have a good look at her. 'Listen. We are going to be married the day after tomorrow. If I don't marry you now, I may never get the chance, and if I do marry you now you may never see me again. Is that all right?'

'I'll marry you anywhere, whenever you say, as often as you like,' said Elsa. 'Oh, Christopher.'

In spite of the piercing cold of a spring late afternoon they walked slowly down the lane, along by the Rising, up past the church, so happy that there was little to say and that little of an incoherent and, to the outsider, uninteresting nature. At last Elsa, who had been summoning her courage for confession, said,

'Christopher, I wasn't listening at the Updikes', but I was in the drawing-room when Father was talking to Mr Updike about Harefield and the Hosiers and your letter about the money, and I couldn't help hearing. I am so ashamed of myself. I was an interfering prig. I can't tell you how miserable and sorry I am. You are an angel.'

'No, I'm not an angel,' said Captain Hornby thoughtfully, 'but I'll probably be an admiral soon if I'm not killed. And then you'll be an admiral's lady and have to behave. I like your people very much, and I have wanted for some time to help them if I could, but it's a bit awkward suddenly to offer people money, and when you tried to bully me it made it all even more awkward. However, that's all over now and everything is all right. Precious darling,' he added violently.

'I'm sorry,' said Elsa in a very small voice.

'I'm glad to hear you say so,' said Captain Hornby, 'as it is the first and probably the last time you have ever behaved sensibly. And now, ANGEL, we are going home to talk about the special licence I've got and break the news to your parents.'

'Yes, Christopher DARLING,' said Elsa, and they turned into the High Street.

It was merely his own selfish feelings that made Captain Hornby think Mr Carton and Miss Sparling might try to overtake him and his affianced. Mr Carton and Miss Sparling were not thinking about them at all, having quite other subjects of conversation. During tea Miss Sparling had a vague uncomfortable feeling that there was between herself and Mr Carton a slight, a very slight barrier, as if during the night a thin sheet of glass had slipped between them. It did not make her unhappy, for that she would not allow; but she felt she would like to dissipate it. And as they happened to leave Clive's Corner at the same time and their roads lay in the same direction, there seemed to be no reason why they should not walk up the High Street as far as the lodge gates together. Miss Sparling, still conscious of the sheet of glass, talked about her approaching holiday and the plans for next term and the Hosiers' schemes for building a new school in the neighbourhood. And so pleasantly did she talk that Mr Carton who was also conscious of the faint barrier between them and knew it was his fault, began to think he had been rather foolish to let Dorothy's confidences influence him. So he began to come out of his shell and Miss Sparling felt that the barrier was only very thin cellophane and might at any moment melt and disappear.

When they came to the lodge gates Miss Sparling stopped.

'I hope we shall see you again next term,' she said. 'Mr Oriel has kindly promised to go on with our Shakespeare readings and the girls want to do some open-air acting.'

Mr Carton said he would like to come to the readings as soon as Oxford came down.

'And I must tell you,' said Miss Sparling, 'that Mr Oriel has my grandfather's copy of Slawkenbergius. He borrowed it in 1902 and never returned it. He was so unhappy about it, poor dear. He said he had wanted to tell me about it for a long time and hadn't the courage.'

'Oh, that was what he said, was it,' said Mr Carton, reflecting on Dorothy's version of the conversation. 'Miss Sparling, if you have time, will you come to Assaye House for a few moments. I have something I want to show you. I think it will interest you. From Sweden.'

The glass, cellophane, summer mist, whatever it was had vanished. Miss Sparling, with a sense of relief for which she did not try to account, said she had plenty of time and would like to come in for a few moments.

As soon as they were in the study, Mr Carton opened a drawer and took out a long envelope.

'I made inquiries,' he said. 'I happen to know a man at Upsala, Professor Ronnquist his name is; Doctor Professor Ronnquist as those foreigners prefer to put it, a poor sort of name, but let that pass. He wants the Oxbridge Press to publish a little book of his on Frederika Bremer's visits to England and America. I happen to be one of the Press Delegates, so,' said Mr Carton thoughtfully, 'I put pressure on him. Here is a photostat copy of the Minucius manuscript. What the censor thought of it, I don't know. I dare say she was thinking of her next cocoa-party and didn't worry,' said Mr Carton, rather unjustly, as the censor who happened to read the Swedish Professor's letter was Geoffrey Harvey's sister Frances Harvey, who thought poorly of cocoa, though she had a good opinion of herself.

'How very good of you,' said Miss Sparling.

'Of course you ought to have been using it, not I,' said Mr Carton. 'But as you have consistently refused, on what I consider very inadequate grounds, to undertake the editing of Minucius, I have done my best with him. If you would care to look through the proofs I shall be honoured; and grateful.'

He handed to Miss Sparling a parcel with her name and address on it.

'This will save time; and postage,' he added sententiously.

'May I look at it now?' said Miss Sparling. She carefully opened the parcel. '*Fluvius Minucius, A Critical Study,*' she read and then turned to the next page. There met her eyes a dedication in elegant Latin to the memory of her grandfather, a man most reverend, most learned, a true son of the Muses, who had brought Fluvius Minucius back from the realm of Dis to the light of day. So overcome with emotion was the headmistress of the Hosiers' Girls' Foundation School and holder of the Freedom of the Worshipful Company of Hosiers, that all she could say at first was a long drawn 'Oh!'

'You do not think it impertinent?' said Mr Carton.

'Oh how pleased my dear grandfather would have been,' said Miss Sparling, finding it strangely difficult to speak or to see.

'I would like to have dedicated my opusculum to you; *Magdalenae doctissimae dilectissimae,*' said Mr Carton. 'But I didn't.'

Miss Sparling looked quickly and questioningly at Mr Carton.

'You see, I feel like that,' said Mr Carton. 'At least I cannot describe my feeling in any other way. But I offend you.'

'No, no; you don't,' said Miss Sparling. 'I do so appreciate your friendship, your affection, if I may call it that.'

'You may call it what you like,' said Mr Carton. 'Catullus, as

376

you will remember,' he continued, looking beyond Miss Sparling to his imaginary audience of third-year men, 'said that his affection for Lesbia was not so much like that of any fellow for any girl, as like that of a father towards his male relations on the paternal side and his sons-in-law. Not our idea of the fondest ties, but he was born a Roman and must please himself. What I would like to express, though feeling myself totally unable to do so, is that I have for you a very deep affection, but it need never trouble you. And that is really all,' said Mr Carton apologetically.

'I don't know what to say,' said Miss Sparling.

'I can't help you there, Madeleine,' said Mr Carton.

'I don't even know your name, so I can't use it,' said Miss Sparling, half laughing.

Mr Carton looked annoyed.

'Your state is the more blessed,' he said, rather snappishly. 'It is Sidney. Yes – after Sydney Carton. My parents were strong admirers of Dickens. The only moment at which I have not loathed the name was when I saw that enchanting actor Martin Harvey, of whom you have probably never heard, acting the part of Sydney Carton. But my parents didn't ever spell it properly,' Mr Carton added angrily. 'Sidney with an "i" is what I am; not but that both forms of the name are equally repugnant. I have no other vices except those that you know.'

'I am not as young as all that,' said Miss Sparling. 'I too have been enamoured of that actor. But it is a dreadful name, I must admit, and I shall go on calling you Mr Carton.'

'Mrs Sidney Carton is a first-class name,' Mr Carton misquoted hopefully.

Miss Sparling was silent.

'I don't know about schoolmistresses,' she said at last, with apparent irrelevance. 'I suppose we are some help. We do a good deal of work and try to do our best. Then suddenly one day we look round and we are no longer young; and the time for retiring is near at hand. What then? Some of us do get married while we are still fairly young; but that seems to me rather like having your cake and eating it. I don't know.'

'And I can't help you,' said Mr Carton. 'If, at any time, now or later, you felt you needed an almshouse, I will not presume to call it a Harbour of Refuge, to retire to, my offer will always hold good. I happen to know that the Wickenses would have no objection, for owing to her deafness, mostly deliberate where her husband is concerned, I hear far more than I am meant to hear, and often more than I wish to hear. But you appear to satisfy their standard.'

Miss Sparling said that was perhaps the most flattering thing that had ever happened to her; even better than being made an honorary Hosier. And now, she said, she must really be going, as there were still a good many odds and ends to be tidied before she and Miss Holly set out next day for Devonshire.

'We might correspond,' said Mr Carton.

Miss Sparling said she would like that, of all things.

'I think,' said Mr Carton, taking both her hands in his, 'that we might call it an understanding, Madeleine. Would that suit you?'

'Thank you, dear Mr Carton, it would suit me very well,' said Miss Sparling.

And at last withdrawing her hands from his she left the house. He watched her cross the road, go through the lodge gates and walk up the drive towards Harefield Park. Then he drew his curtains, turned on the light and settled down to work.

NORTHBRIDGE RECTORY

ANGELA THIRKELL

'The novels are a delight, with touches of E. F. Benson,
E. M. Delafield and P. G. Wodehouse' Christopher Fowler,
Independent on Sunday

Bartsetshire during wartime finds Mr Downing, Miss
Pemberton, and Mrs Turner engaged in a love triangle; a
chorus of officers raucously quartered at the rectory; and
village ladies with violent leanings. In Mrs Major Spender,
Thirkell offers a devastating sketch of the good-natured
egoist, and readers will be pleased that the less-than-articulate
Betty finds a soulmate in Captain Copham.

'You read her, laughing, and want to do your best to protect
her characters from any reality but their own' *New York Times*

'Charming, very funny indeed. Angela Thirkell is
perhaps the most Pym-like of any twentieth-century author,
after Pym herself' Alexander McCall Smith

VIRAGO MODERN CLASSICS

The first Virago Modern Classic, *Frost in May* by Antonia White, was published in 1978. It launched a list dedicated to the celebration of women writers and to the rediscovery and reprinting of their works. Its aim was, and is, to demonstrate the existence of a female tradition in literature, and to broaden the sometimes narrow definition of a 'classic' which has often led to the neglect of interesting books. Published with new introductions by some of today's best writers, the books are chosen for many reasons: they may be great works of literature; they may be wonderful period pieces; they may reveal particular aspects of women's lives; they may be classics of comedy, storytelling, letter-writing or autobiography.

'Good news for everyone writing and reading today' –
Hilary Mantel

'The Virago Modern Classics list is wonderful. It's quite
simply one of the best and most essential things that has
happened in publishing in our time. I hate to think where
we'd be without it' – *Ali Smith*

'The Virago Modern Classics have reshaped literary history
and enriched the reading of us all. No library is complete
without them' – *Margaret Drabble*

'The writers are formidable, the production handsome. The
whole enterprise is thoroughly grand' – *Louise Erdrich*

'A continuingly magnificent imprint' – *Joanna Trollope*

'The Virago Modern Classics are one of the best things
in Britain today' – *Alison Lurie*'

'Masterful works' – *Vogue*